THE PRINCESS
AND THE GOBLIN
AND OTHER FAIRY TALES

broadview editions
series editor: L.W. Conolly

THE PRINCESS
AND THE GOBLIN
AND OTHER FAIRY TALES

George MacDonald

edited by Shelley King and John Pierce

broadview editions

Library and Archives Canada Cataloguing in Publication

Macdonald, George, 1824-1905
[Fairy tales. Selections]
   The princess and the goblin and other fairy tales / George MacDonald ; edited by Shelley King and John Pierce.

(Broadview editions)
Includes bibliographical references.
ISBN 978-1-55481-007-9 (pbk.)

   1. Fairy tales—Scotland. I. King, M. Shelley (Marilyn Shelley), 1954-, editor II. Pierce, John Benjamin, 1957-, editor III. Title. IV. Series: Broadview editions

PR4966.K55 2014   823'.8   C2014-905184-0

Broadview Editions
The Broadview Editions series represents the ever-changing canon of literature in English by bringing together texts long regarded as classics with valuable lesser-known works.

Advisory editor for this volume: Michel Pharand

Broadview Press is an independent, international publishing house, incorporated in 1985.

We welcome comments and suggestions regarding any aspect of our publications—please feel free to contact us at the addresses below or at broadview@broadviewpress.com.

North America
PO Box 1243, Peterborough, Ontario K9J 7H5, Canada
555 Riverwalk Parkway, Tonawanda, NY 14150, USA
Tel: (705) 743-8990; Fax: (705) 743-8353
email: customerservice@broadviewpress.com

UK, Europe, Central Asia, Middle East, Africa, India, and Southeast Asia
Eurospan Group, 3 Henrietta St., London WC2E 8LU, United Kingdom
Tel: 44 (0) 1767 604972; Fax: 44 (0) 1767 601640
email: eurospan@turpin-distribution.com

Australia and New Zealand
NewSouth Books
c/o TL Distribution, 15-23 Helles Ave., Moorebank, NSW 2170, Australia
Tel: (02) 8778 9999; Fax: (02) 8778 9944
email: orders@tldistribution.com.au

www.broadviewpress.com

Broadview Press acknowledges the financial support of the Government of Canada through the Canada Book Fund for our publishing activities.

Typesetting and assembly: True to Type Inc., Claremont, Canada.

PRINTED IN CANADA

Contents

Acknowledgements

Any editor of MacDonald's *The Princess and the Goblin* owes an inestimable debt to the work of Rod McGillis, not only for his meticulous Oxford World's Classics edition of the novel, but for his distinguished body of critical analysis: to work with his edition was to experience the depth and complexity of the cultural milieu expressed in this fairy tale. Scholars are also indebted to Raphael Shaberman for mapping the complicated history of the publication of this author's works in *George MacDonald: A Bibliographical Study*.

We would also like to thank Heather Cyr, our research assistant for this project; Heather Evans, who for many years co-taught the course at Queen's University in the history of Children's Literature that featured *The Princess and the Goblin*; and Anne Heibert Alton, who has been our dear friend and fellow MacDonald enthusiast for more years than either of us likes to remember. Additional credit is due to David Pugh for his help in identifying MacDonald's allusions to German writings.

We would also like to thank Michel Pharand, our Broadview copy-editor and friend, for his meticulous attention to the final preparation of the manuscript. Finally, our sincerest gratitude to Marjorie Mather, Leonard Conolly, and the team at Broadview Press who have demonstrated extraordinary patience with a project that has taken far too long to bring to completion.

Introduction

George MacDonald was among the most prolific writers of the Victorian Age, publishing poems, essays, sermons, and a wide range of novels, but he is known today primarily for his works for children, especially *The Princess and the Goblin* (1872) and its sequel *The Princess and Curdie* (1883), as well as a variety of fairy tales, including *The Light Princess* (1864/1867) and *The Golden Key* (1867). Contemporary critics point to a number of elements in MacDonald's fantasies for children that lend his work continued relevance: his interrogation of Victorian class and gender norms, his frequent inclusion of a mystical eroticism in his tales, and his insistence on the authority of the reader as interpreter of his texts, for although MacDonald writes with a strong narratorial voice, he refuses to provide his readers with definitive answers, preferring instead to stretch their understanding by posing questions and mysteries. He is also remembered for the impact his works of fantasy—both creative and theoretical—had on another important writer for children, C.S. Lewis of Narnia fame, who regarded MacDonald as a major influence, in terms of both Christian theology and fantasy.[1]

Early Life

George MacDonald was born on 10 December 1824 in the small town of Huntly in Aberdeenshire, Scotland. His father, also George, was a handloom weaver by trade, but eventually took a

---

1 Lewis compiled an anthology of MacDonald's writings when they had fallen out of print, and in the preface commented: "I have never concealed the fact that I regarded him as my master; indeed I fancy I have never written a book in which I did not quote from him." Chesterton wrote: "I for one can testify to a book that has made a difference to my whole existence, which helped me to see things in a certain way from the start; a vision of things which even so real a revelation as a change of religious allegiance has substantially only crowned and confirmed. Of all the stories I have read ... it remains the most real, the most like life. It is called *The Princess and the Goblin*, and is by George MacDonald" (quoted in McGillis "Editor's Introduction," vii). W.H. Auden, who wrote an introduction to the 1954 *Visionary Novels of George MacDonald* edited by Anne Fremantle, thought *The Princess and the Goblin* "the only English children's book in the same class as the Alice books" (quoted in Davenport-Hines, 18).

management role in the family thread factory before moving on to agriculture at "The Farm," a location that figures large in MacDonald's youthful memories. A promising student at the local Huntly school where he received a basic grounding in Latin, Greek, and Maths, at age fifteen he was sent to the city of Aberdeen to Aulton Grammar School to prepare for the bursary exams that would enable him to pursue a university degree. A successful effort earned him a Fullarton Bursary, whose £14 per year allowed him to begin classes at King's College in the city in November 1840. At this time, the four-year program leading to a Master's degree took the student through a further foundation in classical studies and then Natural History, Natural Philosophy (what we would call Natural Sciences), and Moral Philosophy.[1] Despite a talent and predilection for literature, MacDonald chose chemistry, a field with clear application to agriculture and business, as his specialty, and in 1845 graduated from King's College, taking third prize in the subject. While there he also explored his own talent as a poet, dedicating his early works to his cousin, Helen McKay, and even considering taking up writing as his profession. As an aspiring author, he studied the works of the previous generation of Romantic poets, fascinated by Coleridge's mystical *The Rime of the Ancient Mariner* and Wordsworth's numinous poetry of nature. MacDonald's son Greville speculated that his father's writing was also shaped in part by work he undertook in 1842, cataloguing the library of a Scottish aristocrat, where he had the opportunity to read works of medieval romance and German Romanticism. Here he encountered the works of a variety of writers, including Novalis, Tieck, and de la Motte Fouqué,[2] whose interest in the Kunstmärchen (or art tale) would be crucial to MacDonald's development of an alternative literary approach to the traditional fairy tale later in his career.[3]

After graduating, MacDonald worked briefly as a tutor in London before returning to school in 1848, this time entering Highbury College to study for the ministry. The MacDonald

---

1 See Raeper 41-54 for an account of MacDonald's university years.

2 All three writers belong to the German Romantic Movement. Novalis is Georg Philipp Friedrich Freiherr von Hardenberg (1772-1801); Johann Ludwig Tieck (1773-1853), poet, writer, and critic of the German Romantic movement; Friedrich Heinrich Karl de la Motte, Baron Fouqué (1777-1843), best known for *Undine: A Romance* (1811), which MacDonald regarded as an exemplary fairy tale.

3 Gillian Lathey writes: "Indeed, the term *Kunstmärchen* was coined in German to distinguish the kind of literary fairy tale with aesthetic aspi-

family were committed Protestants, and he had been raised according to a strict Calvinist doctrine. Despite this background, MacDonald found the Calvinist division of humankind into the elect and the reprobate, the saved and the damned, difficult to reconcile with his own desire for a God who offered salvation to all and not just those predestined to be saved. Nevertheless, he experienced a strong call to ministry, and on completing his course of study in 1850 he took up a charge in Arundel, Sussex. Although his parishioners found him a caring pastor, his persistent radical ideas regarding salvation of the heathen, and his acceptance of the new critical studies suggesting that the Bible was better understood as a composite historical document assembled by men than as the infallibly recorded word of God, alienated the Church elders.[1] It became increasingly clear that the tenets of MacDonald's personal faith were incompatible with working within the system of the Church, and by 1853 he had left Arundel for Manchester, where he reconsidered his options for supporting his growing family.

A Career in Literature

MacDonald had married Louisa Powell in 1851, and over the next two decades they would become the parents of eleven children: Lilia Scott (1852), Mary Josephine (1853), Caroline Grace (1854), Greville (1856), Irene (1857), Winnifred Louisa (1858), Ronald (1860), Robert Falconer (1862), Maurice (1864), Bernard Powell (1865), and George MacKay (1867). Accounts of the household suggest that it was lively and sociable. The family entertained themselves and their guests with amateur theatricals (Louisa MacDonald would publish *Chamber Dramas for*

---

rations from the *Volksmärchen* or folk tales collected by the Grimm brothers or Ashbjørnsen and Moe. First applied to tales for adults ... the term is also used for carefully crafted stories for children and for a mixed adult-child audience" (97).

1   Stephen Prickett writes: "At the final showdown, the deacons of the church charged him with three areas of 'heresy.' First, that he had been unwise enough to speculate about salvation for animals—though he had, modestly enough, added that this was 'for all he knew.' Second, and far worse, he had followed up this piece of liberal agnosticism by suggesting that the same dispensation might even be extended to the heathen. Finally, turning away from specifics altogether, the deacons declared MacDonald to be 'tainted by German theology'" ("Two Worlds of George MacDonald" 21).

Children in 1870) and eventually developed a semi-professional production of Bunyan's *The Pilgrim's Progress* (first performed publicly in 1877) that helped to support the family. As the American children's periodical *Saint Nicholas* notes, Bunyan's "little story is turned into a quaint and beautiful drama, and acted by the family of a favourite writer, in the houses of earls and dukes ..." (Eggleston 301). MacDonald himself was known for his portrayal of Greatheart, and in later years often combined public lecturing with dramatic performance. MacDonald took on a variety of careers throughout his life, but his greatest success came in literary work, whether writing sermons, poetry, and fiction, or in lecturing about literature. In 1859 he became a professor of English Literature at Bedford College, moving six years later to hold the same position at King's College, London.

During his years as a minister, MacDonald had continued to pursue his interest in writing. In 1851 he gave as Christmas presents his own translation of *Twelve of the Spiritual Songs of Novalis*, which he had published privately. After leaving the ministry he worked on original compositions, publishing a long dramatic poem, *Within and Without*, in 1855 and *Poems* in 1857. It was not as a poet, however, that MacDonald was to make his most significant contributions to literature, but as a writer of fiction. His first novel, *Phantastes* (1858), introduced the strain of fantasy that would be central to his lasting reputation.[1] Subtitled *A Faerie Romance for Men and Women*, *Phantastes* offers a narrative made coherent not by plot and character, but rather by association and symbolism. MacDonald's somewhat mystical approach was influenced by his reading of German Romantic writers,[2] in particular Novalis, from whose work MacDonald takes his substantial epigraph to the novel:

One can imagine stories without rational cohesion and yet filled with associations, like dreams; and poems that are merely lovely

---

1 Stephen Prickett comments on the difficulty of classifying the genre of this novel: "We ... have the inestimable advantage of hindsight over the first puzzled and contemptuous reviewers who could hardly have been expected to hail it rapturously as the harbinger of the new literary form that we now call 'Victorian Fantasy'" ("Fictions and Metafictions" 109).

2 Rolland Hein comments, "He composed it during the final two months of 1857, intending to write for his English audience a fairy tale for adults in the tradition of the German *märchen*, such as Novalis's *Heinrich von Ofterdingen* or E.T.A. Hoffmann's *The Golden Pot*, both of which he greatly admired" (77).

*sounding, full of beautiful words, but also without rational sense
and connections—with, at the most, individual verses which are
intelligible, like fragments of the most varied things. This true
Poesie can at most have a general allegorical meaning and an
indirect effect, as music does. Thus is Nature so purely poetic, like
the room of a magician or a physicist; like a children's nursery or
a carpenter's shop....*

*A fairy-story is like a vision without rational connections, a
harmonious whole of miraculous things and events—as, for
example, a musical fantasia, the harmonic sequence of an Aeolian
harp, indeed Nature itself.*

★★★

*In a genuine fairy-story, everything must be miraculous, myste-
rious, and interrelated; everything must be alive, each in its own
way. The whole of Nature must be wondrously blended with the
whole world of the Spirit. In fairy-story the tie of anarchy, lawless-
ness, freedom, the natural state of Nature makes itself felt in the
world.... The world of the fairy-story is that world which is
opposed throughout to the world of rational truth, and precisely for
that reason it is so thoroughly an analogue to it, as Chaos is an
analogue to the finished Creation.*

This substantial epigraph announces what would become the
central tenets of MacDonald's literary art: the elevation of
mystery over rationality, the celebration of meaning acquired intu-
itively through symbol and association, and the insistence on the
interconnection of the natural world and the divine spirit. Such a
view of literature contrasts sharply with the dominant realist mode
of other British novels published that year, such as Dickens's *Little
Dorrit*, Charlotte Brontë's *The Professor*, or even Thomas Hughes's
school story for young readers, *Tom Brown's Schooldays*. Realist
fiction relies on plot lines that are both possible and probable,
characters who respond in recognizably human ways, and settings
that reflect the material world of experience. Although MacDonald would later become recognized as an author of such fiction
with the publication of *David Elginbrod* (1862), *Alec Forbes of
Howglen* (1865), and *Robert Falconer* (1868), his literary fame
remains primarily associated with fairy tales and fantasy.

Dealings with the Fairies

If MacDonald had imagined an audience of "Men and Women"
for *Phantastes*, he would very soon begin thinking in terms of

fairy tales for a broader readership that also included children. By 1862 he had prepared the manuscript for "The Light Princess," a gently satirical tale filled with puns and wry humour about a princess cursed at her christening with literal and metaphorical levity, but he was unable to secure a publisher. His friend Charles Dodgson had better luck with his own manuscript tale of talking rabbits and strange adventures, which he tried out on MacDonald's large family at this time: Greville MacDonald remembers giving "Uncle Dodgson's" story high praise by "wish[ing] there were 60,000 volumes of it"; it was published as *Alice's Adventures in Wonderland* in 1865, under the pseudonym Lewis Carroll (Raeper 173). Undaunted, MacDonald turned to a strategy that had been used by both British moralist writers for children and by his literary model Novalis: he combined romance and realism by embedding fairy tales within the text of a larger realist novel. "The Light Princess" was incorporated into *Adela Cathcart* (1864), along with other tales including "The Shadows" and "The Giant's Heart." In this novel, MacDonald weaves the story of a young woman suffering from a profound malaise with life, whose mental state is eased only when her interest is piqued by anecdotes and stories. MacDonald's narrator, John Smith, explains that a therapeutic process of tale-telling might effect a cure for her disorder, and it is in this context that "The Light Princess" first appeared in print. Paradoxically subtitled "A Fairy Tale Without Fairies" and with a motto—"Your servant, Goody Gravity"—from Samuel Richardson's epistolary novel *Sir Charles Grandison* (1753), from the outset the tale provokes a critical response from Adela's aunt, who "can't make head or tail of it." Smith offers a defence of fairy tales and of the importance of layered meaning, taking his motto from Milton's "Il Penseroso":

'Great bards beside
In sage and solemn times have sung
Of turneys and of trophies hung;
Of forests and inchantments drear,
Where more is meant than meets the ear.'[1]

Smith comments that "what distinguishes the true bard in such work is that *more is meant than meets the ear*; and although I am no

---

1 Milton, "Il Penseroso," lines 116-20. The final line would become the epigraph for *Dealings with the Fairies* (1867), when the fairy tales from *Adela Cathcart* were published separately.

bard, I should scorn to write anything that spoke only to the *ear,* which signifies the surface understanding" (MacDonald 1: 122-23). Readers are directed to interpret the tale beyond the simple letter of the text. *Adela Cathcart* was not, however, well-regarded by many reviewers—the *Athenaeum* sniffed that it is "nothing more than a collection of scraps, woven together by the pretense of a connected narrative" ("Review of *Adela Cathcart*" 644)—but others did recognize the vision that unifies the work: "This book, which is, as to its outside form, a collection of stories, has an inner life that gives it unity. Its author has the poet's sense of harmony that extends far as heaven from earth beyond mere questions of the marshaling of words, though it includes skill to make language musical and apt to the thought or feeling it expresses" ("Review of *Adela Cathcart*" 550). In privileging the "inner life" over the "outside form," the reviewer for the *Examiner* recognized MacDonald's characteristic perspective on the immanence of the Divine in the material. As the reviewer for the *British Quarterly* would write in an omnibus review of MacDonald's works up to 1868,

> The central idea of all his thinking is that the universe is but subject-matter for the love of God, a tree to be penetrated with life to its remotest branch, to be thrown out into the eternal blossoming of holiness and joy, a lamp to be filled with Divine radiance. Nay, the universe is but the embodiment of a Divine idea, and that idea is love. ("Works by George MacDonald" 12)

Even the critical *Athenaeum,* however, conceded that "Of the stories [in *Adela Cathcart*], Mr. Smith's extravagant but quaint fairy tales seem to us the best.... There is a certain grace and beauty about all that Mr. Macdonald [*sic*] writes" (644), and perhaps on the strength of the positive reception of these embedded fairy tales, MacDonald decided to collect a number together in a single volume. Four years later he republished the three fairy tales included in *Adela Cathcart,* along with "Cross Purposes," which had first appeared in *Beeton's Christmas Annual* for 1862, and a new tale, "The Golden Key," as *Dealings with the Fairies.* This collection was received far more positively and established MacDonald's reputation as a writer of literary fairy tales. But what exactly did it mean to be a writer of fairy tales in nineteenth-century Britain?

When MacDonald had begun writing fairy stories in the 1860s, he adopted a genre that had been a popular—but also highly contested—form of children's literature in Britain for well over a century. In his influential *Some Thoughts Concerning Education* (1692), John Locke had warned parents against exposing their children to the dangerous imaginative world of ghost stories and fairy tales, though he did advocate animal fables, with their clear moral allegory, as suitable books for children. Nevertheless, even a cursory examination of works published in the later eighteenth century demonstrates that traditional tales involving the land of faerie, such as medieval romances, continued to be available in chapbook form, and popular adaptations of the French *salon* fairy tales of Charles Perrault, Madame D'Aulnoy, and others found a market in Britain throughout the period. A significant change, however, takes place at the beginning of nineteenth century, for at this time an articulated consciousness of the links between ideology and children's literature begins to emerge, most famously in the writings of Mrs. Sarah Trimmer, whom M.O. Grenby has identified as "perhaps the most important individual influence on late eighteenth- and early nineteenth-century British children's literature" (137). In 1802 she began *The Guardian of Education*, the first periodical dedicated to reviewing works for children,[1] and, like Locke, she had little sympathy with the traditional fairy tale. In her 1803 review of *Histories and Tales of Past Times, Told by Mother Goose* (an English translation of Perrault's *Histoires ou Contes du Temps Passé*), Trimmer relegates the fairy tale to the pleasures of a more primitive literary past not in keeping with modern ideas of child-rearing:

> Though we well remember the interest with which, in our childish days, when books of amusement for children were scarce, we read, or listened to the history of *Little Red Riding Hood*, and *Blue Beard*, &c., we do not wish to have such sensations awakened in the hearts of our grandchildren, by the same means; for the terrific images, which tales of this nature present to the imagination, usually make deep impressions, and injure the tender minds of children, by exciting unreasonable and groundless fears. Neither do the generality of tales of this kind supply any moral instruction to the level of the infantine capacity. (Quoted in Rowe 29)

---

1 Grenby notes: "[*The Guardian*] was published monthly, then quarterly, from June 1802 until September 1806 and, as far as we know, was written entirely by Trimmer" (137).

Rejecting the often brutal morality of the traditional tale—think of *Bluebeard* with its series of dismembered wives punished for their inappropriate curiosity, or versions of *Cinderella* in which the wicked stepmother dances to her death in red-hot iron shoes—Trimmer advocated works for children that offered a more civilized moral education. Indeed, by the beginning of the nineteenth century a parallel tradition of fairy tales had begun to develop in Britain, in which fantastic narratives were embedded within realist fiction for children, their imaginative elements safely contained and interpreted for young readers, their fairies not benevolent godmothers lavishing jewels and ball-gowns, but moral arbiters who provided gifts such as mirrors that reflected the ugliness of vanity and selfishness or the beauty of virtue and sacrifice. By the 1830s, a generation of British writers had continued the process of moralizing the fairy tale, with rather mixed aesthetic results. As Anita Moss points out, "writers of these didactic fairy tales—Francis Edward Paget, Catherine Sinclair, Mark Lemon, and others—used the fairy tale mode to reinforce bourgeois moral lessons on thrift, industry, piety, and other plodding Victorian virtues.... Such writers often profess to believe in the imagination, fairytale, and liberated possibilities for children; yet they give in finally to explicit moral didacticism" (47). Throughout the century Victorian writers continued to adapt and re-imagine the fairy tale and its relationship to entertainment and moral education.

Nevertheless, a parallel fairy-tale tradition was beginning to emerge in Britain that owed more to the fantastic than to the didactic. Mary Howitt's *Wonderful Stories for Children* (1846), a translation of ten of Hans Christian Andersen's tales, was well-received. As William Raeper notes, "Progress was slow, but after 1840 the literary fairy tale—as opposed to rewritten versions of traditional tales—began to make its appearance and with increased leisure time and the acceptance of the novel as entertainment for adults, it became grudgingly accepted that children could have their fun too" (307). A few writers chose to approach the moral fairy tale in a more elevated and literary manner, imbuing the supernatural realm of faerie with a distinctly Christian mysticism. John Ruskin's *The King of the Golden River* (1851) takes the traditional elements of the European fairy tale—three brothers, the youngest of whom is unlikely to succeed, a test of character, and a magical helper in the form of the South West Wind—to create an original tale in which greed and selfishness are punished and kindness and communal feeling rewarded. In

The Gold Thread: A Story for the Young (1861), Norman MacLeod, from whom MacDonald would take over the editorship of *Good Words for the Young*, offers an allegory of Christian faith that closely resembles those created by MacDonald in both Curdie's clue and the magical thread followed by Irene in *The Princess and the Goblin*. Other writers adapted the fairy tale to offer a satiric commentary on contemporary life: William Makepeace Thackeray's *The Rose and the Ring* (1855), subtitled "A Fire-side Pantomime for Great and Small Children," provides a witty critique of aristocratic life and manners through the same kind of lively domestic exchange that MacDonald would use in "The Light Princess."

MacDonald's shorter fairy tales then, form part of a larger cultural discussion of the place of fantasy as a genre and the function of the imagination in works for younger readers. The three tales from *Dealings with the Fairies* included in this Broadview edition offer a good introduction to MacDonald's characteristic themes and literary strategies. "The Light Princess," "The Giant's Heart," and "The Golden Key" illustrate the breadth of MacDonald's approach.

"The Light Princess" offers perhaps the best introduction to MacDonald's art of the fairy tale: gently comic and satirical, the tale acknowledges its debt to the classic fairy tale tradition while challenging its readers to engage imaginatively with the infinite power of love and sacrifice. Like a traditional fairy tale princess, the protagonist is cursed at her christening by her spiteful aunt Princess Makemnoit (who also happens to be a witch):

Light of spirit, by my charms,
Light of body, every part,
    Never weary human arms—
Only crush thy parents' heart! (p. 195)

Her childhood provides multiple comic opportunities for Mac-Donald to explore as the lighter than air princess floats at inopportune moments, her corporeal resistance to gravity matched only by her irrepressible lightness of heart on all occasions. Such lightness is a mixed quality, and as the princess grows older but no more emotionally mature, her parents debate its merits, with the king focusing on the positive nature of being light-hearted, light-handed, light-footed, and light-bodied, while the queen counters with the negative associations of being light-headed, light-fingered, and light-minded. For all its slapstick physical comedy and verbal punning play, MacDonald's tale conveys a serious meaning: mere physical gravity alone is insufficient to reverse Makemnoit's curse—the princess must experience spiritual gravitas as well. The marriage plot, which MacDonald uses repeatedly in his tales as a means of balancing masculine and feminine, material and spiritual desire, provides the impetus for change. Only in the water of the lake can the Light Princess experience the normal physical forces of gravity, and it is thus fitting that the lake becomes the locus of her attainment of a spiritual gravity as well when she learns what it is to love and to grieve. After encountering the Prince of a neighbouring kingdom during one of her midnight swims, the Light Princess discovers the pleasure of falling when he helps her return to the lake after having inadvertently propelled her into the tree-tops. The Prince experiences a pleasurable fall as well, of the romantic kind, but his love is unreciprocated by a princess who is unable to experience such a weighty emotion. When Princess Makemnoit learns of the pleasure taken by her niece in the lake, she retaliates by draining it and offering only one solution: a living man must willingly plug the hole in the bottom of the lake or the kingdom will be parched to oblivion. Faced with watching his Princess die with her beloved lake, the Prince offers to sacrifice himself to save her. Still unable to experience the heaviness of sadness, the Princess cheerfully accepts his offer: "She did not care who the man was; that was nothing to her. The hole wanted stopping; and if only a man would do, why, take one" (p. 224). Not until she experiences care—both the sacramental feeding of the Prince with wine and biscuits as he awaits the rising waters and the concern she unexpectedly experiences as they rise above his head—can the Princess reciprocate his gesture of love and pull him from the hole, willing to sacrifice her lake to his well-being. MacDonald's description of the natural world at the climax of the Prince's restoration to life emphasizes the paradoxical union of opposites:

> All the pent-up crying of her life was spent now. And a rain came on, such as had never been seen in that country. The sun shone all the time, and the great drops, which fell straight to the earth, shone likewise. The palace was in the heart of a rainbow. It was a rain of rubies, and sapphires, and emeralds, and topazes. The torrents poured from the mountains like molten gold; and if it had not been for its subterraneous outlet, the lake would have overflowed and inundated the country. It was full from shore to shore. (p. 228)

The rainbow echoes the Biblical covenant, while the gemstones evoke those found in the walls of the Heavenly City; plenitude is possible only with a balance of outflow and replenishment.

If "The Light Princess" demonstrates MacDonald's talent for combining traditional fairy tale elements with a new mystical meaning, the tale in *Dealings with the Fairies* generally conceded to be most derivative is "The Giant's Heart," the story of Tricksey-Wee and her brother, Buffy Bob, and their defeat of the giant Thunderthump. As Roderick McGillis points out, "the story of a giant who keeps his heart hidden outside his body is familiar to students of folklore" ("Introduction" 6), and MacDonald may have based his tale on George Dasent's translation of one of Asbjørnsen and Moe's *Popular Tales from the Norse*. The tale is unusual in MacDonald's oeuvre in both its violence and its knowingness. Tricksey-Wee, as her name suggests, is a young heroine who acts as a trickster figure, one who actively deceives both the Giant and his wife and who functions as a pragmatic solver of problems. Although it is Buffy Bob who ultimately stabs the Giant's heart to deliver his death blow, it is Tricksey-Wee who anoints it with spider juice to shrink it and who then repeatedly pinches it to torment the Giant into complying with their wishes. She is thus quite unlike the gentle and naïve Irene of *The Princess and the Goblin*, the other-worldly Tangle of "The Golden Key," or the irrepressible Light Princess. In "The Giant's Heart" MacDonald offers little sense of a fantasy world charged with the numinous Divine most frequently associated with his works; rather, he offers the more traditional elements of ogreish giants who consume little children (though this one prefers them pickled like radishes), talking animal helpers, and character tests. Still, as a number of critics have pointed out, the tale remains somewhat unsettling, something other than a simple imitation of the folk tale. Raeper comments "'the Giant's Heart' ... paints an uncomfortable picture of a giant who gorges himself on vegetable-like children, and who is finally outwitted by the embarrassingly named Tricksey-Wee and Buffy Bob.... Perhaps it is the cynicism of the children, their lack of compassion, and their readiness to break their word which makes this story such uncomfortable reading" (315-16). Those who share Raeper's sense of the tale as "clumsy and uneven," judge it according to expectations shaped by the mystery and complex allegory of MacDonald's other tales. What they miss, according to McGillis, is the degree to which "The Giant's Heart" expresses literary characteristics that are equally part of MacDonald's art: "Laughter, parody, and satire feature in many of MacDonald's children's works" ("Introduction" 13), he writes, and "The Giant's Heart" is no exception. The anthropomorphic domestic bickering of the Lark and his wife pokes satiric fun at married life, as does the depiction of the giant's wife as one part Victorian 'angel in the house,' who defends her husband as "a very good man" (though he eats little children) and who darns his Sunday stockings with care, and one part devious schemer who lies concerning the whereabouts of Tricksey-Wee and Buffy Bob, and who tries to gain advantage over her husband by persuading him to move his heart closer to home. Thunderthump's self-righteous morality as he pops a little boy caught in a lie into a pot of boiling water affords similar amusement, as the reader is faced with the choice of sympathizing with the narrator's satisfaction in seeing the tattle-tale punished or the giant's virtuous satisfaction in punishing a liar ("Introduction" 11). As a protagonist, Tricksey-Wee also reflects MacDonald's typical complicating of stereotypical gender roles, especially for girls. She owes much to the folk tradition of practical heroines like Gretel, who is resourceful enough to outwit the witch and save her brother Hansel, and in "The Giant's Heart" she is clearly the dominant intellect in her partnership with Buffy Bob.

The Princess and the Goblin

As he came close to finishing the manuscript for *The Princess and the Goblin*, MacDonald wrote to his wife, "I know it is as good work of the kind as I can do, and I think will be the most complete thing I have done."[1] His confident tone is, however, moderated by anxiety over the question of the commercial potential of the new work. He planned to publish *The Princess and the Goblin* in the monthly magazine *Good Words for the Young*, which he edited for the publisher Alexander Strahan, but, in the same letter to his wife he noted, "I have a bit of bad news. The Magazine, which went up in the beginning of the volume, has fallen very much since. Strahan thinks it is because there is too much of what he calls the fairy element." MacDonald clearly felt divided between his sense of the artistic merits of his work and the need, as an editor, to work in service of a successful commercial enterprise. No doubt this conflict between the confidence

---

1   Qtd. in Greville MacDonald's biography of George MacDonald (412).

he held in his aesthetic sense and uncertainty about the saleability of a marketed product was intensified by the critique from Strahan that "there is too much of ... the fairy element" in MacDonald's work.

MacDonald's sense of conflict expressed in this letter to his wife is representative of a significant debate about the definition, form, content, and marketing of literature for young children that began early in the Victorian period and intensified in the latter half of the nineteenth century. The debate has been well discussed by critics such as Marjory Lang, but it is worth reviewing comments made by Sir Joshua Girling Fitch, a noted educationalist of the time, described as "an admirable example of an open-minded and progressive man with strong traditionalist roots seeking to realign himself to a changing society" (Robertson), since he offers an effective summary of the concerns of the time in an article for *The London Quarterly Review* in 1860:

> The fact is, that while books written for children, and sold for them, are abundant enough, a real child's book is still a comparatively scarce product. Scores of persons who could not succeed in any other branch of letters, are attracted to this by the prospect of certain remuneration, and by the supposed easiness of the task. Any body can write commonplace anecdotes, and diluted history, and sham science, in jargon which, because it is not the language of men and women, is conventionally supposed to be that of children; and when the outward furtherance and embellishment of crimson and gold binding and coloured engravings are added it is easy to mistake the result for a child's book. (470-71)

Central to Fitch's concern is that the rush to feed a rapidly growing demand has led to a debasement of the product and therefore a debasement of those who consume these books as objects, which are now, he writes, "not, in fact *a book*, in any true sense of the word,—only a feeble, showy and worthless substitute" (471). Fitch goes on to argue for the importance of developing a sense of social responsibility, morality, justice, and religious faith in children through the "true sense" of the book. He does not offer a formal definition of children's literature or even its specific subject matter but instead makes an interesting assertion about the education of the child and the object of literature for the young, one that opposes the advocacy by many divines in the period that the best literature for children conveys its values through explicit moral statements or pious religious allegory. The best children's writer

> is content to let the story carry its own moral, and to leave the interpretation to work itself out in due time in his little reader's mind; and this is the wisest course. It is in harmony with the true requirements of a child's imperfectly developed nature. For in early life some of the best lessons which we learn, are learnt unconsciously, and when we are least aware that they are lessons. The lessons which are conveyed in books of amusement, since they are intended to be acquired voluntarily, should all be of this class. Otherwise it may be safely predicted that they will not be acquired at all. (486)

Fitch's position moves the debate from concern for subject matter to a much more engaged approach to the readerly experience of a childlike mind, one open to influences and highly capable of taking in more than the obvious. In this suggestion Fitch points to a childhood power of learning through the potentiality of understanding (whether that comprehension is conscious or unconscious).

Extending his argument about the importance of unconscious learning, Fitch adds the important qualification that there should be a sophistication in writing for children that awakens the mind and presents it with content that stretches perception beyond its immediate understanding. "The great purpose of children's books," he argues, "is not so much to impart instruction, as to promote growth." With this purpose comes a specialized view of the child and the ideal form of literature for the childhood mind:

> We must not think of a child's mind as of a vessel, which it is for us to fill, but as a wonderfully organized instrument, which it is for us to develop and to set in motion. He will be well or ill educated, not according to the accuracy with which he retains the notions which have been impressed upon him from without, but according to the power which he puts forth from within, and the activity and regularity with which the several feelers or *tentacula* of his nature lay hold on all that is to be seen and thought and known around him.... The teaching in our books should be less dogmative than suggestive. It should seek rather to waken appetite than to satiate it. So long as a book makes a child wakeful and interested, it is by no means necessary that he should com-

prehend it all. The thought, 'I cannot understand this now, but when I am older I shall be able to do so,' is not only a natural one to a child, but one which at once betokens modesty, and provides stimulus for future exertion. The excessive care to explain everything clearly, which characterizes many modern books for young people, renders this thought unfamiliar to a child. (486-87)

Fitch's goal is to redefine the purposes of reading, and in particular reading done by children, from one designed to import specific, raw, and "dogmative" lessons to an inspirational and aspirational experience. The importance of the instrumentality of the mind is its active qualities, its ability to reach out even to ideas, images, and stories it can't fully comprehend. MacDonald's approach to his own fiction was an even more sophisticated version of this inspirational and aspirational model as he worked to define, or perhaps, more properly, not define the fairy tale in his essays on the Imagination (see Appendix B, p. 321).

When it came to defining the fairy tale and the importance of the fantastic in the fairy tale, MacDonald approaches the matter through indirection rather than reductive definition. "Were I asked, what is a fairytale?" he writes in an essay on "The Fantastic Imagination," "I should reply, *Read Undine: that is a fairytale*; ... Were I further begged to describe the *fairytale*, or define what it is, I would make answer, that I should as soon think of describing the abstract human face, or stating what must go to constitute a human being. A fairytale is just a fairytale ..." (Appendix B1, p. 322). The circular argument is not designed to deny the value of the inquiry but rather to redirect the attention to a more important question: how does a fairy tale work? Indeed, he redirects the inquiry from definition to hermeneutics, formulating a discussion that explores how fairy tales have meaning and how they are transactional forms designed to awaken something in the reader. He quickly dispels the idea that reading fairy tales is easy or that meaning is the experience of singular meaning: "A fairytale is not an allegory" since the limited correspondence of image to meaning typical of naïve allegory can only bring about "weariness" in the reader. Instead, "A genuine work of art must mean many things; the truer its art, the more things it will mean," and meaning involves an exchange between reader and text: "Everyone, however, who feels the story, will read its meaning after his own nature and development: one man will read one meaning in it, another will read another" (Appendix B1, p. 324).

The claims MacDonald makes for the reading experience, then, are ones that see the interaction between reader and text significant in terms of the degree to which the text awakens something in the reader. Thus, he writes, "The best thing you can do for your fellow, next to rousing his conscience, is—not to give him things to think about, but to wake things up that are in him; or say, to make him think things for himself" (Appendix B1, p. 325). This "rousing" of conscience is, for MacDonald, the essence of learning and a forward-looking expansion of the mind as its circumference of understanding grows. Certainty or "repose is not the end of education; its end is a noble unrest, an ever renewed awaking from the dead, a ceaseless questioning of the past for the interpretation of the future, an urging on of the motions of life, which had better far be accelerated into fever, than retarded into lethargy" (Appendix B2, p. 327). He seats this process of growth and pursuit of the unknown within the faculty of the imagination, a faculty designated "for those infinite lands of uncertainty lying all about the sphere hollowed out of the dark by the glimmering lamp of our knowledge" (Appendix B2, p. 346). And the imagination is fed, he concludes, by the power of fantasy, and fantasy is therefore essential to the writing which most inspires mental growth in youth:

> Seek not that your sons and your daughters should not see visions, should not dream dreams; seek that they should see true visions, that they should dream noble dreams. Such outgoing of the imagination is one with aspiration, and will do more to elevate above what is low and vile than all possible inculcations of morality. Nor can religion herself ever rise up into her own calm home, her crystal shrine, when one of her wings, one of the twain with which she flies, is thus broken or paralyzed. (Appendix B2, p. 347)

While such bold statements about the importance of vision, dreams, and the imagination as a basis for childhood education, when put into practice by MacDonald, did perhaps make his publisher Alexander Strahan uneasy, these basic elements provide a foundation for works such as *The Princess and the Goblin*. Throughout the tale we see a range of narrative strategies designed to waken the appetite, bring about an exertion of the imagination, and promote growth in the understanding. The goal of these narrative strategies is, in keeping with Fitch's dictum, "not so much to impart instruction, as to promote growth."

The first of these strategies appears in the frame narrative established in the periodical version of *The Princess and the Goblin* published in *Good Words for the Young* in 1870-71. It opens with a narrative frame in which a young reader asks the "Editor" of the story a series of questions about some basic assumptions contained in the story's opening. The narrative strategy chosen by MacDonald here is designed to shape the process of reading as one involving engagement, question, and an aspiration of the imagination and understanding in acts of comprehension. From the beginning of the tale MacDonald's text invites exchange between the authorial/editorial persona and his imagined reader:

There once was a little princess, who—
"But, Mr. Editor, why do you always write about princesses?"
"Because every little girl is a princess."
"You will make them vain if you tell them that."
"Not if they understand what I mean."
"Then what do you mean?"
"What do you *mean by a princess?"*
"The daughter of a king."
"Very well; then every little girl is a princess, and there would be no need to say anything about it, except that she is always in danger of forgetting her rank, and behaving as if she had grown out of the mud. I have seen little princesses behave like the children of thieves and lying beggars, and that is why they need to be told they are princesses. And that is why, when I tell a story of this kind, I like to tell it about a princess. Then I can say better what I mean, because I can then give her every beautiful thing I want her to have."
"Please go on." (p. 47)

This brief exchange illustrates a complex interpretive transaction between MacDonald's imagined child reader and the editor. This reader is recognized as sufficiently sophisticated to identify recurrent characters and themes—*"why do you always write about princesses"*—and to suspect that this pattern carries significance beyond mere coincidence. The reader also believes that texts have the power to effect changes in those who read them—for example, little girls will become vain if they are told that they are princesses. Thus the first three lines of the story establish reading as an endeavour that is active rather than passive, that is predicated on previous experience, both textual and literal, and suggests that because they carry social effect, texts assume moral responsibility.

While MacDonald's narrator constructs an active, questioning, meaning-producing reader, he complicates the relationship by challenging the assumptions offered, suggesting that such a response may miss the full significance of his predilection for princesses as his protagonists. Little girls won't be made vain by being called princesses, he asserts, "*if they understand what [he] mean[s].*" There follows a brief discussion of what exactly might be meant/understood by the apparently straightforward term "princess." The child asserts simply that she understands the word literally as meaning "*the daughter of a king,*" which the narrator then paradoxically insists means that "*every little girl is a princess.*" Thus the interpretive challenge is posed: How can it be that "every little girl is princess" unless every little girl is "the daughter of a king"? But in the reader's cultural experience, both in life and in previously encountered texts, not all fathers are kings, so how can the statement be true? MacDonald requires his reader to make an interpretive leap, to understand that he is speaking not in socio-political terms, but in metaphorical/doctrinal images—that according to his theological world view, all little girls are princesses in that they are the daughters of the King of Heaven. But MacDonald refuses to say so explicitly. That such a narrative challenge was a conscious choice on the part of the author is demonstrated by the revisions to the manuscript,[1] which show that the narrator's response initially asserted, "I need hardly say what I mean, for I mean—Is not every little girl the daughter of The King?" Such phrasing directs the reader to the metaphorical answer of Christ as universal Father rather than posing the riddle for the reader to figure out. The revisions take the answer out of the hands of the narrator and places it firmly back in those of the reader.

In "The Fantastic Imagination," MacDonald assures the adult reader that "your children are not likely to trouble you about the meaning [of a fairy tale]. They find what they are capable of finding, and more would be too much" (p. 324). Indeed, the

---

1   The manuscript for the serialized publication of *The Princess and the Goblin* is held in the George MacDonald Collection of the Brander Library in Huntly, Aberdeenshire, Scotland. A digitized version is available at http://www.aberdeenshire.gov.uk/libraries/information/georgemacdonald/ebooks/The%20Princess%20and%20The%20Goblin/index.htm#/-2/. For a brief account of MacDonald's practice of revision, see Appendix D, p. 369.

child reader of *The Princess and the Goblin* doesn't interrogate the narrator further, but simply says "Please go on." Whether this results from an understanding and recognition of MacDonald's metaphor for her as a child of God, or from a complete inability to comprehend, it is not clear; it does, however, illustrate MacDonald's faith that children as readers "will take what they are capable of finding" in the text and move on. MacDonald's prose style, then, with its gaps requiring imagined completion, its mystical suggestiveness, its frequent complex metaphors pointing a meaning outside of the child's immediate experience, enacts his belief that through the act of engaging with this type of text, the child reader will come to an understanding of the Divine both within and without.

Throughout the serial version of *The Princess and the Goblin*, the narrative "fourth wall" is breached as the imagined reader interrogates "Mr. Editor" regarding his narratorial practices. When in the third chapter MacDonald introduces "A very old lady who sat spinning," the imagined reader immediately interrupts to challenge the originality of his story: "*Oh Mr. Editor! I know the story you are going to tell: it's The Sleeping Beauty; only you're spinning too, and making it longer*" (p. 51). A challenge such as this makes explicit the textual transactions recognized by both writer and reader: the child's demand for originality couched in the satisfied knowingness of a cultural literacy (she recognizes the details derived from the tale of *Sleeping Beauty*) is met with adult defensiveness: "*No indeed, it is not that story. Why should I tell one that every properly educated child knows already? More old ladies than one have sat spinning in a garret.*" (The initial response in the manuscript is even more forceful: "I don't tell second-hand stories.") These inserted passages make literal the ideal reader posited by MacDonald: one who actively questions the text and who brings the full weight of her literary experience—no matter how limited—to bear on the narrative at hand.

An additional narrative strategy appears in MacDonald's description, or more properly, his lack of description of a set of toys Irene owns but does not play with. On a dreary "wet day" the princess finds herself essentially trapped within doors, feeling extraordinarily "tired, so tired that even her toys could no longer amuse her." The narrator goes on to depict how this tiredness admits of no distractions:

> You would wonder at that if I had time to describe to you
> one half of the toys she had. But then you wouldn't have the

toys themselves, and that makes all the difference: you can't get tired of a thing before you have it. It was a picture, though, worth seeing—the princess sitting in the nursery with the sky-ceiling over her head, at a great table covered with her toys. If my brother-editor who looks after the pictures,[1] would like to draw this, I should advise him not to meddle with the toys. I am afraid of attempting to describe them, and I think he had better not try to draw them. He had better not. He can do a thousand things I can't, but I don't think he could draw those toys. (pp. 49–50)

The narrator stresses the marvellous nature of these toys, tempting the reader to imagine them, but refusing to describe them in any concrete detail. The invitation, the enticement of phrases such as "It was a picture, though, worth seeing," wakens the appetite, the understanding and draws out the reader's imagination, at the same time as the narrator expresses his fear of "attempting to describe" these toys. To do so would be to "meddle" or to interfere with the imaginative work of the reader as she or he aspires to create pictures of toys that are so entrancing they offer a challenge to the act of representation itself. The challenge to the act of representation becomes a challenge to the reader and in particular to the reader's imagination as it is moved to formulate a picture of the most wonderful toys conceivable. Further, this challenge intensifies the polarity between the misery of the wet day and the implied beauty and attraction of the toys themselves. Ultimately, the strategy of incomplete representation stimulates the imagination, inspiring it to acts of exertion that in turn move the mind towards a state of growth.

In addition to the use of narrative strategies that we have seen in the frame narrative and the strategy of incomplete representation, the narrator offers partial explanations of important events without offering the reader clear or complete rationale for these events. One of the most intriguing of these partial explanations appears in the narrator's first description of the goblins and their origins:

There was a legend current in the country, that at one time they lived above ground, and were very like other people. But for some reason or other, concerning which there were differ-

---

1   MacDonald substitutes "the artist" for "my brother-editor who looks after the pictures" in subsequent editions.

ent legendary theories, the king had laid what they thought too severe taxes upon them, or had required observances of them they did not like, or had begun to treat them with more severity, in some way or other, and impose stricter laws; and the consequence was that they had all disappeared from the face of the country. According to the legend, however, instead of going to some other country, they had all taken refuge in the subterranean caverns, whence they never came out but at night, and then seldom showed themselves in any numbers, and never to many people at once. (p. 48)

This passage serves as a model of the movement of the searching mind. The origins of the goblins are tied up in traditional legends, which have been obscured by time and tradition. When the goblins lived above ground, their king may have taxed them heavily, required what were believed to be onerous "observances" or imposed "stricter laws" or even undertaken a combination of these objectionable actions, but the narrator is unable to specify the causes of such actions (no matter which action might have taken place). The source of these actions is "for some reason or other" and "there were different legendary theories" about how this situation came to unfold. Even the possibility that the king imposed severer laws comes with a qualification. "In some way or other" these laws were imposed, but the mechanisms used to enact them and the nature of these laws remains unaccounted for. In part, MacDonald is showing the nature of legend, tradition, and oral history with the vagaries and accretions that accompany such forms. However, the searching nature of the passage invites the mind to move across a landscape of possibilities not seeking for dogmatic answers but instead inspiring the exploration of a wide range of political and social potential causes for a distortion of the human mind and spirit that manifests itself in the form of goblins and gnomes. As this particular passage progresses, the narrator again invokes a strategy of incomplete representation to describe the goblins as figures whose "hideous" appearance challenges representation: "There was no invention ... of the most lawless imagination expressed by pen or pencil, that could surpass the extravagance of their appearance" (p. 48).

Although the narrative strategies described so far have tended to activate the reader's imagination through incomplete representations, partial explanations, and other acts of verbal indirection, MacDonald's commissioning of illustrations by Arthur Hughes invokes visual enticements for the imagination. Deeply influenced as a young man by the first issue of the *Germ* (1850), which announced the artistic tenets of the Pre-Raphaelite Brotherhood,[1] Hughes became a member of that circle and his paintings reflect the Romantic symbolism and fascination with colour and detail associated with their work. His art was praised by John Ruskin and purchased by William Morris, though it is as an illustrator of works for children that much of his fame rests today. In 1869 he was asked to provide forty-three illustrations for the sixth edition of the popular school novel *Tom Brown's Schooldays*, a commission that "earned the artist celebrity for the rest of the century" (Wildman 24). By that time, however, Hughes had already begun illustrating works for young readers through his association with MacDonald. The two had been introduced in 1859 and shared a common interest in fantasy and family life. MacDonald's household was known for its amateur theatricals and children's parties: one visitor commented that MacDonald "used to cover himself with a skin rug, and pretend to be a bear to the great delight of us all! Arthur Hughes used to join in with great gusto" (quoted in Wildman 26). Thus when MacDonald needed an illustrator for his fairy tale, he turned to Hughes to strike just the right note. The two had worked together previously on *At the Back of the Northwind*, serialized in *Good Words for the Young* between November 1868 and October 1870.[2] Stephen Wildman, in *Arthur Hughes: His Life and Works*, comments of the seventy-seven designs, "these are among the most extraordinary

---

1 The Pre-Raphaelite Brotherhood is the name adopted by a group of English poets, painters, and critics who hoped to reform contemporary art by advocating a return to fourteenth-century Italian aesthetic values of attention to detail, intense colour palette, and high mimetic purpose. Founded in 1848 by William Holman Hunt, John Everett Millais, and Dante Gabriel Rossetti, the group soon grew to include a broad range of artists and writers. Their work was championed by influential critic John Ruskin. The tenets focussed on attitude as much as technique: artists should have serious and important ideas to express and should avoid the merely academic or conventional in expressing them, rather returning to close attention to Nature for inspiration.

2 Following this initial collaboration, Hughes illustrated *Ranald Bannerman's Boyhood* (1869-70), as well as stories by a number of other authors commissioned by MacDonald after he became editor of the journal in 1868.

illustrations of their age" (26).[1] Described as "one of a number of artists who provided the pictures for wood engravings that supplied illustrations for a growing list of Victorian periodicals, which typifies them as illustrators of the 1860s" (Bodmer 124), Hughes worked with the constraints imposed by the medium of the nineteenth-century periodical. The format of a journal such as *Good Words for the Young* and the technical requirements of the woodcut production method posed a challenge to the artist:

> Because of the prevalence of this hatching and texture, certain motifs developed to contrast the light and dark of the image, such as an external light source provided by a fireplace or a window, the latter of which set up a dichotomy of outside and inside.... This built-in claustrophobia was emphasized by the odd-shaped or limited sized pictures, usually strictly framed, required for the narrower double columns of journal publication, as well as the extended or bent necks common to the Pre-Raphaelite images. (Bodmer 123)

When *The Princess and the Goblin* appeared in *Good Words for the Young*, Hughes once more was chosen as illustrator. He provided thirty images, all designed as partial page illustrations to fit the double-column format.

The illustrations themselves provide another instance of a narrative strategy that sets in motion the power of the imagination by depicting the process of interpretive action. In the passage quoted above concerning the incomplete representation of Irene's toys, the narrator pauses to say, "If my brother-editor [later changed by MacDonald to "the artist"] who looks after the pictures, would like to draw this, I should advise him not to meddle with the toys" (pp. 49-50). While this injunction seems restrictive and accuses the illustrator of potentially interfering with the work of imagining, it also directs attention to the immediate relationship between writer and artist. The visual accompa-

---

1 He is less complimentary regarding the illustrations for *The Princess and the Goblin*: "succeeding illustrations became more workmanlike than impressive, although this is not entirely surprising given the often tedious nature of the text. Hughes did his best with the uninspiring writing of *The Princess and the Goblin...*, but clearly preferred the odder, more succinct stories ... where he could concentrate on a few strong images, using dramatic chiaroscuro effects" (26).

niments to the text are not accidental and are engaged in the same process of activating an exertion of the imagination and inspiring a growth of understanding. The illustrations, in the first instance, provide an interpretation of MacDonald's text. As George Bodmer points out, Hughes's illustrations heighten the medieval context of the story and "are sharp, controlled and hard-edged, and fill their columnwide frame with action and emotion. Rather than explaining the motives, they tend to suggest the mystery of the actions. Much of the drama takes place inside, underground, or at night, and Hughes's engravings add to the darkness" (Bodmer 128). Moreover, for the modern reader the interconnection of this interpretive relationship between author and illustrator has become fully intertwined so that "the illustrator and ... writer's works are so closely identified that later interpreters of MacDonald cannot help but be influenced by Hughes's pictures and presentation of the text" (Bodmer 124).

The illustrations entice the reader's imagination. Figure 17 (p. 104), for instance, depicts the princess heading up the winding stair to her great grandmother's room, drawn by the light coming from above. At this point in the story, both she and the reader are in a state of suspense about what or who will be at the top of the staircase. Hughes harnesses the power of anticipation in the written narrative and heightens expectation in the reader as she or he is propelled forward in the narrative towards discovery of the grandmother figure and the potentials she represents. The verbal motif of stretching the mind forward and outward to a greater understanding is maintained in these illustrations to inspire growth that leads to comprehension. Elsewhere, Hughes depicts the need to break the outside borders of his designs and thereby to consider the extension of meaning beyond the confines of the illustration. Figures 15 (p. 102) and 31 (p. 185) each depict the king on his horse with Irene, and both illustrations break through the top edge of the picture frame, suggesting that expansiveness of the king's soul cannot be fully contained within conventional boundaries, especially when he and Irene are together. In contrast, Hughes shows us the other extreme, the closing down of opportunity and the constriction of the imagination in Figure 4 (p. 56), a depiction of Irene's boredom on the rainy day in which even the wonder of her own toys cannot distract her. Hughes follows the narrator's injunction that the illustrator should not depict these toys, so he turns instead to an image of Irene and her nurse, both bent within the confines of the picture frame. The compression of their bodies and the down-turned faces of both represent the world of mental entropy and an imagination oppressed by its dreary circumstance.

Beyond the commentary in the sequence of illustrations provided by Hughes and the specific narrative strategies used by MacDonald, the overall structural dimensions of *The Princess and the Goblin* engage and at times frustrate the attempt at simplistic or dogmatic interpretation. Stephen Prickett notes that *The Princess and the Goblin* repeatedly invites the reader to interpret the text as a sustained and consistent allegory of ideas, but at the same time frustrates such a reading. For instance, the setting of the story appears to have "the makings of a medieval three-story universe" (*Victorian Fantasy* 166) with a heavenly setting portrayed though the grandmother, a middle earth inhabited by the princess Irene and a hellish world of demonish goblins. A reading of this type would lead to analogies with a Freudian system of superego, ego, and id; however, such elaborate schemes quickly break down since, as Prickett points out, "Too strong an allegorical consistency is always in danger of threatening the reality of the surface narrative" (*Victorian Fantasy* 167). The vestiges of a consistent allegory that depicts the goblins as representations of debased passions, for instance, dissipates in "The Last Chapter" where they are reclaimed with little explanation and become part of middle earth again:

> A good many of the goblins with their creatures escaped from the inundation out upon the mountain. But most of them soon left that part of the country, and most of those who remained grew milder in character, and indeed became very much like the Scotch Brownies. Their skulls became softer as well as their hearts, and their feet grew harder, and by degrees they became friendly with the inhabitants of the mountain and even with the miners. But the latter were merciless to any of the *cobs' creatures* that came in their way, until at length they all but disappeared. (pp. 190-91)

As we have seen, the goblins themselves originate in middle earth and the causes of their devolution are not specified. The hints we get from the narrator point to a political revolution against tyrannical actions by the king, and this political revolution may be viewed as providing a positive origin for such actions and no clear sign of debased motivation. Rather than being driven by will, passion, or base desire, they act in opposition to what appear to be arbitrary imperatives from an oppressive government.

The closing frame in the serial form of the story concludes with a caution about attempts to bring complete acts of interpretation with the end of this or any narrative. In part the final use of the frame narrative with its interrogation of Mr. Editor by the young female reader prepares for the continuation of the story in *The Princess and Curdie*. Mr. Editor tells the reader, "'*Some day, perhaps, I may tell you the further history of both of them; how Curdie came to visit Irene's grandmother, and what she did for him; and how the princess and he met again after they were older—and how—But there! I don't mean to go any farther at present.*'" This story would appear as *The Princess and Curdie* (1877), but the final comment by Mr. Editor indicates that the end of *The Princess and the Goblin* does not necessarily bring closure to the narrative. To the young reader's exclamation, "'*Then you're leaving the story unfinished, Mr. Editor!*'" he replies:

'*Not more unfinished than a story ought to be, I hope. If you ever knew a story finished, all I can say is, I never did. Somehow stories won't finish. I think I know why, but I won't say that either now.*' (p. 191)

Closure of this story, or any story, would mean an end to the work of the imagination and to the intellectual growth that MacDonald prized throughout his writings. Stories, he indicates, always go on in the mind of the reader, and the final statement—"'*I think I know why, but I won't say that either now*'"—draws the reader's mind onward to discovery of her own possibilities.

Works Cited

Bodmer, George. "Arthur Hughes, Walter Crane, and Maurice Sendak: The Picture as Literary Fairy Tale." *Marvels and Tales* 17.1 (2003): 120-37.

Eggleston, Edward. "A Curious Drama." *Saint Nicholas* 9.1 (1882): 300-02.

Davenport-Hines, Richard. *Auden*. London: Heinemann, 1995.

Fitch, Joshua Girling. "Children's Literature." *The London Quarterly Review, 1853-1900* 13 (1860): 469-500.

Grenby, M.O. "'A Conservative Woman Doing Radical Things': Sarah Trimmer and the Guardian of Education." *Culturing the Child, 1690-1914: Essays in Memory of Mitzi Meyers*. Ed.

Donelle Ruwe. Lanham: Children's Literature Association and Scarecrow Press, 2005. 137-61.

Hein, Rolland. *Christian Mythmakers: C.S. Lewis, Madeleine L'Engle, J.R. Tolkien, George MacDonald, G.K. Chesterton, Charles Williams, Dante Alighieri, John Bunyan, Walter Wangerin, Robert Siegel, and Hannah Hurnard.* 2nd ed. Chicago: Cornerstone, 2002.

Lang, Marjory. "Childhood's Champions: Mid-Victorian Children's Periodicals and the Critics." *Victorian Periodicals Review* 13.1/2 (1980): 17-31.

Lathey, Gillian. *The Role of Translators in Children's Literature: Invisible Storytellers.* London: Routledge, 2010.

MacDonald, George. *Adela Cathcart.* 3 vols. London: Hurst and Blackett, 1864.

MacDonald, Greville. *George MacDonald and His Wife with an Introduction by G. K. Chesterton.* London: G. Allen & Unwin, 1924.

McGillis, Roderick. "Introduction." *The Princess and the Goblin and The Princess and Curdie.* Ed. Roderick McGillis. Oxford: Oxford UP, 1990. vii-xxiii.

———. "Introduction." *For the Childlike: George MacDonald's Fantasies for Children.* Ed. Roderick McGillis. Metuchen, NJ: Scarecrow, 1992. 1-15.

Moss, Anita West. "Varieties of Literary Fairy Tale." *Children's Literature Association Quarterly* 7.2 (1982): 15-17.

Prickett, Stephen. "Fictions and Metafictions: *Phantastes, Wilhelm Meister,* and the Idea of the *Bildungsroman.*" *The Gold Thread: Essays on George MacDonald.* Ed. William Raeper. Edinburgh: Edinburgh UP, 1990. 109-25.

———. "The Two Worlds of George MacDonald." *For the Childlike: George MacDonald's Fantasies for Children.* Ed. Roderick McGillis. Metuchen, NJ: Scarecrow, 1992. 17-29.

———. *Victorian Fantasy.* 2nd rev. and expanded ed. Waco, TX: Baylor UP, 2005.

Raeper, William. *George MacDonald.* Tring: Lion, 1987.

"Review of *Adela Cathcart.*" *The Athenaeum.* 1906 (1864): 644.

"Review of *Adela Cathcart.*" *Examiner* 2952 (1864): 550.

Robertson, A.B. "Fitch, Sir Joshua Girling (1824-1903)." *Oxford Dictionary of National Biography.* Ed. H.C.G. Matthew and Brian Harrison. Oxford: Oxford UP, 2004. Online ed. Ed. Lawrence Goldman. Jan. 2008. 8 May 2014 <www.oxforddnb.com/view/article/33149>.

Rowe, Karen E. "Virtue in the Guise of Vice: The Making and Unmaking of Morality from Fairy Tale Fantasy." *Culturing the Child, 1690-1914: Essays in Memory of Mitzi Meyers*. Ed. Donelle Ruwe. Lanham: Children's Literature Association and Scarecrow, 2005. 22-66.

Wildman, Stephen. "Introduction." *Arthur Hughes: His Life and Works*. Ed. Leonard Roberts. Woodbridge: Antique Collectors' Club, 1997.

"Works by George MacDonald." *The British Quarterly Review* 47.93 (1868): 1-34.

George MacDonald: A Brief Chronology

[Works for children in **bold italics**.]

1824	Born in village of Huntly, West Aberdeenshire, on 10 December, the son of George MacDonald and Helen MacKay.
1832	Death of his mother.
1840-41	Attends Aberdeen University.
1842	Catalogues library on an unidentified estate in northern Scotland.
1844-45	Attends Aberdeen University, taking prizes in chemistry and natural philosophy.
1845-47	Works as tutor in London.
c. 1848-49	Studies for the Congregationalist ministry at Independent College, Highbury.
1850	Pastor at Arundel.
1851	Marries Louisa Powell.
1853	Forced to resign his parish because members of the congregation are dissatisfied with his gentle Christianity; travels to Algiers for health; returns to England determined to become a writer.
1855	*Within and Without* (poem).
1857	*Poems.*
1858	*Phantastes, a Faerie Romance for Men and Women.*
1860	Converts to Church of England.
1863	*David Elginbrod.*
1864	*Adela Cathcart; The Portent.*
1865	*Alec Forbes of Howglen.*
1867	**Dealings with the Fairies** (first published as part of *Adela Cathcart*); *Unspoken Sermons* (1st series); *Annals of a Quiet Neighbourhood.*
1868	*Robert Falconer; The Seabord Parish*; receives LLD degree from Aberdeen University.
1870	Alexander Strahan offers MacDonald the editorship of *Good Words for the Young*, a periodical magazine for young readers; first installment of *The Princess and the Goblin* appears in November; *The Miracle of our Lord.*

1871	Final installment of *The Princess and the Goblin* appears in June; *Ranald Bannerman's Boyhood*; ***At the Back of the Northwind***.
1872	Undertakes American lecture tour; publishes ***The Princess and the Goblin***; *The Vicar's Daughter*; *Wilfred Cumbermede*.
1873	*Gutta Percha Willie, The Working Genius*.
1875	*Malcolm*.
1876	*Thomas Wingfold, Curate*; *Saint George*; *Saint Michael*.
1877	Queen Victoria arranges for pension; *The Marquis of Lossie*. *The Princess and Curdie* serialized in *Good Things: A Picturesque Magazine for Boys and Girls* January-June.
1879	*Sir Gibbie*; *Paul Faber, Surgeon*.
1880	*A Book of Strife in the Form of The Diary of an Old Soul* (poem).
1881-1902	*Mary Marston*; spends part of each year in Bordighera, in Casa Coraggio.
1882	*Gifts of the Christ Child*; *Castle Warlock*; *Weighed and Wanting*.
1883	***The Princess and Curdie***; *Donal Grant*.
1885	*Unspoken Sermons* (2nd series).
1886	*What's Mine's Mine*.
1887	*Home Again*.
1888	*The Elect Lady*.
1889	*Unspoken Sermons* (3rd series).
1890	***The Light Princess and Other Fairy Stories***; *A Rough Shaking, A Tale*.
1891	*There and Back*.
1892	*The Hope of the Gospel*.
1893	*A Dish of Orts* (essays and reflections); *Heather and Snow*; *Poetical Works of George MacDonald*.
1895	*Lilith, a Romance*; ***The Lost Princess***.
1897	*Salted with Fire, A Tale*.
1902	Death of his wife Louisa.
1905	Dies at Ashstead in England after long illness.

A Note on the Illustrations

When *The Princess and the Goblin* appeared in *Good Words for the Young*, the text was accompanied by a series of woodcut illustrations designed by Arthur Hughes (1832-1913), a friend of MacDonald who by 1871 was recognized as one of the foremost illustrators of works for children and who had previously worked with the author illustrating *At the Back of the Northwind* in 1869-70. Hughes provided thirty images, all designed as partial page illustrations to fit the double-column format of the periodical. This Broadview edition includes all thirty designs, printed in the order in which they appeared in *Good Words for the Young* and placed as closely as possible, within the constraints imposed by the single-column Broadview format, to the text they originally followed. The exact placement of the original illustrations is indicated within the text by a †. In the rare instances where illustrations appeared in the midst of a hyphenated word, we have placed the symbol at the end of the word.

The illustrations from *Good Words for the Young* are reproduced courtesy of the editors.

Images of George MacDonald's manuscript of *The Princess and the Goblin* are from the Brander Library, Huntly. Image courtesy of the Aberdeenshire Library and Information Service: The George MacDonald Collection:
http://www.aberdeenshire.gov.uk/libraries/information/
georgemacdonald/ebooks/The%20Princess%20and%20The
%20Goblin/index.htm

A Note on the Texts

This edition of *The Princess and the Goblin* is based on the first appearance of the work as a serial publication in *Good Words for the Young*, which was edited by George MacDonald. *The Princess and the Goblin* appeared in volume 3 of *Good Words for the Young* between November 1870 and June 1871 (pages 1-5, 65-72, 129-36, 185-91, 279-86, 301-05, 353-63, 409-20). Our only modification to the text has been to standardize matters of punctuation, including the uses of exclamation points, semi-colons, colons, and quotation marks. A slightly modified version appeared a year later in book form published by Strahan & Co. of London. A frame narrative, in which an adult Editor tells the story to a child reader who has occasional conversations with him, appears in the first serial publication but was removed from the book form published by Strahan in 1872. Our notes indicate substantive variations between the text of the serial publication and that of the 1872 single-volume edition. The frame appears in two American editions but was not part of the English editions in book form or other editions after 1924. It does appear in the surviving version of the manuscript held in The George MacDonald Collection, Brander Library, Huntly, Aberdeenshire (see Appendix D).

"The Light Princess," "The Giant's Heart," and "The Golden Key" are all based on the versions included in *Dealings with the Fairies* published by Alexander Strahan in 1867. "The History of Photogen and Nycteris: A Day and Night Märchen" is based on the version appearing in *The Gifts of the Christ Child, and Other Tales* published by Sampson Low, Marston, Searle & Rivington, in 1882.

As for the works not by MacDonald, William Makepeace Thackeray's *The Rose and the Ring: Or, the History of Prince Giglio and Prince Bulbo. A Fire-Side Pantomime for Great and Small Children* is based on the version published by Smith, Elder, and Co. of London in 1855. Norman Macleod's *The Gold Thread: A Story for the Young* is based on the seventh edition produced in London by Alexander Strahan in 1867. John Ruskin's *The King of the Golden River* is based on the fourth edition published by Smith, Elder in 1859 (see Appendix C).

We have standardized the spelling of MacDonald and Macleod throughout.

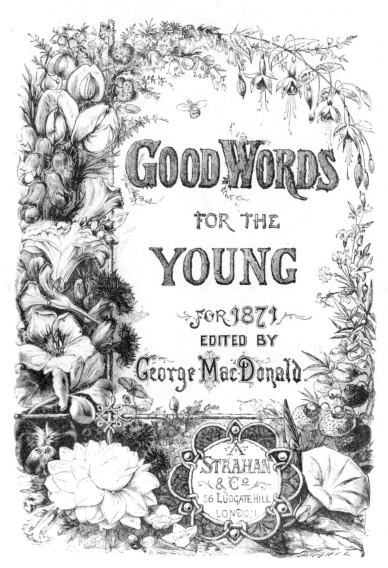

Figure 1: Cover for the serial *Good Words for the Young* (1871) in which *The Princess and the Goblin* first appeared.

THE PRINCESS AND THE GOBLIN

I.—WHY THE PRINCESS HAS A STORY ABOUT HER.

There was once a little princess, who—

"But, Mr. Editor, why do you always write about princesses?"

"Because every little girl is a princess."

"You will make them vain if you tell them that."

"Not if they understand what I mean."

"Then what do you mean?"

"What do you mean by a princess?"

"The daughter of a king."

"Very well; then every little girl is a princess, and there would be no need to say anything about it, except that she is always in danger of forgetting her rank, and behaving as if she had grown out of the mud. I have seen little princesses behave like the children of thieves and lying beggars, and that is why they need to be told they are princesses. And that is why, when I tell a story of this kind, I like to tell it about a princess. Then I can say better what I mean, because I can then give her every beautiful thing I want her to have."

"Please go on." [1]

There was once a little princess whose father was king over a great country full of mountains and valleys. His palace was built upon one of the mountains, and was very grand and beautiful. The princess, whose name was Irene, was born there, but she was sent soon after her birth, because her mother was not very strong, to be brought up by country people in a large house, half castle, half farm-house, on the side of another mountain, about halfway between its base and its peak.

The princess was a sweet little creature, and at the time my story begins, was about eight years old, I think, but she got older very fast. Her face was fair and pretty, with eyes like two bits of night-sky, each with a star dissolved in the blue. Those eyes you would have thought must have known they came from there, so often were they turned up in that direction. The ceiling of her nursery was blue, with stars in it, as like the sky as they could

---

1   The narrative frame beginning the tale appeared in the first serialized version of the story in *Good Words for the Young* (1870-71). In subsequent editions the frame was removed. The narrative frame provided by the "Editor" and the reader reappears in Chapter 3 (pp. 51-52) and in Chapter 32 (p. 191).

make it. But I doubt if ever she saw the real sky with the stars in it, for a reason which I had better mention at once.

These mountains were full of hollow places underneath; huge caverns, and winding ways, some with water running through them, and some shining with all colours of the rainbow when a light was taken in. There would not have been much known about them, had there not been mines there, great deep pits, with long galleries and passages running off from them, which had been dug to get at the ore of which the mountains were full. In the course of digging, the miners came upon many of these natural caverns. A few of them had far-off openings out on the side of a mountain, or into a ravine.

Now in these subterranean caverns lived a strange race of beings, called by some gnomes, by some kobolds,[1] by some goblins. There was a legend current in the country, that at one time they lived above ground, and were very like other people. But for some reason or other, concerning which there were different legendary theories, the king had laid what they thought too severe taxes upon them, or had required observances of them they did not like, or had begun to treat them with more severity, in some way or other, and impose stricter laws; and the consequence was that they had all disappeared from the face of the country. According to the legend, however, instead of going to some other country, they had all taken refuge in the subterranean caverns, whence they never came out but at night, and then seldom showed themselves in any numbers, and never to many people at once. It was only in the least frequented and most difficult parts of the mountains that they were said to gather even at night in the open air. Those who had caught sight of any of them said that they had greatly altered in the course of generations; and no wonder, seeing they lived away from the sun, in cold and wet and dark places. They were now, not ordinarily ugly, but either absolutely hideous, or ludicrously grotesque both in face and form. There was no invention, they said, of the most lawless imagination expressed by pen or pencil, that could surpass the extravagance of their appearance.[2] And as they grew mis-shapen in body, they had grown in knowledge and cleverness, and now were able to do things no mortal could see the possibility

---

1 In German folklore, "a familiar spirit, haunting houses and rendering services to the inmates, but often of a tricky disposition" or "an underground spirit haunting mines or caves" (*OED*).

2 When the tale was published in volume form by Strahan & Co. in 1872, MacDonald added, "But I suspect those who said so, had mistaken

of. But as they grew in cunning, they grew in mischief, and their great delight was in every way they could think of to annoy the people who lived in the open-air-story above them. They had enough of affection left for each other, to preserve them from being absolutely cruel for cruelty's sake to those that came in their way; but still they so heartily cherished the ancestral grudge against those who occupied their former possessions, and especially against the descendants of the king who had caused their expulsion, that they sought every opportunity of tormenting them in ways that were as odd as their inventors; and although dwarfed and mis-shapen, they had strength equal to their cunning. In the process of time they had got a king and a government of their own, whose chief business, beyond their own simple affairs, was to devise trouble for their neighbours. It will now be pretty evident why the little princess had never seen the sky at night. They were much too afraid of the goblins to let her out of the house then, even in company with ever so many attendants; and they had good reason, as we shall see by-and-by.

II.—THE PRINCESS LOSES HERSELF.

I have said the princess Irene was about eight years old when my story begins. And this is how it begins.

One very wet day, when the mountain was covered with mist which was constantly gathering itself together into rain-drops, and pouring down on the roofs of the great old house, whence it fell in a fringe of water from the eaves all round about it, the princess could not of course go out. She got very tired, so tired that even her toys could no longer amuse her. You would wonder at that if I had time to describe to you one half of the toys she had. But then you wouldn't have the toys themselves, and that makes all the difference: you can't get tired of a thing before you have it. It was a picture, though, worth seeing—the princess sitting in the nursery with the sky-ceiling over her head, at a great table covered with her toys. If my brother-editor who looks after the pictures,[1] would like to draw this, I should advise him not to

---

some of their animal companions for the goblins themselves—of which more by and by. The goblins themselves were not so far removed from the human as such a description would imply."

1 MacDonald substituted "the artist" for "my brother-editor who looks after the pictures" in later editions.

meddle with the toys. I am afraid of attempting to describe them, and I think he had better not try to draw them. He had better not. He can do a thousand things I can't, but I don't think he could draw those toys. No man could better make the princess herself than he could, though—leaning with her back bowed into the back of the chair, her head hanging down, and her hands in her lap, very miserable as she would say herself, not even knowing what she would like, except it were to go out and get thoroughly wet, and catch a particularly nice cold, and have to go to bed and take gruel. The next moment after you see her sitting there, her nurse goes out of the room.

Even that is a change, and the princess wakes up a little, and looks about her. Then she tumbles off her chair, and runs out of the door, not the same door the nurse went out of, but one which opened at the foot of a curious old stair of worm-eaten oak, which looked as if never any one had set foot upon it. She had once before been up six steps, and that was sufficient reason, in such a day, for trying to find out what was at the top of it.

Up and up she ran—such a long way it seemed to her! until she came to the top of the third flight. There she found the landing was the end of a long passage. Into this she ran. It was full of doors on each side. There were so many that she did not care to open any, but ran on to the end, where she turned into another passage, also full of doors. When she had turned twice more, and still saw doors and only doors about her, she began to get frightened. It was so silent! And all those doors must hide rooms with nobody in them! That was dreadful. Also the rain made a great trampling noise on the roof. She turned and started at full speed, her little footsteps echoing through the sounds of the rain—back for the stairs and her safe nursery. So she thought, but she had lost herself long ago. It doesn't follow that she *was* lost, because she had lost herself, though.

She ran for some distance, turned several times, and then began to be afraid. Very soon she was sure that she had lost the way back. Rooms everywhere, and no stair! Her little heart beat as fast as her little feet ran, and a lump of tears was growing in her throat. But she was too eager and perhaps too frightened to cry for some time. At last her hope failed her. Nothing but passages and doors everywhere! She threw herself on the floor, and burst into a wailing cry broken by sobs.

She did not cry long, however, for she was as brave as could be expected of a princess of her age. After a good cry, she got up, and brushed the dust from her frock. Oh what old dust it was!

Then she wiped her eyes with her hands, for princesses don't always have their handkerchiefs in their pockets, any more than some other little girls I know of. Next, like a true princess, she resolved on going wisely to work to find her way back: she would walk through the passages, and look in every direction for the stair. This she did, but without success. She went over the same ground again and again without knowing it, for the passages and doors were all alike. At last, in a corner, through a half open door, she did see a stair. But alas! it went the wrong way: instead of going down, it went up. Frightened as she was, however, she could not help wishing to see where yet further the stair could lead. It was very narrow, and so steep that she went up like a four-legged creature on her hands and feet.

III.—THE PRINCESS AND—WE SHALL SEE WHO.

When she came to the top, she found herself in a little square place, with three doors, two opposite each other, and one opposite the top of the stair. She stood for a moment, without an idea in her little head what to do next. But as she stood, she began to hear a curious humming sound. Could it be the rain? No. It was much more gentle and even monotonous than the sound of the rain, which now she scarcely heard. The low sweet humming sound went on, sometimes stopping for a little while and then beginning again. It was more like the hum of a very happy bee that had found a rich well of honey in some globular flower, than anything else I can think of at this moment. Where could it come from? She laid her ear first to one of the doors to hearken if it was there—then to another. When she laid her ear against the third door, there could be no doubt where it came from: it must be from something in that room. What could it be? She was rather afraid, but her curiosity was stronger than her fear, and she opened the door very gently and peeped in. What do you think she saw? A very old lady who sat spinning.

"*Oh Mr. Editor! I know the story you are going to tell: it's The Sleeping Beauty; only you're spinning too, and making it longer.*"[1]

"*No indeed, it is not that story. Why should I tell one that every properly educated child knows already? More old ladies than one have*

---

1   *La Belle au Bois Dormant* (*The Sleeping Beauty*) is a classic fairy tale (1697) by Charles Perrault (1628-1703). Its plot hinges on the curse placed upon the young princess by a disgruntled fairy not (*continued*)

sat spinning in a garret. Besides, the old lady in that story was only spinning with a spindle, and this one was spinning with a spinning-wheel, else how could the princess have heard the sweet noise through the door? Do you know the difference? Did you ever see a spindle or a spinning-wheel? I dare say you never did. Well, ask your mamma to explain to you the difference. Between ourselves, however, I shouldn't wonder if she didn't know much better than you. Another thing is, that this is not a fairy story; but a goblin story. And one thing more, this old lady spinning was not an old nurse—but—you shall see who. I think I have now made it quite plain that this is not that lovely story of The Sleeping Beauty. It is quite a new one, I assure you, and I will try to tell it as prettily as I can."[1]

Perhaps you will wonder how the princess could tell that the old lady was an old lady, when I inform you that not only was she beautiful, but her skin was smooth and white. I will tell you more. Her hair was combed back from her forehead and face, and hung loose far down and all over her back. That is not much like an old lady—is it? Ah! but it was white almost as snow. And although her face was so smooth, her eyes looked so wise that you could not have helped seeing she must be old. The princess, though she could not have told you why, did think her very old indeed—quite fifty—she said to herself. But she was rather older than that, as you shall hear.

While the princess stared bewildered, with her head just inside the door, the old lady lifted hers, and said, in a sweet, but old and rather shaky voice, which mingled very pleasantly with the continued hum of her wheel: "Come in, my dear; come in. I am glad to see you."

That the princess was a real princess, you might see now quite plainly; for she didn't hang on to the handle of the door, and stare without moving, as I have known some do who ought to have

---

invited to the christening, who declares that the princess will prick her finger with a spindle, and die. A younger fairy mitigates this fate by changing it from death to a sleep of a hundred years. MacDonald here alludes to the tale to draw attention to the need to focus on accurate empirical observation. Unlike the quiet spindle, a simple tapered wooden rod used in spinning by hand, the more complex spinning wheel would produce an audible hum in the process of making thread; similarly, the drop spindle usually featured a sharp metal hook capable of pricking a finger, unlike the spinning wheel. Both devices, he makes clear, are found more frequently in literary tales than in modern Victorian households.

1 For the appearance of an editorial narrative frame in the work, see p. 26.

Figure 2

instruction on how to be more like a princess → *didactic*

been princesses but†[1] were only rather vulgar[2] little girls. She did as she was told, stepped inside the door at once, and shut it gently behind her.

"Come to me, my dear," said the old lady.

And again the princess did as she was told. She approached the old lady—rather slowly, I confess, but did not stop until she stood by her side, and looked up in her face with her blue eyes and the two melted stars in them.

---

* 1 A † indicates the original placement of the illustration in the serial version.
  2 Common or ordinary.

"Why, what have you been doing with your eyes, child?" asked the old lady.

"Crying," answered the princess.

"Why, child?"

"Because I couldn't find my way down again."

"But you could find your way up."†

Figure 3

"Not at first—not for a long time."

"But your face is streaked like the back of a zebra. Hadn't you a handkerchief to wipe your eyes with?"

"No."

"Then why didn't you come to me to wipe them for you?"

"Please, I didn't know you were here. I will next time."

"There's a good child!" said the old lady.

Then she stopped her wheel, and rose, and, going out of the room, returned with a little silver basin and a soft white towel, with which she washed and wiped the bright little face. And the princess thought her hands were so smooth and nice!

When she carried away the basin and towel, the little princess wondered to see how straight and tall she was, for, although she was so old, she didn't stoop a bit. She was dressed in black velvet with thick white heavy-looking lace about it; and on the black dress, her hair shone like silver. There was hardly any more furniture in the room than there might have been in that of the poorest old woman who made her bread by her spinning. There was no carpet on the floor—no table anywhere—nothing but the spinning-wheel and the chair beside it. When she came back, she sat down again, and without a word began her spinning once more, while Irene, who had never seen a spinning-wheel, stood by her side and looked on. When the old lady had got her thread fairly going again, she said to the princess, but without looking at her:

"Do you know my name, child?"

"No, I don't know it," answered the princess.

"My name is Irene."

"That's *my* name!" cried the princess.

"I know that. I let you have mine. I haven't got your name. You've got mine."

"How can that be?" asked the princess, bewildered. "I've always had my name."

"Your papa, the king, asked me if I had any objection to your having it; and of course I hadn't. I let you have it with pleasure."

"It was very kind of you to give me your name—and such a pretty one," said the princess.

"Oh, not so *very* kind!" said the old† lady. "A name is one of those things one can give away and keep all the same. I have a good many such things. Wouldn't you like to know who I am, child?"

"Yes, that I should—very much."

"I'm your great-great-grandmother," said the lady.

"What's that?" asked the princess.

"I'm your father's mother's father's mother."

"Oh dear! I can't understand that," said the princess.

"I daresay not. I didn't expect you would. But that's no reason why I shouldn't say it."

"Oh, no!" answered the princess.

Figure 4

"I will explain it all to you when you are† older," the lady went on. "But you will be able to understand this much now: I came here to take care of you."

"Is it long since you came? Was it yesterday? Or was it to-day, because it was so wet that I couldn't get out?"

"I've been here ever since you came yourself."

"What a long time!" said the princess. "I don't remember it at all."

"No. I suppose not."

"But I never saw you before."

Figure 5

"No. But you shall see me again."

"Do you live in this room always?"

"I don't sleep in it. I sleep on the opposite side of the landing. I sit here most of the day."

"I shouldn't like it. My nursery is much prettier. You must be a queen too, if you are my great big grandmother."

"Yes, I am a queen."

"Where is your crown then?"

"In my bed-room."

"I *should* like to see it."

"You shall some day—not to-day."

"I wonder why nursie never told me."

"Nursie doesn't know. She never saw me."

"But somebody knows that you are in the house?"

"No; nobody."

"How do you get your dinner then?"

"I keep poultry—of a sort."

"Where do you keep them?"

"I will show you."

"And who makes the chicken-broth for you?"

"I never kill any of my chickens."

"Then I can't understand."

"What did you have for breakfast this morning?" asked the lady.

"Oh! I had bread and milk, and an egg.—I daresay you eat their eggs."

"Yes, that's it. I eat their eggs."

"Is that what makes your hair so white?"

"No, my dear. It's old age. I am very old."

"I thought so. Are you fifty?"

"Yes—more than that."

"Are you a hundred?"

"Yes—more than that. I am too old for you to guess. Come and see my chickens."

Again she stopped her spinning. She rose, took the princess by the hand, led her out of the room, and opened the door opposite the stair. The princess expected to see a lot of hens and chickens, but instead of that, she saw the blue sky first, and then the roofs of the house, with a multitude of the loveliest pigeons, mostly white, but of all colours, walking about, making bows to each other, and talking a language she could not understand. She clapped her hands with delight, and up rose such a flapping of wings, that she in her turn was startled.

"You've frightened my poultry," said the old lady, smiling.

"And they've frightened me," said the princess, smiling too. "But what very nice poultry! Are the eggs nice?"

"Yes, very nice."

"What a small egg-spoon you must have! Wouldn't it be better to keep hens, and get bigger eggs?"

"How should I feed them, though?"

"I see," said the princess. "The pigeons feed themselves. They've got wings."

"Just so. If they couldn't fly, I couldn't eat their eggs."

"But how do you get at the eggs? Where are their nests?"

The lady took hold of a little loop of string in the wall at the side of the door, and lifting a shutter, showed a great many pigeon-holes with nests, some with young ones and some with eggs in them. The birds came in at the other side, and she took out the eggs on this side. She closed it again quickly, lest the young ones should be frightened.

"Oh what a nice way!" cried the princess. "Will you give me an egg to eat, I'm rather hungry."

"I will some day, but now you must go back, or nursie will be miserable about you. I daresay she's looking for you everywhere."

"Except here," answered the princess. "Oh how surprised she *will* be when I tell her about my great big grand-grandmother!"

"Yes, that she will!" said the old lady with a curious smile. "Mind you tell her all about it exactly."

"That I will. Please will you take me back to her?"

"I can't go all the way, but I will take you to the top of the stair, and then you must run down quite fast into your own room."

The little princess put her hand in the old lady's who, looking this way and that, brought her to the top of the first stair, and thence to the bottom of the second, and did not leave her till she saw her half way down the third. When she heard the cry of her nurse's pleasure at finding her, she turned and walked up the stairs again, very fast indeed for such a very great grandmother, and sat down to her spinning with another strange smile on her sweet old face.

About this spinning of hers I will tell you more next time. Guess what she was spinning.[1]

IV.—WHAT THE NURSE THOUGHT OF IT.

"Why, where can you have been, princess?" asked the nurse, taking her in her arms. "It's very unkind of you to hide away so long. I began to be afraid—"

Here she checked herself.

"What were you afraid of, nursie?" asked the princess.

"Never mind," she answered. "Perhaps I will tell you another day. Now tell me where you have been?"

---

1 End of the first instalment appearing in *Good Words for the Young*, 1 November 1870, pp. 1-5.

"I've been up a long way to see my very great, huge, old grand-mother," said the princess.

"What do you mean by that?" asked the nurse, who thought she was making fun.

"I mean that I've been a long way up and up to see my GREAT grandmother. Ah, nursie, you don't know what a beautiful mother of grandmothers I've got up stairs. She is *such* an old lady! with such lovely white hair!—as white as my silver cup. Now, when I think of it, I think her hair must be silver."

"What nonsense you are talking, princess!" said the nurse.

"I'm not talking nonsense," returned Irene, rather offended. "I will tell you all about her. She's much taller than you, and much prettier."

"Oh, I daresay!" remarked the nurse.

"And she lives upon pigeons' eggs."

"Most likely," said the nurse.

"And she sits in an empty room, spin-spinning all day long."

"Not a doubt of it," said the nurse.

"And she keeps her crown in her bed-room."

"Of course—quite the proper place to keep her crown in. She wears it in bed, I'll be bound."

"She didn't say that. And I don't think she does. That wouldn't be comfortable—would it? I don't think my papa wears his crown for a night cap. Does he, nursie?"

"I never asked him. I daresay he does."

"And she's been there ever since I came here—ever so many years."

"Anybody could have told you that," said the nurse, who did not believe a word Irene was saying.

"Why didn't you tell me then?"

"There was no necessity. You could make it all up for yourself."

"You don't believe me then!" exclaimed the princess, astonished and angry, as she well might be.

"Did you expect me to believe you, princess?" asked the nurse coldly. "I know princesses are in the habit of telling make-believes, but you are the first I ever heard of who expected to have them believed," she added, seeing that the child was strangely in earnest.

The princess burst into tears.

"Well, I must say," remarked the nurse, now thoroughly vexed with her for crying, "it is not at all becoming in a princess to tell stories *and* expect to be believed just because she's a princess."

"But it's quite true, I tell you, nursie."

"You've dreamt it, then, child."

"No, I didn't dream it. I went up stairs, and I lost myself, and if I hadn't found the beautiful lady, I should never have found myself."

"Oh, I daresay!"

"Well, you just come up with me, and see if I'm not telling the truth."

"Indeed I have other work to do. It's your dinner-time, and I won't have any more such nonsense."

The princess wiped her eyes, and her face grew so hot that they were soon quite dry. She sat down to her dinner, but ate next to nothing. Not to be believed does not at all agree with princesses; for a real princess cannot tell a lie. So all the after- *didacti*◡ noon she did not speak a word. Only when the nurse spoke to her, she answered her, for a real princess is never rude—even when she does well to be offended.

Of course the nurse was not comfortable in her mind—not that she suspected the least truth in Irene's story, but that she loved her dearly, and was vexed with herself for having been cross to her.

She thought her crossness was the cause of the princess's unhap- piness, and had no idea that she was really and deeply hurt at not being believed. But, as it became more and more plain during the evening in her every motion and look, that, although she tried to amuse herself with her toys, her heart was too vexed and troubled to enjoy them, her nurse's discomfort grew and grew. When bedtime came, she undressed and laid her down, but the child, instead of holding up her little mouth to be kissed, turned away from her and lay still. Then nursie's heart gave way altogether, and she began to cry. At the sound of her first sob, the princess turned again, and held her face to kiss her as usual. But the nurse had her handkerchief to her eyes, and did not see the movement.

"Nursie," said the princess, "why won't you believe me?"

"Because I can't believe you," said the nurse, getting angry again.

"Ah! then, you can't help it," said Irene, "and I will not be vexed with you any more. I will give you a kiss and go to sleep."

"You little angel!" cried the nurse, and caught her out of bed, and walked about the room with her in her arms, kissing and hugging her.

"You *will* let me take you to see my dear old great big grand- mother? won't you?" said the princess, as she laid her down again.

"And *you* won't say I'm ugly, any more—will you, princess?"

"Nursie! I never said you were ugly. What can you mean?"

"Well, if you didn't say it, you meant it."

"Indeed, I never did."

"You said I wasn't so pretty as that—"

"As my beautiful grandmother—yes, I did say that; and I say it again, for it's quite true."

"Then I *do* think you *are* unkind!" said the nurse, and put her handkerchief to her eyes again.

"Nursie, dear, everybody can't be as beautiful as every other body, you know. You are *very* nice-looking, but if you had been as beautiful as my grandmother—"

"Bother your grandmother!" said the nurse.

"Nurse, that's very rude. You are not fit to be spoken to—till you can behave better."

The princess turned away once more, and again the nurse was ashamed of herself.

"I'm sure I beg your pardon, princess," she said, though still in an offended tone. But the princess let the tone pass, and heeded only the words.

"You won't say it again, I am sure," she answered, once more turning towards her nurse.

"I was only going to say that if you had been twice as nice-looking as you are, some king or other would have married you, and then what would have become of me?"

"You are an angel!" repeated the nurse, again embracing her.

"Now," insisted Irene, "you *will* come and see my grandmother—won't you?"

"I will go with you anywhere you like, my cherub," she answered; and in two minutes the weary little princess was fast asleep.

V.—THE PRINCESS LETS WELL ALONE.

When she woke the next morning, the first thing she heard was the rain still falling. Indeed, this day was so like the last, that it would have been difficult to tell where was the use of it. The first thing she thought of, however, was not the rain, but the lady in the tower; and the first question that occupied her thoughts was whether she should not ask the nurse to fulfil her promise this very morning, and go with her to find her grandmother as soon as she had had her breakfast. But she came to the conclusion that perhaps the lady would not be pleased if she took anyone to see her without first asking leave; especially as it was pretty evident, seeing she lived on pigeons' eggs, and cooked them herself, that she did not want the household to know she was there. So the princess resolved to take the first opportunity of running up alone and asking whether she might bring her nurse. She believed the fact that she could not otherwise convince her she was telling the truth, would have much weight with her grandmother.

The princess and her nurse were the best of friends all dressing time, and the princess in consequence ate an enormous little breakfast.

"I wonder, Lootie"—that was her pet-name for her nurse— "What pigeons' eggs taste like?" she said, as she was eating her egg—not quite a common one, for they always picked out the pinky ones for her.

"We'll get you a pigeon's egg, and you shall judge for yourself," said the nurse.

"Oh, no, no!" returned Irene, suddenly reflecting they might disturb the old lady in getting it, and that even if they did not, she would have one less in consequence.

"What a strange creature you are," said the nurse—"first to want a thing and then to refuse it!"

But she did not say it crossly, and the princess never minded any remarks that were not unfriendly.

"Well, you see, Lootie, there are reasons," she returned, and said no more, for she did not want to bring up the subject of their former strife, lest her nurse should offer to go before she had had her grandmother's permission to bring her. Of course she could refuse to take her, but then she would believe her less than ever.

Now the nurse, as she said herself afterwards, could not be every moment in the room, and as never before yesterday had the princess given her the smallest reason for anxiety, it had not yet come into her head to watch her more closely. So she soon gave her a chance, and, the very first that offered, Irene was off and up the stairs again.

This day's adventure, however, did not turn out like yesterday's, although it began like it; and indeed to-day is very seldom like yesterday, if people would note the differences—even when it rains. The princess ran through passage after passage, and could not find the stair of the tower. My own suspicion is that she had not gone up high enough, and was searching on the second instead of the third floor. When she turned to go back, she failed equally in her search after the stair. She was lost once more.

Something made it even worse to bear this time, and it was no wonder that she cried again. Suddenly it occurred to her that it was after having cried before that she had found her grandmother's stair. She got up at once, wiped her eyes, and started upon a fresh quest. This time, although she did not find what she hoped, she found what was next best: she did not come on a stair that went up, but she came upon one that went down. It was evidently not the stair she had come up, yet it was a good deal better than none; so down she went, and was singing merrily before she reached the bottom. There, to her surprise, she found herself in the kitchen. Although she was not allowed to go there alone, her nurse had often taken her, and she was a great favourite with the servants. So there was a general rush at her the moment she appeared, for every one wanted to have her; and the report of where she was soon reached the nurse's ears. She came at once to fetch her; but she never suspected how she had got there, and the princess kept her own counsel.

Her failure to find the old lady not only disappointed her, but made her very thoughtful. Sometimes she came almost to the nurse's opinion that she had dreamed all about her; but that fancy never lasted very long. She wondered much whether she should ever see her again, and thought it very sad not to have been able to find her when she particularly wanted her. She resolved to say nothing more to her nurse on the subject, seeing it was so little in her power to prove her words.

VI.—THE LITTLE MINER.

The next day the great cloud still hung over the mountain, and the rain poured like water from a full sponge. The princess was very fond of being out of doors, and she nearly cried when she saw that the weather was no better. But the mist was not of such a dark dingy gray; there was light in it; and as the hours went on, it grew brighter and brighter, until it was almost too brilliant to look at; and late in the afternoon, the sun broke out so gloriously that Irene clapped her hands, crying,

"See, see, Lootie! The sun has had his face washed. Look how bright he is! Do get my hat, and let us go out for a walk. Oh dear! oh dear! how happy I am!"

Lootie was very glad to please the princess. She got her hat and cloak, and they set out together for a walk up the mountain; for the road was so hard and steep that the water could not rest upon it, and it was always dry enough for walking a few minutes after the rain ceased. The clouds were rolling away in broken pieces, like great, over-woolly sheep, whose wool the sun had bleached till it was almost too white for the eyes to bear. Between them the sky shone with a deeper and purer blue, because of the rain. The trees on the road-side were hung all over with drops, which sparkled in the sun like jewels. The only things that were no brighter for the rain, were the brooks that ran down the mountain; they had changed from the clearness of crystal to a muddy brown; but what they lost in colour they gained in sound—or at least in noise, for a brook when it is swollen is not so musical as before. But Irene was in raptures with the great brown streams tumbling down everywhere; and Lootie shared in her delight, for she too had been confined to the house for three days. At length she observed that the sun was getting low, and said it was time to be going back. She made the remark again and again, but, every time, the princess begged her to go on just a little farther and a little farther; reminding her that it was much easier to go downhill, and saying that when they did turn, they would be at home in a moment. So on and on they did go, now to look at a group of ferns over whose tops a stream was pouring in a watery arch, now to pick a shining stone from a rock by the wayside, now to watch the flight of some bird. Suddenly the shadow of a great mountain peak came up from behind, and shot in front of them. When the nurse saw it, she started and shook, and catching hold of the princess's hand turned and began to run down the hill.

"What's all the haste, nursie?" asked Irene, running alongside of her.

"We must not be out a moment longer."

"But we can't help being out a good many moments longer."

It was too true. The nurse almost cried. They were much too far from home. It was against express orders to be out with the princess one moment after the sun was down; and they were nearly a mile up the mountain! If his majesty, Irene's papa, were to hear of it, Lootie would certainly be dismissed; and to leave the princess would break her heart. It was no wonder she ran. But Irene was not in the least† frightened, not knowing anything to be frightened at. She kept on chattering as well as she could, but it was not easy.

"Lootie! Lootie! why do you run so fast? It shakes my teeth when I talk."

"Then don't talk," said Lootie.

Figure 6

But the princess went on talking. She was always saying, "Look, look, Lootie," but Lootie paid no more heed to anything she said, only ran on.

"Look, look, Lootie! Don't you see that funny man peeping over the rock?"

Lootie only ran the faster. They had to pass the rock, and when they came nearer, the princess saw it was only a lump of the rock itself that she had taken for a man.

"Look, look, Lootie! There's *such* a curious creature at the foot of that old tree. Look at it, Lootie! It's making faces at us, I do think."

Lootie gave a stifled cry, and ran faster still—so fast, that Irene's little legs could not keep up with her, and she fell with a clash. It was a hard down-hill road, and she had been running very fast—so it was no wonder she began to cry. This put the nurse nearly beside herself; but all she could do was to run on, the moment she got the princess on her feet again.

"Who's that laughing at me?" said the princess, trying to keep in her sobs, and running too fast for her grazed knees.

"Nobody, child," said the nurse, almost angrily.

But that instant there came a burst of coarse tittering from somewhere near, and a hoarse indistinct voice that seemed to say, "Lies! lies! lies!"

"Oh!" cried the nurse with a sigh that was almost a scream, and ran on faster than ever.

"Nursie! Lootie! I can't run any more. Do let us walk a bit."

"What *am* I to do?" said the nurse. "Here, I will carry you."

She caught her up; but found her much too heavy to run with, and had to set her down again. Then she looked wildly about her, gave a great cry, and said—

"We've taken the wrong turning somewhere, and I don't know where we are. We are lost, lost!"

The terror she was in had quite bewildered her. It was true enough they had lost the way. They had been running down into a little valley in which there was no house to be seen.

Now Irene did not know what good reason there was for her nurse's terror, for the servants had all strict orders never to mention the goblins to her, but it was very discomposing† to see her nurse in such a fright. Before, however, she had time to grow thoroughly alarmed like her, she heard the sound of whistling, and that revived her. Presently she saw a boy coming up the road from the valley to meet them. He was the whistler; but before they met, his whistling changed to singing. And this is something like what he sang.†

> "Ring! dod! bang!
> Go the hammers' clang!
> Hit and turn and bore!
> Whizz and puff and roar!
> Thus we rive the rocks,
> Force the goblin locks.—
> See the shining ore!
> One, two, three—
> Bright as gold can be!

Figure 7

Four, five, six—
Shovels, mattocks, picks!
Seven, eight, nine—
Light your lamp at mine.
Ten, eleven, twelve—
Loosely hold the helve.[1]

---

1 "The handle of a weapon or tool, as an axe, chisel, hammer" (*OED*).

Figure 8

We're the merry miner-boys,
  Make the goblins hold their noise."

"I wish you would hold *your* noise," said the nurse rudely, for
the very word goblin at such a time and in such a place made her
tremble. It would bring the goblins upon them to a certainty, she
thought, to defy them in that way. But whether the boy heard her
or not, he did not stop his singing.

"Thirteen, fourteen, fifteen—
This is worth the siftin';
Sixteen, seventeen, eighteen—
There's the match, and lay't in.
Nineteen, twenty—
Goblins in a plenty."

"Do be quiet," cried the nurse, in a whispered shriek. But the boy, who was now close at hand, still went on.

"Hush! scush! scurry!
There you go in a hurry!
Gobble! gobble! goblin!
There you go a' wobblin';
Hobble, hobble, hobblin'!
Cobble! cobble! cobblin!
Hob-bob-goblin!—Huuuuuh!"

"There!" said the boy, as he stood still opposite them. "There! that'll do for them. They can't bear singing, and they can't stand that song. They can't sing themselves, for they have no more voice than a crow; and they don't like other people to sing." The boy was dressed in a miner's dress, with a curious cap on his head. He was a very nice-looking boy, with eyes as dark as the mines in which he worked, and as sparkling as the crystals in their rocks. He was about twelve years old. His face was almost too pale for beauty, which came of his being so little in the open air and the sunlight—for even vegetables grown in the dark are white; but he looked happy, merry indeed—perhaps at the thought of having routed the goblins; and his bearing as he stood before them had nothing clownish or rude about it.

"I saw them," he went on, "as I came up; and I'm very glad I did. I knew they were after somebody, but I couldn't see who it was. They won't touch you so long as I'm with you."†

"Why, who are you?" asked the nurse, offended at the freedom with which he spoke to them.

"I'm Peter's son."

"Who's Peter?"

"Peter the miner."

"I don't know him."

"I'm his son though."

"And why should the goblins mind *you*, pray?"

"Because I don't mind them. I'm used to them."

Figure 9

"What difference does that make?"

"If you're not afraid of them, they're afraid of you. I'm not afraid of them. That's all. But it's all that's wanted—up here, that is. It's a different thing down there. They won't always mind that song even, down there. And if any one sings it, they stand grinning at him awfully; and if he gets frightened, and misses a word, or says a wrong one, they—oh! don't they give it him!"

"What do they do to him?" asked Irene, with a trembling voice.

"Don't go frightening the princess," said the nurse.

"The princess!" repeated the little miner, taking off his curious cap. "I beg your pardon; but you oughtn't to be out so late. Everybody knows that's against the law."

"Yes, indeed it is!" said the nurse, beginning to cry again. "And I shall have to suffer for it."

"What does that matter?" said the boy. "It must be your fault. It is the princess who will suffer for it. I hope they didn't hear you call her the princess. If they did, they're sure to know her again: they're awfully sharp."

"Lootie! Lootie!" cried the princess. "Take me home."

"Don't go on like that," said the nurse to the boy, almost fiercely. "How could I help it? I lost my way."

"You shouldn't have been out so late. You wouldn't have lost your way if you hadn't been frightened," said the boy. "Come along. I'll soon set you right again. Shall I carry your little highness?"

"Impertinence!" murmured the nurse, but she did not say it aloud, for she thought if she made him angry, he might take his revenge by telling some one belonging to the house, and then it would be sure to come to the king's ears.

"No, thank you," said Irene. "I can walk very well, though I can't run so fast as nursie. If you will give me one hand, Lootie will give me another, and then I shall get on famously."

They soon had her between them, holding a hand of each.

"Now let's run," said the nurse.

"No, no," said the little miner. "That's the worst thing you can do. If you hadn't run before, you would not have lost your way. And if you run now, they will be after you in a moment."

"I don't want to run," said Irene.

"You don't think of *me*," said the nurse.

"Yes, I do, Lootie. The boy says they won't touch us if we don't run."

"Yes, but if they know at the house that I've kept you out so late, I shall be turned away, and that would break my heart."

"Turned away, Lootie! Who would turn you away?"

"Your papa, child."

"But I'll tell him it was all my fault. And you know it was, Lootie."

"He won't mind that. I am sure he won't."

"Then I'll cry, and go down on my knees to him, and beg him not to take away my own dear Lootie."

The nurse was comforted at hearing this, and said no more. They went on, walking pretty fast, but taking care not to run a step.

"I want to talk to you," said Irene to the little miner; "but it's so awkward! I don't know your name."

"My name's Curdie, little princess."

"What a funny name! Curdie! What more?"

"Curdie Peterson. What's your name, please?"

"Irene."

"What more?"

"I don't know what more.—What more is my name, Lootie?"

"Princesses haven't got more than one name. They don't want it."

"Oh then, Curdie, you must call me just Irene and no more."

"No, indeed," said the nurse indignantly. "He shall do no such thing."

"What shall he call me, then, Lootie?"

"Your royal Highness."

"My royal Highness! What's that? No, no, Lootie. I won't be called names. I don't like them. You told me once yourself it's only rude children that call names; and I'm sure Curdie wouldn't be rude.—Curdie, my name's Irene."

"Well, Irene," said Curdie, with a glance at the nurse which showed he enjoyed teasing her, "it is very kind of you to let me call you anything. I like your name very much."

He expected the nurse to interfere again; but he soon saw that she was too frightened to speak. She was staring at something a few yards before them, in the middle of the path, where it narrowed between rocks so that only one could pass at a time.

"It is very much kinder of you to go out of your way to take us home," said Irene.

"I'm not going out of my way yet," said Curdie. "It's on the other side those rocks the path turns off to my father's."

"You wouldn't think of leaving us till we're safe home, I'm sure," gasped the nurse.

"Of course not," said Curdie.

"You dear, good, kind Curdie! I'll give you a kiss when we get home," said the princess.

The nurse gave her a great pull by the hand she held. But at that instant the something in the middle of the way, which had looked like a great lump of earth brought down by the rain, began to move. One after another it shot out four long things, like two arms and two legs, but it was now too dark to tell what they were. The nurse began to tremble from head to foot. Irene clasped Curdie's hand yet faster, and Curdie began to sing again.

"One, two—
Hit and hew!
Three, four—
Blast and bore!
Five, six—
There's a fix!
Seven, eight—
Hold it straight.
Nine, ten—
Hit again!
Hurry! scurry!
Bother! smother!
There's a toad
In the road!
Smash it!
Squash it!
Fry it!
Dry it!
You're another!
Up and off!
There's enough!—Huuuuh!"

As he uttered the last words, Curdie let go his hold of his companion, and rushed at the thing in the road, as if he would trample it under his feet. It gave a great spring, and ran straight up one of the rocks like a huge spider. Curdie turned back laughing, and took Irene's hand again. She grasped his very tight, but said nothing till they had passed the rocks. A few yards more and she found herself on a part of the road she knew, and was able to speak again.

"Do you know, Curdie, I don't quite like your song: it sounds to me rather rude," she said.

"Well, perhaps it is," answered Curdie. "I never thought of that; it's a way we have. We do it because they don't like it."

"Who don't like it?"

"The cobs, as we call them."

"Don't!" said the nurse.

"Why not?" said Curdie.

"I beg you won't. Please don't."

"Oh! if you ask me that way, of course I won't; though I don't a bit know why.—Look! there are the lights of your great house down below. You'll be at home in five minutes now."

Nothing more happened. They reached home in safety. Nobody had missed them, or even known they had gone out; and they arrived at the door belonging to their part of the house without any one seeing them. The nurse was rushing in with a hurried and not over gracious good night to Curdie; but the princess pulled her hand from hers, and was just throwing her arms round Curdie's neck, when she caught her again and dragged her away.

"Lootie! Lootie! I promised Curdie a kiss," cried Irene.

"A princess mustn't give kisses. It's not at all proper," said Lootie.

"But I promised," said the princess.

"There's no occasion: he's only a miner-boy."

"He's a good boy, and a brave boy, and he has been very kind to us. Lootie! Lootie! I *promised.*"

"Then you shouldn't have promised."

"Lootie, I promised him a kiss."

"Your royal Highness," said Lootie, suddenly grown very respectful, "must come in directly."

"Nurse, a princess must *not* break her word," said Irene, drawing herself up and standing stock-still.

Lootie did not know which the king might count the worst—to let the princess be out after sunset, or to let her kiss a miner-boy. She did not know that, being a gentleman, as many kings have been, he would have counted neither of them the worse. However much he might have disliked his daughter to kiss the miner-boy, he would not have had her break her word for all the goblins in creation. But, as I say, the nurse was not lady enough to understand this, and so she was in a great difficulty, for, if she insisted, some one might hear the princess cry and run to see, and then all would come out. But here Curdie came again to the rescue.

"Never mind, Princess Irene," he said. "You mustn't kiss me to-night. But you sha'n't break your word. I will come another time. You may be sure I will."

"Oh, thank you, Curdie!" said the princess, and stopped crying.

"Good night, Irene; good night, Lootie," said Curdie, and turned and was out of sight in a moment.

"I should like to see him!" muttered the nurse, as she carried the princess to the nursery.

"You *will* see him," said Irene. "You may be sure Curdie will keep his word. He's *sure* to come again."

"I should like to see him!" repeated the nurse, and said no more. She did not want to open a new cause of strife with the princess by saying more plainly what she meant. Glad enough that she had succeeded both in getting home unseen, and in keeping the princess from kissing the miner's boy, she resolved to watch her far better in future. Her carelessness had already doubled the danger she was in. Formerly the goblins were her only fear: now she had to protect her charge from Curdie as well.[1]

VII.—THE MINES.

Curdie went home whistling. He resolved to say nothing about the princess for fear of getting the nurse into trouble, for while he enjoyed teasing her because of her absurdity, he was careful not to do her any harm. He saw no more of the goblins, and was soon fast asleep in his bed.

He woke in the middle of the night, and thought he heard curious noises outside. He sat up and listened; then got up, and, opening the door very quietly, went out. When he peeped round the corner, he saw, under his own window, a group of stumpy creatures, whom he at once recognized by their shape. Hardly, however, had he begun his "One, two, three!" when they broke asunder, scurried away, and were out of sight. He returned laughing, got into bed again, and was fast asleep in a moment.

Reflecting a little over the matter in the morning, he came to the conclusion that, as nothing of the kind had ever happened before, they must be annoyed with him for interfering to protect the princess. By the time he was dressed, however, he was thinking of something quite different, for he did not value the enmity of the goblins in the least.

As soon as they had had breakfast, he set off with his father for the mine.

They entered the hill by a natural opening under a huge rock, where a little stream rushed out. They followed its course for a few yards, when the passage took a turn, and sloped steeply into the heart of the hill. With many angles and windings and branch-

---

1   End of the second instalment published in *Good Words for the Young*, 1 December 1870, pp. 65-72.

ings off, and sometimes with steps where it came upon a natural gulf, it led them deep into the hill before they arrived at the place where they were at present digging out the precious ore. This was of various kinds, for the mountain was very rich in the better sorts of metals. With flint and steel, and tinder-box, they lighted their lamps, then fixed them on their heads, and were soon hard at work with their pickaxes and shovels and hammers. Father and son were at work near each other, but not in the same *gang*—the passages out of which the ore was dug, they called *gangs*[1]—for when the *lode*, or vein of ore, was small, one miner would have to dig away alone in a passage no bigger than gave him just room to work—sometimes in uncomfortable cramped positions. If they stopped for a moment they could hear everywhere around them, some nearer, some farther off, the sounds of their companions burrowing away in all directions in the inside of the great mountain—some boring holes in the rock in order to blow it up with gunpowder, others shovelling the broken ore into baskets to be carried to the mouth of the mine, others hitting away with their pickaxes. Sometimes, if the miner was in a very lonely part, he would hear only a tap-tapping, no louder than that of a woodpecker, for the sound would come from a great distance off through the solid mountain-rock.

The work was hard at best, for it is very warm underground; but it was not particularly unpleasant, and some of the miners, when they wanted to earn a little more money for a particular purpose, would stop behind the rest, and work all night. But you could not tell night from day down there, except from feeling tired and sleepy; for no light of the sun ever came into those gloomy regions. Some who had thus remained behind during the night, although certain there were none of their companions at work, would declare the next morning that they heard, every time they halted for a moment to take breath, a tap-tapping all about them, as if the mountain were then more full of miners than ever it was during the day; and some in consequence would never stay over night, for all knew those were the sounds of the goblins. They worked only at night, for the miners' night was the goblins' day. Indeed the greater number of the miners were afraid of the

---

1   A northern dialect word meaning a narrow passage or pathway. C.C. Clough, in his *Glossary of Words Pertaining to the Dialect of Mid Yorkshire* (1876), defines "gang" as "a division of a mine.... Lead-mines are principally worked upward, from the base of a hill, so that there are a continuous succession of galleries, or gangs."

goblins; for there were strange stories well known amongst them of the treatment some had received whom the goblins had surprised at their work during the night. The more courageous of them, however, amongst them Peter Peterson and Curdie, who in this took after his father, had stayed in the mine all night again and again, and although they had several times encountered a few stray goblins, had never yet failed in driving them away. As I have indicated already, the chief defence against them was verse, for they hated verse of every kind, and some kinds they could not endure at all. I suspect they could not make any themselves, and that was why they disliked it so much. At all events, those who were most afraid of them were those who could neither make verses themselves, nor remember the verses that other people made for them; while those who were never afraid were those who could make verses for themselves; for although there were certain old rhymes which were very effectual, yet it was well known that a new rhyme, if of the right sort, was even more distasteful to them, and therefore more effectual in putting them to flight.

Perhaps my readers may be wondering what the goblins could be about, working all night long, seeing they never carried up the ore and sold it; but when I have informed them concerning what Curdie learned the very next night, they will be able to understand.

For Curdie had determined, if his father would permit him, to remain there alone this night—and that for two reasons: first, he wanted to get extra wages that he might buy a very warm red petticoat for his mother, who had begun to complain of the cold of the mountain air sooner than usual this autumn; and second, he had just a faint hope of finding out what the goblins were about under his window the night before.

When he told his father, he made no objection, for he had great confidence in his boy's courage and resources.

"I'm sorry I can't stay with you," said Peter; "but I want to go and pay the parson a visit this evening, and besides I've had a bit of a headache all day."

"I'm sorry for that, father," said Curdie.

"Oh! it's not much. You'll be sure to take care of yourself, won't you?"

"Yes, father; I will. I'll keep a sharp look out, I promise you."

Curdie was the only one who remained in the mine. About six o'clock the rest went away, every one bidding him good night, and telling him to take care of himself; for he was a great favourite with them all.

"Don't forget your rhymes," said one.

"No, no," answered Curdie.

"It's no matter if he does," said another, "for he'll only have to make a new one."

"Yes; but he mightn't be able to make it fast enough," said another; "and while it was cooking in his head, they might take a mean advantage and set upon him."

"I'll do my best," said Curdie. "I'm not afraid."

"We all know that," they returned, and left him.

VIII.—THE GOBLINS.

For some time Curdie worked away briskly, throwing all the ore he had disengaged on one side behind him, to be ready for carrying out in the morning. He heard a good deal of goblin-tapping, but it all sounded far away in the hill, and he paid it little heed. Towards midnight he began to feel rather hungry; so he dropped his pickaxe, got out a lump of bread which in the morning he had laid in a damp hole in the rock, sat down on the heap of ore, and ate his supper. Then he leaned back for five minutes' rest before beginning his work again, and laid his head against the rock. He had not kept the position for one minute before he heard something which made him sharpen his ears. It sounded like a voice inside the rock. After a while he heard it again. It was a goblin-voice—there could be no doubt about that—and this time he could make out the words.

"Hadn't we better be moving?" it said.

A rougher and deeper voice replied—

"There's no hurry. That wretched little mole won't be through to-night, if he work ever so hard. He's not by any means at the thinnest place."

"But you still think the lode does come through into our house?" said the first voice.

"Yes, but a good bit farther on than he has got to yet. If he had struck a stroke more to the side just here," said the goblin, tapping the very stone, as it seemed to Curdie, against which his head lay, "he would have been through; but he's a couple of yards past it now, and if he follow the lode it will be a week before it leads him in. You see it back there—a long way. Still, perhaps, in case of accident, it would be as well to be getting out of this. Helfer, you'll take the great chest. That's your business, you know."

"Yes, dad," said a third voice. "But you must help me to get it on my back. It's awfully heavy, you know."

"Well, it isn't just a bag of smoke, I admit. But you're as strong as a mountain, Helfer."

"You say so, dad. I think myself I'm all right. But I could carry ten times as much if it wasn't for my feet."

"That *is* your weak point, I confess, my boy."

"Ain't it yours too, father?"

"Well, to be honest, it is a goblin-weakness. Why *they* come so soft, I declare I haven't an idea."

"Specially when your head's so hard, you know, father."

"Yes, my boy. The goblin's glory is his head. To think how the fellows up above there have to put on helmets and things when they go fighting! Ha! ha!"

"But why don't we wear shoes like them, father? I should like it—specially when I've got a chest like that on my head."

"Well, you see, it's not the fashion. The king never wears shoes."

"The queen does."

"Yes; but that's for distinction. The first queen, you see—I mean the king's first wife—wore shoes of course, because she came from up stairs; and so, when she died, the next queen would not be inferior to her as she called it, and would wear shoes too. It was all pride. She is the hardest in forbidding them to the rest of the women."

"I'm sure I wouldn't wear them—no, not for—that I would-n't!" said the first voice, which was evidently that of the mother of the family. "I can't think why either of them should."

"Didn't I tell you the first was from up stairs?" said the other. "That was the only silly thing I ever knew his majesty guilty of. Why should he marry an outlandish woman like that—one of our natural enemies too?"

"I suppose he fell in love with her."

"Pooh! pooh! He's just as happy now with one of his own people."

"Did she die *very* soon? They didn't tease her to death, did they?"

"Oh dear no! The king worshipped her very footmarks."

"What made her die, then? Didn't the air agree with her?"

"She died when the young prince was born."

"How silly of her! *We* never do that. It must have been because she wore shoes."

"I don't know that."

"Why do they wear shoes up there?"

"Ah! now that's a sensible question, and I will answer it. But in order to do so, I must first tell you a secret. I once saw the queen's feet."

"Without her shoes?"

"Yes—without her shoes."

"No! Did you? How was it?"

"Never you mind how it was. *She* didn't know I saw them. And what do you think!—they had *toes*!"

"Toes! What's that?"

"You may well ask! I should never have known if I had not seen the queen's feet. Just imagine! the ends of her feet were split up into five or six thin pieces!"

"Oh, horrid! How *could* the king have fallen in love with her?"

"You forget that she wore shoes. That is just why she wore them. That is why all the men, and women too, up stairs wear shoes. They can't bear the sight of their own feet without them."

"Ah! now I understand. If ever you wish for shoes again, Helfer, I'll hit your feet—I will."

"No, no, mother; pray don't."

"Then don't you."

"But with such a big box on my head—"

A horrid scream followed, which Curdie interpreted as in reply to a blow from his mother upon the feet of her eldest goblin.

"Well, I never knew so much before!" remarked a fourth voice.

"Your knowledge is not universal quite yet," said the father. "You were only fifty last month. Mind you see to the bed and bedding. As soon as we've finished our supper, we'll be up and going. Ha! ha! ha!"

"What are you laughing at husband?"

"I'm laughing to think what a mess the miners will find themselves in—somewhere before this day ten years."

"Why, what do you mean?"

"Oh, nothing."

"Oh yes, you do mean something. You always do mean something."

"It's more than you do, then, wife."

"That may be; but it's not more than I find out, you know."

"Ha! ha! You're a sharp one. What a mother you've got, Helfer!"

"Yes, father."

"Well, I suppose I must tell you. They're all at the palace consulting about it to-night; and as soon as we've got away from this thin place, I'm going there to hear what night they fix upon. I should like to see that young ruffian there on the other side, struggling in the agonies of—"

He dropped his voice so low that Curdie could hear only a growl. The growl went on in the low bass for a good while, as inarticulate as if the goblin's tongue had been a sausage; and it was not until his wife spoke again that it rose to its former pitch:

"But what shall we do when you are at the palace?" she asked.

"I will see you safe in the new house I've been digging for you for the last two months. Podge, you mind the table and chairs. I commit them to your care. The table has seven legs—each chair three. I shall require them all at your hands."

After this arose a confused conversation about the various household goods and their transport; and Curdie heard nothing more that was of any importance.

He now knew at least one of the reasons for the constant sound of the goblin hammers and pickaxes at night. They were making new houses for themselves, to which they might retreat when the miners should threaten to break into their dwellings. But he had learned two things of far greater importance. The first was, that some grievous calamity was preparing, and almost ready to fall upon the heads of the miners; the second was—the one weak point of a goblin's body: he had not known that their feet were so tender as he had now reason to suspect. He had heard it said that they† had no toes: he had never had opportunity of inspecting them closely enough in the dusk in which they always appeared, to satisfy himself whether it was a correct report. Indeed, he had not been able even to satisfy himself as to whether they had no fingers, although that also was commonly said to be the fact. One of the miners, indeed, who had had more schooling than the rest, was wont to argue that such must have been the primordial condition of humanity, and that education and handicraft had developed both toes and fingers—with which proposition Curdie had once heard his father sarcastically agree, alleging in support of it the probability that babies' gloves were a traditional remnant of the old state of things; while the stockings of all ages, no regard being paid in them to the toes, pointed in the same direction. But what was of importance was the fact concerning the softness of the goblin-feet, which he foresaw might be useful to all miners. What he had to do in the meantime, however,

Figure 10

was to discover, if possible, the special evil design the goblins had now in their heads.

Although he knew all the gangs and all the natural galleries with which they communicated in the mined part of the mountain, he had not the least idea where the palace of the king of the gnomes was; otherwise he would have set out at once on the enterprise of discovering what the said design was. He judged, and rightly, that it must lie in a further part of the mountain, between which and the mine there was as yet no communication. There must be one nearly completed, however; for it could be but a thin partition which now separated them. If only he could get through in time to follow the goblins as they retreated! A few blows would doubtless be sufficient—just where his ear now lay; but if he attempted to strike there with his pickaxe, he would only hasten the departure of the family, put them on their guard, and perhaps lose their involuntary guidance. He therefore began to feel the wall with his hands, and soon found that some of the stones were loose enough to be drawn out with little noise.

Figure 11

Laying hold of a large one with both his hands, he drew it gently out, and let it down softly.

"What was that noise?" said the goblin-father.

Curdie blew out his light, lest it should shine through.

"It must be that one miner that stayed behind the rest," said the mother.†

"No; he's been gone a good while. I haven't heard a blow for an hour. Besides, it wasn't like that."

"Then I suppose it must have been a stone carried down the brook inside."

"Perhaps. It will have more room by and by."

Figure 12

Curdie kept quite still. After a little while, hearing nothing but the sounds of their preparations for departure, mingled with an occasional† word of direction, and anxious to know whether the removal of the stone had made an opening into the goblins' house, he put in his hand to feel. It went in a good way, and then came in contact with something soft. He had but a moment to feel it over, it was so quickly withdrawn: it was one of the toeless goblin-feet. The owner of it gave a cry of fright.

"What's the matter, Helfer?" asked his mother.

"A beast came out of the wall and licked my foot."

"Nonsense! There are no wild beasts in our country," said his father.

"But it was, father. I felt it."

"Nonsense, I say. Will you malign your native realms and reduce them to a level with the country up stairs? That is swarming with wild beasts of every description."

"But I did feel it, father."

"I tell you to hold your tongue. You are no patriot."

Curdie suppressed his laughter, and lay still as a mouse—but no stiller, for every moment he kept nibbling away with his fingers at the edges of the hole. He was slowly making it bigger, for here the rock had been very much shattered with the blasting.

There seemed to be a good many in the family, to judge from the mass of confused talk which now and then came through the hole; but when all were speaking together, and just as if they had bottle-brushes—each at least one—in their throats, it was not easy to make out much that was said. At length he heard once more what the father-goblin was saying.

"Now then," he said, "get your bundles on your backs. Here, Helfer, I'll help you up with your chest."

"I wish it *was* my chest, father."

"Your turn will come in good time enough! Make haste. I *must* go to the meeting at the palace to-night. When that's over, we can come back and clear out the last of the things before our enemies return in the morning. Now light your torches, and come along. What a distinction it is to provide our own light, instead of being dependent on a thing hung up in the air—a most disagreeable contrivance—intended no doubt to blind us when we venture out under its baleful influence! Quite glaring and vulgar, I call it, though no doubt useful to poor creatures who haven't the wit to make light for themselves!"

Figure 13

Curdie could hardly keep himself from calling through to know whether they made† the fire to light their torches by. But a moment's reflection showed him that they would have said they did, inasmuch as they struck two stones together, and the fire came.

IX.—THE HALL OF THE GOBLIN PALACE.

A sound of many soft feet followed, but soon ceased. Then Curdie flew at the hole like a tiger, and tore and pulled. The sides gave way, and it was soon large enough for him to crawl through. He would not betray himself by rekindling his lamp, but the torches of the retreating company, which he found departing in a straight line up a long avenue from the door of their cave, threw back light enough to afford him a glance round the deserted home of the goblins. To his surprise, he could discover nothing to distinguish it from an ordinary natural cave in the rock, upon many of which he had come with the rest of the miners in the progress of their excavations. The goblins had talked of coming back for the rest of their household gear: he saw nothing that would have made him suspect a family had taken shelter there for a single night. The floor was rough and stony; the walls full of projecting corners; the roof in one place twenty feet high, in another endangering his forehead; while on one side a stream, no thicker than a needle, it is true, but still sufficient to spread a wide dampness over the wall,[1] flowed down the face of the rock. But the troop in front of him was toiling under heavy burdens. He could distinguish Helfer now and then, in the flickering light and shade, with his heavy chest on his bending shoulders; while the second brother was almost buried in what looked like a great feather-bed. "Where do they get the feathers?" thought Curdie; but in a moment the troop disappeared at a turn of the way, and it was now both safe and necessary for Curdie to follow them, lest they should be round the next turning before he saw them again, for so he might lose them altogether. He darted after them like a greyhound. When he reached the corner and looked cautiously round, he saw them again at some distance down another long passage. None of the galleries he saw that night bore signs of the work of man—or of goblin either. Stalactites far older than the mines, hung from their roofs; and their floors were rough with boulders and large round stones, showing that there water must have once run. He waited again at this corner till they had disappeared round the next, and so followed them a long way through one passage after another. The passages grew more and more lofty, and were more and more covered in the roof with shining stalactites.

---

1   The phrase "no thicker than a needle, it is true, but still sufficient to spread a wide dampness over the wall" is replaced by "now" in later editions.

It was a strange enough procession which he followed. But the strangest part of it was the household animals which crowded amongst the feet of the goblins. It was true they had no wild animals down there—at least they did not know of any; but they had a wonderful number of tame ones. I must, however, reserve any contributions towards the natural history of these for a later position in my story.

At length, turning a corner too abruptly, he had almost rushed into the middle of the goblin family; for there they had already set down all their burdens on the floor of a cave considerably larger than that which they had left. They were as yet too breathless to speak, else he would have had warning of their arrest. He started back, however, before any one saw him, and retreating a good way, stood watching till the father should come out to go to the palace. Before very long, both he and his son Helfer appeared and kept on in the same direction as before, while Curdie followed them again with renewed precaution. For a long time he heard no sound except something like the rush of a river inside the rock; but at length what seemed the far-off noise of a great shouting reached his ears, which however presently ceased. After advancing a good way further, he thought he heard a single voice. It sounded clearer and clearer as he went on, until at last he could almost distinguish the words. In a moment or two, keeping after the goblins round another corner, he once more started back— this time in amazement.

He was at the entrance of a magnificent cavern, of an oval shape, once probably a huge natural reservoir of water, now the great palace hall of the goblins. It rose to a tremendous height, but the roof was composed of such shining materials, and the multitude of torches carried by the goblins who crowded the floor lighted up the place so brilliantly, that Curdie could see to the top quite well. But he had no idea how immense the place was, until his eyes had got accustomed to it, which was not for a good many minutes. The rough projections on the walls, and the shadows thrown upwards from them by the torches, made the sides of the chamber look as if they were crowded with statues upon brackets and pedestals, reaching in irregular tiers from floor to roof. The walls themselves were, in many parts, of gloriously shining substances, some of them gorgeously coloured besides, which powerfully contrasted with the shadows. Curdie could not help wondering whether his rhymes would be of any use against such a multitude of goblins as filled the floor of the hall, and indeed felt considerably tempted to begin his shout of *One, two, three!* but as there was no reason for routing them, and much for endeavouring to discover their designs, he kept himself perfectly quiet, and peeping round the edge of the doorway, listened with both his sharp ears.

At the other end of the hall, high above the heads of the multitude, was a terrace-like ledge of considerable height, caused by the receding of the upper part of the cavern wall. Upon this sat the king and his court, the king on a throne hollowed out of a huge block of green copper ore, and his court upon lower seats around it. The king had been making them a speech, and the applause which followed it was what Curdie had heard. One of the court was now addressing the multitude. What he heard him say was to the following effect:—

"Hence it appears that two plans have been for some time together working in the strong head of his majesty for the deliverance of his people. Regardless of the fact that we were the first possessors of the regions they now inhabit, regardless equally of the fact that we abandoned that region from the loftiest motives; regardless also of the self-evident fact that we excel them as far in mental ability as they excel us in stature, they look upon us as a degraded race, and make a mockery of all our finer feelings. But the time has almost arrived when—thanks to his majesty's inventive genius—it will be in our power to take a thorough revenge upon them once for all, in respect of their unfriendly behaviour."

"May it please your majesty—" cried a voice close by the door, which Curdie recognised as that of the goblin he had followed.

"Who is he that interrupts the chancellor?" cried another from near the throne.

"Glump," answered several voices.

"He is our trusty subject," said the king himself, in a slow and stately voice: "let him come forward and speak."

A lane was parted through the crowd, and Glump having ascended the platform and bowed to the king, spoke as follows:—

"Sire, I would have held my peace, had I not known that I only knew how near was the moment to which the chancellor had just referred. In all probability, before another day is past, the enemy will have broken through into my house—the partition between being even now not more than a foot in thickness."

"Not quite so much," thought Curdie to himself.

"This very evening I have had to remove my household effects; therefore the sooner we are ready to carry out the plan, for the execution of which his majesty has been making such magnificent preparations, the better. I may just add, that within the last few days I have perceived a small outbreak in my dining-room, which, combined with observations upon the course of the river escaping where the evil men enter, has convinced me that close to the spot must lie a deep gulf in its channel. This discovery will, I trust, add considerably to the otherwise immense forces at his majesty's disposal."

He ceased, and the king graciously acknowledged his speech with a bend of his head; whereupon Glump, after a bow to his majesty, slid down amongst the rest of the undistinguished multitude. Then the chancellor rose and resumed.

"The information which the worthy Glump has given us," he said, "might have been of considerable import at the present moment, but for that other design already referred to, which naturally takes precedence. His majesty, unwilling to proceed to extremities, and well aware that such measures sooner or later result in violent reactions, has excogitated[1] a more fundamental and comprehensive measure, of which I need say no more. Should his majesty be successful—as who dares to doubt?—then a peace, all to the advantage of the goblin kingdom, will be established for a generation at least, rendered absolutely secure by the pledge which his royal highness the prince will have and hold for the good behaviour of her relatives. Should his majesty fail—which who shall dare even to imagine in his most secret thoughts?—then will be the time for carrying out with rigour the design to which Glump referred, and for which our preparations are even now all but completed. The failure of the former will render the latter imperative."

Curdie perceiving that the assembly was drawing to a close, and that there was little chance of either plan being more fully discovered, now thought it prudent to make his escape before the goblins began to disperse, and slipped quietly away.

There was not much danger of meeting any goblins, for all the men at least were left behind him in the palace; but there was considerable danger of his taking a wrong turning, for he had now no light, and had therefore to depend upon his memory and his hands. After he had left behind him the glow that issued from the door of Glump's new abode, he was utterly without guide, so far as his eyes were concerned.

He was most anxious to get back through the hole before the goblins should return to fetch the remains of their furniture. It was not that he was in the least afraid of them, but, as it was of

---

1 "Thought out, contrived, devised" (*OED*).

the utmost importance that he should thoroughly discover what the plans they were cherishing were, he must not occasion the slightest suspicion that they were watched by a miner.

He hurried on, feeling his way along the walls of rock. Had he not been very courageous, he must have been very anxious, for he could not but know that if he lost his way it would be the most difficult thing in the world to find it again. Morning would bring no light into these regions; and towards him least of all, who was known as a special rhymster and persecutor, could goblins be expected to exercise courtesy. Well might he wish that he had brought his lamp and tinder-box with him, of which he had not thought when he crept so eagerly after the goblins! He wished it all the more when, after a while, he found his way blocked up, and could get no further. It was of no use to turn back, for he had not the least idea where he had begun to go wrong. Mechanically, however, he kept feeling about the walls that hemmed him in. His hand came upon a place where a tiny stream of water was running down the face of the rock. "What a stupid I am!" he said to himself. "I am actually at the end of my journey!—And there are the goblins coming back to fetch their things!" he added, as the red glimmer of their torches appeared at the end of the long avenue that led up to the cave. In a moment he had thrown himself on the floor, and wriggled backwards through the hole. The floor on the other side was several feet lower, which made it easier to get back. It was all he could do to lift the largest stone he had taken out of the hole, but he did manage to shove it in again. He sat down on the ore-heap and thought.

He was pretty sure that the latter plan of the goblins was to inundate the mine by breaking outlets for the water accumulated in the natural reservoirs of the mountain, as well as running through portions of it. While the part hollowed by the miners remained shut off from that inhabited by the goblins, they had had no opportunity of injuring them thus; but now that a passage was broken through, and the goblins' part proved the higher in the mountain, it was clear to Curdie that the mine could be destroyed in an hour. Water was always the chief danger to which the miners were exposed. They met with a little choke-damp[1]

---

1 "A miner's term for the carbonic acid gas (or air largely mixed therewith) which accumulates in old workings in coal-pits, and at the bottom of wells, quarries, and caves; after an explosion in a coal-mine, it often rises and mingling with the remaining nitrogen, steam, smoke and dust, constitutes the after-damp, which suffocates the survivors from the deflagration of the fire-damp" (*OED*).

sometimes, but never with the explosive fire-damp[1] so common in coal mines. Hence they were careful as soon as they saw any appearance of water.

As the result of his reflections while the goblins were busy in their old home, it seemed to Curdie that it would be best to build up the whole of this gang, filling it with stone, and clay or lime, so that there should be no smallest channel for the water to get into. There was not, however, any immediate danger, for the execution of the goblins' plan was contingent upon the failure of that unknown design which was to take precedence of it; and he was most anxious to keep the door of communication open, that he might if possible discover what that former plan was. At the same time they could not then resume their intermitted labours for the inundation without his finding it out; when by putting all hands to the work, the one existing outlet might in a single night be rendered impenetrable to any weight of water; for by filling the gang entirely up, their embankment would be buttressed by the sides of the mountain itself.

As soon as he found that the goblins had again retired, he lighted his lamp, and proceeded to fill the hole he had made, with such stones as he could withdraw when he pleased. He then thought it better, as he might have occasion to be up a good many nights after this, to go home and have some sleep.

How pleasant the night air felt upon the outside of the mountain after what he had gone through in the inside of it! He hurried up the hill, without meeting a single goblin on the way, and called and tapped at the window until he woke his father, who soon rose and let him in. He told him the whole story, and, just as he had expected, his father thought it best to work that lode no further, but at the same time to pretend occasionally to be at work there still, in order that the goblins might have no suspicions. Both father and son went then to bed, and slept soundly until the morning.[2]

X.—THE PRINCESS'S KING-PAPA.

The weather continued fine for weeks, and the little princess went out every day. So long a period of fine weather had indeed

---

1 "A miner's term for carburetted hydrogen or marsh-gas, which is given off by coal and is explosive when mixed in certain proportions with atmospheric air" (*OED*).

2 End of the third instalment appearing in *Good Words for the Young*, 1 January 1871, pp. 129-36.

never been known upon that mountain. The only uncomfortable thing was that her nurse was so nervous and particular about being in before the sun was down, that often she would take to her heels when nothing worse than a fleecy cloud crossing the sun threw a shadow on the hill-side; and many an evening they were home a full hour before the sunlight had left the weather-cock on the stables. If it had not been for such odd behaviour, Irene would by this time have almost forgotten the goblins. She never forgot Curdie, but him she remembered for his own sake, and indeed would have remembered him if only because a princess never forgets her debts until they are paid.

One splendid sunshiny day, about an hour after noon, Irene, who was playing on a lawn in the garden, heard the distant blast of a bugle. She jumped up with a cry of joy, for she knew by that particular blast that her father was on his way to see her. This part of the garden lay on the slope of the hill, and allowed a full view of the country below. So she shaded her eyes with her hand, and looked far away to catch the first glimpse of shining armour. In a few moments a little troop came glittering round the shoulder of a hill. Spears and helmets were sparkling and gleaming, banners were flying, horses prancing, and again came the bugle-blast, which was to her like the voice of her father calling across the distance, "Irene, I'm coming." On and on they came, until she could clearly distinguish the king. He rode a white horse, and was taller than any of the men with him. He wore a narrow circle of gold set with jewels around his helmet, and as he came still nearer, Irene could discern the flashing of the stones in the sun. It was a long time since he had been to see her, and her little heart beat faster and faster as the shining troop approached, for she loved her king-papa very dearly, and was nowhere so happy as in his arms. When they reached a certain point, after which she could see them no more from the garden, she ran to the gate, and there stood till up they came clanging and stamping, with one more bright bugle-blast which said "Irene, I am come."

By this time the people of the house were all gathered at the gate, but Irene stood alone in front of them. When the horsemen pulled up, she ran to the side of the white horse, and held up her arms. The king stooped, and took her hands. In an instant she was on the saddle, and clasped in his great strong arms. I wish I could describe the king, so that you could see him in your mind. He had gentle blue eyes, but a nose that made him look like an eagle. A long dark beard, streaked with silvery lines, flowed from his mouth almost to his waist, and as Irene sat on the saddle and hid her glad face upon his bosom, it mingled with the golden hair which her mother had given her, and the two together were like a cloud with streaks of the sun woven through it. After he had held her to his heart for a minute, he spoke to his white horse, and the great beautiful creature, which had been prancing so proudly a little while before, walked as gently as a lady—for he knew he had a little lady on his back—through the gate and up to the door of the house. Then the king set her on the ground, and dismounting, took her hand and walked with her into the great hall, which was hardly ever entered except when he came to see his little princess. There he sat down with two of his councillors who had accompanied him, to have some refreshment, and Irene sat on his right hand, and drank her milk out of a wooden bowl, curiously carved.

After the king had eaten and drunk, he turned to the princess and said, stroking her hair—

"Now, my child, what shall we do next?"

This was the question he almost always put to her first after their meal together; and Irene had been waiting for it with some impatience, for now, she thought, she should be able to settle a question which constantly perplexed her.

"I should like you to take me to see my great old grand-mother."

The king looked grave, and said—

"What does my little daughter mean?"

"I mean the Queen Irene that lives up in the tower—the very old lady, you know, with the long hair of silver."

The king only gazed at his little princess with a look which she could not understand.

"She's got her crown in her bedroom," she went on; "but I've not been in there yet. You know she's here, don't you?"

"No," said the king very quietly.

"Then it must be all a dream," said Irene. "I half thought it was; but I couldn't be sure. Now I *am* sure of it. Besides, I could-n't find her the next time I went up."

At that moment a snow-white pigeon flew in at an open window and settled upon Irene's head. She broke into a merry laugh, cowered a little, and put up her hands to her head, saying—

"Dear dovey, don't peck me. You'll pull out my hair with your long claws if you don't mind."

The king stretched out his hand to take the pigeon, but it spread its wings and flew again through the open window, when its whiteness made one flash in the sun and vanished. The king laid his hand on his princess's head, held it back a little, gazed in her face, smiled half a smile, and sighed half a sigh.

"Come, my child; we'll have a walk in the garden together," he said.

"You won't come up and see my huge, great beautiful grand-mother, then, king-papa?" said the princess.

"Not this time," said the king very gently. "She has not invited me, you know, and great old ladies like her do not choose to be visited without leave asked and given."

The garden was a very lovely place. Being upon a mountain side there were parts in it where the rocks came through in great masses, and all immediately about them remained quite wild. Tufts of heather grew upon them, and other hardy mountain plants and flowers, while near them would be lovely roses and lilies, and all pleasant garden flowers. This mingling of the wild mountain with the civilized garden was very quaint, and it was impossible for any number of gardeners to make such a garden look formal and stiff.

Against one of these rocks was a garden-seat, shadowed from the afternoon sun by the overhanging of the rock itself. There was a little winding path up to the top of the rock, and on the top another seat; but they sat on the seat at its foot, because the sun was hot; and there they talked together of many things. At length the king said—

"You were out late one evening, Irene."

"Yes, papa. It was my fault; and Lootie was very sorry."

"I must talk to Lootie about it," said the king.

"Don't speak loud to her, please, papa," said Irene. "She's been so afraid of being late ever since! Indeed she has not been naughty. It was only a mistake for once."

"Once might be too often," murmured the king to himself, as he stroked his child's head.

I cannot tell you how he had come to know. I am sure Curdie had not told him. Some one about the palace must have seen them, after all. He sat for a good while thinking. There was no sound to be heard except that of a little stream which ran merrily out of an opening in the rock by where they sat, and sped away down the hill through the garden. Then he rose, and leaving Irene where she was, went into the house and sent for Lootie, with whom he had a talk that made her cry.

When in the evening he rode away upon his great white horse, he left six of his attendants behind him, with orders that three of

them should watch outside the house every night, walking rour
and round it from sunset to sunrise. It was clear he was not quite
comfortable about the princess.

XI.—THE OLD LADY'S BEDROOM.

Nothing more happened worth telling for some time. The autumn
came and went by. There were no more flowers in the garden. The
winds blew strong, and howled among the rocks. The rain fell, and
drenched the few yellow and red leaves that could not get off the
bare branches. Again and again there would be a glorious morning
followed by a pouring afternoon, and sometimes, for a week
together, there would be rain, nothing but rain, all day, and then
the most lovely cloudless night, with the sky all out in full-blown
stars—not one missing. But the princess could not see much of
them, for she went to bed early. The winter drew on, and she
found things growing dreary. When it was too stormy to go out,
and she had got tired of her toys, Lootie would take her about the
house, sometimes to the housekeeper's room, where the housekeeper, who was a good, kind old woman, made much of her—
sometimes to the servants' hall or the kitchen, where she was not
princess merely, but absolute queen, and ran a great risk of being
spoiled. Sometimes she would run of herself to the room where
the men-at-arms whom the king had left, sat, and they showed her
their arms and accoutrements, and did what they could to amuse
her. Still at times she found it very dreary, and often and often
wished that her huge great grandmother had not been a dream.

One morning the nurse left her with the housekeeper for a
while. To amuse her, she turned out the contents of an old
cabinet upon the table. The little princess found her treasures,
queer ancient ornaments, and many things the uses of which she
could not imagine, far more interesting than her own toys, and
sat playing with them for two hours or more. But at length, in
handling a curious old-fashioned brooch, she ran the pin of it
into her thumb, and gave a little scream with the sharpness of the
pain, but would have thought little more of it, had not the pain
increased and her thumb begun to swell. This alarmed the housekeeper greatly. The nurse was fetched; the doctor was sent for;
her hand was poulticed, and long before her usual time she was
put to bed. The pain still continued, and although she fell asleep
and dreamed a good many dreams, there was the pain always in
every dream. At last it woke her up.

The moon was shining brightly into the room. The poultice had fallen off her hand, and it was burning hot. She fancied if she could hold it into the moonlight, that would cool it. So she got out of bed, without waking the nurse who lay at the other end of the room, and went to the window. When she looked out, she saw one of the men-at-arms walking in the garden, with the moonlight glancing on his armour. She was just going to tap on the window and call him, for she wanted to tell him all about it, when she bethought herself that that might wake Lootie, and she would put her into her bed again. So she resolved to go to the window of another room, and call him from there. It was so much nicer to have somebody to talk to than to lie awake in bed with the burning pain in her hand. She opened the door very gently and went through the nursery, which did not look into the garden, to go to the other window. But when she came to the foot of the old staircase, there was the moon shining down from some window high up, and making the worm-eaten oak look very strange and delicate and lovely. In a moment she was putting her little feet one after the other in the silvery path up the stair, looking behind as she went, to see the shadow they made in the middle of the silver. Some little girls would have been afraid to find themselves thus alone in the middle of the night, but Irene was a princess.

As she went slowly up the stair, not quite sure that she was not dreaming, suddenly a great longing woke up in her heart to try once more whether she could not find the old old lady with the silvery hair.

"If she is a dream," she said to herself, "then I am the likelier to find her, if I am dreaming."

So up and up she went, stair after stair, until she came to the many rooms—all just as she had seen them before. Through passage after passage she softly sped, comforting herself that if she should lose her way it would not matter much, because when she woke she would find herself in her own bed, with Lootie not far off. But as if she had known every step of the way, she walked straight to the door at the foot of the narrow stair that led to the tower.

"What if I should realliality-really find my beautiful old grandmother up there!" she said to herself, as she crept up the steep steps.

When she reached the top, she stood a moment listening in the dark, for there was no moon there. Yes! it was! it was the hum of the spinning-wheel! What a diligent grandmother to work both day and night!

She tapped gently at the door.

"Come in, Irene," said the sweet voice.

The princess opened the door, and entered. There was the moonlight streaming in at the window, and in the middle of the moonlight sat the old lady in her black dress with the white lace, and her silvery hair mingling with the moonlight, so that you could not have told which was which.

"Come in, Irene," she said again. "Can you tell me what I am spinning?"

"She speaks," thought Irene, "just as if she had seen me five minutes ago, or yesterday at the farthest.—No," she answered; "I don't know what you are spinning. Please, I thought you were a dream. Why couldn't I find you before, great-great-grand-mother?"

"That you are hardly old enough to understand. But you would have found me sooner if you hadn't come to think I was a dream. I will give you one reason though why you couldn't find me. I didn't want you to find me."

"Why, please?"

"Because I did not want Lootie to know I was here."

"But you told me to tell Lootie."

"Yes. But I knew Lootie would not believe you. If she were to see me sitting spinning here, she wouldn't believe me either."

"Why?"

"Because she couldn't. She would rub her eyes, and go away and say she felt queer, and forget half of it and more, and then say it had been all a dream."

"Just like me," said Irene, feeling very much ashamed of herself.

"Yes, a good deal like you, but not just like you; for you've come again; and Lootie wouldn't have come again. She would have said, No no—she had had enough of such nonsense."

"Is it naughty of Lootie then?"

"It would be naughty of you. I've never done anything for Lootie."

"And you did wash my face and hands for me," said Irene, beginning to cry.

The old lady smiled a sweet smile and said—†

"I'm not vexed with you, my child—nor with Lootie either. But I don't want you to say anything more to Lootie about me. If she should ask you, you must just be silent. But I do not think she will ask you."

All the time they talked, the old lady kept on spinning.

Figure 14

"You haven't told me yet what I am spinning," she said.

"Because I don't know. It's very pretty stuff."

It was indeed very pretty stuff. There was a good bunch of it on the distaff attached to the spinning-wheel, and in the moonlight it shone like—what shall I say it was like? It was not white enough for silver—yes, it was like silver, but shone gray rather than white, and glittered only a little. And the thread the old lady drew out from it was so fine that Irene could hardly see it.

"I am spinning this for you, my child."

"For me! What am I to do with it, please?"

"I will tell you by-and-by. But first I will tell you what it is. It is spider-webs—of a particular kind. My pigeons bring it me from over the great sea. There is only one forest where the spiders live who make this particular kind—the finest and strongest of any. I have nearly finished my present job. What is on the rock now will be enough. I have a week's work there yet, though," she added, looking at the bunch.

"Do you work all day and all night too, great-great-great-great grandmother?" said the princess, thinking to be very polite with so many *greats*.

"I am not quite so great as all that," she answered, smiling almost merrily. "If you call me grandmother, that will do.—No, I don't work every night—only moonlit nights, and then no longer than the moon shines upon my wheel. I shan't work much longer to-night."

"And what will you do next, grandmother?"

"Go to bed. Would you like to see my bedroom?"

"Yes, that I should."

"Then I think I won't work any longer to-night. I shall be in good time."

The old lady rose, and left her wheel standing just as it was. You see there was no good in putting it away, for where there was not any furniture, there was no danger of being untidy.

Then she took Irene by the hand, but it was her bad hand, and Irene gave a little cry of pain.†

"My child!" said her grandmother, "what is the matter?"

Irene held her hand into the moonlight, that the old lady might see it, and told her all about it, at which she looked grave. But she only said—"Give me your other hand;" and, having led her out upon the little dark landing, opened the door on the opposite side of it. What was Irene's surprise to see the loveliest room she had ever seen† in her life! It was large and lofty, and dome-shaped. From the centre hung a lamp as round as a ball, shining as if with the brightest moonlight, which made everything visible in the room, though not so clearly that the princess could tell what many of the things were. A large oval bed stood in the middle, with a coverlid of rose-colour, and velvet curtains all round it of a lovely pale blue. The walls were also blue—spangled all over with what looked like stars of silver.

The old lady left her, and going to a strange looking cabinet, opened it and took out a curious silver casket. Then she sat down on a low chair, and calling Irene, made her kneel before her while she looked at her hand. Having examined it, she opened the casket and took from it a little ointment. The sweetest odour

Figure 15

filled the room—like that of roses and lilies—as she rubbed the ointment gently all over the hot swollen hand. Her touch was so pleasant and cool, that it seemed to drive away the pain and heat wherever it came.

"Oh, grandmother! it is *so* nice!" said Irene. "Thank you; thank you."

Then the old lady went to a chest of drawers, and took out a large handkerchief of gossamer-like cambric,[1] which she tied round her hand.

---

1 "A kind of fine white linen, originally made at Cambray in Flanders" (*OED*).

Figure 16

"I don't think I can let you go away to-night," she said. "Would you like to sleep with me?"

"Oh, yes, yes, dear grandmother!" said Irene, and would have clapped her hands, forgetting that she could not.

"You won't be afraid then to go to bed with such an old woman?"

"No. You are so beautiful, grandmother!"

"But I am *very* old."

"And I suppose I am very young. You won't mind sleeping with such a *very* young woman, grandmother?"

"You sweet little pertness!" said the old lady, and drew her towards her, and kissed her on the forehead and the cheek and the mouth.

Then she got a large silver basin, and having poured some water into it, made Irene sit on the chair, and washed her feet. This done, she was ready for bed. And oh, what a delicious bed it was into which her grandmother laid her! She hardly could have told she was lying upon anything: she felt nothing but the

Figure 17

softness. The old lady having undressed herself lay down beside her.†

"Why don't you put out your moon?" asked the princess.

"That never goes out, night or day," she answered. "In the darkest night, if any of my pigeons are out on a message, they always see my moon, and know where to fly to."

"But if somebody besides the pigeons were to see it—somebody about the house, I mean—they would come to look what it was, and find you."

"The better for them then," said the old lady. "But it does not happen above five times in a hundred years that any one does see it. The greater part of those who do, take it for a meteor, wink their eyes and forget it again. Besides, nobody could find the room except I pleased. Besides again—I will tell you a secret—if that light were to go out, you would fancy yourself lying in a bare garret, on a heap of old straw, and would not see one of the pleasant things round about you all the time."

"I hope it will never go out," said the princess.

"I hope not. But it is time we both went to sleep. Shall I take you in my arms?"

The little princess nestled close up to the old lady, who took her in both her arms, and held her close to her bosom.

"Oh dear! this is so nice!" said the princess. "I didn't know anything in the whole world could be so comfortable. I should like to lie here for ever."

"You may if you will," said the old lady. "But I must put you to one trial—not a *very* hard one, I hope.—This night week you must come back to me. If you don't, I do not know when you may find me again, and you will soon want me very much."

"Oh! please, don't let me forget."

"You shall not forget. The only question is whether you will believe I am anywhere—whether you will believe I am anything but a dream. You may be sure I will do all I can to help you to come. But it will rest with yourself after all. On the night of next Friday, you must come to me. Mind now."

"I *will* try," said the princess.

"Then good night," said the old lady, and kissed the forehead which lay in her bosom.

In a moment more the little princess was dreaming in the midst of the loveliest dreams—of summer seas and moonlight and mossy springs and great murmuring trees, and beds of wild flowers with such odours as she had never smelled before. But after all, no dream could be more lovely than what she had left behind when she fell asleep.

In the morning she found herself in her own bed. There was no handkerchief or anything else on her hand, only a sweet odour lingered about it. The swelling had all gone down; the prick of the brooch had vanished;—in fact her hand was perfectly well.

XII.—A SHORT CHAPTER ABOUT CURDIE.

Curdie spent many nights in the mine. His father and he had taken Mrs. Peterson into the secret, for they knew mother could hold her tongue, which was more than could be said of all the miners' wives. But Curdie did not tell her that every night he spent in the mine, part of it went in earning a new red petticoat for her.

Mrs. Peterson was such a nice good mother! All mothers are nice and good more or less, but Mrs. Peterson was nice and good all *more* and no *less*. She made and kept a little heaven in that poor cottage on the high hill-side—for her husband and son to go home to out of the low and rather dreary earth in which they worked. I doubt if the princess was very much happier even in the arms of her huge-great-grandmother than Peter and Curdie were in the arms of Mrs. Peterson. True, her hands were hard and chapped and large, but it was with work for them; and therefore in the sight of the angels, her hands were so much the more beautiful. And if Curdie worked hard to get her a petticoat, she worked hard every day to get him comforts which he would have missed much more than she would a new petticoat even in winter. Not that she and Curdie ever thought of how much they worked for each other: that would have spoiled everything.

When left alone in the mine, Curdie always worked on for an hour or two first, following the lode which, according to Glump, would lead at last into the deserted habitation. After that, he would set out on a reconnoitring expedition. In order to manage this, or rather the return from it, better than the first time, he had bought a huge ball of fine string, having learned the trick from Hop-o'-my-Thumb,[1] whose history his mother had often told him. Not that Hop-o'-my-Thumb had ever used a ball of string— I should be sorry to be supposed so far out in my classics—but

---

1 Hop-o'-my-Thumb is a diminutive character appearing in Perrault's "Le Petit Poucet" in his *Contes de ma mère l'Oye* (1697).

the principle was the same as that of the pebbles. The end of this string he fastened to his pickaxe, which figured no bad anchor, and then, with the ball in his hand, unrolling it as he went, set out in the dark through the natural gangs of the goblins' territory. The first night or two he came upon nothing worth remembering; saw only a little of the home-life of the *cobs* in the various caves they called houses; failed in coming upon anything to cast light upon the foregoing design which kept the inundation for the present in the background. But at length, I think on the third or fourth night, he found, partly guided by the noise of their implements, a company of evidently the best sappers[1] and miners amongst them, hard at work. What were they about? It could not well be the inundation, seeing that had in the meantime been postponed to something else. Then what was it? He lurked and watched, every now and then in the greatest risk of being detected, but without success. He had again and again to retreat in haste, a proceeding rendered the more difficult that he had to gather up his string as he returned upon its course. It was not that he was afraid of the goblins, but that he was afraid of their finding out that they were watched, which might have prevented the discovery at which he aimed. Sometimes his haste had to be such that, when he reached home towards morning, his string, for lack of time to wind it up as he "dodged the cobs," would be in what seemed the most hopeless entanglement; but after a good sleep though a short one, he always found his mother had got it right again. There it was, wound in a most respectable ball, ready for use the moment he should want it!

"I can't think how you do it, mother," he would say.

"I follow the thread," she would answer—"just as you do in the mine."

She never had more to say about it; but the less clever she was with her words, the more clever she was with her hands; and the less his mother said, the more, Curdie believed, she had to say.

But still he had made no discovery as to what the goblin miners were about.[2]

---

1 "A soldier employed in working at saps, the building and repairing of fortifications, the execution of field-works, and the like." The verb "to sap" means "To dig a sap or covered trench; to approach a besieged place by means of a sap" (*OED*).

2 End of the fourth instalment appearing in *Good Words for the Young*, 1 February 1871, pp. 185-91.

XIII.—THE COBS' CREATURES.

About this time, the gentlemen whom the king had left behind him to watch over the princess, had each occasion to doubt the testimony of his own eyes, for more than strange were the objects to which they would bear witness. They were of one sort—creatures—but so grotesque and misshapen as to be more like a child's drawings upon his slate than anything natural. They saw them only at night, while on guard about the house. The testimony of the man who first reported having seen one of them was that, as he was walking slowly round the house, while yet in the shadow, he caught sight of a creature standing on its hind legs in the moonlight, with its fore feet upon a window-ledge, staring in at the window. Its body might have been that of a dog or wolf—he thought, but he declared on his honour that its head was twice the size it ought to have been for the size of its body, and as round as a ball, while the face, which it turned upon him as it fled, was more like one carved by a boy upon the turnip inside which he is going to put a candle, than anything else he could think of.[1] It rushed into the garden. He sent an arrow after it, and thought he must have struck it; for it gave an unearthly howl, and he could not find his arrow any more than the beast, although he searched all about the place where it vanished. They laughed at him until he was driven to hold his tongue; and said he must have taken too long a pull at the ale-jug. But before two nights were over, he had one to side with him; for he too had seen something strange, only quite different from that reported by the other. The description the second man gave of the creature he had seen, was yet more grotesque and unlikely. They were both laughed at by the rest; but night after night another came over to their side, until at last there was only one left to laugh at all his companions. Two nights more passed, and he saw nothing; but on the third, he came rushing from the garden to the other two before the house, in such an agitation that they declared—for it was their turn now—that the band of his helmet was cracking under his chin with the rising of his hair inside it. Running with him into that part of the garden which I have already described, they saw a score of creatures, to not one of which they could give a name, and not one of which was like another, hideous and ludicrous at once, gambolling on the lawn in the moonlight. The supernatural or rather

---

1 According to Irish and Scottish tradition, the lanterns carved at Hallowe'en were made from turnips.

subnatural ugliness of their faces, the length of legs and necks in some, and the apparent absence of both or either in others, made the spectators, although in one consent as to what they saw, yet doubtful, as I have said, of the evidence of their own eyes—and ears as well; for the noises they made, although not loud, were as uncouth and varied as their forms, and could be described neither as grunts nor squeaks nor roars nor howls nor barks nor yells nor screams nor croaks nor hisses nor mews nor shrieks, but only as something like all of them mingled in one horrible dissonance. Keeping in the shade, the watchers had a few moments to recover themselves before the hideous assembly suspected their presence; but all at once, as if by common consent, they scampered off in the direction of a great rock, and vanished before the men had come to themselves sufficiently to think of following them.

My readers will suspect what these were; but I will now give them full information concerning them. They were of course household animals belonging to the goblins, whose ancestors had taken their ancestors many centuries before from the upper regions of light into the lower regions of darkness. The original stocks of these horrible creatures were very much the same as the animals now seen about farms and homes in the country, with the exception of a few of them, which had been wild creatures, such as foxes, and indeed wolves and small bears, which the goblins, from their proclivity towards the animal creation, had caught when cubs and tamed. But in the course of time, all had undergone even greater changes than had passed upon their owners. They had altered—that is, their descendants had altered—into such creatures as I have not attempted to describe except in the vaguest manner—the various parts of their bodies assuming, in an apparently arbitrary and self-willed manner, the most abnormal developments. Indeed so little did any distinct type predominate in some of the bewildering results, that you could only have guessed at any known animal as the original, and even then, what likeness remained would be more one of general expression than of definable conformation. But what increased the gruesomeness tenfold, was that, from constant domestic, or indeed rather family association with the goblins, their countenances had grown in grotesque resemblance to the† human. No one understands animals who does not see that every one of them, even amongst the fishes, it may be with a dimness and vagueness infinitely remote, yet shadows the human: in the case of these the human resemblance had greatly increased: while

Figure 18

their owners had sunk towards them, they had risen towards their owners. But the conditions of subterranean life being equally unnatural for both, while the goblins were worse, the creatures had not improved by the approximation, and its result would have appeared far more ludicrous than consoling to the warmest lover of animal nature. I shall now explain how it was that just then these animals began to show themselves about the king's country-house.

The goblins, as Curdie had discovered, were mining on—at work both day and night, in divisions, urging the scheme after which he lay in wait. In the course of their tunnelling, they had broken into the channel of a small stream, but the break being in the top of it, no water had escaped to interfere with their work. Some of the creatures, hovering as they often did about their masters, had found the hole, and had, with the curiosity which had grown to a passion from the restraints of their unnatural circumstances, proceeded to explore the channel. The stream was the same which ran out by the seat on which Irene and her king-papa had sat as I have told, and the goblin-creatures found it jolly fun to get out for a romp on a smooth lawn such as they had never seen in all their poor miserable lives. But although they had

Figure 19

partaken enough of the nature of their owners to delight in annoying and alarming any of the people whom they met on the mountain, they were of course incapable of designs of their own, or of intentionally furthering those of their masters.

For several nights after the men-at-arms were at length of one mind as to the fact of the visits of some horrible creatures, whether bodily or spectral they could not yet say, they watched with special attention that part of the garden where they had last seen them. Perhaps indeed they gave in consequence too little attention to the house. But the creatures were too cunning to be easily caught; nor were the watchers quick-eyed enough to descry the head, or the keen eyes in it, which, from the opening whence the stream issued, would watch them in turn, ready, the moment they should leave the lawn, to report the place clear.†

XIV.—THAT NIGHT WEEK.

During the whole of the week, Irene had been thinking every other moment of her promise to the old lady, although even now she could not feel quite sure that she had not been dreaming. Could it really be that an old lady lived up in the top of the house, with pigeons and a spinning-wheel and a lamp that never went out? She was, however, none the less determined, on the coming Friday, to ascend the three stairs, walk through the passages with the many doors,† and try to find the tower in which she had either seen or dreamed her grandmother.

Her nurse could not help wondering what had come to the child—she would sit so thoughtfully silent, and even in the midst of a game with her, would so suddenly fall into a dreamy mood. But Irene took care to betray nothing, whatever efforts Lootie might make to get at her thoughts. And Lootie had to say to herself, "What an odd child she is!" and give it up.

At length the longed-for Friday arrived, and lest Lootie should be moved to watch her, Irene endeavoured to keep herself as quiet as possible. In the afternoon she asked for her doll's-house, and went on arranging and re-arranging the various rooms and their inhabitants for a whole hour. Then she gave a sigh and threw herself back in her chair. One of the dolls would not sit, and another would not stand, and they were all very tiresome. Indeed there was one would not even lie down, which was too bad. But it was now getting dark, and the darker it got the more excited Irene became, and the more she felt it necessary to be composed.

Figure 20

"I see you want your tea, princess," said the nurse: "I will go and get it. The room feels close: I will open the window a little. The evening is mild: it won't hurt you."

"There's no fear of that, Lootie," said Irene, wishing she had put off going for the tea till it was darker, when she might have made her attempt with every advantage.

I fancy Lootie was longer in returning than she had intended; for when Irene, who had been lost in thought, looked up, she saw it was nearly dark, and at the same moment caught sight of a pair of eyes, bright with a green light, glowering at her through the open window. The next instant, something leaped into the room. It was like a cat, with legs as long as a horse's, Irene said, but its body no bigger and its legs no thicker than those of a cat. She was too frightened to cry out, but not too frightened to jump from her chair and run from the room.

It is plain enough to every one of my readers what she ought to have done—and indeed Irene thought of it herself; but when she came to the foot of the old stair, just outside the nursery door, she imagined the creature running up those long ascents after her, and pursuing her through the dark passages—*which,*

Figure 21

after all, might lead to no tower! That thought was too much. Her heart failed her, and turning from the stair, she rushed along to the hall, whence, finding the front-door open, she darted into the court,† pursued—at least she thought so—by the creature. No one happening to see her, on she ran, unable to think for fear, and ready to run anywhere to elude the awful creature with the stilt-legs. Not daring to look behind her, she rushed straight out of the gate, and up the mountain. It was foolish indeed—thus to run farther and farther from all who could help her, as if she had been seeking a fit spot for the goblin-creature to eat her in at his leisure; but that is the way fear serves us: it always sides with the thing we are afraid of.

The princess was soon out of breath with running up hill; but she ran on, for she fancied the horrible creature just behind her, forgetting that, had it been after her, such legs as those must have overtaken her long ago. At last she could run no longer, and fell, unable even to scream, by the roadside, where she lay for some time, half dead with terror. But finding nothing lay hold of her, and her breath beginning to come back, she ventured at length to get half up, and peer anxiously about her. It was now so dark that she could see nothing. Not a single star was out. She could not even tell in what direction the house lay, and between her and home she fancied the dreadful creature lying ready to pounce upon her. She saw now that she ought to have run up the stairs at once. It was well she did not scream; for, although very few of the goblins had come out for weeks, a stray idler or two might have heard her. She sat down upon a stone, and nobody but one who had done something wrong could have been more miserable. She had quite forgotten her promise to visit her grandmother. A rain-drop fell on her face. She looked up, and for a moment her terror was lost in astonishment. At first she thought the rising moon had left her place, and drawn nigh to see what could be the matter with the little girl, sitting alone, without hat or cloak, on the dark bare mountain; but she soon saw she was mistaken, for there was no light on the ground at her feet, and no shadow anywhere. But a great silvery globe was hanging in the air; and as she gazed at the lovely thing, her courage revived. If she were but in doors again, she would fear nothing, not even the terrible creature with the long legs! But how was she to find her way back? What could that light be? Could it be—? No, it couldn't. But what if it should be—yes—it must be—her great-great-grandmother's lamp, which guided her pigeons home through the darkest night! She jumped up: she had but to keep that light in view, and she must find the house.

Her heart grew strong. Speedily, yet softly, she walked down the hill, hoping to pass the watching creature unseen. Dark as it was, there was little danger now of choosing the wrong road. And—which was most strange—the light that filled her eyes from the lamp, instead of blinding them for a moment to the object upon which they next fell, enabled her for a moment to see it, despite the darkness. By looking at the lamp and then dropping her eyes, she could see the road for a yard or two in front of her, and this saved her from several falls, for the road was very rough. But all at once, to her dismay, it vanished, and the terror of the beast, which had left her the moment she began to return, again laid hold of her heart. The same instant, however, she caught the light of the windows, and knew exactly where she was. It was too dark to run, but she made what haste she could, and reached the gate in safety. She found the house-door still open, ran through the hall, and, without even looking into the nursery, bounded straight up the stair, and the next, and the next; then turning to the right, ran through the long avenue of silent rooms, and found her way at once to the door at the foot of the tower stair.

When first the nurse missed her, she fancied she was playing her a trick, and for some time took no trouble about her; but at last, getting frightened, she had begun to search; and when the princess entered, the whole household was hither and thither over the house, hunting for her. A few seconds after she reached the stair of the tower, they had even begun to search the neglected rooms, in which they would never have thought of looking had they not already searched every other place they could think of in vain. But by this time she was knocking at the old lady's door.

XV.—WOVEN AND THEN SPUN.

"Come in, Irene," said the silvery voice of her grandmother.

The princess opened the door, and peeped in. But the room was quite dark, and there was no sound of the spinning-wheel. She grew frightened once more, thinking that, although the room was there, the old lady might be a dream after all. Every little girl knows how dreadful it is to find a room empty where she thought somebody was; but Irene had to fancy for a moment that the person she came to find was nowhere at all. She remembered however that at night she spun only in the moonlight, and concluded that must be why there was no sweet, bee-like humming:

the old lady might be somewhere in the darkness. Before she had time to think another thought, she heard her voice again, saying as before,

"Come in, Irene."

From the sound, she understood at once that she was not in the room beside her. Perhaps she was in her bedroom. She turned across the passage, feeling her way to the other door. When her hand fell on the lock, again the old lady spoke—

"Shut the other door behind you, Irene. I always close the door of my workroom when I go to my chamber."

Irene wondered to hear her voice so plainly through the door: having shut the other, she opened it and went in. Oh, what a lovely haven to reach from the darkness and fear through which she had come! The soft light made her feel as if she were going into the heart of the milkiest pearl; while the blue walls and their silver stars for a moment perplexed her with the fancy that they were in reality the sky which she had left outside a minute ago covered with rain-clouds.

"I've lighted a fire for you, Irene: you're cold and wet," said her grandmother.

Then Irene looked again, and saw that what she had taken for a huge bouquet of red roses on a low stand against the wall, was in fact a fire which burned in the shapes of the loveliest and reddest roses, glowing gorgeously between the heads and wings of two cherubs of shining silver. And when she came nearer, she found that the smell of roses with which the room was filled, came from the fire-roses on the hearth. Her grandmother was dressed in the loveliest pale-blue velvet, over which her hair, no longer white, but of a rich golden colour, streamed like a cataract, here falling in dull gathered heaps, there rushing away in smooth shining falls. And ever as she looked, the hair seemed pouring down from her head, and vanishing in a golden mist ere it reached the floor. It flowed from under the edge of a circle of shining silver, set with alternated pearls and opals. On her dress was no ornament whatever, neither was there a ring on her hand, or a necklace or carcanet about her neck. But her slippers glimmered with the light of the milky way, for they were covered with seed-pearls and opals in one mass. Her face was that of a woman of three-and-twenty.

The princess was so bewildered with astonishment and admiration that she could hardly thank her, and drew nigh with timidity, feeling dirty and uncomfortable. The lady was seated on a low chair by the side of the fire, with hands outstretched to take her, but the princess hung back with a troubled smile.

"Why, what's the matter?" asked her grandmother. "You haven't been doing anything wrong—I know that by your face, though it *is* rather miserable. What's the matter, my dear?"

And she still held out her arms.

"Dear grandmother," said Irene, "I'm not so sure that I haven't done something wrong. I ought to have run up to you at once when the long-legged cat came in at the window, instead of running out on the mountain, and making myself such a fright."

"You were taken by surprise, my child, and are not so likely to do it again. It is when people do wrong things wilfully that they are the more likely to do them again. Come."

And still she held out her arms.

"But, grandmother, you're so beautiful and grand with your crown on! and I am so dirty with mud and rain!—I should quite spoil your beautiful blue dress."

With a merry little laugh, the lady sprung from her chair, more lightly far than Irene herself could, caught the child to her bosom, and kissing the tear-stained face over and over, sat down with her in her lap.

"Oh, grandmother! you'll make yourself such a mess!" cried Irene, clinging to her.

"You darling! do you think I care more for my dress than for my little girl? Besides—look here."

As she spoke she set her down, and Irene saw to her dismay that the lovely dress was covered with the mud of her fall on the mountain road. But the lady stooped to the fire, and taking from it, by the stalk in her fingers, one of the burning roses, passed it once and again and a third time over the front of her dress; and when Irene looked, not a single stain was to be discovered.

"There!" said her grandmother, "you won't mind coming to me now?"

But Irene again hung back, eyeing the flaming rose which the lady held in her hand.

"You're not afraid of the rose—are you?" she said, about to throw it on the hearth again.

"Oh! don't, please!" cried Irene. "Won't you hold it to my frock and my hands and my face? And I'm afraid my feet and my knees want it too!"

"No," answered her grandmother, smiling a little sadly, as she threw the rose from her; "it is too hot for you yet. It would set *your* frock in a flame. Besides, I don't want to make you clean to-night. I want your nurse and the rest of the people to see you as you are, for you will have to tell them how you ran away for fear of the long-legged cat. I should like to wash you, but they would not believe you then. Do you see that bath behind you?"

The princess looked, and saw a large oval tub of silver, shining brilliantly in the light of the wonderful lamp.

"Go and look into it," said the lady.

Irene went, and came back very silent, with her eyes shining.

"What did you see?" asked her grandmother.

"The sky and the moon and the stars," she answered. "It looked as if there was no bottom to it."

The lady smiled a pleased satisfied smile, and was silent also for a few moments. Then she said,

"Any time you want a bath, come to me. I know you have a bath every morning, but sometimes you want one at night too."

"Thank you, grandmother; I will—I will indeed," answered Irene, and was again silent for some moments thinking. Then she said, "How was it, grandmother, that I saw your beautiful lamp—not the light of it only—but the great round silvery lamp itself, hanging alone in the great open air high up? It was your lamp I saw—wasn't it?"

"Yes, my child; it was my lamp."

"Then how was it? I don't see a window all round."

"When I please, I can make the lamp shine through the walls—shine so strong that it melts them away from before the sight, and shows itself as you saw it. But, as I told you, it is not everybody can see it."

"How is it that I can then? I'm sure I don't know."

"It is a gift born with you. And one day I hope everybody will have it."

"But how do you make it shine through the walls?"

"Ah! that you would not understand if I were to try ever so much to make you—not yet—not yet. But," added the lady rising, "you must sit in my chair while I get you the present I have been preparing for you. I told you my spinning was for you. It is finished now, and I am going to fetch it. I have been keeping it warm under one of my brooding pigeons."

Irene sat down in the low chair, and her grandmother left her, shutting the door behind her. The child sat gazing, now at the rose-fire, now at the starry walls, now at the silvery light; and a great quietness grew in her heart. If all the long-legged cats in the world had come rushing at her then, she would not have been afraid of them for a moment. How this was she could not tell;— she only knew there was no fear in her, and everything was so right and safe that it could not get in.

She had been gazing at the lovely lamp for some minutes fixedly: turning her eyes, she found the wall had vanished, for she was looking out on the dark cloudy night. But though she heard the wind blowing, none of it blew upon her. In a moment more, the clouds themselves parted, or rather vanished like the wall, and she looked straight into the starry herds, flashing gloriously in the dark blue. It was but for a moment. The clouds gathered again and shut out the stars; the wall gathered again and shut out the clouds; and there stood the lady beside her with the loveliest smile on her face, and a shimmering ball in her hand, about the size of a pigeon's egg.

"There, Irene; there is my work for you!" she said, holding out the ball to the princess.

She took it in her hand, and looked at it all over. It sparkled a little, and shone here and shone there, but not much. It was of a sort of gray whiteness, something like spun glass.

"Is this *all* your spinning, grandmother?" she asked.

"All since you came to the house. There is more there than you think."

"How pretty it is! What am I to do with it, please?"

"That I will now explain to you," answered the lady, turning from her, and going to her cabinet.

She came back with a small ring in her hand. Then she took the ball from Irene's, and did something with the two—Irene could not tell what.

"Give me your hand," she said.

Irene held up her right hand.

"Yes, that is the hand I want," said the lady, and put the ring on the forefinger of it.

"What a beautiful ring!" said Irene. "What is the stone called?"

"It is a fire-opal."[1]

"Please, am I to keep it?"

"Always."

"Oh, thank you, grandmother! It's prettier than anything I ever saw, except those—of all colours—in your—Please, is that your crown?"

"Yes, it is my crown. The stone in your ring is of the same sort—only not so good. It has only red, but mine have all colours, you see."

"Yes, grandmother. I will take such care of it!—But—" she added, hesitating.

---

1 "A variety of opal showing flame-coloured internal reflections" (*OED*).

"But what?" asked her grandmother.

"What am I to say when Lootie asks me where I got it?"

"*You* will ask *her* where you got it," answered the lady smiling.

"I don't see how I can do that."

"You will though."

"Of course I will if you say so. But you know I can't pretend not to know."

"Of course not. But don't trouble yourself about it. You will see when the time comes."

So saying, the lady turned, and threw the little ball into the rose-fire.

"Oh, grandmother!" exclaimed Irene; "I thought you had spun it for me."

"So I did my child. And you've got it."

"No; it's burnt in the fire!"

The lady put her hand in the fire, brought out the ball, glimmering as before, and held it towards her. Irene stretched out her hand to take it, but the lady turned, and going to her cabinet, opened a drawer, and laid the ball in it.

"Have I done anything to vex you, grandmother?" said Irene pitifully.

"No, my darling. But you must understand that no one ever gives anything to another properly and really without keeping it. That ball is yours."

"Oh! I'm not to take it with me! You are going to keep it for me!"

"You are to take it with you. I've fastened the end of it to the ring on your finger."

Irene looked at the ring.

"I can't see it there, grandmother," she said.

"Feel—a little way from the ring—towards the cabinet," said the lady.

"Oh! I do feel it!" exclaimed the princess. "But I can't see it," she added, looking close to her outstretched hand.

"No. The thread is too fine for you to see it. You can only feel it. Now you can fancy how much spinning that took, although it does seem such a little ball."

"But what use can I make of it, if it lies in your cabinet?"

"That is what I will explain to you. It would be of no use to you—it wouldn't be yours at all if it did not lie in my cabinet.— Now listen.—If ever you find yourself in any danger—such, for example, as you were in this same evening—you must take off your ring and put it under the pillow of your bed. Then you must lay your forefinger, the same that wore the ring, upon the thread, and follow the thread wherever it leads you."

"Oh, how delightful! It will lead me to you, grandmother, I know!"

"Yes. But, remember, it may seem to you a very roundabout way indeed, and you must not doubt the thread. Of one thing you may be sure, that while you hold it, I hold it too."

"It is very wonderful!" said Irene, thoughtfully. Then suddenly becoming aware, she jumped up, crying—"Oh, grandmother! here have I been sitting all this time in your chair, and you standing! I *beg* your pardon."

The lady laid her hand on her shoulder, and said,

"Sit down again, Irene. Nothing pleases me better than to see any one sit in my chair. I am only too glad to stand so long as any one will sit in it."

"How kind of you!" said the princess, and sat down again.

"It makes me happy," said the lady.

"But," said Irene, still puzzled, "won't the thread get in somebody's way and be broken, if the one end is fast to my ring, and the other laid in your cabinet?"

"You will find all that arrange itself.—I am afraid it is time for you to go."

"Mightn't I stay and sleep with you to-night, grandmother?"

"No, not to-night. If I had meant you to stay to-night, I should have given you a bath; but you know everybody in the house is miserable about you, and it would be cruel to keep them so all night. You must go down stairs."

"I'm so glad, grandmother, you didn't say—*go home*—for this is my home. Mayn't I call this my home?"

"You may, my child. And I trust you will always think it your home. Now come. I must take you back without any one seeing you."

"Please, I want to ask you one question more," said Irene. "Is it because you have your crown on that you look so young?"

"No, child," answered her grandmother; "it is because I felt so young this evening, that I put my crown on. And I thought you would like to see your old grandmother in her best."

"Why do you call yourself old? You're not old, grandmother."

"I am very old indeed. It is so silly of people—I don't mean you, for you are such a tiny, and couldn't know better—but it *is* so silly of people to fancy that old age means crookedness and witheredness and feebleness and sticks and spectacles and rheumatism and forgetfulness! It is so silly! Old age has nothing whatever to do with all that. The right old age means strength and beauty and mirth and courage and clear eyes and strong painless limbs. I am older than you are able to think, and—"

"And look at you, grandmother!" cried Irene, jumping up, and flinging her arms about her neck. "I won't be so silly again, I promise you. At least—I'm rather afraid to promise—but if I am, I promise to be sorry for it—I do.—I wish I were as old as you, grandmother. I don't think you are ever afraid of anything."

"Not for long, at least, my child. Perhaps by the time I am two thousand years of age, I shall, indeed, never be afraid of anything. But I confess I have sometimes been afraid about my children— sometimes about you, Irene."

"Oh, I'm *so* sorry, grandmother!—To-night, I suppose, you mean."

"Yes—a little to-night; but a good deal when you had all but made up your mind that I was a dream, and no real great-great-grandmother.—You must not suppose I am blaming you for that. I daresay you could not help it."

"I don't know, grandmother," said the princess, beginning to cry. "I can't always do myself as I should like. And I don't always try.—I'm very sorry anyhow."

The lady stooped, lifted her in her arms, and sat down with her in her chair, holding her close to her bosom. In a few minutes the princess had sobbed herself to sleep. How long she slept, I do not know. When she came to herself she was sitting in her own high chair at the nursery table, with her doll's-house before her.

XVI.—THE RING.

The same moment her nurse came into the room, sobbing. When she saw her sitting there, she started back with a loud cry of amazement and joy. Then running to her, she caught her in her arms and covered her with kisses.

"My precious darling princess! where have you been? What has happened to you? We've all been crying our eyes out, and searching the house from top to bottom for you."

"Not quite from the top," thought Irene to herself; and she might have added—"not quite to the bottom," perhaps, if she had known all. But the one she would not, and the other she could not say.

"Oh, Lootie! I've had such a dreadful adventure!" she replied, and told her all about the cat with the long legs, and how she ran out upon the mountain, and came back again. But she said nothing of her grandmother or her lamp.

"And there we've been searching for you all over the house for more than an hour and a half!" exclaimed the nurse. "But that's no matter, now we've got you! Only, princess, I must say," she added, her mood changing, "what you ought to have done was to call for your own Lootie to come and help you, instead of running out of the house, and up the mountain, in that wild—I must say, foolish fashion."

"Well, Lootie," said Irene quietly, "perhaps if you had a big cat, all legs, running at you, you mightn't exactly know which was the wisest thing to do at the moment."

"I wouldn't run up the mountain, anyhow," returned Lootie.

"Not if you had time to think about it. But when those creatures came at you that night on the mountain, you were so frightened yourself that you lost your way home."

This put a stop to Lootie's reproaches. She had been on the point of saying that the long-legged cat must have been a twilight fancy of the princess's, but the memory of the horrors of that night, and of the talking-to which the king had given her in consequence, prevented her from saying what after all she did not half believe—having a strong suspicion that the cat was a goblin; for she knew nothing of the difference between the goblins and their creatures: she counted them all just goblins.

Without another word she went and got some fresh tea and bread and butter for the princess. Before she returned, the whole household, headed by the housekeeper, burst into the nursery to exult over their darling. The gentlemen-at-arms followed, and were ready enough to believe all she told them about the long-legged cat. Indeed, though wise enough to say nothing about it, they remembered, with no little horror, just such a creature amongst those they had surprised at their gambols upon the princess's lawn. In their own hearts they blamed themselves for not having kept better watch. And their captain gave order that from this night the front door and all the windows on the ground floor, should be locked immediately the sun set, and opened after upon no pretence whatever. The men-at-arms redoubled their vigilance, and for some time there was no further cause of alarm.

When the princess woke the next morning, her nurse was bending over her.

"How your ring does glow this morning, princess!—just like a fiery rose!" she said.

"Does it, Lootie?" returned Irene. "Who gave me the ring, Lootie? I know I've had it a long time, but where did I get it? I don't remember."

"I think it must have been your mother gave it you, princess; but really, for as long as you have worn it, I don't remember that ever I heard," answered her nurse.

"I will ask my king-papa the next time he comes," said Irene.[1]

XVII.—SPRING-TIME.

The spring so dear to all creatures, young and old, came at last, and before the first few days of it had gone, the king rode through its budding valleys to see his little daughter. He had been in a distant part of his dominions all the winter, for he was not in the habit of stopping in one great city, or of visiting only his favourite country-houses, but he moved from place to place, that all his people might know him. Wherever he journeyed, he kept a constant look out for the ablest and best men to put into office; and wherever he found himself mistaken, and those he had appointed incapable or unjust, he removed them at once. Hence you see it was his care of the people that kept him from seeing his princess so often as he would have liked. You may wonder why he did not take her about with him; but there were several reasons against his doing so, and I suspect her great-great-grandmother had had a principal hand in preventing it. Once more, Irene heard the bugle-blast, and once more she was at the gate to meet her father as he rode up on his great white horse.

After they had been alone for a little while, she thought of what she had resolved to ask him.

"Please, king-papa," she said, "will you tell me where I got this pretty ring? I can't remember."

The king looked at it. A strange beautiful smile spread like sunshine over his face, and an answering smile, but at the same time a questioning one, spread like moonlight over Irene's.

"It was your queen-mamma's once," he said.

"And why isn't it hers now?" asked Irene.

"She does not want it now," said the king, looking grave.

"Why doesn't she want it now?"

"Because she's gone where all those rings are made."

"And when shall I see her?" asked the princess.

"Not for some time yet," answered the king, and the tears came in his eyes.

1 End of the fifth instalment appearing in *Good Words for the Young*, 1 March 1871, pp. 279-89.

Irene did not remember her mother, and did not know why her father looked so, and why the tears came in his eyes; but she put her arms round his neck and kissed him, and asked no more questions.

The king was much disturbed on hearing the report of the gentlemen-at-arms concerning the creatures they had seen; and I presume would have taken Irene with him that very day, but for what the presence of the ring on her finger assured him of. About an hour before he left, Irene saw him go up the old stair; and he did not come down again till they were just ready to start; and she thought with herself that he had been up to see the old lady. When he went away, he left other six gentlemen behind him, that there might be six of them always on guard.

And now, in the lovely spring-weather, Irene was out on the mountain the greater part of the day. In the warmer hollows there were lovely primroses, and not so many that she ever got tired of them. As often as she saw a new one opening an eye of light in the blind earth, she would clap her hands with gladness, and, unlike some children I know, instead of pulling it, would touch it as tenderly as if it had been a new baby, and, having made its acquaintance, would leave it as happy as she found it. She treated the plants on which they grew like birds' nests; every fresh flower was like a new little bird to her. She would pay visits to all the flower-nests she knew, remembering each by itself. She would go down on her hands and knees beside one and say "Good morning! Are you all smelling very sweet this morning? Good-bye!" And then she would go to another nest, and say the same. It was a favourite amusement with her. There were many flowers up and down, and she loved them all, but the primroses were her favourites.

"They're not too shy, and they're not a bit forward," she would say to Lootie.

There were goats too about, over the mountain, and when the little kids came, she was as pleased with them as with the flowers. The goats belonged to the miners mostly—a few of them to Curdie's mother; but there were a good many wild ones that seemed to belong to nobody. These the goblins counted theirs, and it was upon them partly that they lived. They set snares and dug pits for them; and did not scruple to take what tame ones happened to be caught; but they did not try to steal them in any other manner, because they were afraid of the dogs the hill-people kept to watch them, for the knowing dogs always tried to bite their feet. But the goblins had a kind of sheep of their own—

very queer creatures, which they drove out to feed at night, and the other goblin-creatures were wise enough to keep good watch over them, for they knew they should have their bones by-and-by.

XVIII.—CURDIE'S CLUE.

Curdie was as watchful as ever, but was almost getting tired of his ill-success. Every other night or so, he followed the goblins about, as they went on digging and boring, and getting as near them as he could, watched them from behind stones and rocks; but as yet he seemed no nearer finding out what they had in view. As at first, he always kept hold of the end of his string, while his pickaxe, left just outside the hole by which he entered the goblins' country from the mine, continued to serve as an anchor and hold fast the other end. The goblins hearing no more noise in that quarter, had ceased to apprehend an immediate invasion, and kept no watch.

One night, after dodging about and listening till he was nearly falling asleep with weariness, he began to roll up his ball, for he had resolved to go home to bed. It was not long, however, before he began to feel bewildered. One after another he passed goblin-houses, caves that is, occupied by goblin families, and at length was sure they were many more than he had passed as he came. He had to use great caution to pass unseen—they lay so close together. Could his string have led him wrong? He still followed winding it, and still it led him into more thickly populated quarters, until he became quite uneasy, and indeed apprehensive; for although he was not afraid of the *cobs*, he was afraid of not finding his way out. But what could he do? It was of no use to sit down and wait for the morning—the morning made no difference here. It was all dark, and always dark; and if his string failed him, he was helpless. He might even arrive within a yard of the mine, and never know it. Seeing he could do nothing better, he would at least find where the end of his string was, and if possible how it had come to play him such a trick. He knew by the size of the ball, that he was getting pretty near the last of it, when he began to feel a tugging and pulling at it. What could it mean? Turning a sharp corner, he thought he heard strange sounds. These grew, as he went on, to a scuffling and growling and squeaking; and the noise increased, until, turning a second sharp corner, he found himself in the midst of it, and the same moment tumbled over a wallowing mass, which he knew must be a knot of the cobs' creatures. Before he could recover his feet, he had caught some great scratches on his face, and several severe bites on his legs and arms. But as he scrambled to get up, his hand fell upon his pickaxe, and before the horrid beasts could do him any serious harm, he was laying about with it right and left in the dark. The hideous cries which followed gave him the satisfaction of knowing that he had punished some of them pretty smartly for their rudeness, and by their scampering and their retreating howls, he perceived that he had routed them. He stood for a little, weighing his battle-axe in his hand as if it had been the most precious lump of metal—but indeed no lump of gold itself could have been so precious at the time as that common tool—then untied the end of the string from it, put the ball in his pocket, and still stood thinking. It was clear that the cobs' creatures had found his axe, had between them carried it off, and had so led him he knew not where. But for all his thinking he could not tell what he ought to do, until suddenly he became aware of a glimmer of light in the distance. Without a moment's hesitation he set out for it, as fast as the unknown and rugged way would permit. Yet again turning a corner, led by the dim light, he spied something quite new in his experience of the underground regions—a small irregular shape of something shining. Going up to it, he found it was a piece of mica, or Muscovy glass,[1] called sheep-silver in Scotland, and the light flickered as if from a fire behind it. After trying in vain for some time to discover an entrance to the place where it was burning, he came at length to a small chamber in which an opening high in the wall, revealed a glow beyond. To this opening he managed to scramble up, and then he saw a strange sight.

Below sat a little group of goblins around a fire, the smoke of which vanished in the darkness far aloft. The sides of the cave were full of shining minerals like those of the palace-hall; and the company was evidently of a superior order, for every one wore stones about head, or arms, or waist, shining dull gorgeous colours in the light of the fire. Nor had Curdie looked long before he recognized the king himself, and found that he had made his way into the inner apartment of the royal family. He had never had such a good chance of hearing something! He crept through the hole as softly as he could, scrambled a good way down the

---

1   Mica is "a small glistening particle of talc, selenite, or other crystalline substance present in large numbers in the structure of a rock"; Muscovy glass is "the mineral muscovite, esp. as used to make translucent windows" (*OED*).

wall towards them without attracting attention, and then sat down and listened. The king, evidently the queen, and probably the crown-prince and the prime minister, were talking together. He was sure of the queen by her shoes, for as she warmed her feet at the fire, he saw them quite plainly.

"That *will* be fun!" said the one he took for the crown-prince. It was the first whole sentence he heard.

"I don't see why you should think it such a grand affair!" said his stepmother, tossing her head backward.

"You must remember, my spouse," interposed his majesty, as if making excuse for his son, "he has got the same blood in him. His mother—"

"Don't talk to me of his mother! You positively encourage his unnatural fancies. Whatever belongs to *that* mother, ought to be cut out of him."

"You forget yourself, my dear!" said the king.

"I don't," said the queen, "nor you either. If you expect *me* to approve of such coarse tastes, you will find yourself mistaken. *I* don't wear shoes for nothing."

"You must acknowledge, however," the king said, with a little groan, "that this at least is no whim of Harelip's, but a matter of state-policy. You are well aware that his gratification comes purely from the pleasure of sacrificing himself to the public good.— Does it not, Harelip?"

"Yes, father; of course it does. Only it *will* be nice to make her cry. I'll have the skin taken off between her toes, and tie them up till they grow together. Then her feet will be like other people's, and there will be no occasion for her to wear shoes."

"Do you mean to insinuate *I've* got toes, you unnatural wretch?" cried the queen; and she moved angrily towards Harelip. The councillor, however, who was betwixt them, leaned forward so as to prevent her touching him, but only as if to address the prince.

"Your royal highness," he said, "possibly requires to be reminded that you have got three toes yourself—one on one foot, two on the other."

"Ha! ha! ha!" shouted the queen triumphantly.

The councillor, encouraged by this mark of favour, went on.

"It seems to me, your royal highness, it would greatly endear you to your future people, proving to them that you are not the less one of themselves that you had the misfortune to be born of a sun-mother, if you were to command upon yourself the comparatively slight operation which, in a more extended form, you so wisely meditate with regard to your future princess."

"Ha! ha! ha!" laughed the queen, louder than before, and the king and the minister joined in the laugh. Harelip growled, and for a few moments the others continued to express their enjoyment of his discomfiture.

The queen was the only one Curdie could see with any distinctness. She sat sideways to him, and the light of the fire shone full upon her face. He could not consider her handsome. Her nose was certainly broader at the end than its extreme length, and her eyes, instead of being horizontal, were set up like two perpendicular eggs, one on the broad, the other on the small end. Her mouth was no bigger than a small button-hole until she laughed, when it stretched from ear to ear—only to be sure her ears were very nearly in the middle of her cheeks.

Anxious to hear everything they might say, Curdie ventured to slide down a smooth part of the rock just under him, to a projection below, upon which he thought to rest. But whether he was not careful enough, or the projection gave way, down he came with a rush on the floor of the cavern, bringing with him a great rumbling shower of stones.

The goblins jumped from their seats in more anger than consternation, for they had never yet seen anything to be afraid of in the palace. But when they saw Curdie with his pick in his hand, their rage was mingled with fear, for they took him for the first of an invasion of miners. The king notwithstanding drew himself up to his full height of four feet, spread himself to his full breadth of three and a half, for he was the handsomest and squarest of all the goblins, and strutting up to Curdie, planted himself with outspread feet before him, and said with dignity,

"Pray what right have you in my palace?"

"The right of necessity, your majesty," answered Curdie. "I lost my way, and did not know where I was wandering to."

"How did you get in?"

"By a hole in the mountain."

"But you are a miner! Look at your pickaxe!"

Curdie did look at it, answering,

"I came upon it, lying on the ground, a little way from here. I tumbled over some wild beasts who were playing with it. Look, your majesty." And Curdie showed him how he was scratched and bitten.

The king was pleased to find him behave more politely than he had expected from what his people had told him concerning the miners, for he attributed it to the power of his own presence; but he did not therefore feel friendly to the intruder.

"You will oblige me by walking out of my dominions at once," he said, well knowing what a mockery lay in the words.

"With pleasure, if your majesty will give me a guide," said Curdie.

"I will give you a thousand," said the king, with a scoffing air of magnificent liberality.

"One will be quite sufficient," said Curdie.†

Figure 22

But the king uttered a strange shout, half halloo, half roar, and in rushed goblins till the cave was swarming. He said something to the first of them which Curdie could not hear, and it was passed from one to another till in a moment the farthest in the crowd had evidently heard and understood it. They began to gather about him in a way he did not relish, and he retreated towards the wall. They pressed upon him.

"Stand back," said Curdie, grasping his pick-axe tighter by his knee.

They only grinned and pressed closer. Curdie bethought himself, and began to rhyme.

> "Ten, twenty, thirty—
> You're all so very dirty!
> Twenty, thirty, forty—
> You're all so thick and snorty!
>
> Thirty, forty, fifty—
> You're all so puff-and-snifty!
> Forty, fifty, sixty—
> Beast and man so mixty!
>
> Fifty, sixty, seventy—
> Mixty, maxty, leaventy!
> Sixty, seventy, eighty—
> All your cheeks so slaty!
>
> Seventy, eighty, ninety,
> All your heads[1] so flinty!
> Eighty, ninety, hundred,
> Altogether dundred!"

The goblins fell back a little when he began, and made horrible grimaces all though the rhyme, as if eating something so disagreeable that it set their teeth on edge and gave them the creeps; but whether it was that the rhyming words were most of them no words at all, for, a new rhyme being considered the more efficacious, Curdie had made it on the spur of the moment, or whether it was that the presence of the king and queen gave them courage, I cannot tell; but the moment the rhyme was over, they crowded on him again, and out shot a hundred long arms, with a multitude of thick nailless fingers at the ends of them, to lay hold upon him. Then Curdie heaved up his axe. But being as gentle as courageous and not wishing to kill any of them, he turned the end which was square and blunt like a hammer, and with that came

---

1 "Heads" was changed to "hands" in later editions. ·

down a great blow on the head of the goblin nearest him. Hard as the heads of all goblins are, he thought he must feel that. And so he did, no doubt; but he only gave a horrible cry, and sprung at Curdie's throat. Curdie however drew back in time, and just at that critical moment, remembered the vulnerable part of the goblin-body. He made a sudden rush at the king, and stamped with all his might on his majesty's feet. The king gave a most un-kingly howl, and almost fell into the fire. Curdie then rushed into

Figure 23

the crowd,† stamping right and left. The goblins drew back howling on every side as he approached, but they were so crowded that few of those he attacked could escape his tread; and

the shrieking and roaring that filled the cave would have appalled
Curdie, but for the good hope it gave him. They were tumbling
over each other in heaps in their eagerness to rush from the cave,
when a new assailant suddenly faced him:—the queen, with
flaming eyes and expanded nostrils, her hair standing half up

Figure 24

from her head, rushed† at him. She trusted in her shoes: they were
of granite—hollowed like French *sabots*.[1] Curdie would have
endured much rather than hurt a woman, even if she was a

---

1 "A wooden shoe made of a single piece of wood shaped and hollowed
   out to fit the foot" (*OED*).

goblin; but here was an affair of life and death: forgetting her shoes, he made a great stamp on one of her feet. But she instantly returned it with very different effect, causing him frightful pain, and almost disabling him. His only chance with her would have been to attack the granite shoes with his pickaxe, but before he could think of that, she had caught him up in her arms, and was rushing with him across the cave. She dashed him into a hole in the wall, with a force that almost stunned him. But although he could not move, he was not too far gone to hear her great cry, and the rush of multitudes of soft feet, followed by the sounds of something heaved up against the rock; after which came a multitudinous patter of stones falling near him. The last had not ceased when he grew very faint, for his head had been badly cut, and at last insensible.

When he came to himself, there was perfect silence about him, and utter darkness, but for the merest glimmer in one tiny spot. He crawled to it, and found that they had heaved a slab against the mouth of the hole, past the edge of which a poor little gleam found its way from the fire. He could not move it a hair's breadth, for they had piled a great heap of stones against it. He crawled back to where he had been lying, in the faint hope of finding his pickaxe. But after a vain search, he was at last compelled to acknowledge himself in an evil plight. He sat down and tried to think, but soon fell fast asleep.

XIX.—GOBLIN COUNSELS.

He must have slept a long time, for when he awoke, he felt wonderfully restored—indeed almost well, and very hungry. There were voices in the outer cave.

Once more then, it was night; for the goblins slept during the day, and went about their affairs during the night.

In the universal and constant darkness of their dwelling, they had no reason to prefer the one arrangement to the other; but from aversion to the sun-people, they chose to be busy when there was least chance of their being met either by the miners below, when they were burrowing, or by the people of the mountain above, when they were feeding their sheep or catching their goats. And indeed it was only when the sun was away that the outside of the mountain was sufficiently like their own dismal regions to be endurable to their mole-eyes, so thoroughly† had they become disused to any light beyond that of their own fires and torches.

Figure 25

Curdie listened, and soon found that they were talking of himself.

"How long will it take?" asked Harelip.

"Not many days, I should think," answered the king. "They are poor feeble creatures, those sun-people, and want to be always eating. *We* can go a week at a time without food, and be all the better for it; but I've been told *they* eat two or three times every day! Can you believe it?—They must be quite hollow inside—not at all like us, nine-tenths of whose bulk is solid flesh and bone. Yes—I judge a week of starvation will do for him."

"If *I* may be allowed a word," interposed the queen, "—and I think I ought to have some voice in the matter—"

"The wretch is entirely at your disposal, my spouse," interrupted the king. "He is your property. You caught him yourself. We should never have done it."

The queen laughed. She seemed in far better humour than the night before.

"I was about to say," she resumed, "that it does seem a pity to waste so much fresh meat."

"What are you thinking of, my love?" said the king. "The very notion of starving him implies that we are not going to give him any meat, either salt or fresh."[1]

"I'm not such a stupid as that comes to," returned her majesty. "What I mean is, that by the time he is starved, there will hardly be a picking upon his bones."

The king gave a great laugh.

"Well, my spouse, you may have him when you like," he said. "I don't fancy him for my part. I am pretty sure he is tough eating."

"That would be to honour instead of punish his insolence," returned the queen. "But why should our poor creatures be deprived of so much nourishment? Our little dogs and cats and pigs and small bears would enjoy him very much."

"You are the best of housekeepers, my lovely queen!" said her husband. "Let it be so by all means. Let us have our people in, and get him out and kill him at once. He deserves it. The mischief he might have brought upon us, now that he had penetrated so far as our most retired citadel, is incalculable. Or rather let us tie him hand and foot, and have the pleasure of seeing him torn to pieces by full torchlight in the great hall."

"Better and better!" cried the queen and the prince together, both of them clapping their hands. And the prince made an ugly noise with his hare-lip, just as if he had intended to be one at the feast.

"But," added the queen, bethinking herself, "he is so troublesome. For as poor creatures as they are, there is something about those sun-people that is *very* troublesome. I cannot imagine how it is that with such superior strength and skill and understanding as ours, we permit them to exist at all. Why do we not destroy them entirely, and use their cattle and grazing lands at our pleas-

---

1 The alternatives are between meat preserved by being cured with salt (before the age of refrigeration) or freshly killed meat.

ure? Of course, we don't want to live in their horrid country! It is far too glaring for our quieter and more refined tastes. But we might use it for a sort of outhouse,[1] you know. Even our creatures' eyes might get used to it, and if they did grow blind, that would be of no consequence, provided they grew fat as well. But we might even keep their great cows and other creatures, and then we should have a few more luxuries, such as cream and cheese, which at present we only taste occasionally, when our brave men have succeeded in carrying some off from their farms."

"It is worth thinking of," said the king; "and I don't know why *you* should be the first to suggest it, except that you have a positive genius for conquest. But still, as you say, there is something very troublesome about them; and it would be better, as I understand you to suggest, that we should starve him for a day or two first, so that he may be a little less frisky when we take him out."

> "Once there was a goblin
> Living in a hole;
> Busy he was cobblin'
> A shoe without a sole.
>
> By came a birdie:
> 'Goblin, what do you do?'
> 'Cobble at a sturdie
> Upper leather shoe.'
>
> 'What's the good o' that, sir?'
> Said the little bird.
> 'Why it's very pat, sir—
> Plain without a word.'
>
> 'Where 'tis all a hill,[2] sir,
> Never can be holes:
> Why should their shoes have soles, sir,
> When *they*'ve got no souls?'"

---

1 "A subsidiary building in the grounds of or adjoining a house, as a barn, shed, etc." (*OED*). The sense of outhouse as an outdoor toilet is primarily an American usage.

2 "Hill" was changed to "hole" in later editions.

"What's that horrible noise?" cried the queen, shuddering from pot-metal head to granite shoes.

"I declare," said the king with solemn indignation, "it's the sun-creature in the hole!"

"Stop that disgusting noise!" cried the crown-prince valiantly, getting up and standing in front of the heap of stones, with his face towards Curdie's prison.—"Do now, or I'll break your head."

"Break away," shouted Curdie, and began singing again—

> "Once there was a goblin,
> Living in a hole—"

"I really can*not* bear it," said the queen. "If I could only get at his horrid toes with my slippers again!"

"I think we had better go to bed," said the king.

"It's not time to go to bed," said the queen.

"I would if I was you," said Curdie.

"Impertinent wretch!" said the queen, with the utmost scorn in her voice.

"An impossible *if*," said his majesty with dignity.

"Quite," returned Curdie, and began singing again—

> "Go to bed,
> Goblin, do.
> Help the queen
> Take off her shoe.
>
> If you do,
> It will disclose
> A horrid set
> Of sprouting toes."

"What a lie!" roared the queen in a rage.

"By the way, that reminds me," said the king, "that, for as long as we have been married, I have never seen your feet, queen. I think you might take off your shoes when you go to bed! They positively hurt me sometimes."

"I will do as I like," retorted the queen sulkily.

"You ought to do as your own hubby wishes you," said the king.

"I will not," said the queen.

"Then I insist upon it," said the king.

Apparently his majesty approached the queen for the purpose of following the advice given by Curdie, for the latter heard a scuffle, and then a great roar from the king.

"Will you be quiet then?" said the queen wickedly.

"Yes, yes, queen. I only meant to coax you."

"Hands off!" cried the queen triumphantly. "I'm going to bed. You may come when you like. But as long as I am queen, I will sleep in my shoes. It is my royal privilege. Harelip, go to bed."

"I'm going," said Harelip sleepily.

"So am I," said the king.

"Come along then," said the queen; "and mind you are good, or I'll—"

"Oh, no, no, no!" screamed the king, in the most supplicating of tones.

Curdie heard only a muttered reply in the distance; and then the cave was quite still.

They had left the fire burning, and the light came through brighter than before. Curdie thought it was time to try again if anything could be done. But he found he could not get even a finger through the chink between the slab and the rock. He gave a great rush with his shoulder against the slab, but it yielded no more than if it had been part of the rock. All he could do, was to sit down and think again.

By-and-by he came to the resolution to pretend to be dying, in the hope they might take him out before his strength was too much exhausted to let him have a chance. Then, for the creatures, if he could but find his axe again, he would have no fear of them; and if it were not for the queen's horrid shoes, he would have no fear at all.

Meantime, until they should come again at night, there was nothing for him to do but forge new rhymes, now his only weapons. He had no intention of using them at present, of course; but it was well to have a stock, for he might live to want them, and the manufacture of them would help to while away the time.

XX.—IRENE'S CLUE.

That same morning early, the princess woke in a terrible fright. There was a hideous noise in her room—of creatures snarling and hissing and racketing about as if they were fighting. The moment she came to herself, she remembered something she had never thought of again—what her grandmother told her to do when she was frightened. She immediately took off her ring and put it under her pillow. As she did so, she fancied she felt a finger and thumb take it gently from under her palm. "It must be my grandmother!" she said to herself, and the thought gave her such courage that she stopped to put on her dainty little slippers before running from the room. While doing this, she caught sight of a long cloak of sky-blue, thrown over the back of a chair by her bedside. She had never seen it before, but it was evidently waiting for her. She put it on, and then, feeling with the forefinger of her right hand, soon found her grandmother's thread, which she proceeded at once to follow, expecting it would lead her straight up the old stair. When she reached the door, she found it went down and ran along the floor, so that she had almost to crawl in order to keep a hold of it. Then, to her surprise, and somewhat to her dismay, she found that instead of leading her towards the stair it turned in quite the opposite direction. It led her through certain narrow passages towards the kitchen, turning aside ere she reached it, and guiding her to a door which communicated with a small back yard. Some of the maids were already up, and this door was standing open. Across the yard the thread still ran along the ground, until it brought her to a door in the wall which opened upon the mountain-side. When she had passed through, the thread rose to about half her height, and she could hold it with ease as she walked. It led her straight up the mountain.

The cause of her alarm was less frightful than she supposed. The cook's great black cat, pursued by the housekeeper's terrier, had bounced against her bedroom door, which had not been properly fastened, and the two had burst into the room together and commenced a battle royal. How the nurse came to sleep through it, was a mystery, but I suspect the old lady had something to do with it.

It was a clear warm morning. The wind blew deliciously over the mountain-side. Here and there she saw a late primrose, but she did not stop to call upon them. The sky was mottled with small clouds. The sun was not yet up, but some of their fluffy edges had caught his light, and hung out orange and gold-coloured fringes upon the air. The dew lay in round drops upon the leaves, and hung like tiny diamond earrings from the blades of grass about her path.

"How lovely that bit of gossamer is!" thought the princess, looking at a long undulating line that shone at some distance from her up the hill. It was not the time for gossamers though;

and Irene soon discovered it was her own thread she saw shining on before her in the light of the morning. It was leading her she knew not whither; but she had never in her life been out before sunrise, and everything was so fresh and cool and lively and full of something coming, that she felt too happy to be afraid of anything.

After leading her up a good distance, the thread turned to the left, and down the path upon which she and Lootie had met Curdie. But she never thought of that, for now in the morning light, with its far outlook over the country, no path could have been more open and airy and cheerful. She could see the road almost to the horizon, along which she had so often watched her king-papa and his troop come shining, with the bugle blast cleaving the air before them; and it was like a companion to her. Down and down the path went, then up, and then down and then up again, getting rugged and more rugged as it went; and still along the path went the silvery thread, and still along the thread went Irene's little rosy-tipped forefinger.

By and by she came to a little stream that jabbered and prattled down the hill, and up the side of the stream went both path and thread. And still the path grew rougher and steeper, and the mountain grew wilder, till Irene began to think she was going a very long way from home; and when she turned to look back, she saw that the level country had vanished and the rough bare mountain had closed in about her. But still on went the thread, and on went the princess. Everything around her was getting brighter and brighter as the sun came nearer; till at length his first rays all at once alighted on the top of a rock before her, like some golden creature fresh from the sky. Then she saw that the little stream ran out of a hole in that rock, that the path did not go past the rock, and that the thread was leading her straight up to it. A shudder ran through her from head to foot when she found that the thread was actually taking her into the hole out of which the stream ran. It ran out babbling joyously, but she had to go in.

She did not hesitate. Right into the hole she went, which was high enough to let her walk without stooping. For a little way there was a brown glimmer, but at the first turn it all but ceased, and before she had gone many paces she was in total darkness. Then she began to be frightened indeed. Every moment she kept feeling the thread backwards and forwards, and as she went farther and farther into the darkness of the great hollow mountain, she kept thinking more and more about her grandmother, and all that she had said to her, and how kind she had been, and how beautiful she was, and all about her lovely room, and the fire of roses, and the great lamp that sent its light through stone walls. And she became more and more sure that the thread could not have gone there of itself, and that her grandmother must have sent it. But it tried her dreadfully when the path went down very steep, and especially when she came to places where she had to go down rough stairs, and even sometimes a ladder. Through one narrow passage after another, over lumps of rock and sand and clay, the thread guided her, until she came to a small hole through which she had to creep. Finding no change on the other side—"Shall I ever get back?" she thought, over and over again, wondering at herself that she was not ten times more frightened, and often feeling as if she were only walking in the story of a dream. Sometimes she heard the noise of water, a dull gurgling inside the rock. By-and-by she heard the sounds of blows, which came nearer and nearer; but again they grew duller, and almost died away. In a hundred directions she turned, obedient to the guiding thread.

At last she spied a dull red shine, and came up to the mica-window,[1] and thence away and round about, and right into a cavern, where glowed the red embers of a fire. Here the thread began to rise. It rose as high as her head, and higher still. What *should* she do if she lost her hold? She was pulling it down! She might break it! She could see it far up, glowing as red as her fire-opal in the light of the embers.

But presently she came to a huge heap of stones, piled in a slope against the wall of the cavern. On these she climbed, and soon recovered the level of the thread—only however to find, the next moment, that it vanished through the heap of stones, and left her standing on it, with her face to the solid rock. For one terrible moment, she felt as if her grandmother had forsaken her. The thread which the spiders had spun far over the seas, which her grandmother had sat in the moonlight and spun again for her, which she had tempered in the rose-fire, and tied to her opal ring, had left her—had gone where she could no longer follow it—had brought her into a horrible cavern, and there left her! She was forsaken indeed!

"When *shall* I wake?" she said to herself in an agony, but the same moment knew that it was no dream. She threw herself upon the heap, and began to cry. It was well she did not know

---

1   Mica is a kind of mineral that occurs as small glittering plates or scales in granite and other rocks. If large enough, the crystals can be split into thin, transparent sheets that can be used as a substitute for glass. See note p. 128.

what creatures, one of them with stone shoes on her feet, were lying in the next cave. But neither did she know who was on the other side of the slab.

At length the thought struck her, that at least she could follow the thread backwards, and thus get out of the mountain, and home. She rose at once, and found the thread. But the instant she tried to feel it backwards, it vanished from her touch. Forwards, it led her hand up to the heap of stones—backwards it seemed nowhere. Neither could she see it as before in the light of the fire. She burst into a wailing cry, and again threw herself down on the stones.[1]

XXI.—THE ESCAPE.

As the princess lay and sobbed, she kept feeling the thread mechanically, following it with her finger many times up to the stones in which it disappeared. By and by she began, still mechanically, to poke her finger in after it between the stones as far as she could. All at once it came into her head that she might remove some of the stones and see where the thread went next. Almost laughing at herself for never having thought of this before, she jumped to her feet. Her fear vanished; once more she was certain her grandmother's thread could not have brought her there just to leave her there; and she began to throw away the stones from the top as fast as she could, sometimes two or three at a handful, sometimes taking both hands to lift one. After clearing them away a little, she found that the thread turned and went straight downwards. Hence, as the heap sloped a good deal, growing of course wider towards its base, she had to throw away a multitude of stones to follow the thread. But this was not all, for she soon found that the thread, after going straight down for a little way, turned first sideways in one direction, then sideways in another, and then shot, at various angles, hither and thither inside the heap, so that she began to be afraid that to clear the thread, she must remove the whole huge gathering. She was dismayed at the very idea, but, losing no time, set to work with a will; and with aching back, and bleeding fingers and hands, she worked on, sustained by the pleasure of seeing the heap slowly diminish, and begin to show itself on the opposite side of the fire. Another thing which helped to keep up her courage was, that as often as she uncovered a turn of the thread, instead of lying loose

---

1 End of the sixth instalment appearing in *Good Words for the Young*, 1 April 1871, pp. 297-305.

upon the stones, it tightened up: this made her sure that her grandmother was at the end of it somewhere.

She had got about half way down when she started, and nearly fell with fright. Close to her ear as it seemed, a voice broke out singing—

> "Jabber, bother, smash!
> You'll have it all in a crash.
> Jabber, smash, bother!
> You'll have the worst of the pother.[1]
> Smash, bother, jabber!—"

Here Curdie stopped, either because he could not find a rhyme to *jabber*, or because he remembered what he had forgotten when he woke up at the sound of Irene's labours, that his plan was to make the goblins think he was getting weak. But he had uttered enough to let Irene know who he was.

"It's Curdie!" she cried joyfully.

"Hush! hush!" came Curdie's voice again from somewhere. "Speak softly."

"Why, you were singing loud!" said Irene.

"Yes. But they know I am here, and they don't know you are. Who are you?"

"I'm Irene," answered the princess. "I know who you are quite well. You're Curdie."

"Why, however did you come here, Irene?"

"My great-great-grandmother sent me; and I think I've found out why. You can't get out, I suppose?"

"No, I can't. What are you doing?"

"Clearing away a huge heap of stones."

"There's a princess!" exclaimed Curdie, in a tone of delight, but still speaking in little more than a whisper. "I can't think how you got here though."

"My grandmother sent me after her thread."

"I don't know what you mean," said Curdie: "but so you're there, it doesn't much matter."

"Oh, yes it does!" returned Irene. "I should never have been here but for her."

"You can tell me all about it when we get out, then. There's no time to lose now," said Curdie.

And Irene went to work, as fresh as when she began.

---

1 "Disturbance, turmoil, bustle; noise, tumult" (*OED*).

"There's such a lot of stones!" she said. "It will take me a long time to get them all away."

"How far on have you got?" asked Curdie.

"I've got about the half away, but the other half is ever so much bigger."

"I don't think you will have to move the lower half. Do you see a slab laid up against the wall?"

Irene looked, and felt about with her hands, and soon perceived the outlines of the slab.

"Yes," she answered, "I do."

"Then, I think," rejoined Curdie, "when you have cleared the slab about half way down, or a little more, I shall be able to push it over."

"I must follow my thread," returned Irene, "whatever I do."

"What *do* you mean?" exclaimed Curdie.

"You will see when you get out," answered the princess, and went on harder than ever.

But she was soon satisfied that what Curdie wanted done, and what the thread wanted done, were one and the same thing. For she not only saw that by following the turns of the thread she had been clearing the face of the slab, but that, a little more than half way down, the thread went through the chink between the slab and the wall into the place where Curdie was confined, so that she could not follow it any farther until the slab was out of her way. As soon as she found this, she said in a right joyous whisper—

"Now, Curdie! I think if you were to give a great push, the slab would tumble over."

"Stand quite clear of it then," said Curdie, "and let me know when you are ready."

Irene got off the heap, and stood on one side of it.

"Now, Curdie!" she cried.

Curdie gave a great rush with his shoulder against it. Out tumbled the slab on the heap, and out crept Curdie over the top of it.

"You've saved my life, Irene!" he whispered.

"Oh, Curdie! I'm so glad! Let's get out of this horrid place as fast as we can."

"That's easier said than done," returned he.

"Oh, no! it's quite easy," said Irene. "We have only to follow my thread. I am sure that it's going to take us out now."

She had already begun to follow it over the fallen slab into the hole, while Curdie was searching the floor of the cavern for his pickaxe.

"Here it is!" he cried. "No, it is not!" he added, in a disappointed tone. "What can it be then?—I declare it's a torch. That is jolly! It's better almost than my pickaxe. Much better if it weren't for those stone shoes!" he went on, as he lighted the torch by blowing the last embers of the expiring fire.

When he looked up, with the lighted torch casting a glare into the great darkness of the huge cavern, he caught sight of Irene disappearing in the hole out of which he had himself just come.

"Where are you going there?" he cried. "That's not the way out. That's where I couldn't get out."

"I know that," whispered Irene. "But this is the way my thread goes, and I must follow it."

"What nonsense the child talks!" said Curdie to himself. "I must follow her, though, and see that she comes to no harm. She will soon find she can't get out that way, and then she will come with me."

So he crept over the slab once more into the hole with his torch in his hand. But when he looked about in it, he could see her nowhere. And now he discovered that although the hole was narrow, it was much longer than he had supposed; for in one direction the roof came down very low, and the hole went off in a narrow passage, of which he could not see the end. The princess must have crept in there. He got on his knees and one hand, holding the torch with the other, and crept after her. The hole twisted about, in some parts so low that he could hardly get through, in others so high that he could not see the roof, but everywhere it was narrow—far too narrow for a goblin to get through, and so I presume they never thought that Curdie might. He was beginning to feel very uncomfortable lest something should have befallen the princess, when he heard her voice almost close to his ear, whispering—

"Aren't you coming, Curdie?"

And when he turned the next corner, there she stood waiting for him.

"I knew you couldn't go wrong in that narrow hole, but now you must keep by me, for here is a great wide place," she said.

"I can't understand it," said Curdie, half to himself, half to Irene.

"Never mind," she returned. "Wait till we get out."

Curdie, utterly astonished that she had already got so far, and by a path he had known nothing of, thought it better to let her do as she pleased.

"At all events," he said again to himself, "I know nothing about the way, miner as I am; and she seems to think she does know something about it, though how she should, passes my comprehension. So she's just as likely to find her way as I am, and as she insists on taking the lead, I must follow. We can't be much worse off than we are, anyhow."

Reasoning thus, he followed her a few steps, and came out in another great cavern, across which Irene walked in a straight line, as confidently as if she knew every step of the way. Curdie went on after her, flashing his torch about, and trying to see something of what lay around them. Suddenly he started back a pace as the light fell upon something close by which Irene was passing. It was a platform of rock raised a few feet from the floor and covered with sheep skins, upon which lay two horrible figures asleep, at once recognised by Curdie as the king and queen of the goblins. He lowered his torch instantly lest the light should awake them. As he did so, it flashed upon his pickaxe, lying by the side of the queen, whose hand lay close by the handle of it.

"Stop one moment," he whispered. "Hold my torch, and don't let the light on their faces."

Irene shuddered when she saw the frightful creatures, whom she had passed without observing them, but she did as he requested, and turning her back, held the torch low in front of her. Curdie drew his pickaxe carefully away, and as he did so, spied one of her feet, projecting from under the skins. The great clumsy granite shoe, exposed thus to his hand, was a temptation not to be resisted. He laid hold of it, and, with cautious efforts, drew it off. The moment he succeeded, he saw to his astonishment that what he had sung in ignorance, to annoy the queen, was actually true: she had six horrible toes. Overjoyed at his success, and seeing by the huge bump in the sheep skins where the other foot was, he proceeded to lift them gently, for, if he could only succeed in carrying away the other shoe as well, he would be no more afraid of the goblins than of so many flies. But as he pulled at the second shoe, the queen gave a growl and sat up in bed. The same instant the king awoke also, and sat up beside her.

"Run, Irene!" cried Curdie, for though he was not now in the least afraid for himself, he was for the princess.

Irene looked once round, saw the fearful creatures awake, and like the wise princess she was, dashed the torch on the ground and extinguished it, crying out—

"Here, Curdie, take my hand."

He darted to her side, forgetting neither the queen's shoe nor his pickaxe, and caught hold of her hand, as she sped fearlessly where her thread guided her. They heard the queen give a great bellow; but they had a good start, for it would be some time before they could get torches lighted to pursue them. Just as they thought they saw a gleam behind them, the thread brought them to a very narrow opening, through which Irene crept easily, and Curdie with difficulty.

"Now," said Curdie; "I think we shall be safe."

"Of course we shall," returned Irene.

"Why do you think so?" asked Curdie.

"Because my grandmother is taking care of us."

"That's all nonsense," said Curdie. "I don't know what you mean."

"Then if you don't know what I mean, what right have you to call it nonsense?" asked the princess, a little offended.

"I beg your pardon, Irene," said Curdie; "I did not mean to vex you."

"Of course not," returned the princess. "But why do *you* think we shall be safe?"

"Because the king and queen are far too stout to get through that hole."

"There might be ways round," said the princess.

"To be sure there might: we are not out of it yet," acknowledged Curdie.

"But what do you mean by the king and queen?" asked the princess. "I should never call such creatures as those a king and a queen."

"Their own people do, though," answered Curdie.

The princess asked more questions, and Curdie, as they walked leisurely along, gave her a full account, not only of the character and habits of the goblins, so far as he knew them, but of his own adventures with them, beginning from the very night after that in which he had met her and Lootie upon the mountain. When he had finished, he begged Irene to tell him how it was that she had come to his rescue. So Irene too had to tell a long story, which she did in rather a roundabout manner, interrupted by many questions concerning things she had not explained. But her tale, as he did not believe more than half of it, left everything as unaccountable to him as before, and he was nearly as much perplexed as to what he must think of the princess. He could not believe that she was deliberately telling stories, and the only conclusion he could come to was that Lootie had been playing the child tricks, inventing no end of lies to frighten her for her own purposes.

"But how ever did Lootie come to let you go into the mountain alone?" he asked.

"Lootie knows nothing about it. I left her fast asleep—at least I think so. I hope my grandmother won't let her get into trouble, for it wasn't her fault at all, as my grandmother very well knows."

"But how *did* you find your way to me?" persisted Curdie.

"I told you already," answered Irene;—"by keeping my finger upon my grandmother's thread, as I am doing now."

"You don't mean you've got the thread there?"

"Of course I do. I have told you so ten times already. I have hardly—except when I was removing the stones—taken my finger off it. There!" she added, guiding Curdie's hand to the thread, "you feel it yourself—don't you?"

"I feel nothing at all," replied Curdie.

"Then what *can* be the matter with your finger? *I* feel it perfectly. To be sure it is very thin, and in the sunlight looks just like the thread of a spider, though there are many of them twisted together to make it—but for all that I can't think why you shouldn't feel it as well as I do."

Curdie was too polite to say he did not believe there was any thread there at all. What he did say was—

"Well, I can make nothing of it."

"I can though, and you must be glad of that, for it will do for both of us."

"We're not out yet," said Curdie.

"We soon shall be," returned Irene confidently.

And now the thread went downwards, and led Irene's hand to a hole in the floor of the cavern, whence came a sound of running water which they had been hearing for some time.

"It goes into the ground now, Curdie," she said, stopping.

He had been listening to another sound, which his practised ear had caught long ago, and which also had been growing louder. It was the noise the goblin miners made at their work, and they seemed to be at no great distance now. Irene heard it the moment she stopped.

"What is that noise?" she asked. "Do you know, Curdie?"

"Yes. It is the goblins digging and burrowing," he answered.

"And you don't know what they do it for?"

"No; I haven't the least idea. Would you like to see them?" he asked, wishing to have another try after their secret.

"If my thread took me there, I shouldn't much mind; but I don't want to see them, and I can't leave my thread. It leads me down into the hole, and we had better go at once."

"Very well. Shall I go in first?" said Curdie.

"No; better not. You can't feel the thread," she answered, stepping down through a narrow break in the floor of the cavern. "Oh!" she cried, "I am in the water. It is running strong—but it is not deep, and there is just room to walk. Make haste, Curdie."

He tried, but the hole was too small for him to get in.

"Go on a little bit," he said, shouldering his pickaxe.

In a few moments he had cleared a larger opening and followed her. They went on, down and down with the running water, Curdie getting more and more afraid it was leading them to some terrible gulf in the heart of the mountain. In one or two places he had to break away the rock to make room before even Irene could get through—at least without hurting herself. But at length they spied a glimmer of light, and in a minute more, they were almost blinded by the full sunlight into which they emerged. It was some little time before the princess could see well enough to discover that they stood in her own garden, close by the seat on which she and her king-papa had sat that afternoon. They had come out by the channel of the little stream. She danced and clapped her hands with delight.

"Now, Curdie!" she cried, "won't you believe what I told you about my grandmother and her thread?"

For she had felt all the time that Curdie was not believing what she told him.

"There!—don't you see it shining on before us?" she added.

"I don't see anything," persisted Curdie.

"Then you must believe without seeing," said the princess; "for you can't deny it has brought us out of the mountain."

"I can't deny we *are* out of the mountain, and I should be very ungrateful indeed to deny that *you* had brought *me* out of it."

"I couldn't have done it but for the thread," persisted Irene.

"That's the part I don't understand."

"Well, come along, and Lootie will get you something to eat. I am sure you must want it very much."

"Indeed I do. But my father and mother will be so anxious about me, I must make haste—first up the mountain to tell my mother, and then down into the mine again to let my father know."

"Very well, Curdie; but you can't get out without coming this way, and I will take you through the house, for that is nearest."

They met no one by the way, for indeed, as before, the people were here and there and everywhere searching for the princess. When they got in, Irene found that the thread, as she had half expected, went up the old staircase, and a new thought struck her. She turned to Curdie and said—

"My grandmother wants me. Do come up with me, and see her. Then you will know that I have been telling you the truth. Do come—to please me, Curdie. I can't bear you should think I say what is not true."

"I never doubted you believed what you said," returned Curdie. "I only thought you had some fancy in your head that was not correct."

"But do come, dear Curdie."

The little miner could not withstand this appeal, and though he felt shy in what seemed to him such a huge grand house, he yielded, and followed her up the stair.

XXII.—THE OLD LADY AND CURDIE.

Up the stair then they went, and the next and the next, and through the long rows of empty rooms, and up the little tower stair, Irene growing happier and happier as she ascended. There was no answer when she knocked at length at the door of the work-room, nor could she hear any sound of the spinning-wheel, and once more her heart sunk within her—but only for one moment, as she turned and knocked at the other door.

"Come in," answered the sweet voice of her grandmother, and Irene opened the door and entered, followed by Curdie.

"You darling!" cried the lady, who was seated by a fire of red roses mingled with white—"I've been waiting for you, and indeed getting a little anxious about you, and beginning to think whether I had not better go and fetch you myself."

As she spoke she took the little princess in her arms and placed her upon her lap. She was dressed in white now, and looking if possible more lovely than ever.

"I've brought Curdie, grandmother. He wouldn't believe what I told him, and so I've brought him."

"Yes—I see him. He is a good boy, Curdie, and a brave boy. Aren't you glad you've got him out?"

"Yes, grandmother. But it wasn't very good of him not to believe me when I was telling him the truth."

"People must believe what they can, and those who believe more must not be hard upon those who believe less. I doubt if you would have believed it all yourself if you hadn't seen some of it."

"Ah! yes, grandmother, I daresay. I'm sure you are right. But he'll believe now."

"I don't know that," replied her grandmother.

"Won't you, Curdie?" said Irene, looking round at him as she asked the question.

He was standing in the middle of the floor, staring, and looking strangely bewildered. This she thought came of his astonishment at the beauty of the lady.

"Make a bow to my grandmother, Curdie," she said.

"I don't see any grandmother," answered Curdie rather gruffly.

"Don't see my grandmother, when I'm sitting in her lap!" exclaimed the princess.

"No, I don't," reiterated Curdie, in an offended tone.

"Don't you see the lovely fire of roses—white ones amongst them this time?" asked Irene, almost as bewildered as he.

"No, I don't," answered Curdie, almost sulkily.

"Nor the blue bed? Nor the rose-coloured counterpane?[1] Nor the beautiful light, like the moon, hanging from the roof?"

"You're making game of me, your royal highness; and after what we have come through together this day, I don't think it is kind of you," said Curdie, feeling very much hurt.

"Then what *do* you see?" asked Irene, who perceived at once that for her not to believe him was at least as bad as for him not to believe her.

"I see a big, bare, garret-room—like the one in mother's cottage, only big enough to take the cottage itself in, and leave a good margin all round," answered Curdie.

"And what more do you see?"

"I see a tub, and a heap of musty straw, and a withered apple, and a ray of sunlight coming through a hole in the middle of the roof, and shining on your head, and making all the place look a curious dusky brown. I think you had better drop it, princess, and go down to the nursery, like a good girl."

---

1 "The outer covering of a bed, generally more or less ornamental, being woven in a raised pattern, quilted, made of patch-work, etc.; a coverlet, a quilt" (*OED*).

"But don't you hear my grandmother talking to me?" asked Irene, almost crying.

"No. I hear the cooing of a lot of pigeons. If you won't come down, I will go without you. I think that will be better anyhow, for I'm sure nobody who met us would believe a word we said to them. They would think we made it all up. I don't expect anybody but my own father and mother to believe me. They *know* I wouldn't tell a story."

"And yet *you* won't believe *me*, Curdie?" expostulated the princess, now fairly crying with vexation, and sorrow at the gulf between her and Curdie.

"No. I *can't*, and I can't help it," said Curdie, turning to leave the room.

"What *shall* I do, grandmother?" sobbed the princess, turning her face round upon the lady's bosom, and shaking with suppressed sobs.

"You must give him time," said her grandmother; "and you must be content not to be believed for a while. It is very hard to bear; but I have had to bear it, and shall have to bear it many a time yet. I will take care of what Curdie thinks of you in the end. You must let him go now."

"You're not coming, are you?" asked Curdie.

"No, Curdie; my grandmother says I must let you go. Turn to the right when you get to the bottom of all the stairs, and that will take you to the hall where the great door is."

"Oh! I don't doubt I can find my way—without you, princess, or your old grannie's thread either," said Curdie quite rudely.

"Oh! Curdie! Curdie!"

"I wish I had gone home at once. I'm very much obliged to you, Irene, for getting me out of that hole, but I wish you hadn't made a fool of me afterwards."

He said this as he opened the door, which he left open, and, without another word, went down the stair. Irene listened with dismay to his departing footsteps. Then turning again to the lady—

"What does it all mean, grandmother?" she sobbed, and burst into fresh tears.

"It means, my love, that I did not mean to show myself. Curdie is not yet able to believe some things. Seeing is not believing—it is only seeing. You remember I told you that if Lootie were to see me, she would rub her eyes, forget the half she saw, and call the other half nonsense."

"Yes; but I should have thought Curdie—"

"You are right. Curdie is much farther on than Lootie, and you will see what will come of it. But in the meantime, you must be content, I say, to be misunderstood for a while. We are all very anxious to be understood, and it is very hard not to be. But there is one thing much more necessary."

"What is that, grandmother?"

"To understand other people."

"Yes, grandmother. I must be fair—for if I'm not fair to other people, I'm not worth being understood myself. I see. So as Curdie can't help it, I will not be vexed with him, but just wait."

"There's my own dear child," said her grandmother, and pressed her close to her bosom.

"Why weren't you in your workroom, when we came up, grandmother?" asked Irene, after a few moments' silence.

"If I had been there, Curdie would have seen me well enough. But why should I be there rather than in this beautiful room?"

"I thought you would be spinning."

"I've nobody to spin for just at present. I never spin without knowing for whom I am spinning."

"That reminds me—there is one thing that puzzles me," said the princess: "how are you to get the thread out of the mountain again? Surely you won't have to make another for *me*! That would be such a trouble!"

The lady set her down, and rose, and went to the fire. Putting in her hand, she drew it out again, and held up the shining ball between her finger and thumb.

"I've got it now, you see," she said, coming back to the princess, "all ready for you when you want it."

Going to her cabinet, she laid it in the same drawer as before.

"And here is your ring," she added, taking it from the little finger of her left hand, and putting it on the forefinger of Irene's right hand.

"Oh! thank you, grandmother. I feel so safe now!"

"You are very tired, my child," the lady went on. "Your hands are hurt with the stones, and I have counted nine bruises on you. Just look what you are like."

And she held up to her a little mirror which she had brought from the cabinet. The princess burst into a merry laugh at the sight. She was so draggled with the stream, and dirty with creeping through narrow places, that if she had seen the reflection without knowing it was a reflection, she would have taken herself for some gypsy-child whose face was washed and hair combed about once in a month. The lady laughed too, and lifting her again upon her knee, took off her cloak and night gown. Then she carried her to the side of the room. Irene wondered what she was going to do with her, but asked no questions—only starting a little when she found that she was going to lay her in the large silver bath; for as she looked into it, again she saw no bottom, but the stars shining miles away, as it seemed, in a great blue gulf. Her hands closed involuntarily on the beautiful arms that held her, and that was all.

The lady pressed her once more to her bosom, saying—

"Do not be afraid, my child."

"No, grandmother," answered the princess, with a little gasp; and the next instant she sank in the clear cool water.

When she opened her eyes, she saw nothing but a strange lovely blue over and beneath and all about her. The lady and the beautiful room had vanished from her sight, and she seemed utterly alone. But instead of being afraid, she felt more than happy—perfectly blissful. And from somewhere came the voice of the lady, singing a strange sweet song, of which she could distinguish every word; but of the sense she had only a feeling—no understanding. Nor could she remember a single line after it was gone. It vanished, like the poetry in a dream, as fast as it came. In after years, however, she would sometimes fancy that snatches of melody suddenly rising in her brain, must be little phrases and fragments of the air of that song; and the very fancy would make her happier, and abler to do her duty.

How long she lay in the water, she did not know. It seemed a long time—not from weariness, but from pleasure. But at last she felt the beautiful hands lay hold of her, and through the gurgling water she was lifted out into the lovely room. The lady carried her to the fire, and sat down with her in her lap, and dried her tenderly with the softest towel. It was so different from Lootie's drying! When the lady had done, she stooped to the fire, and drew from it her night-gown, as white as snow.

"How delicious!" exclaimed the princess. "It smells of all the roses in the world, I think."

When she stood up on the floor, she felt as if she had been made over again. Every bruise and all weariness were gone, and her hands were soft and whole as ever.

"Now I am going to put you to bed for a good sleep," said her grandmother.

"But what will Lootie be thinking? And what am I to say to her when she asks me where I have been?"

"Don't trouble yourself about it. You will find it all come right," said her grandmother, and laid her into the blue bed, under the rosy counterpane.

"There is just one thing more," said Irene. "I am a little anxious about Curdie. As I brought him into the house, I ought to have seen him safe on his way home."

"I took care of all that," answered the lady. "I told you to let him go, and therefore I was bound to look after him. Nobody saw him, and he is now eating a good dinner in his mother's cottage, far up the mountain."

"Then I will go to sleep," said Irene, and in a few minutes, she was fast asleep.

XXIII.—CURDIE AND HIS MOTHER.

Curdie went up the mountain neither whistling nor singing, for he was vexed with Irene for taking him in, as he called it; and he was vexed with himself for having spoken to her so angrily. His mother gave a cry of joy when she saw him, and at once set about getting him something to eat, asking him questions all the time, which he did not answer so cheerfully as usual. When his meal was ready, she left him to eat it, and hurried to the mine to let his father know he was safe. When she came back, she found him fast asleep upon her bed; nor did he wake until his father came home in the evening.

"Now, Curdie," his mother said, as they sat at supper, "tell us the whole story from beginning to end, just as it all happened."

Curdie obeyed, and told everything to the point where they came out upon the lawn in the garden of the king's house.

"And what happened after that?" asked his mother. "You haven't told us all. You ought to be very happy at having got away from those demons, and instead of that, I never saw you so gloomy. There must be something more. Besides, you do not speak of that lovely child as I should like to hear you. She saved your life at the risk of her own, and yet somehow you don't seem to think much of it."

"She talked such nonsense!" answered Curdie, "and told me a pack of things that weren't a bit true; and I can't get over it."

"What were they?" asked his father. "Your mother may be able to throw some light upon them."

Then Curdie made a clean breast of it, and told them everything.

They all sat silent for some time, pondering the strange tale. At last Curdie's mother spoke.

"You confess, my boy," she said, "there is something about the whole affair you do not understand?"

"Yes, of course, mother," he answered. "I cannot understand how a child knowing nothing about the mountain, or even that I was shut up in it, should come all that way alone, straight to where I was; and then, after getting me out of the hole, lead me out of the mountain too, where I should not have known a step of the way if it had been as light as in the open air."

"Then you have no right to say that what she told you was not true. She did take you out, and she must have had something to guide her: why not a thread as well as a rope, or anything else? There is something you cannot explain, and her explanation may be the right one."

"It's no explanation at all, mother; and I can't believe it."

"That may be only because you do not understand it. If you did, you would probably find it was an explanation, and believe it thoroughly. I don't blame you for not being able to believe it, but I do blame you for fancying such a child would try to deceive you. Why should she? Depend upon it, she told you all she knew. Until you had found a better way of accounting for it all, you might at least have been more sparing of your judgment."

"That is what something inside me has been saying all the time," said Curdie, hanging down his head. "But what do you make of the grandmother? That is what I can't get over. To take me up to an old garret, and try to persuade me against the sight of my own eyes that it was a beautiful room, with blue walls and silver stars, and no end of things in it, when there was nothing there but an old tub and a withered apple and† a heap of straw and a sunbeam! It was too bad! She *might* have had some old woman there at least to pass for her precious grandmother!"

"Didn't she speak as if she saw those other things herself, Curdie?"

"Yes. That's what bothers me. You would have thought she really meant and believed that she saw every one of the things she talked about. And not one of them there! It was too bad, I say."

"Perhaps some people can see things other people can't see, Curdie," said his mother very gravely. "I think I will tell you something I saw myself once—only perhaps you won't believe me either!"

"Oh, mother, mother!" cried Curdie, bursting into tears; "I don't deserve that, surely!"

Figure 26

"But what I am going to tell you is very strange," persisted his mother; "and if having heard it you were to say I must have been dreaming, I don't know that I should have any right to be vexed with you, though I know at least that I was not asleep."

"Do tell me, mother. Perhaps it will help me to think better of the princess."

"That's why I am tempted to tell you," replied his mother. "But first, I may as well mention, that according to old whispers, there is something more than common about the king's family; and the queen was of the same blood, for they were cousins of some degree. There were strange stories told concerning them— all good stories—but strange, very strange. What they were I cannot tell, for I only remember the faces of my grandmother and my mother as they talked together about them. There was wonder and awe—not fear, in their eyes, and they whispered, and never spoke aloud. But what I saw myself, was this: Your father was going to work in the mine, one night, and I had been down with his supper. It was soon after we were married, and not very long before you were born. He came with me to the mouth of the mine, and left me to go home alone, for I knew the way almost as well as the floor of our own cottage. It was pretty dark, and in some parts of the road where the rocks overhung, nearly quite dark. But I got along perfectly well, never thinking of being afraid, until I reached a spot you know well enough, Curdie, where the path has to make a sharp turn out of the way of a great rock on the left hand side. When I got there, I was suddenly surrounded by about half-a-dozen of the cobs, the first I had ever seen, although I had heard tell of them often enough. One of them blocked up the path, and they all began tormenting and teasing me in a way it makes me shudder to think of even now."

"If I had only been with you!" cried father and son in a breath.

The mother gave a funny little smile, and went on.

"They had some of their horrible creatures with them too, and I must confess I was dreadfully frightened. They had torn my clothes very much, and I was afraid they were going to tear myself to pieces, when suddenly a great white soft light shone upon me. I looked up. A broad ray, like a shining road, came down from a large globe of silvery light, not very high up, indeed not quite so high as the horizon—so it could not have been a new star or another moon or anything of that sort. The cobs dropped persecuting me, and looked dazed, and I thought they were going to run away, but presently they began again. The same moment, however, down the path from the globe of light came a bird, shining like silver in the sun. It gave a few rapid flaps first, and then, with its wings straight out, shot sliding down the slope of the light. It looked to me just like a white pigeon. But whatever it was, when the cobs caught sight of it coming straight down upon them, they took to their heels and scampered away across the mountain, leaving me safe, only much frightened. As soon as it had sent them off, the bird went gliding again up the light, and the moment it reached the globe, the light disappeared, just as if a shutter had been closed over a window, and I saw it no more. But I had no more trouble with the cobs that night, or ever after."

"How strange!" exclaimed Curdie.

"Yes, it is strange; but I can't help believing it, whether you do or not," said his mother.

"It's exactly as your mother told it to me the very next morning," said his father.

"You don't think I'm doubting my own mother!" cried Curdie.

"There are other people in the world quite as well worth believing as your own mother," said his mother. "I don't know that she's so much the fitter to be believed that she happens to be *your* mother, Mr. Curdie. There are mothers far more likely to tell lies than that little girl I saw talking to the primroses a few weeks ago. If she were to lie I should begin to doubt my own word."

"But princesses *have* told lies as well as other people," said Curdie.

"Yes, but not princesses like that child. She's a good girl, I am certain, and that's more than being a princess. Depend upon it you will have to be sorry for behaving so to her, Curdie. You ought at least to have held your tongue."

"I am sorry now," answered Curdie.

"You ought to go and tell her so, then."

"I don't see how I could manage that. They wouldn't let a miner boy like me have a word with her alone; and I couldn't tell her before that nurse of hers. She'd be asking ever so many questions, and I don't know how many of them the little princess would like me to answer. She told me that Lootie didn't know anything about her coming to get me out of the mountain. I am certain she would have prevented her somehow if she had known of it. But I may have a chance before long, and meantime I must try to do something for her. I think, father, I have got on the track at last."

"Have you, indeed, my boy?" said Peter. "I am sure you deserve some success; you have worked very hard for it. What have you found out?"

"It's difficult you know, father, inside the mountain, especially in the dark, and not knowing what turns you have taken, to tell the lie of things outside."

"Impossible, my boy, without a chart, or at least a compass," returned his father.

"Well, I think I have nearly discovered in what direction the cobs are mining. If I am right, I know something else that I can put to it, and then one and one will make three."

"They very often do, Curdie, as we miners ought to be well aware. Now tell us, my boy, what the two things are, and see whether we guess at the same third as you."

"I don't see what that has to do with the princess," interposed his mother.

"I will soon let you see that, mother. Perhaps you may think me foolish, but until I am sure there is nothing in my present fancy, I am more determined than ever to go on with my observations. Just as we came to the channel by which we got out, I heard the miners at work somewhere near—I think down below

Figure 27

us. Now since I began to watch them, they have mined a good half mile, in a straight line; and so far as I am aware, they are working in no other part of the mountain. But I never could tell in what direction they were going. When we came out in the king's garden, however, I thought at once whether it was possible they were working towards the king's house; and what I want to do to-night is to make sure whether they are or not. I will take a light with me—"

"Oh Curdie!" cried his mother, "then they will see you."

"I'm no more afraid of them now than I was before," rejoined Curdie, "—now that I've got this precious shoe. They can't make† another such in a hurry, and one bare foot will do for my purpose. Woman as she may be, I won't spare her next time. But I shall be careful with my light, for I don't want them to see me. I won't stick it in my hat."

"Go on then, and tell us what you mean to do."

"I mean to take a bit of paper with me and a pencil, and go in at the mouth of the stream by which we came out. I shall mark on the paper as near as I can the angle of every turning I take until I find the cobs at work, and so get a good idea in what direction they are going. If it should prove to be nearly parallel with the stream, I shall know it is towards the king's house they are working."

"And what if you should? How much wiser will you be then?"

"Wait a minute, mother, dear. I told you that when I came upon the royal family in the cave, they were talking of their prince—Harelip, they called him—marrying a sun-woman—that means one of us—one with toes to her feet. Now in the speech one of them made that night at their great gathering, of which I heard only a part, he said that peace would be secured for a generation at least by the pledge the prince would hold for the good behaviour of *her* relatives: that's what he said, and he must have meant the sun-woman the prince was to marry. I am quite sure the king is much too proud to wish his son to marry any but a princess, and much too knowing to fancy that his having a peasant woman for a wife would be of any great advantage to them."

"I see what you are driving at now," said his mother.

"But," said his father, "the king would dig the mountain to the plain before he would have his princess the wife of a cob, if he were ten times a prince."

"Yes; but they think so much of themselves!" said the mother. "Small creatures always do. The bantam is the proudest cock in my little yard."

"And I fancy," said Curdie, "if they once got her, they would tell the king they would kill her except he consented to the marriage."

"They might say so," said his father, "but they wouldn't kill her; they would keep her alive for the sake of the hold it gave them over our king. Whatever he did to them, they would threaten to do the same to the princess."

"And they are bad enough to torment her just for their own amusement—I know that," said his mother.

"Anyhow, I will keep a watch on them, and see what they are up to," said Curdie. "It's too horrible to think of. I daren't let myself do it. But they shan't have her—at least if I can help it. So, mother dear—my clue is all right—will you get me a bit of paper and a pencil and a lump of pease-pudding, and I will set out at once. I saw a place where I can climb over the wall of the garden quite easily."

"You must mind and keep out of the way of the men on the watch," said his mother.

"That I will. I don't want them to know anything about it. They would spoil it all. The cobs would only try some other plan—they are such obstinate creatures! I shall take good care, mother. They won't kill and eat me either if they should come upon me. So you needn't mind them."

His mother got him what he had asked for, and Curdie set out. Close beside the door by which the princess left the garden for the mountain, stood a great rock, and by climbing it Curdie got over the wall. He tied his clue to a stone just inside the channel of the stream, and took his pickaxe with him. He had not gone far before he encountered a horrid creature coming towards the mouth. The spot was too narrow for two of almost any size or shape, and besides Curdie had no wish to let the creature pass. Not being able to use his pickaxe, however, he had a severe struggle with him, and it was only after receiving many bites, some of them bad, that he succeeded in killing him with his pocket-knife. Having dragged him out, he made haste to get in again before another should stop up the way.

I need not follow him farther in this night's adventures. He returned to his breakfast, satisfied that the goblins were mining in the direction of the palace—on so low a level that their intention must, he thought, be to burrow under the walls of the king's house, and rise up inside it—in order, he fully believed, to lay hands on the little princess, and carry her off for a wife to their horrid Harelip.

XXIV.—IRENE BEHAVES LIKE A PRINCESS.

When the princess awoke from the sweetest of sleeps, she found her nurse bending above her, the housekeeper looking over the nurse's shoulder, and the laundry-maid looking over the housekeeper's. The room was full of women-servants; and the gentlemen-at-arms, with a long column of men-servants behind them, were peeping, or trying to peep in at the door of the nursery.

"Are those horrid creatures gone?" asked the princess, remembering first what had terrified her in the morning.

"You naughty, naughty little princess!" cried Lootie.

Her face was very pale, with red streaks in it, and she looked as if she were going to shake her; but Irene said nothing—only waited to hear what should come next.

"How *could* you get under the clothes like that, and make us all fancy you were lost! And keep it up all day too! You *are* the most obstinate child! It's anything but fun to us, I can tell you!"

It was the only way the nurse could account for her disappearance.

"I didn't do that, Lootie," said Irene, very quietly.

"Don't tell stories!" cried her nurse quite rudely.

"I shall tell you nothing at all," said Irene.

"That's just as bad," said the nurse.

"Just as bad to say nothing at all as to tell stories!" exclaimed the princess. "I will ask my papa about that. He won't say so. And I don't think he will like you to say so."

"Tell me directly what you mean by it!" screamed the nurse, half wild with anger at the princess, and fright at the possible consequences to herself.

"When I tell you the truth, Lootie," said the princess, who somehow did not feel at all angry, "you say to me *Don't tell stories*: it seems I must tell stories before you will believe me."

"You are very rude, princess," said the nurse.

"You are so rude, Lootie, that I will not speak to you again till you are sorry. Why should I, when I know you will not believe me?" returned the princess.

For she did know perfectly well that if she were to tell Lootie what she had been about, the more she went on to tell her, the less would she believe her.

"You are the most provoking child!" cried her nurse. "You deserve to be well punished for your wicked behaviour."

"Please, Mrs. Housekeeper," said the princess, "will you take me to your room, and keep me till my king-papa comes? I will ask him to come as soon as he can."

Every one stared at these words. Up to this moment, they had all regarded her as little more than a baby.

But the housekeeper was afraid of the nurse, and sought to patch matters up, saying—

"I am sure, princess, nursey did not mean to be rude to you."

"I do not think my papa would wish me to have a nurse who spoke to me as Lootie does. If she thinks I tell lies, she had better either say so to my papa, or go away. Sir Walter, will you take charge of me?"

"With the greatest of pleasure, princess," answered the captain of the gentlemen-at-arms, walking with his great stride into the room. The crowd of servants made eager way for him, and he bowed low before the little princess's bed. "I shall send my servant at once, on the fastest horse in the stable, to tell your king-papa that your royal highness desires his presence. When you have chosen one of these under-servants to wait upon you, I shall order the room to be cleared."

"Thank you very much, Sir Walter," said the princess, and her eye glanced towards a rosy-cheeked girl who had lately come to the house as a scullery maid.

But when Lootie saw the eyes of her dear princess going in search of another instead of her, she fell upon her knees by the bedside, and burst into a great cry of distress.

"I think, Sir Walter," said the princess, "I will keep Lootie. But I put myself under your care; and you need not trouble my king-papa until I speak to you again. Will you all please to go away. I am quite safe and well, and I did not hide myself for the sake either of amusing myself, or of troubling my people.—Lootie, will you please to dress me."[1]

XXV.—CURDIE COMES TO GRIEF.

Everything was for some time quiet above ground. The king was still away in a distant part of his dominions. The men-at-arms kept watching about the house. They had been considerably astonished by finding at the foot of the rock in the garden, the hideous body of the goblin creature killed by Curdie; but they came to the con-

---

1 End of the seventh instalment appearing in *Good Words for the Young*,
   1 May 1871, pp. 353-63.

clusion that it had been slain in the mines, and had crept out there to die; and except an occasional glimpse of a live one they saw nothing to cause alarm. Curdie kept watching in the mountain, and the goblins kept burrowing deeper into the earth. As long as they went deeper, there was, Curdie judged, no immediate danger.

To Irene, the summer was as full of pleasure as ever, and for a long time, although she often thought of her grandmother during the day, and often dreamed about her at night, she did not see her. The kids and the flowers were as much her delight as ever, and she made as much friendship with the miners' children she met on the mountain as Lootie would permit; but Lootie had very foolish notions concerning the dignity of a princess, not understanding that the truest princess is just the one who loves all her brothers and sisters best, and who is most able to do them good by being humble towards them. At the same time she was considerably altered for the better in her behaviour to the princess. She could not help seeing that she was no longer a mere child, but wiser than her age would account for. She kept foolishly whispering to the servants, however—sometimes that the princess was not right in her mind, sometimes that she was too good to live, and other nonsense of the same sort.

All this time, Curdie had to be sorry, without a chance of confessing, that he had behaved so unkindly to the princess. This perhaps made him the more diligent in his endeavours to serve her. His mother and he often talked on the subject, and she comforted him, and told him she was sure he would some day have the opportunity he so much desired.

Here I should like to remark, for the sake of princes and princesses in general, that it is a low and contemptible thing to refuse to confess a fault, or even an error. If a true princess has done wrong, she is always uneasy until she has had an opportunity of throwing the wrongness away from her by saying, "I did it; and I wish I had not; and I am sorry for having done it." So you see there is some ground for supposing that Curdie was not a miner only, but a prince as well. Many such instances have been known in the world's history.

At length, however, he began to see signs of a change in the proceedings of the goblin excavators: they were going no deeper, but had commenced running on a level; and he watched them, therefore, more closely than ever. All at once, one night, coming to a slope of very hard rock, they began to ascend along the inclined plane of its surface. Having reached its top, they went again on a level for a night or two, after which they began to ascend once more, and kept on, at a pretty steep angle. At length Curdie judged it time to transfer his observation to another quarter, and the next night, he did not go to the mine at all; but, leaving his pickaxe and clue at home, and taking only his usual lumps of bread and pease-pudding, went down the mountain to the king's house. He climbed over the wall, and remained in the garden the whole night, creeping on hands and knees from one spot to the other, and lying at full length with his ear to the ground, listening. But he heard nothing except the tread of the men-at-arms as they marched about, whose observation, as the night was cloudy and there was no moon, he had little difficulty in avoiding. For several following nights, he continued to haunt the garden and listen, but with no success.

At length, early one evening, whether it was that he had got careless of his own safety, or that the growing moon had become strong enough to expose him, his watching came to a sudden end. He was creeping from behind the rock where the stream ran out, for he had been listening all round it in the hope it might convey to his ear some indication of the whereabouts of the goblin miners, when just as he came into the moonlight on the lawn, a whizz in his ear and a blow upon his leg startled him. He instantly squatted in the hope of eluding further notice. But when he heard the sound of running feet, he jumped up to take the chance of escape by flight. He fell, however, with a keen shoot of pain, for the bolt of a cross-bow had wounded his leg, and the blood was now streaming from it. He was instantly laid hold of by two or three of the men-at-arms. It was useless to struggle, and he submitted in silence.

"It's a boy!" cried several of them together, in a tone of amazement. "I thought it was one of those demons."

"What are you about here?"

"Going to have a little rough usage, apparently," said Curdie laughing, as the men shook him.

"Impertinence will do you no good. You have no business here in the king's grounds, and if you don't give a true account of yourself, you shall fare as a thief."

"Why, what else could he be?" said one.

"He might have been after a lost kid, you know," suggested another.

"I see no good in trying to excuse him. He has no business here, anyhow."

"Let me go away then, if you please," said Curdie.

"But we don't please—not except you give a good account of yourself."

"I don't feel quite sure whether I can trust you," said Curdie.

"We are the king's own men-at-arms," said the captain courteously, for he was taken with Curdie's appearance and courage.

"Well, I will tell you all about it—if you will promise to listen to me and not do anything rash."

"I call that cool!" said one of the party laughing. "He will tell us what mischief he was about, if we promise to do as pleases him."

"I was about no mischief," said Curdie.

But ere he could say more he turned faint, and fell senseless on the grass. Then first they discovered that the bolt they had shot, taking him for one of the goblin creatures, had wounded him.

They carried him into the house, and laid him down in the hall. The report spread that they had caught a robber, and the servants crowded in to see the villain. Amongst the rest came the nurse. The moment she saw him she exclaimed with indignation:

"I declare it's the same young rascal of a miner that was rude to me and the princess on the mountain. He actually wanted to kiss the princess. *I* took good care of that—the wretch! And *he* was prowling about—was he? Just like his impudence!"

The princess being fast asleep, and Curdie in a faint, she could misrepresent at her pleasure.

When he heard this, the captain, although he had considerable doubt of its truth, resolved to keep Curdie a prisoner until they could search into the affair. So, after they had brought him round a little, and attended to his wound, which was rather a bad one, they laid him, still exhausted from the loss of blood, upon a mattress in a disused room—one of those already so often mentioned—and locked the door, and left him. He passed a troubled night, and in the morning they found him talking wildly. In the evening he came to himself, but felt very weak, and his leg was exceedingly painful. Wondering where he was, and seeing one of the men-at-arms in the room, he began to question him, and soon recalled the events of the preceding night. As he was himself unable to watch any more, he told the soldier all he knew about the goblins, and begged him to tell his companions, and stir them up to watch with tenfold vigilance; but whether it was that he did not talk quite coherently, or that the whole thing appeared incredible, certainly the man concluded that Curdie was only raving still, and tried to coax him into holding his tongue. This, of course, annoyed Curdie dreadfully, who now felt in his turn what it was not to be believed, and the consequence was that his fever returned, and by the time when, at his persistent entreaties, the captain was called, there could be no doubt that he was raving. They did for him what they could, and promised everything he wanted, but with no intention of fulfilment. At last he went to sleep, and when at length his sleep grew profound and peaceful, they left him, locked the door again, and withdrew, intending to revisit him early in the morning.

XXVI.—THE GOBLIN-MINERS.

That same night several of the servants were having a chat together before going to bed.

"What can that noise be?" said one of the housemaids, who had been listening for a moment or two.

"I've heard it the last two nights," said the cook. "If there were any about the place, I should have taken it for rats, but my Tom keeps them far enough."

"I've heard though," said the scullery-maid, "that rats move about in great companies sometimes. There may be an army of them invading us. I've heard the noises yesterday and to-day too."

"It'll be grand fun then for my Tom and Mrs. Housekeeper's Bob," said the cook. "They'll be friends for once in their lives, and fight on the same side. I'll engage Tom and Bob together will put to flight any number of rats."

"It seems to me," said the nurse, "that the noises are much too loud for that. I have heard them all day, and my princess has asked me several times what they could be. Sometimes they sound like distant thunder, and sometimes like the noises you hear in the mountain from those horrid miners underneath."

"I shouldn't wonder," said the cook, "if it was the miners after all. They may have come on some hole in the mountain through which the noises reach to us. They are always boring and blasting and breaking, you know."

As he spoke, there came a great rolling rumble beneath them, and the house quivered. They all started up in affright, and rushing to the hall found the gentlemen-at-arms in consternation also. They had sent to wake their captain, who said from their description that it must have been an earthquake, an occurrence which, although very rare in that country, had taken place almost within the century; and then went to bed again, strange to say, and fell fast asleep without once thinking of Curdie, or associating the noises they had heard with what he had told them. He had not believed Curdie. If he had, he would at once have thought of what he had said, and would have taken precautions. As they heard nothing more, they concluded that Sir Walter was right, and that the danger was over for perhaps another hundred years. The fact, as discovered afterwards, was that the goblins had, in working up a second sloping face of stone, arrived at a huge block which lay under the cellars of the house, within the line of the foundations. It was so round that when they succeeded, after hard work, in dislodging it without blasting, it rolled thundering down the slope with a bounding, jarring roll, which shook the foundations of the house. The goblins were themselves dismayed at the noise, for they knew, by careful spying and measuring, that they must now be very near, if not under, the king's house, and they feared giving an alarm. They, therefore, remained quiet for a while, and when they began to work again, they no doubt thought themselves very fortunate in coming upon a vein of sand which filled a winding fissure in the rock on which the house was built. By scooping this away they soon came out in the king's wine-cellar.

No sooner did they find where they were, than they scurried back again, like rats into their holes, and running at full speed to the goblin palace, announced their success to the king and queen with shouts of triumph. In a moment the goblin royal family and the whole goblin people were on their way in hot haste to the king's house, each eager to have a share in the glory of carrying off that same night the Princess Irene.

The queen went stumping along in one shoe of stone and one of skin. This could not have been pleasant, and my readers may wonder that, with such skilful workmen about her, she had not yet replaced the shoe carried off by Curdie. As the king however had more than one ground of objection to her stone shoes, he no doubt took advantage of the discovery of her toes, and threatened to expose her deformity if she had another made. I presume he insisted on her being content with skin-shoes, and allowed her to wear the remaining granite one on the present occasion only because she was going out to war.

They soon arrived in the king's wine-cellar, and regardless of its huge vessels, of which they did not know the use, proceeded at once, but as quietly as they could, to force the door that led upwards.

XXVII.—THE GOBLINS IN THE KING'S HOUSE.

When Curdie fell asleep he began at once to dream. He thought he was ascending the mountain-side from the mouth of the mine, whistling and singing *"Ring, dod, bang!"* when he came upon a woman and child who had lost their way; and from that point he went on dreaming everything that had happened to him since he thus met the princess and Lootie; how he had watched the goblins, how he had been taken by them, how he had been rescued by the princess; everything indeed, until he was wounded, captured, and imprisoned by the men-at-arms. And now he thought he was lying wide awake where they had laid him, when suddenly he heard a great thundering sound.

"The cobs are coming!" he said. "They didn't believe a word I told them! The cobs 'll be carrying off the princess from under their stupid noses! But they shan't! that they shan't!"

He jumped up, as he thought, and began to dress, but, to his dismay, found that he was still lying in bed.

"Now then I will!" he said. "Here goes! I *am* up now!"

But yet again he found himself snug in bed. Twenty times he tried, and twenty times he failed; for in fact he was not awake, only dreaming that he was. At length in an agony of despair, fancying he heard the goblins all over the house, he gave a great cry. Then there came, as he thought, a hand upon the lock of his door. It opened, and, looking up, he saw a lady with white hair, carrying a silver box in her hand, enter the room. She came to his bed, he thought, stroked his head and face with cool, soft hands, took the dressing from his leg, rubbed it with something that smelt like roses, and then waved her hands over him three times. At the last wave of her hands everything vanished, he felt himself sinking into the profoundest slumber, and remembered nothing more until he woke in earnest.

The setting moon was throwing a feeble light through the casement, and the house was full of uproar. There was soft heavy multitudinous stamping, a clashing and clanging of weapons, the voices of men and the cries of women, mixed with a hideous bellowing, which sounded victorious. The cobs were in the house! He sprung from his bed, hurried on some of his clothes, not forgetting his shoes, which were armed with nails; then spying an old hunting-knife, or short sword, hanging on the wall, he caught it, and rushed down the stairs, guided by the sounds of strife, which grew louder and louder.

When he reached the ground floor he found the whole place swarming. All the goblins of the mountain seemed gathered there. He rushed amongst them, shouting—

> "One, two,
> Hit and hew!
> Three, four,
> Blast and bore!"

and with every rhyme he came down a great stamp upon a foot, cutting at the same time at their faces—executing, indeed, a sword dance of the wildest description. Away scattered the goblins in every direction,—into closets, up stairs, into chimneys, up on rafters, and down to the cellars. Curdie went on stamping and slashing and singing, but saw nothing of the people of the house until he came to the great hall, in which, the moment he entered it, arose a great goblin shout. The last of the men-at-arms, the captain himself, was on the floor, buried beneath a wallowing crowd of goblins. For, while each knight was busy defending himself as well as he could, by stabs in the thick bodies of the goblins, for he had soon found their heads all but invulnerable, the queen had attacked his legs and feet with her horrible granite shoe, and he was soon down; but the captain had got his back to the wall and stood out longer. The goblins would have torn them all to pieces, but the king had given orders to carry them away alive, and over each of them, in twelve groups, was standing a knot of goblins, while as many as could find room were sitting upon their prostrate bodies.

Curdie burst in dancing and gyrating and stamping and singing like a small incarnate whirlwind.

> "Where 'tis all a hole, sir,
> Never can be holes:
> Why should their shoes have soles, sir,
> When they've got no souls?

> "But she upon her foot, sir,
> Has a granite shoe:
> The strongest leather boot, sir,
> Six would soon be through."

The queen gave a howl of rage and dismay; and before she recovered her presence of mind, Curdie, having begun with the group nearest him, had eleven of the knights on their legs again.

"Stamp on their feet!" he cried as each man rose, and in a few minutes the hall was nearly empty, the goblins running from it as fast as they could, howling and shrieking and limping, and cowering every now and then as they ran to cuddle their wounded feet in their hard hands, or to protect them from the frightful stamp-stamp of the armed men.

And now Curdie approached the group which, trusting in the queen and her shoe, kept their guard over the prostrate captain. The king sat on the captain's head, but the queen stood in front, like an infuriated cat, with her perpendicular eyes gleaming green, and her hair standing half up from her horrid head. Her heart was quaking however, and she kept moving about her skin-shod foot with nervous apprehension. When Curdie was within a few paces, she rushed at him, made one tremendous stamp at his opposing foot, which happily he withdrew in time, and caught him round the waist, to dash him on the marble floor. But just as she caught him, he came down with all the weight of his iron-shod shoe upon her skin-shod foot, and with a hideous howl she dropped him, squatted on the floor and took her foot in both her hands. Meanwhile the rest rushed on the king and the body-guard, sent them flying, and lifted the prostrate captain, who was all but pressed to death. It was some moments before he recovered breath and consciousness.

"Where's the princess?" cried Curdie, again and again.

No one knew, and off they all rushed in search of her.

Through every room in the house they went, but nowhere was she to be found. Neither was one of the servants to be seen. But Curdie, who had kept to the lower part of the house, which was now quiet enough, began to hear a confused sound as of a distant hubbub, and set out to find where it came from. The noise grew as his sharp ears guided him to a stair and so to the wine cellar. It was full of goblins, whom the butler was supplying with wine as fast as he could draw it.

While the queen and her party had encountered the men-at-arms, Harelip with another company had gone off to search the house. They captured every one they met, and when they could find no more, they hurried away to carry them safe to the caverns below. But when the butler, who was amongst them, found that their path lay through the wine cellar, he bethought himself of persuading them to taste the wine, and, as he had hoped, they no sooner tasted than they wanted more. The routed goblins, on their way below, joined them, and when Curdie entered, they were all, with outstretched hands, in which were vessels of every description from saucepan to silver cup, pressing around the butler, who sat at the tap of a huge cask, filling and filling. Curdie cast one glance around the place before commencing his attack, and saw in the furthest corner a terrified group of the domestics unwatched, but cowering without courage to attempt their escape. Amongst them was the terror-stricken face of Lootie; but nowhere could he see the princess. Seized with the horrible conviction that Harelip had already carried her off, he rushed amongst them, unable for wrath to sing any more, but stamping and cutting with greater fury than ever.

"Stamp on their feet; stamp on their feet!" he shouted, and in a moment the goblins were disappearing through the hole in the floor like rats and mice.

They could not vanish so fast, however, but that many more goblin-feet had to go limping back over the underground ways of the mountain that morning.

Presently however they were reinforced from above by the king and his party, with the redoubtable queen at their head. Finding Curdie again busy amongst her unfortunate subjects, she rushed at him once more with the rage of despair, and this time gave him a bad bruise on the foot. Then a regular stamping fight got up between them, Curdie with the point of his hunting knife keeping her from clasping her mighty arms about him, as he watched his opportunity of getting once more a good stamp at her skin-shod foot. But the queen was more wary as well as more agile than hitherto.

The rest meantime, finding their adversary thus matched for the moment, paused in their headlong hurry, and turned to the shivering group of women in the corner. As if determined to emulate his father and have a sun-woman of some sort to share his future throne, Harelip rushed at them, caught up Lootie and sped with her to the hole. She gave a great shriek, and Curdie heard her, and saw the plight she was in. Gathering all his strength, he gave the queen a sudden cut across the face with his weapon, came down, as she started back, with all his weight on the proper foot, and sprung to Lootie's rescue. The prince had two defenceless feet, and on both of them Curdie stamped just as he reached the hole. He dropped his burden and rolled shrieking into the earth. Curdie made one stab at him as he disappeared, caught hold of the senseless Lootie, and having dragged her back to the corner, there mounted guard over her, preparing once more to encounter the queen. Her face streaming with blood, and her eyes flashing green lightning through it, she came on with her mouth open and her teeth grinning like a tiger's, followed by the king and her bodyguard of the thickest goblins. But the same moment in rushed the captain and his men, and ran at them stamping furiously. They dared not encounter such an onset. Away they scurried, the queen foremost. Of course the right thing would have been to take the king and queen prisoners, and hold them hostages for the princess, but they were so anxious to find her that no one thought of detaining them until it was too late.

Having thus rescued the servants, they set about searching the house once more. None of them could give the least information concerning the princess. Lootie was almost silly with terror, and although scarcely able to walk, would not leave Curdie's side for a single moment. Again he allowed the others to search the rest of the house—where, except a dismayed goblin lurking here and there, they found no one—while he requested Lootie to take him to the princess's room. She was as submissive and obedient as if he had been the king.

He found the bed-clothes tossed about, and most of them on the floor, while the princess's garments were scattered all over the room, which was in the greatest confusion. It was only too evident that the goblins had been there, and Curdie had no longer any doubt that she had been carried off at the very first of the inroad. With a pang of despair he saw how wrong they had been in not securing the king and queen and prince; but he determined to find and rescue the princess as she had found and rescued him, or meet the worst fate to which the goblins could doom him.

XXVIII.—CURDIE'S GUIDE.

Just as the consolation of this resolve dawned upon his mind, and he was turning away for the cellar to follow the goblins into their hole, something touched his hand. It was the slightest touch, and when he looked he could see nothing. Feeling and peering about in the gray of the dawn, his fingers came upon a tight thread. He looked again, and narrowly, but still could see nothing. It flashed upon him that this must be the princess's thread. Without saying a word, for he knew no one would believe him any more than he had believed the princess, he followed the thread with his finger, contrived to give Lootie the slip, and was soon out of the house, and on the mountain-side—surprised that, if the thread were indeed her grandmother's messenger, it should have led the princess as he supposed it must, into the mountain where she would be certain to meet the goblins rushing back enraged from their defeat. But he hurried on in the hope of overtaking her first. When he arrived however at the place where the path turned off for the mine, he found that the thread did not turn with it, but went straight up the mountain. Could it be that the thread was leading him home to his mother's cottage? Could the princess be there? He bounded up the mountain like one of its own goats, and before the sun was up, the thread had brought him indeed to his mother's door. There it vanished from his fingers, and he could not find it, search as he might.

The door was on the latch, and he entered. There sat his mother by the fire, and in her arms lay the princess fast asleep.

"Hush, Curdie!" said his mother. "Do not wake her. I'm so glad you're come! I thought the cobs must have got you again!"

With a heart full of delight, Curdie sat down at a corner of the hearth, on a stool opposite his mother's chair, and gazed at the princess, who slept as peacefully as if she had been in her own bed. All at once she opened her eyes and fixed them on him.

"Oh, Curdie! you're come!" she said quietly. "I thought you would!"

Curdie rose and stood before her with downcast eyes.

"Irene," he said, "I am very sorry I did not believe you."

"Oh, never mind, Curdie!" answered the princess. "You couldn't, you know. You do believe me now, don't you?"

"I can't help it now. I ought to have helped it before."

"Why can't you help it now?"

"Because, just as I was going into the mountain to look for you, I got a hold of your thread, and it brought me here."

"Then you've come from my house, have you?"

"Yes, I have."

"I didn't know you were there."

"I've been there two or three days, I believe."

"And I never knew it!—Then perhaps you can tell me why my grandmother has brought me here? I can't think. Something woke me—I didn't know what, but I was frightened, and I felt for the thread, and there it was! I was more frightened still when it brought me out on the mountain, for I thought it was going to take me into it again, and I like the outside of it best. I supposed you were in trouble again, and I had to get you out. But it brought me here instead; and, oh Curdie! your mother has been so kind to me—just like my own grandmother!"

Here Curdie's mother gave the princess a hug, and the princess turned and gave her a sweet smile, and held up her mouth to kiss her.

"Then you didn't see the cobs?" asked Curdie.

"No; I haven't been into the mountain, I told you, Curdie."

"But the cobs have been into your house—all over it—and into your bedroom, making such a row!"

"What did they want there? It was very rude of them."

"They wanted you—to carry you off into the mountain with them, for a wife to their Prince Harelip."

"Oh, how dreadful!" cried the princess, shuddering.

"But you needn't be afraid, you know. Your grandmother takes care of you."

"Ah! you do believe in my grandmother then? I'm so glad! She made me think you would some day."

All at once Curdie remembered his dream, and was silent, thinking.

"But how did you come to be in my house, and me not know it?" asked the princess.

Then Curdie had to explain everything—how he had watched for her sake, how he had been wounded and shut up by the soldiers, how he heard the noises and could not rise, and how the beautiful old lady had come to him, and all that followed.

"Poor Curdie! to lie there hurt and ill, and me never to know it!" exclaimed the princess, stroking his rough hand. "I would have come and nursed you, if they had told me."

"I didn't see you were lame," said his mother.

"Am I, mother? Oh—yes—I suppose I ought to be. I declare I've never thought of it since I got up to go down amongst the cobs!"

"Let me see the wound," said his mother.

He pulled down his stocking—when behold, except a great scar, his leg was perfectly sound!

Curdie and his mother gazed in each other's eyes, full of wonder, but Irene called out—

"I thought so, Curdie! I was sure it wasn't a dream. I was sure my grandmother had been to see you.—Don't you smell the roses? It was my grandmother healed your leg, and sent you to help me."

"No, Princess Irene," said Curdie; "I wasn't good enough to be allowed to help you: I didn't believe you. Your grandmother took care of you without me."

"She sent you to help my people, anyhow. I wish my king-papa would come. I do want so to tell him how good you have been!"

"But," said the mother, "we are forgetting how frightened your people must be.—You must take the princess home at once, Curdie—or at least go and tell them where she is."

"Yes, mother. Only I'm dreadfully hungry. Do let me have some breakfast first. They ought to have listened to me, and then they wouldn't have been taken by surprise as they were."

"That is true, Curdie; but it is not for you to blame them much. You remember?"

"Yes, mother, I do. Only I must really have something to eat."

"You shall, my boy—as fast as I can get it," said his mother, rising and setting the princess on her chair.

But before his breakfast was ready, Curdie jumped up so suddenly as to startle both his companions.

"Mother, mother!" he cried, "I was forgetting. You must take the princess home yourself. I must go and wake my father."

Without a word of explanation, he rushed to the place where his father was sleeping. Having thoroughly roused him with what he told him, he darted out of the cottage.

XXIX.—MASON-WORK.

He had all at once remembered the resolution of the goblins to carry out their second plan upon the failure of the first. No doubt they were already busy, and the mine was therefore in the greatest danger of being flooded and rendered useless—not to speak of the lives of the miners.

When he reached the mouth of the mine, after rousing all the miners within reach, he found his father and a good many more just entering. They all hurried to the gang by which he had found a way into the goblin country. There the foresight of Peter had already collected a great many blocks of stone, with cement, ready for building up the weak place—well enough known to the goblins. Although there was not room for more than two to be actually building at once, they managed, by setting all the rest to work in preparing the cement and passing the stones, to finish in the course of the day a huge buttress filling the whole gang, and supported everywhere by the live rock. Before the hour when they usually dropped work, they were satisfied the mine was secure.

They had heard goblin hammers and pickaxes busy all the time, and at length fancied they heard sounds of water they had never heard before. But that was otherwise accounted for when they left the mine; for they stepped out into a tremendous storm which was raging all over the mountain. The thunder was bellowing, and the lightning lancing out of a huge black cloud which lay above it, and hung down its edges of thick mist over its sides. The lightning was breaking out of the mountain, too, and flashing up into the cloud. From the state of the brooks, now swollen into raging torrents, it was evident that the storm had been storming all day.

The wind was blowing as if it would blow him off the mountain, but, anxious about his mother and the princess, Curdie darted up through the thick of the tempest. Even if they had not set out before the storm came on, he did not judge them safe, for, in such a storm even their poor little house was in danger. Indeed he soon found that but for a huge rock against which it was built, and which protected it both from the blasts and the waters, it must have been swept if it was not blown away; for the two torrents into which this rock parted the rush of water behind it united again in front of the cottage—two roaring and dangerous streams, which his mother and the princess could not possibly have passed. It was with great difficulty that he forced his way through one of them, and up to the door.

The moment his hand fell on the latch, through all the uproar of winds and waters came the joyous cry of the princess:—

"There's Curdie! Curdie! Curdie!"

She was sitting wrapped in blankets on the bed, his mother trying for the hundredth time to light the fire which had been drowned by the rain that came down the chimney. The clay floor was one mass of mud, and the whole place looked wretched. But the faces of the mother and the princess shone as if their troubles only made them the merrier. Curdie burst out laughing at the sight of them.

"I never *had* such fun!" said the princess, her eyes twinkling and her pretty teeth shining. "How nice it must be to live in a cottage on the mountain!"†

"It all depends on what kind your inside house is," said the mother.

"I know what you mean," said Irene. "That's the kind of thing my grandmother says."

Figure 28

By the time Peter returned, the storm was nearly over, but the streams were so fierce and so swollen, that it was not only out of the question for the princess to go down the mountain, but most dangerous for Peter even or Curdie to make the attempt in the gathering darkness.

"They will be dreadfully frightened about you," said Peter to the princess, "but we cannot help it. We must wait till the morning."

With Curdie's help, the fire was lighted at last, and the mother set about making their supper; and after supper they all told the princess stories till she grew sleepy. Then Curdie's mother laid her in Curdie's bed, which was in a tiny little garret-room. As soon as she was in bed, through a little window low down in the roof she caught sight of her grandmother's lamp shining far away beneath, and she gazed at the beautiful silvery globe until she fell fast asleep.

XXX.—THE KING AND THE KISS.

The next morning the sun rose so bright that Irene said the rain had washed his face and let the light out clean. The torrents were still roaring down the side of the mountain, but they were so much smaller as not to be dangerous in the daylight. After an early breakfast, Peter went to his work, and Curdie and his mother set out to take the princess home. They had difficulty in getting her dry across the streams, and Curdie had again and again to carry her, but at last they got safe on the broader part of the road, and walked gently down towards the king's house. And what should they see as they turned the last corner, but the last of the king's troop riding through the gate!

"Oh Curdie!" cried Irene, clapping her hands right joyfully, "my king-papa is come."

The moment Curdie heard that, he caught her up in his arms, and set off at full speed, crying—

"Come on, mother dear! The king may break his heart before he knows that she is safe."

Irene clung round his neck, and he ran with her like a deer. When he entered the gate into the court, there sat the king on his horse, with all the people of the house about him, weeping and hanging their heads. The king was not weeping, but his face was white† as a dead man's, and he looked as if the life had gone out of him. The men-at-arms he had brought with him, sat with horror-stricken faces, but eyes flashing with rage, waiting only for the word of the king to do something—they did not know what, and nobody knew what.

The day before, the men-at-arms belonging to the house, as soon as they were satisfied the princess had been carried away, rushed after the goblins into the hole, but found that they had already so skilfully blockaded the narrowest part, not many feet below the cellar,† that without miners and their tools they could

Figure 29

do nothing. Not one of them knew where the mouth of the mine lay, and some of those who had set out to find it had been overtaken by the storm and had not even yet returned. Poor Sir Walter was especially filled with shame, and almost hoped the king would order his head to be cut off, for to think of that sweet little face down amongst the goblins was unendurable.

When Curdie ran in at the gate with the princess in his arms, they were all so absorbed in their own misery and awed by the king's presence and grief, that no one observed his arrival. He went straight up to the king, where he sat on his horse.

Figure 30

"Papa! papa!" the princess cried, stretching out her arms to him; "here I am!"

The king started. The colour rushed to his face. He gave an inarticulate cry. Curdie held up the princess, and the king bent down and took her from his arms. As he clasped her to his bosom, the big tears went dropping down his cheeks and his beard. And such a shout arose from all the bystanders, that the startled horses pranced and capered, and the armour rang and clattered, and the rocks of the mountain echoed back the noises.

Figure 31

The princess greeted them all as she nestled in her father's bosom, and the king did not set her down until she had told them all the story. But she had more to tell about Curdie than about herself, and what she did tell about herself none of them could understand except the king and Curdie, who stood by the king's knee stroking the neck of the great white horse. And still as she told what Curdie had done, Sir Walter and others added to what she told, even Lootie joining in the praises of his courage and energy.

Curdie held his peace, looking quietly up in the king's face. And his mother stood on the outskirts of the crowd listening with delight, for her son's deeds were pleasant in her ears, until the princess caught sight of her.

"And there is his mother, king-papa!" she said. "See—there. She is such a nice mother, and has been so kind to me!"

They all parted asunder as the king made a sign to her to come forward. She obeyed, and he gave her his hand, but could not speak.

"And now, king-papa," the princess went on, "I must tell you another thing. One night long ago Curdie drove the goblins away and brought Lootie and me safe from the mountain. And I promised him a kiss when we got home, but Lootie wouldn't let me give it him. I don't want you to scold Lootie,† but I want you to tell her that a princess *must* do as she promises."

"Indeed she must, my child—except it be wrong," said the king.—"There, give Curdie a kiss."

And as he spoke he held her towards him.

The princess reached down, threw her arms round Curdie's neck, and kissed him on the mouth, saying—

"There, Curdie! There's the kiss I promised you!"

Then they all went into the house, and the cook rushed to the kitchen, and the servants to their work. Lootie dressed Irene in her shiningest clothes, and the king put off his armour, and put on purple and gold; and a messenger was sent for Peter and all the miners, and there was a great and a grand feast, which continued long after the princess was put to bed.

XXXI.—THE SUBTERRANEAN WATERS.

The king's harper, who always formed a part of his escort, was chanting a ballad which he made as he went on playing on his instrument—about the princess and the goblins, and the prowess of Curdie, when all at once he ceased, with his eyes on one of the doors of the hall. Thereupon the eyes of the king and his guests turned thitherward also. The next moment, through the open doorway came the princess Irene. She went straight up to her father, with her right hand stretched out a little sideways, and her forefinger, as her father and Curdie understood, feeling its way along the invisible thread. The king took her on his knee, and she said in his ear—

"King-papa, do you hear that noise?"

"I hear nothing," said the king.

"Listen," she said, holding up her forefinger.

The king listened, and a great stillness fell upon the company. Each man, seeing that the king listened, listened also, and the harper sat with his harp between his arms, and his fingers silent upon the strings.

"I do hear a noise," said the king at length—"a noise as of distant thunder. It is coming nearer and nearer. What can it be?"

They all heard it now, and each seemed ready to start to his feet as he listened. Yet all sat perfectly still. The noise came rapidly nearer.

"What *can* it be?" said the king again.

"I think it must be another storm coming over the mountain," said Sir Walter.

Then Curdie, who at the first word of the king had slipped from his seat, and laid his ear to the ground, rose up quickly, and approaching the king said, speaking very fast—

"Please your majesty, I think I know what it is. I have no time to explain, for that might make it too late for some of us. Will your majesty give orders that everybody leave the house as quickly as possible, and get up the mountain."

The king, who was the wisest man in the kingdom, knew well there was a time when things must be done, and questions left till afterwards. He had faith in Curdie, and rose instantly, with Irene in his arms.

"Every man and woman follow me," he said, and strode out into the darkness.

Before he had reached the gate, the noise had grown to a great thundering roar, and the ground trembled beneath their feet, and before the last of them had crossed the court, out after them from the great hall-door came a huge rush of turbid water, and almost swept them away. But they got safe out of the gate and up the mountain, while the torrent went roaring down the road into the valley beneath.

Curdie had left the king and the princess to look after his mother, whom he and his father, one on each side, caught up when the stream overtook them and carried safe and dry.

When the king had got out of the way of the water, a little up the mountain, he stood with the princess in his arms, looking back with amazement on the issuing torrent, which glimmered fierce and foamy through the night. There Curdie rejoined them.

"Now, Curdie," said the king, "what does it mean? Is this what you expected?"

"It is, your majesty," said Curdie; and proceeded to tell him about the second scheme of the goblins, who, fancying the miners of more importance to the upper world than they were, had resolved, if they should fail in carrying off the king's daughter, to flood the mine and drown the miners. Then he explained what the miners had done to prevent it. The goblins had, in pursuance of their design, let loose all the underground reservoirs and streams, expecting the water to run down into the mine, which was lower than their part of the mountain, for they had, as they supposed, not knowing of the solid wall close behind, broken a passage through into it. But the readiest outlet the water could find had turned out to be the tunnel they had made to the king's house, the possibility of which catastrophe had not occurred to the young miner until he laid his ear to the floor of the hall.

What was then to be done? The house appeared in danger of falling, and every moment the torrent was increasing.

"We must set out at once," said the king. "But how to get at the horses!"

"Shall I see if we can manage that?" said Curdie.

"Do," said the king.

Curdie gathered the men-at-arms, and took them over the garden wall, and so to the stables. They found their horses in terror; the water was rising fast around them, and it was quite time they were got out. But there was no way to get them out, except by riding them through the stream, which was now pouring from the lower windows as well as the door. As one horse was quite enough for any man to manage through such a torrent, Curdie got on the king's white charger, and leading the way, brought them all in safety to the rising ground.

"Look, look, Curdie!" cried Irene, the moment that, having dismounted, he led the horse up to the king.

Curdie did look, and saw, high in the air, somewhere about the top of the king's house, a great globe of light, shining like the purest silver.

"Oh!" he cried in some consternation, "that is your grandmother's lamp! We *must* get her out. I will go and find her. The house may fall, you know."

"My grandmother is in no danger," said Irene, smiling.

"Here, Curdie, take the princess while I get on my horse," said the king.

Curdie took the princess again, and both turned their eyes to the globe of light. The same moment there shot from it a white bird, which, descending with outstretched wings, made one circle round the king and Curdie and the princess, and then glided up again. The light and the pigeon vanished together.

"Now, Curdie," said the princess, as he lifted her to her father's arms, "you see my grandmother knows all about it, and isn't frightened. I believe she could walk through that water and it wouldn't wet her a bit."

"But, my child," said the king, "you will be cold if you haven't something more on. Run, Curdie, my boy, and fetch anything you can lay your hands on, to keep the princess warm. We have a long ride before us."

Curdie was gone in a moment, and soon returned with a great rich fur, and the news that dead goblins were tossing about in the current through the house. They had been caught in their own snare; instead of the mine they had flooded their own country, whence they were now swept up drowned. Irene shuddered, but the king held her close to his bosom. Then he turned to Sir Walter, and said—

"Bring Curdie's father and mother here."

"I wish," said the king, when they stood before him, "to take your son with me. He shall enter my body-guard at once, and wait further promotion."

Peter and his wife, overcome, only murmured almost inaudible thanks. But Curdie spoke aloud.

"Please your majesty," he said, "I cannot leave my father and mother."

"That's right, Curdie!" cried the princess. "*I* wouldn't if I was you."

The king looked at the princess and then at Curdie with a glow of satisfaction on his countenance.

"I too think you are right, Curdie," he said, "and I will not ask you again. But I shall have a chance of doing something for you some time."

"Your majesty has already allowed me to serve you," said Curdie.

"But, Curdie!" said his mother, "why shouldn't you go with the king? We can get on very well without you."

"But I can't get on very well without you," said Curdie. "The king is very kind, but I could not be half the use to him that I am to you. Please your majesty, if you wouldn't mind giving my mother a red petticoat! I should have got her one long ago, but for the goblins."

"As soon as we get home," said the king, "Irene and I will search out the warmest one to be found, and send it by one of the gentlemen."

"Yes, that we will, Curdie!" said the princess. "And next summer we'll come back and see you wear it, Curdie's mother," she added. "Shan't we, king-papa?"

"Yes, my love; I hope so," said the king.

Then turning to the miners, he said—

"Will you do the best you can for my servants to-night. I hope they will be able to return to the house to-morrow."

The miners with one voice promised their hospitality.

Then the king commanded his servants to mind whatever Curdie should say to them, and after shaking hands with him and his father and mother, the king and the princess and all their company rode away down the side of the new stream which had already devoured half the road, into the starry night.

XXXII.—THE LAST CHAPTER.

All the rest went up the mountain, and separated in groups to the homes of the miners. Curdie and his father and mother took Lootie with them. And the whole way, a light, of which all but Lootie understood the origin, shone upon their path. But when they looked round they could see nothing of the silvery globe.

For days and days the water continued to rush from the doors and windows of the king's house, and a few goblin bodies were swept out into the road.

Curdie saw that something must be done. He spoke to his father and the rest of the miners, and they at once proceeded to make another outlet for the waters. By setting all hands to the work, tunnelling here and building there, they soon succeeded; and having also made a little tunnel to drain the water away from under the king's house, they were soon able to get into the wine cellar, where they found a multitude of dead goblins—among the rest the queen, with the skin-shoe gone, and the stone one fast to her ancle—for the water had swept away the barricade which pre-vented the men-at-arms from following the goblins, and had greatly widened the passage. They built it securely up, and then went back to their labours in the mine.

A good many of the goblins with their creatures escaped from the inundation out upon the mountain. But most of them soon left that part of the country, and most of those who remained grew milder in character, and indeed became very much like the Scotch Brownies.[1] Their skulls became softer as well as their hearts, and their feet grew harder, and by degrees they became friendly with the inhabitants of the mountain and even with the miners. But the latter were merciless to any of the *cobs' creatures* that came in their way, until at length they all but disappeared.[2] Still—

"*But Mr. Editor, we would rather hear more about the Princess and Curdie. We don't care about the goblins and their nasty creatures. They frighten us—rather.*"

"*But you know if you once get rid of the goblins there is no fear of the princess or of Curdie.*"

"*But we want to know more about them.*"

"*Some day, perhaps, I may tell you the further history of both of them; how Curdie came to visit Irene's grandmother, and what she did for him; and how the princess and he met again after they were older— and how—But there! I don't mean to go any farther at present.*"

"*Then you're leaving the story unfinished, Mr. Editor!*"

"*Not more unfinished than a story ought to be, I hope. If you ever knew a story finished, all I can say is, I never did. Somehow stories won't finish. I think I know why, but I won't say that either now.*"[3]

---

1 A Brownie is "A benevolent spirit or goblin, of shaggy appearance, supposed to haunt old houses, esp. farmhouses, in Scotland, and sometimes to perform useful household work while the family were asleep" (*OED*).

2 The final appearance of the narrative frame included in the serialized version of the novel was removed in subsequent editions. These later editions end with the statement, "The rest of the history of *The Princess and Curdie* must be kept for another volume." *The Princess and Curdie* was first published in *Good Things: A Picturesque Magazine for Boys and Girls* from January to June 1877; it first appeared in volume form in 1883.

3 End of the eighth and final instalment appearing in *Good Words for the Young*, 1 June 1871, pp. 409-20.

Other Fairy Tales[1]
From *Dealings with the Fairies*

THE LIGHT PRINCESS[2]

I. WHAT! NO CHILDREN?

Once upon a time, so long ago that I have quite forgotten the date, there lived a king and queen who had no children.

And the king said to himself, "All the queens of my acquaintance have children, some three, some seven, and some as many as twelve; and my queen has not one. I feel ill-used." So he made up his mind to be cross with his wife about it. But she bore it all like a good patient queen as she was. Then the king grew very cross indeed. But the queen pretended to take it all as a joke, and a very good one too.

"Why don't you have any daughters, at least?" said he. "I don't say *sons*; that might be too much to expect."

"I am sure, dear king, I am very sorry," said the queen.

"So you ought to be," retorted the king; "you are not going to make a virtue of *that*, surely."

But he was not an ill-tempered king, and in any matter of less moment would have let the queen have her own way with all his heart. This, however, was an affair of state.

The queen smiled.

"You must have patience with a lady, you know, dear king," said she.

---

1 By the late 1860s MacDonald had made preliminary ventures into fantasy writing, but they had been largely commercially unsuccessful. *Phantastes* (1858), his fantasy novel for adults, had not been well received, nor had his inclusion of several fairy tales in *Adela Cathcart* (1864) pleased the critics. In 1867, he published the latter tales, along with some others from early in the decade, in *Dealings with the Fairies*. This selection opens with three of the best known tales—"The Light Princess," "The Giant's Heart," and "The Golden Key"—as well as the later "The History of Photogen and Nycteris: A Day and Night Märchen" (1879).

2 "The Light Princess" first appeared in *Adela Cathcart* (1864) interspersed with commentary from a listening audience. The story later appeared in *Dealings with the Fairies* (1867) and *The Light Princess and Other Fairy Stories* (1890). The text reproduced here is based on that published in *Dealings with the Fairies*.

She was, indeed, a very nice queen, and heartily sorry that she could not oblige the king immediately.

The king tried to have patience, but he succeeded very badly. It was more than he deserved, therefore, when, at last, the queen gave him a daughter—as lovely a little princess as ever cried.

II. WON'T I, JUST?

The day drew near when the infant must be christened. The king wrote all the invitations with his own hand. Of course somebody was forgotten.

Now it does not generally matter if somebody *is* forgotten, only you must mind who. Unfortunately, the king forgot without intending to forget; and so the chance fell upon the Princess Makemnoit, which was awkward. For the princess was the king's own sister; and he ought not to have forgotten her. But she had made herself so disagreeable to the old king, their father, that he had forgotten her in making his will; and so it was no wonder that her brother forgot her in writing his invitations. But poor relations don't do anything to keep you in mind of them. Why don't they? The king could not see into the garret she lived in, could he?

She was a sour, spiteful creature. The wrinkles of contempt crossed the wrinkles of peevishness, and made her face as full of wrinkles as a pat of butter. If ever a king could be justified in forgetting anybody, this king was justified in forgetting his sister, even at a christening. She looked very odd, too. Her forehead was as large as all the rest of her face, and projected over it like a precipice. When she was angry, her little eyes flashed blue. When she hated anybody, they shone yellow and green. What they looked like when she loved anybody, I do not know; for I never heard of her loving anybody but herself, and I do not think she could have managed that if she had not somehow got used to herself. But what made it highly imprudent in the king to forget her was—that she was awfully clever. In fact, she was a witch; and when she bewitched anybody, he very soon had enough of it; for she beat all the wicked fairies in wickedness, and all the clever ones in cleverness. She despised all the modes we read of in history, in which offended fairies and witches have taken their revenges; and therefore, after waiting and waiting in vain for an invitation, she made up her mind at last to go without one, and make the whole family miserable, like a princess as she was.

So she put on her best gown, went to the palace, was kindly received by the happy monarch, who forgot that he had forgotten her, and took her place in the procession to the royal chapel. When they were all gathered about the font, she contrived to get next to it, and throw something into the water; after which she maintained a very respectful demeanour till the water was applied to the child's face. But at that moment she turned round in her place three times, and muttered the following words, loud enough for those beside her to hear:—

> "Light of spirit, by my charms,
>   Light of body, every part,
> Never weary human arms—
>   Only crush thy parents' heart!"

They all thought she had lost her wits, and was repeating some foolish nursery rhyme; but a shudder went through the whole of them notwithstanding. The baby, on the contrary, began to laugh and crow; while the nurse gave a start and a smothered cry, for she thought she was struck with paralysis: she could not feel the baby in her arms. But she clasped it tight and said nothing.

The mischief was done.

III. SHE CAN'T BE OURS.

Her atrocious aunt had deprived the child of all her gravity. If you ask me how this was effected, I answer, "In the easiest way in the world. She had only to destroy gravitation." For the princess was a philosopher, and knew all the *ins* and *outs* of the laws of gravitation as well as the *ins* and *outs* of her boot-lace. And being a witch as well, she could abrogate those laws in a moment; or at least so clog their wheels and rust their bearings, that they would not work at all. But we have more to do with what followed than with how it was done.

The first awkwardness that resulted from this unhappy privation was, that the moment the nurse began to float the baby up and down, she flew from her arms towards the ceiling. Happily, the resistance of the air brought her ascending career to a close within a foot of it. There she remained, horizontal as when she left her nurse's arms, kicking and laughing amazingly. The nurse in terror flew to the bell, and begged the footman, who answered it, to bring up the house-steps directly. Trembling in every limb, she climbed upon the steps, and had to stand upon the very top, and reach up, before she could catch the floating tail of the baby's long clothes.

When the strange fact came to be known, there was a terrible commotion in the palace. The occasion of its discovery by the king was naturally a repetition of the nurse's experience. Astonished that he felt no weight when the child was laid in his arms, he began to wave her up and—not down; for she slowly ascended to the ceiling as before, and there remained floating in perfect comfort and satisfaction, as was testified by her peals of tiny laughter. The king stood staring up in speechless amazement, and trembled so that his beard shook like grass in the wind. At last, turning to the queen, who was just as horror-struck as himself, he said, gasping, staring, and stammering,—

"She *can't* be ours, queen!"

Now the queen was much cleverer than the king, and had begun already to suspect that "this effect defective came by cause."[1]

"I am sure she is ours," answered she. "But we ought to have taken better care of her at the christening. People who were never invited ought not to have been present."

"Oh, ho!" said the king, tapping his forehead with his forefinger, "I have it all. I've found her out. Don't you see it, queen? Princess Makemnoit has bewitched her."

"That's just what I say," answered the queen.

"I beg your pardon, my love; I did not hear you.—John! bring the steps I get on my throne with."

For he was a little king with a great throne, like many other kings.

The throne-steps were brought, and set upon the dining-table, and John got upon the top of them. But he could not reach the little princess, who lay like a baby-laughter-cloud in the air, exploding continuously.

"Take the tongs, John," said his Majesty; and getting up on the table, he handed them to him.

John could reach the baby now, and the little princess was handed down by the tongs.

---

1 Shakespeare, *Hamlet* II.ii.101-03: Polonius "Find out the cause of this effect, / Or rather say, the cause of this defect / For this effect defective comes by cause."

IV. WHERE IS SHE?

One fine summer day, a month after these her first adventures, during which time she had been very carefully watched, the princess was lying on the bed in the queen's own chamber, fast asleep. One of the windows was open, for it was noon, and the day so sultry that the little girl was wrapped in nothing less ethereal than slumber itself. The queen came into the room, and not observing that the baby was on the bed, opened another window. A frolicsome fairy wind, which had been watching for a chance of mischief, rushed in at the one window, and taking its way over the bed where the child was lying, caught her up, and rolling and floating her along like a piece of flue,[1] or a dandelion-seed, carried her with it through the opposite window, and away. The queen went down-stairs, quite ignorant of the loss she had herself occasioned.

When the nurse returned, she supposed that her Majesty had carried her off, and, dreading a scolding, delayed making inquiry about her. But hearing nothing, she grew uneasy, and went at length to the queen's boudoir, where she found her Majesty.

"Please, your Majesty, shall I take the baby?" said she.

"Where is she?" asked the queen.

"Please forgive me. I know it was wrong."

"What do you mean?" said the queen, looking grave.

"Oh! don't frighten me, your Majesty!" exclaimed the nurse, clasping her hands.

The queen saw that something was amiss, and fell down in a faint. The nurse rushed about the palace, screaming, "My baby! my baby!"

Every one ran to the queen's room. But the queen could give no orders. They soon found out, however, that the princess was missing, and in a moment the palace was like a beehive in a garden; and in one minute more the queen was brought to herself by a great shout and a clapping of hands. They had found the princess fast asleep under a rose-bush, to which the elvish little wind-puff had carried her, finishing its mischief by shaking a shower of red rose-leaves all over the little white sleeper. Startled by the noise the servants made, she woke, and, furious with glee, scattered the rose-leaves in all directions, like a shower of spray in the sunset.

---

1 Floating bits of cotton, down, or fluff, hence generally "any light, floating particle" (*OED*).

She was watched more carefully after this, no doubt; yet it would be endless to relate all the odd incidents resulting from this peculiarity of the young princess. But there never was a baby in a house, not to say a palace, that kept the household in such constant good-humour, at least below-stairs. If it was not easy for her nurses to hold her, at least she made neither their arms nor their hearts ache. And she was so nice to play at ball with! There was positively no danger of letting her fall. They might throw her down, or knock her down, or push her down, but couldn't *let* her down. It is true, they might let her fly into the fire or the coal-hole, or through the window; but none of these accidents had happened as yet. If you heard peals of laughter resounding from some unknown region, you might be sure enough of the cause. Going down into the kitchen, or *the room*, you would find Jane and Thomas, and Robert and Susan, all and sum, playing at ball with the little princess. She was the ball herself, and did not enjoy it the less for that. Away she went, flying from one to another, screeching with laughter. And the servants loved the ball itself better even than the game. But they had to take some care how they threw her, for if she received an upward direction, she would never come down again without being fetched.

V. WHAT IS TO BE DONE?

But above-stairs it was different. One day, for instance, after breakfast, the king went into his counting-house, and counted out his money.[1]

The operation gave him no pleasure.

"To think," said he to himself, "that every one of these gold sovereigns weighs a quarter of an ounce, and my real, live, flesh-and-blood princess weighs nothing at all!"

And he hated his gold sovereigns, as they lay with a broad smile of self-satisfaction all over their yellow faces.

---

1 A reference to the beginning of an extended allusion to the nursery rhyme "Sing a Song of Sixpence," the third quatrain of which reads,

> The king was in his counting house,
> Counting out his money;
> The queen was in the parlour,
> Eating bread and honey.

The queen was in the parlour, eating bread and honey. But at the second mouthful she burst out crying, and could not swallow it. The king heard her sobbing. Glad of anybody, but especially of his queen, to quarrel with, he clashed his gold sovereigns into his money-box, clapped his crown on his head, and rushed into the parlour.

"What is all this about?" exclaimed he. "What are you crying for, queen?"

"I can't eat it," said the queen, looking ruefully at the honey-pot.

"No wonder!" retorted the king. "You've just eaten your breakfast—two turkey eggs, and three anchovies."

"Oh, that's not it!" sobbed her Majesty. "It's my child, my child!"

"Well, what's the matter with your child? She's neither up the chimney nor down the draw-well. Just hear her laughing."

Yet the king could not help a sigh, which he tried to turn into a cough, saying,—

"It is a good thing to be light-hearted, I am sure, whether she be ours or not."

"It is a bad thing to be light-headed," answered the queen, looking with prophetic soul far into the future.

"'Tis a good thing to be light-handed," said the king.

"'Tis a bad thing to be light-fingered," answered the queen.

"'Tis a good thing to be light-footed," said the king.

"'Tis a bad thing—" began the queen; but the king interrupted her.

"In fact," said he, with the tone of one who concludes an argument in which he has had only imaginary opponents, and in which, therefore, he has come off triumphant—"in fact, it is a good thing altogether to be light-bodied."

"But it is a bad thing altogether to be light-minded," retorted the queen, who was beginning to lose her temper.

This last answer quite discomfited his Majesty, who turned on his heel, and betook himself to his counting-house again. But he was not half-way towards it, when the voice of his queen overtook him.

"And it's a bad thing to be light-haired," screamed she, determined to have more last words, now that her spirit was roused.

The queen's hair was black as night; and the king's had been, and his daughter's was, golden as morning. But it was not this reflection on his hair that arrested him; it was the double use of the word *light*. For the king hated all witticisms, and punning especially. And besides, he could not tell whether the queen meant light-*haired* or light-*heired*; for why might she not aspirate her vowels when she was ex-asperated herself?

He turned upon his other heel, and rejoined her. She looked angry still, because she knew that she was guilty, or, what was much the same, knew that he thought so.

"My dear queen," said he, "duplicity of any sort is exceedingly objectionable between married people of any rank, not to say kings and queens; and the most objectionable form duplicity can assume is that of punning."

"There!" said the queen, "I never made a jest, but I broke it in the making. I am the most unfortunate woman in the world!"

She looked so rueful, that the king took her in his arms; and they sat down to consult.

"Can you bear this?" said the king.

"No, I can't," said the queen.

"Well, what's to be done?" said the king.

"I'm sure I don't know," said the queen. "But might you not try an apology?"

"To my old sister, I suppose you mean?" said the king.

"Yes," said the queen.

"Well, I don't mind," said the king.

So he went the next morning to the house of the princess, and, making a very humble apology, begged her to undo the spell. But the princess declared, with a grave face, that she knew nothing at all about it. Her eyes, however, shone pink, which was a sign that she was happy. She advised the king and queen to have patience, and to mend their ways. The king returned disconsolate. The queen tried to comfort him.

"We will wait till she is older. She may then be able to suggest something herself. She will know at least how she feels, and explain things to us."

"But what if she should marry?" exclaimed the king, in sudden consternation at the idea.

"Well, what of that?" rejoined the queen.

"Just think! If she were to have children! In the course of a hundred years the air might be as full of floating children as of gossamers in autumn."

"That is no business of ours," replied the queen. "Besides, by that time they will have learned to take care of themselves."

A sigh was the king's only answer.

He would have consulted the court physicians; but he was afraid they would try experiments upon her.

VI. SHE LAUGHS TOO MUCH.

Meantime, notwithstanding awkward occurrences, and griefs that she brought upon her parents, the little princess laughed and grew—not fat, but plump and tall. She reached the age of seventeen, without having fallen into any worse scrape than a chimney; by rescuing her from which, a little bird-nesting urchin got fame and a black face. Nor, thoughtless as she was, had she committed anything worse than laughter at everybody and everything that came in her way. When she was told, for the sake of experiment, that General Clanrunfort was cut to pieces with all his troops, she laughed; when she heard that the enemy was on his way to besiege her papa's capital, she laughed hugely; but when she was told that the city would certainly be abandoned to the mercy of the enemy's soldiery—why, then she laughed immoderately. She never could be brought to see the serious side of anything. When her mother cried, she said,—

"What queer faces mamma makes! And she squeezes water out of her cheeks! Funny mamma!"

And when her papa stormed at her, she laughed, and danced round and round him, clapping her hands, and crying,—

"Do it again, papa. Do it again! It's such fun! Dear, funny papa!"

And if he tried to catch her, she glided from him in an instant, not in the least afraid of him, but thinking it part of the game not to be caught. With one push of her foot, she would be floating in the air above his head; or she would go dancing backwards and forwards and sideways, like a great butterfly. It happened several times, when her father and mother were holding a consultation about her in private, that they were interrupted by vainly repressed outbursts of laughter over their heads; and looking up with indignation, saw her floating at full length in the air above them, whence she regarded them with the most comical appreciation of the position.

One day an awkward accident happened. The princess had come out upon the lawn with one of her attendants, who held her by the hand. Spying her father at the other side of the lawn, she snatched her hand from the maid's, and sped across to him. Now when she wanted to run alone, her custom was to catch up a stone in each hand, so that she might come down again after a bound. Whatever she wore as part of her attire had no effect in this way: even gold, when it thus became as it were a part of herself, lost all its weight for the time. But whatever she only held in her hands retained its downward tendency. On this occasion she could see nothing to catch up but a huge toad, that was walking across the lawn as if he had a hundred years to do it in. Not knowing what disgust meant, for this was one of her peculiarities, she snatched up the toad and bounded away. She had almost reached her father, and he was holding out his arms to receive her, and take from her lips the kiss which hovered on them like a butterfly on a rosebud, when a puff of wind blew her aside into the arms of a young page, who had just been receiving a message from his Majesty. Now it was no great peculiarity in the princess that, once she was set agoing, it always cost her time and trouble to check herself. On this occasion there was no time. She *must* kiss—and she kissed the page. She did not mind it much; for she had no shyness in her composition; and she knew, besides, that she could not help it. So she only laughed, like a musical box. The poor page fared the worst. For the princess, trying to correct the unfortunate tendency of the kiss, put out her hands to keep her off the page; so that, along with the kiss, he received, on the other cheek, a slap with the huge black toad, which she poked right into his eye. He tried to laugh, too, but the attempt resulted in such an odd contortion of countenance, as showed that there was no danger of his pluming himself on the kiss. As for the king, his dignity was greatly hurt, and he did not speak to the page for a whole month.

I may here remark that it was very amusing to see her run, if her mode of progression could properly be called running. For first she would make a bound; then, having alighted, she would run a few steps, and make another bound. Sometimes she would fancy she had reached the ground before she actually had, and her feet would go backwards and forwards, running upon nothing at all, like those of a chicken on its back. Then she would laugh like the very spirit of fun; only in her laugh there was something missing. What it was, I find myself unable to describe. I think it was a certain tone, depending upon the possibility of sorrow—*morbidezza*,[1] perhaps. She never smiled.

---

1   "Delicacy, softness, esp. in musical performance; sensibility, smoothness. Also occas. with negative connotation: unwholesomeness, effeminacy, sickliness" (*OED*).

VII. TRY METAPHYSICS.[1]

After a long avoidance of the painful subject, the king and queen resolved to hold a council of three upon it; and so they sent for the princess. In she came, sliding and flitting and gliding from one piece of furniture to another, and put herself at last in an arm-chair, in a sitting posture. Whether she could be said *to sit*, seeing she received no support from the seat of the chair, I do not pretend to determine.

"My dear child," said the king, "you must be aware by this time that you are not exactly like other people."

"Oh, you dear funny papa! I have got a nose, and two eyes, and all the rest. So have you. So has mamma."

"Now be serious, my dear, for once," said the queen.

"No, thank you, mamma; I had rather not."

"Would you not like to be able to walk like other people?" said the king.

"No indeed, I should think not. You only crawl. You are such slow coaches!"

"How do you feel, my child?" he resumed, after a pause of discomfiture.

"Quite well, thank you."

"I mean, what do you feel like?"

"Like nothing at all, that I know of."

"You must feel like something."

"I feel like a princess with such a funny papa, and such a dear pet of a queen-mamma!"

"Now really!" began the queen; but the princess interrupted her.

"Oh yes," she added, "I remember. I have a curious feeling sometimes, as if I were the only person that had any sense in the whole world."

She had been trying to behave herself with dignity; but now she burst into a violent fit of laughter, threw herself backwards over the chair, and went rolling about the floor in an ecstasy of enjoyment. The king picked her up easier than one does a down quilt, and replaced her in her former relation to the chair. The

---

1 "The branch of philosophy that deals with the first principles of things or reality, including questions about being, substance, time and space, causation, change, and identity (which are presupposed in the special sciences but do not belong to any one of them); theoretical philosophy as the ultimate science of being and knowing" (*OED*).

exact preposition expressing this relation I do not happen to know.

"Is there nothing you wish for?" resumed the king, who had learned by this time that it was quite useless to be angry with her.

"Oh, you dear papa!—yes," answered she.

"What is it, my darling?"

"I have been longing for it—oh, such a time! Ever since last night."

"Tell me what it is."

"Will you promise to let me have it?"

The king was on the point of saying *Yes*; but the wiser queen checked him with a single motion of her head.

"Tell me what it is first," said he.

"No, no. Promise first."

"I dare not. What is it?"

"Mind, I hold you to your promise.—It is—to be tied to the end of a string—a very long string indeed, and be flown like a kite. Oh, such fun! I would rain rose-water, and hail sugar-plums, and snow whipped-cream, and—and—and—"

A fit of laughing checked her; and she would have been off again over the floor, had not the king started up and caught her just in time. Seeing that nothing but talk could be got out of her, he rang the bell, and sent her away with two of her ladies-in-waiting.

"Now, queen," he said, turning to her Majesty, "what *is* to be done?"

"There is but one thing left," answered she. "Let us consult the college of Metaphysicians."

"Bravo!" cried the king; "we will."

Now at the head of this college were two very wise Chinese philosophers—by name, Hum-Drum and Kopy-Keck. For them the king sent; and straightway they came. In a long speech he communicated to them what they knew very well already—as who did not?—namely, the peculiar condition of his daughter in relation to the globe on which she dwelt; and requested them to consult together as to what might be the cause and probable cure of her *infirmity*. The king laid stress upon the word, but failed to discover his own pun. The queen laughed; but Hum-Drum and Kopy-Keck heard with humility and retired in silence.

Their consultation consisted chiefly in propounding and supporting, for the thousandth time, each his favourite theories. For the condition of the princess afforded delightful scope for the discussion of every question arising from the division of thought—

in fact, of all the Metaphysics of the Chinese Empire. But it is only justice to say that they did not altogether neglect the discussion of the practical question, *what was to be done*.

Hum-Drum was a Materialist, and Kopy-Keck was a Spiritualist. The former was slow and sententious; the latter was quick and flighty: the latter had generally the first word; the former the last.

"I reassert my former assertion," began Kopy-Keck, with a plunge. "There is not a fault in the princess, body or soul; only they are wrong put together. Listen to me now, Hum-Drum, and I will tell you in brief what I think. Don't speak. Don't answer me. I *won't* hear you till I have done.—At that decisive moment, when souls seek their appointed habitations, two eager souls met, struck, rebounded, lost their way, and arrived each at the wrong place. The soul of the princess was one of those, and she went far astray. She does not belong by rights to this world at all, but to some other planet, probably Mercury. Her proclivity to her true sphere destroys all the natural influence which this orb would otherwise possess over her corporeal frame. She cares for nothing here. There is no relation between her and this world.

"She must therefore be taught, by the sternest compulsion, to take an interest in the earth as the earth. She must study every department of its history—its animal history; its vegetable history; its mineral history; its social history; its moral history; its political history; its scientific history; its literary history; its musical history; its artistical history; above all, its metaphysical history. She must begin with the Chinese dynasty and end with Japan. But first of all she must study geology, and especially the history of the extinct races of animals—their natures, their habits, their loves, their hates, their revenges. She must—"

"Hold, h-o-o-old!" roared Hum-Drum. "It is certainly my turn now. My rooted and insubvertible conviction is, that the causes of the anomalies evident in the princess's condition are strictly and solely physical. But that is only tantamount to acknowledging that they exist. Hear my opinion.—From some cause or other, of no importance to our inquiry, the motion of her heart has been reversed. That remarkable combination of the suction and the force-pump works the wrong way—I mean in the case of the unfortunate princess: it draws in where it should force out, and forces out where it should draw in. The offices of the auricles and the ventricles are subverted. The blood is sent forth by the veins, and returns by the arteries. Consequently it is running the wrong way through all her corporeal organism—

lungs and all. Is it then at all mysterious, seeing that such is the case, that on the other particular of gravitation as well, she should differ from normal humanity? My proposal for the cure is this:—

"Phlebotomize[1] until she is reduced to the last point of safety. Let it be effected, if necessary, in a warm bath. When she is reduced to a state of perfect asphyxy, apply a ligature to the left ankle, drawing it as tight as the bone will bear. Apply, at the same moment, another of equal tension around the right wrist. By means of plates constructed for the purpose, place the other foot and hand under the receivers of two air-pumps. Exhaust the receivers.[2] Exhibit a pint of French brandy, and await the result."

"Which would presently arrive in the form of grim Death," said Kopy-Keck.

"If it should, she would yet die in doing our duty," retorted Hum-Drum.

But their Majesties had too much tenderness for their volatile offspring to subject her to either of the schemes of the equally unscrupulous philosophers. Indeed, the most complete knowledge of the laws of nature would have been unserviceable in her case; for it was impossible to classify her. She was a fifth imponderable body, sharing all the other properties of the ponderable.

VIII. TRY A DROP OF WATER.

Perhaps the best thing for the princess would have been to fall in love. But how a princess who had no gravity could fall into anything is a difficulty—perhaps *the* difficulty. As for her own feelings on the subject, she did not even know that there was such a beehive of honey and stings to be fallen into. But now I come to mention another curious fact about her.

The palace was built on the shore of the loveliest lake in the world; and the princess loved this lake more than father or mother. The root of this preference no doubt, although the princess did not recognize it as such, was, that the moment she

---

1 A "phlebotomy" is "the action or practice of extracting blood from a vein for therapeutic or diagnostic purposes (originally by surgical incision of the vein, later by means of a needle and syringe, cannula, etc.)" (*OED*).

2 Early experiments with the elements of air involved the use of large glass vessels or receivers that could be used to create a vacuum by means of air pumps.

got into it, she recovered the natural right of which she had been so wickedly deprived—namely, gravity. Whether this was owing to the fact that water had been employed as the means of conveying the injury, I do not know. But it is certain that she could swim and dive like the duck that her old nurse said she was. The manner in which this alleviation of her misfortune was discovered was as follows.

One summer evening, during the carnival of the country, she had been taken upon the lake by the king and queen, in the royal barge. They were accompanied by many of the courtiers in a fleet of little boats. In the middle of the lake she wanted to get into the lord chancellor's barge, for his daughter, who was a great favourite with her, was in it with her father. Now though the old king rarely condescended to make light of his misfortune, yet, happening on this occasion to be in a particularly good humour, as the barges approached each other, he caught up the princess to throw her into the chancellor's barge. He lost his balance, however, and, dropping into the bottom of the barge, lost his hold of his daughter; not, however, before imparting to her the downward tendency of his own person, though in a somewhat different direction; for, as the king fell into the boat, she fell into the water. With a burst of delighted laughter she disappeared in the lake. A cry of horror ascended from the boats. They had never seen the princess go down before. Half the men were under water in a moment; but they had all, one after another, come up to the surface again for breath, when—tinkle, tinkle, babble, and gush! came the princess's laugh over the water from far away. There she was, swimming like a swan. Nor would she come out for king or queen, chancellor or daughter. She was perfectly obstinate.

But at the same time she seemed more sedate than usual. Perhaps that was because a great pleasure spoils laughing. At all events, after this, the passion of her life was to get into the water, and she was always the better behaved and the more beautiful the more she had of it. Summer and winter it was quite the same; only she could not stay so long in the water when they had to break the ice to let her in. Any day, from morning till evening in summer, she might be descried—a streak of white in the blue water—lying as still as the shadow of a cloud, or shooting along like a dolphin; disappearing, and coming up again far off, just where one did not expect her. She would have been in the lake of a night too, if she could have had her way; for the balcony of her window overhung a deep pool in it; and through a shallow reedy passage she could have swum out into the wide wet water, and no one would have been any the wiser. Indeed, when she happened to wake in the moonlight, she could hardly resist the temptation. But there was the sad difficulty of getting into it. She had as great a dread of the air as some children have of the water. For the slightest gust of wind would blow her away; and a gust might arise in the stillest moment. And if she gave herself a push towards the water and just failed of reaching it, her situation would be dreadfully awkward, irrespective of the wind; for at best there she would have to remain, suspended in her night-gown, till she was seen and angled for by somebody from the window.

"Oh! if I had my gravity," thought she, contemplating the water, "I would flash off this balcony like a long white sea-bird, headlong into the darling wetness. Heigh-ho!"

This was the only consideration that made her wish to be like other people.

Another reason for her being fond of the water was that in it alone she enjoyed any freedom. For she could not walk out without a *cortège*, consisting in part of a troop of light horse, for fear of the liberties which the wind might take with her. And the king grew more apprehensive with increasing years, till at last he would not allow her to walk abroad at all without some twenty silken cords fastened to as many parts of her dress, and held by twenty noblemen. Of course horseback was out of the question. But she bade good-bye to all this ceremony when she got into the water.

And so remarkable were its effects upon her, especially in restoring her for the time to the ordinary human gravity, that Hum-Drum and Kopy-Keck agreed in recommending the king to bury her alive for three years; in the hope that, as the water did her so much good, the earth would do her yet more. But the king had some vulgar prejudices against the experiment, and would not give his consent. Foiled in this, they yet agreed in another recommendation; which, seeing that the one imported his opinions from China and the other from Thibet, was very remarkable indeed. They argued that, if water of external origin and application could be so efficacious, water from a deeper source might work a perfect cure; in short, that if the poor afflicted princess could by any means be made to cry, she might recover her lost gravity.

But how was this to be brought about? Therein lay all the difficulty—to meet which the philosophers were not wise enough. To make the princess cry was as impossible as to make her weigh. They sent for a professional beggar; commanded him to prepare his most touching oracle of woe; helped him, out of the court charade-box, to whatever he wanted for dressing up, and promised great rewards in the event of his success. But it was all in vain. She listened to the mendicant artist's story, and gazed at his marvellous make-up, till she could contain herself no longer, and went into the most undignified contortions for relief, shrieking, positively screeching with laughter.

When she had a little recovered herself, she ordered her attendants to drive him away, and not give him a single copper; whereupon his look of mortified discomfiture wrought her punishment and his revenge, for it sent her into violent hysterics, from which she was with difficulty recovered.

But so anxious was the king that the suggestion should have a fair trial, that he put himself in a rage one day, and, rushing up to her room, gave her an awful whipping. Yet not a tear would flow. She looked grave, and her laughing sounded uncommonly like screaming—that was all. The good old tyrant, though he put on his best gold spectacles to look, could not discover the smallest cloud in the serene blue of her eyes.

IX. PUT ME IN AGAIN.

It must have been about this time that the son of a king, who lived a thousand miles from Lagobel, set out to look for the daughter of a queen. He travelled far and wide, but as sure as he found a princess, he found some fault in her. Of course he could not marry a mere woman, however beautiful; and there was no princess to be found worthy of him. Whether the prince was so near perfection that he had a right to demand perfection itself, I cannot pretend to say. All I know is, that he was a fine, handsome, brave, generous, well-bred, and well-behaved youth, as all princes are.

In his wanderings he had come across some reports about our princess; but as everybody said she was bewitched, he never dreamed that she could bewitch him. For what indeed could a prince do with a princess that had lost her gravity? Who could tell what she might not lose next? She might lose her visibility, or her tangibility; or, in short, the power of making impressions upon the radical sensorium; so that he should never be able to tell whether she was dead or alive. Of course he made no further inquiries about her.

One day he lost sight of his retinue in a great forest. These forests are very useful in delivering princes from their courtiers, like a sieve that keeps back the bran. Then the princes get away to follow their fortunes. In this they have the advantage of the princesses, who are forced to marry before they have had a bit of fun. I wish our princesses got lost in a forest sometimes.

One lovely evening, after wandering about for many days, he found that he was approaching the outskirts of this forest; for the trees had got so thin that he could see the sunset through them; and he soon came upon a kind of heath. Next he came upon signs of human neighbourhood; but by this time it was getting late, and there was nobody in the fields to direct him.

After travelling for another hour, his horse, quite worn out with long labour and lack of food, fell, and was unable to rise again. So he continued his journey on foot. At length he entered another wood—not a wild forest, but a civilized wood, through which a footpath led him to the side of a lake. Along this path the prince pursued his way through the gathering darkness. Suddenly he paused, and listened. Strange sounds came across the water. It was, in fact, the princess laughing. Now there was something odd in her laugh, as I have already hinted, for the hatching of a real hearty laugh requires the incubation of gravity; and perhaps this was how the prince mistook the laughter for screaming. Looking over the lake, he saw something white in the water; and, in an instant, he had torn off his tunic, kicked off his sandals, and plunged in. He soon reached the white object, and found that it was a woman. There was not light enough to show that she was a princess, but quite enough to show that she was a lady, for it does not want much light to see that.

Now I cannot tell how it came about,—whether she pretended to be drowning, or whether he frightened her, or caught her so as to embarrass her,—but certainly he brought her to shore in a fashion ignominious to a swimmer, and more nearly drowned than she had ever expected to be; for the water had got into her throat as often as she had tried to speak.

At the place to which he bore her, the bank was only a foot or two above the water; so he gave her a strong lift out of the water, to lay her on the bank. But, her gravitation ceasing the moment she left the water, away she went up into the air, scolding and screaming.

"You naughty, *naughty*, NAUGHTY, NAUGHTY man!" she cried.

No one had ever succeeded in putting her into a passion before.—When the prince saw her ascend, he thought he must have been bewitched, and have mistaken a great swan for a lady.

But the princess caught hold of the topmost cone upon a lofty fir. This came off; but she caught at another; and, in fact, stopped herself by gathering cones, dropping them as the stocks gave way. The prince, meantime, stood in the water, staring, and forgetting to get out. But the princess disappearing, he scrambled on shore, and went in the direction of the tree. There he found her climbing down one of the branches towards the stem. But in the darkness of the wood, the prince continued in some bewilderment as to what the phenomenon could be; until, reaching the ground, and seeing him standing there, she caught hold of him, and said,—

"I'll tell papa."

"Oh no, you won't!" returned the prince.

"Yes, I will," she persisted. "What business had you to pull me down out of the water, and throw me to the bottom of the air? I never did you any harm."

"Pardon me. I did not mean to hurt you."

"I don't believe you have any brains; and that is a worse loss than your wretched gravity. I pity you."

The prince now saw that he had come upon the bewitched princess, and had already offended her. But before he could think what to say next, she burst out angrily, giving a stamp with her foot that would have sent her aloft again but for the hold she had of his arm,—

"Put me up directly."

"Put you up where, you beauty?" asked the prince.

He had fallen in love with her almost, already; for her anger made her more charming than any one else had ever beheld her; and, as far as he could see, which certainly was not far, she had not a single fault about her, except, of course, that she had not any gravity. No prince, however, would judge of a princess by weight. The loveliness of her foot he would hardly estimate by the depth of the impression it could make in mud.

"Put you up where, you beauty?" asked the prince.

"In the water, you stupid!" answered the princess.

"Come, then," said the prince.

The condition of her dress, increasing her usual difficulty in walking, compelled her to cling to him; and he could hardly persuade himself that he was not in a delightful dream, notwithstanding the torrent of musical abuse with which she overwhelmed him. The prince being therefore in no hurry, they came upon the lake at quite another part, where the bank was twenty-five feet high at least; and when they had reached the edge, he turned towards the princess, and said,—

"How am I to put you in?"

"That is your business," she answered, quite snappishly. "You took me out—put me in again."

"Very well," said the prince; and, catching her up in his arms, he sprang with her from the rock. The princess had just time to give one delighted shriek of laughter before the water closed over them. When they came to the surface, she found that, for a moment or two, she could not even laugh, for she had gone down with such a rush, that it was with difficulty she recovered her breath. The instant they reached the surface—

"How do you like falling in?" said the prince.

After some effort the princess panted out,—

"Is that what you call *falling in*?"

"Yes," answered the prince, "I should think it a very tolerable specimen."

"It seemed to me like going up," rejoined she.

"My feeling was certainly one of elevation too," the prince conceded.

The princess did not appear to understand him, for she retorted his question:—

"How do *you* like falling in?" said the princess.

"Beyond everything," answered he; "for I have fallen in with the only perfect creature I ever saw."

"No more of that: I am tired of it," said the princess.

Perhaps she shared her father's aversion to punning.

"Don't you like falling in, then?" said the prince.

"It is the most delightful fun I ever had in my life," answered she. "I never fell before. I wish I could learn. To think I am the only person in my father's kingdom that can't fall!"

Here the poor princess looked almost sad.

"I shall be most happy to fall in with you any time you like," said the prince, devotedly.

"Thank you. I don't know. Perhaps it would not be proper. But I don't care. At all events, as we have fallen in, let us have a swim together."

"With all my heart," responded the prince.

And away they went, swimming, and diving, and floating, until at last they heard cries along the shore, and saw lights glancing in all directions. It was now quite late, and there was no moon.

"I must go home," said the princess. "I am very sorry, for this is delightful."

"So am I," returned the prince. "But I am glad I haven't a home to go to—at least, I don't exactly know where it is."

"I wish I hadn't one either," rejoined the princess; "it is so stupid! I have a great mind," she continued, "to play them all a trick. Why couldn't they leave me alone? They won't trust me in the lake for a single night!—You see where that green light is burning? That is the window of my room. Now if you would just swim there with me very quietly, and when we are all but under the balcony, give me such a push—*up* you call it—as you did a little while ago, I should be able to catch hold of the balcony, and get in at the window; and then they may look for me till to-morrow morning!"

"With more obedience than pleasure," said the prince, gallantly; and away they swam, very gently.

"Will you be in the lake to-morrow-night?" the prince ventured to ask.

"To be sure I will. I don't think so. Perhaps," was the princess's somewhat strange answer.

But the prince was intelligent enough not to press her further; and merely whispered, as he gave her the parting lift, "Don't tell." The only answer the princess returned was a roguish look. She was already a yard above his head. The look seemed to say, "Never fear. It is too good fun to spoil that way."

So perfectly like other people had she been in the water, that even yet the prince could scarcely believe his eyes when he saw her ascend slowly, grasp the balcony, and disappear through the window. He turned, almost expecting to see her still by his side. But he was alone in the water. So he swam away quietly, and watched the lights roving about the shore for hours after the princess was safe in her chamber. As soon as they disappeared, he landed in search of his tunic and sword, and, after some trouble, found them again. Then he made the best of his way round the lake to the other side. There the wood was wilder, and the shore steeper—rising more immediately towards the mountains which surrounded the lake on all sides, and kept sending it messages of silvery streams from morning to night, and all night long. He soon found a spot whence he could see the green light in the princess's room, and where, even in the broad daylight, he would be in no danger of being discovered from the opposite shore. It was a sort of cave in the rock, where he provided himself a bed of withered leaves, and lay down too tired for hunger to keep him awake. All night long he dreamed that he was swimming with the princess.

X. LOOK AT THE MOON.

Early the next morning the prince set out to look for something to eat, which he soon found at a forester's hut, where for many following days he was supplied with all that a brave prince could consider necessary. And having plenty to keep him alive for the present, he would not think of wants not yet in existence. Whenever Care intruded, this prince always bowed him out in the most princely manner.

When he returned from his breakfast to his watch-cave, he saw the princess already floating about in the lake, attended by the king and queen—whom he knew by their crowns—and a great company in lovely little boats, with canopies of all the colours of the rainbow, and flags and streamers of a great many more. It was a very bright day, and soon the prince, burned up with the heat, began to long for the cold water and the cool princess. But he had to endure till twilight; for the boats had provisions on board, and it was not till the sun went down that the gay party began to vanish. Boat after boat drew away to the shore, following that of the king and queen, till only one, apparently the princess's own boat, remained. But she did not want to go home even yet, and the prince thought he saw her order the boat to the shore without her. At all events, it rowed away; and now, of all the radiant company, only one white speck remained. Then the prince began to sing. And this is what he sang:—

> "Lady fair,
> Swan-white,
> Lift thine eyes,
> Banish night
> By the might
> Of thine eyes.
>
> "Snowy arms,
> Oars of snow,
> Oar her hither,
> Plashing low.
> Soft and slow,
> Oar her hither.
>
> "Stream behind her
> O'er the lake,
> Radiant whiteness!

In her wake
Following, following for her sake,
Radiant whiteness!

"Cling about her,
Waters blue;
Part not from her,
But renew
Cold and true
Kisses round her.

"Lap me round,
Waters sad
That have left her;
Make me glad,
For ye had
Kissed her ere ye left her."

Before he had finished his song, the princess was just under the place where he sat, and looking up to find him. Her ears had led her truly.

"Would you like a fall, princess?" said the prince, looking down.

"Ah! there you are! Yes, if you please, prince," said the princess, looking up.

"How do you know I am a prince, princess?" said the prince.

"Because you are a very nice young man, prince," said the princess.

"Come up then, princess."

"Fetch me, prince."

The prince took off his scarf, then his sword-belt, then his tunic, and tied them all together, and let them down. But the line was far too short. He unwound his turban, and added it to the rest, when it was all but long enough; and his purse completed it. The princess just managed to lay hold of the knot of money, and was beside him in a moment. This rock was much higher than the other, and the splash and the dive were tremendous. The princess was in ecstasies of delight, and their swim was delicious.

Night after night they met, and swam about in the dark clear lake; where such was the prince's gladness, that (whether the princess's way of looking at things infected him, or he was actually getting light-headed) he often fancied that he was swimming in the sky instead of the lake. But when he talked about being in heaven, the princess laughed at him dreadfully.

When the moon came, she brought them fresh pleasure. Everything looked strange and new in her light, with an old, withered, yet unfading newness. When the moon was nearly full, one of their great delights was, to dive deep in the water, and then, turning round, look up through it at the great blot of light close above them, shimmering and trembling and wavering, spreading and contracting, seeming to melt away, and again grow solid. Then they would shoot up through the blot; and lo! there was the moon, far off, clear and steady and cold, and very lovely, at the bottom of a deeper and bluer lake than theirs, as the princess said.

The prince soon found out that while in the water the princess was very like other people. And besides this, she was not so forward in her questions or pert in her replies at sea as on shore. Neither did she laugh so much; and when she did laugh, it was more gently. She seemed altogether more modest and maidenly in the water than out of it. But when the prince, who had really fallen in love when he fell in the lake, began to talk to her about love, she always turned her head towards him and laughed. After a while she began to look puzzled, as if she were trying to understand what he meant, but could not—revealing a notion that he meant something. But as soon as ever she left the lake, she was so altered, that the prince said to himself, "If I marry her, I see no help for it: we must turn merman and mermaid, and go out to sea at once."

XI. HISS!

The princess's pleasure in the lake had grown to a passion, and she could scarcely bear to be out of it for an hour. Imagine then her consternation, when, diving with the prince one night, a sudden suspicion seized her that the lake was not so deep as it used to be. The prince could not imagine what had happened. She shot to the surface, and, without a word, swam at full speed towards the higher side of the lake. He followed, begging to know if she was ill, or what was the matter. She never turned her head, or took the smallest notice of his question. Arrived at the shore, she coasted the rocks with minute inspection. But she was not able to come to a conclusion, for the moon was very small, and so she could not see well. She turned therefore and swam home, without saying a word to explain her conduct to the prince, of whose presence she seemed no longer conscious. He withdrew to his cave, in great perplexity and distress.

Next day she made many observations, which, alas! strengthened her fears. She saw that the banks were too dry; and that the grass on the shore, and the trailing plants on the rocks, were withering away. She caused marks to be made along the borders, and examined them, day after day, in all directions of the wind; till at last the horrible idea became a certain fact—that the surface of the lake was slowly sinking.

The poor princess nearly went out of the little mind she had. It was awful to her to see the lake, which she loved more than any living thing, lie dying before her eyes. It sank away, slowly vanishing. The tops of rocks that had never been seen till now, began to appear far down in the clear water. Before long they were dry in the sun. It was fearful to think of the mud that would soon lie there baking and festering, full of lovely creatures dying, and ugly creatures coming to life, like the unmaking of a world. And how hot the sun would be without any lake! She could not bear to swim in it any more, and began to pine away. Her life seemed bound up with it; and ever as the lake sank, she pined. People said she would not live an hour after the lake was gone.

But she never cried.

Proclamation was made to all the kingdom, that whosoever should discover the cause of the lake's decrease, would be rewarded after a princely fashion. Hum-Drum and Kopy-Keck applied themselves to their physics and metaphysics; but in vain. Not even they could suggest a cause.

Now the fact was that the old princess was at the root of the mischief. When she heard that her niece found more pleasure in the water than anyone else out of it, she went into a rage, and cursed herself for her want of foresight.

"But," said she, "I will soon set all right. The king and the people shall die of thirst; their brains shall boil and frizzle in their skulls before I will lose my revenge."

And she laughed a ferocious laugh, that made the hairs on the back of her black cat stand erect with terror.

Then she went to an old chest in the room, and opening it, took out what looked like a piece of dried seaweed. This she threw into a tub of water. Then she threw some powder into the water, and stirred it with her bare arm, muttering over it words of hideous sound, and yet more hideous import. Then she set the tub aside, and took from the chest a huge bunch of a hundred rusty keys, that clattered in her shaking hands. Then she sat down and proceeded to oil them all. Before she had finished, out from the tub, the water of which had kept on a slow motion ever since she had ceased stirring it, came the head and half the body of a huge gray snake. But the witch did not look round. It grew out of the tub, waving itself backwards and forwards with a slow horizontal motion, till it reached the princess, when it laid its head upon her shoulder, and gave a low hiss in her ear. She started—but with joy; and seeing the head resting on her shoulder, drew it towards her and kissed it. Then she drew it all out of the tub, and wound it round her body. It was one of those dreadful creatures which few have ever beheld—the White Snakes of Darkness.

Then she took the keys and went down to her cellar; and as she unlocked the door she said to herself,—

"This *is* worth living for!"

Locking the door behind her, she descended a few steps into the cellar, and crossing it, unlocked another door into a dark, narrow passage. She locked this also behind her, and descended a few more steps. If any one had followed the witch-princess, he would have heard her unlock exactly one hundred doors, and descend a few steps after unlocking each. When she had unlocked the last, she entered a vast cave, the roof of which was supported by huge natural pillars of rock. Now this roof was the under side of the bottom of the lake.

She then untwined the snake from her body, and held it by the tail high above her. The hideous creature stretched up its head towards the roof of the cavern, which it was just able to reach. It then began to move its head backwards and forwards, with a slow oscillating motion, as if looking for something. At the same moment the witch began to walk round and round the cavern, coming nearer to the centre every circuit; while the head of the snake described the same path over the roof that she did over the floor, for she kept holding it up. And still it kept slowly oscillating. Round and round the cavern they went, ever lessening the circuit, till at last the snake made a sudden dart, and clung to the roof with its mouth.

"That's right, my beauty!" cried the princess; "drain it dry."

She let it go, left it hanging, and sat down on a great stone, with her black cat, which had followed her all round the cave, by her side. Then she began to knit and mutter awful words. The snake hung like a huge leech, sucking at the stone; the cat stood with his back arched, and his tail like a piece of cable, looking up at the snake; and the old woman sat and knitted and muttered. Seven days and seven nights they remained thus; when suddenly the serpent dropped from the roof as if exhausted, and shrivelled up till it was again like a piece of dried seaweed. The witch started to her feet, picked it up, put it in her pocket, and looked up at the roof. One drop of water was trembling on the spot where the snake had been sucking. As soon as she saw that, she turned and fled, followed by her cat. Shutting the door in a terrible hurry, she locked it, and having muttered some frightful words, sped to the next, which also she locked and muttered over; and so with all the hundred doors, till she arrived in her own cellar. There she sat down on the floor ready to faint, but listening with malicious delight to the rushing of the water, which she could hear distinctly through all the hundred doors.

But this was not enough. Now that she had tasted revenge, she lost her patience. Without further measures, the lake would be too long in disappearing. So the next night, with the last shred of the dying old moon rising, she took some of the water in which she had revived the snake, put it in a bottle, and set out, accompanied by her cat. Before morning she had made the entire circuit of the lake, muttering fearful words as she crossed every stream, and casting into it some of the water out of her bottle. When she had finished the circuit she muttered yet again, and flung a handful of water towards the moon. Thereupon every spring in the country ceased to throb and bubble, dying away like the pulse of a dying man. The next day there was no sound of falling water to be heard along the borders of the lake. The very courses were dry; and the mountains showed no silvery streaks down their dark sides. And not alone had the fountains of mother Earth ceased to flow; for all the babies throughout the country were crying dreadfully—only without tears.

XII. WHERE IS THE PRINCE?

Never since the night when the princess left him so abruptly had the prince had a single interview with her. He had seen her once or twice in the lake; but as far as he could discover, she had not been in it any more at night. He had sat and sung, and looked in vain for his Nereid; while she, like a true Nereid, was wasting away with her lake, sinking as it sank, withering as it dried. When at length he discovered the change that was taking place in the level of the water, he was in great alarm and perplexity. He could not tell whether the lake was dying because the lady had forsaken it; or whether the lady would not come because the lake had begun to sink. But he resolved to know so much at least.

He disguised himself, and, going to the palace, requested to see the lord chamberlain. His appearance at once gained his request; and the lord chamberlain, being a man of some insight, perceived that there was more in the prince's solicitation than met the ear. He felt likewise that no one could tell whence a solution of the present difficulties might arise. So he granted the prince's prayer to be made shoe-black to the princess. It was rather cunning in the prince to request such an easy post, for the princess could not possibly soil as many shoes as other princesses.

He soon learned all that could be told about the princess. He went nearly distracted; but after roaming about the lake for days, and diving in every depth that remained, all that he could do was to put an extra polish on the dainty pair of boots that was never called for.

For the princess kept her room, with the curtains drawn to shut out the dying lake. But she could not shut it out of her mind for a moment. It haunted her imagination so that she felt as if the lake were her soul, drying up within her, first to mud, then to madness and death. She thus brooded over the change, with all its dreadful accompaniments, till she was nearly distracted. As for the prince, she had forgotten him. However much she had enjoyed his company in the water, she did not care for him without it. But she seemed to have forgotten her father and mother too. The lake went on sinking. Small slimy spots began to appear, which glittered steadily amidst the changeful shine of the water. These grew to broad patches of mud, which widened and spread, with rocks here and there, and floundering fishes and crawling eels swarming. The people went everywhere catching these, and looking for anything that might have dropped from the royal boats.

At length the lake was all but gone, only a few of the deepest pools remaining unexhausted.

It happened one day that a party of youngsters found themselves on the brink of one of these pools in the very centre of the lake. It was a rocky basin of considerable depth. Looking in, they saw at the bottom something that shone yellow in the sun. A little boy jumped in and dived for it. It was a plate of gold covered with writing. They carried it to the king.

On one side of it stood these words:—

"Death alone from death can save.
Love is death, and so is brave.

Love can fill the deepest grave.
Love loves on beneath the wave."

Now this was enigmatical enough to the king and courtiers. But the reverse of the plate explained it a little. Its writing amounted to this:—

"If the lake should disappear, they must find the hole through which the water ran. But it would be useless to try to stop it by any ordinary means. There was but one effectual mode.—The body of a living man could alone stanch the flow. The man must give himself of his own will; and the lake must take his life as it filled. Otherwise the offering would be of no avail. If the nation could not provide one hero, it was time it should perish."

XIII. HERE I AM.

This was a very disheartening revelation to the king—not that he was unwilling to sacrifice a subject, but that he was hopeless of finding a man willing to sacrifice himself. No time was to be lost, however, for the princess was lying motionless on her bed, and taking no nourishment but lake-water, which was now none of the best. Therefore the king caused the contents of the wonderful plate of gold to be published throughout the country.

No one, however, came forward.

The prince, having gone several days' journey into the forest, to consult a hermit whom he had met there on his way to Lagobel, knew nothing of the oracle till his return.

When he had acquainted himself with all the particulars, he sat down and thought,—

"She will die if I don't do it, and life would be nothing to me without her; so I shall lose nothing by doing it. And life will be as pleasant to her as ever, for she will soon forget me. And there will be so much more beauty and happiness in the world!—To be sure, I shall not see it." (Here the poor prince gave a sigh.) "How lovely the lake will be in the moonlight, with that glorious creature sporting in it like a wild goddess!—It is rather hard to be drowned by inches, though. Let me see—that will be seventy inches of me to drown." (Here he tried to laugh, but could not.) "The longer the better, however," he resumed; "for can I not bargain that the princess shall be beside me all the time? So I shall see her once more, kiss her perhaps,—who knows? and die looking in her eyes. It will be no death. At least, I shall not feel it.

And to see the lake filling for the beauty again!—All right! I am ready."

He kissed the princess's boot, laid it down, and hurried to the king's apartment. But feeling, as he went, that anything sentimental would be disagreeable, he resolved to carry off the whole affair with nonchalance. So he knocked at the door of the king's counting-house, where it was all but a capital crime to disturb him.

When the king heard the knock he started up, and opened the door in a rage. Seeing only the shoeblack,[1] he drew his sword. This, I am sorry to say, was his usual mode of asserting his regality when he thought his dignity was in danger. But the prince was not in the least alarmed.

"Please your majesty, I'm your butler," said he.

"My butler! you lying rascal? What do you mean?"

"I mean, I will cork your big bottle."

"Is the fellow mad?" bawled the king, raising the point of his sword.

"I will put a stopper—plug—what you call it, in your leaky lake, grand monarch," said the prince.

The king was in such a rage that before he could speak he had time to cool, and to reflect that it would be great waste to kill the only man who was willing to be useful in the present emergency, seeing that in the end the insolent fellow would be as dead as if he had died by his majesty's own hand.

"Oh!" said he at last, putting up his sword with difficulty, it was so long; "I am obliged to you, you young fool! Take a glass of wine?"

"No, thank you," replied the prince.

"Very well," said the king. "Would you like to run and see your parents before you make your experiment?"

"No, thank you," said the prince.

"Then we will go and look for the hole at once," said his majesty, and proceeded to call some attendants.

"Stop, please your majesty; I have a condition to make," interposed the prince.

"What!" exclaimed the king, "a condition! and with me! How dare you?"

"As you please," returned the prince, coolly. "I wish your majesty a good morning."

---

1 "One who cleans boots and shoes for a livelihood" (*OED*).

"You wretch! I will have you put in a sack, and stuck in the hole."

"Very well, your majesty," replied the prince, becoming a little more respectful, lest the wrath of the king should deprive him of the pleasure of dying for the princess. "But what good will that do your majesty? Please to remember that the oracle says the victim must offer himself."

"Well, you *have* offered yourself," retorted the king.

"Yes, upon one condition."

"Condition again!" roared the king, once more drawing his sword. "Begone! Somebody else will be glad enough to take the honour off your shoulders."

"Your majesty knows it will not be easy to get another to take my place."

"Well, what is your condition?" growled the king, feeling that the prince was right.

"Only this," replied the prince: "that, as I must on no account die before I am fairly drowned, and the waiting will be rather wearisome, the princess, your daughter, shall go with me, feed me with her own hands, and look at me now and then, to comfort me; for you must confess it *is* rather hard. As soon as the water is up to my eyes, she may go and be happy, and forget her poor shoeblack."

Here the prince's voice faltered, and he very nearly grew sentimental, in spite of his resolution.

"Why didn't you tell me before what your condition was? Such a fuss about nothing!" exclaimed the king.

"Do you grant it?" persisted the prince.

"Of course I do," replied the king.

"Very well. I am ready."

"Go and have some dinner, then, while I set my people to find the place."

The king ordered out his guards, and gave directions to the officers to find the hole in the lake at once. So the bed of the lake was marked out in divisions and thoroughly examined, and in an hour or so the hole was discovered. It was in the middle of a stone, near the centre of the lake, in the very pool where the golden plate had been found. It was a three-cornered hole of no great size. There was water all round the stone, but very little was flowing through the hole.

The prince went to dress for the occasion; for he was resolved to die like a prince.

When the princess heard that a man had offered to die for her, she was so transported that she jumped off the bed, feeble as she was, and danced about the room for joy. She did not care who the man was; that was nothing to her. The hole wanted stopping; and if only a man would do, why, take one. In an hour or two more everything was ready. Her maid dressed her in haste, and they carried her to the side of the lake. When she saw it she shrieked, and covered her face with her hands. They bore her across to the stone, where they had already placed a little boat for her. The water was not deep enough to float it, but they hoped it would be, before long. They laid her on cushions, placed in the boat wines and fruits and other nice things, and stretched a canopy over all.

In a few minutes the prince appeared. The princess recognized him at once, but did not think it worth while to acknowledge him.

"Here I am," said the prince. "Put me in."

"They told me it was a shoeblack," said the princess.

"So I am," said the prince. "I blacked your little boots three times a day, because they were all I could get of you. Put me in."

The courtiers did not resent his bluntness, except by saying to each other that he was taking it out in impudence.

But how was he to be put in? The golden plate contained no instructions on this point. The prince looked at the hole, and saw but one way. He put both his legs into it, sitting on the stone and, stooping forward, covered the corner that remained open with his two hands. In this uncomfortable position he resolved to abide his fate, and turning to the people, said,—

"Now you can go."

The king had already gone home to dinner.

"Now you can go," repeated the princess after him, like a parrot.

The people obeyed her and went.

Presently a little wave flowed over the stone, and wetted one of the prince's knees. But he did not mind it much. He began to sing, and the song he sang was this:—

> "As a world that has no well,
> Darkly bright in forest dell;
> As a world without the gleam

Of the downward-going stream;
As a world without the glance
Of the ocean's fair expanse;
As a world where never rain
Glittered on the sunny plain;—
Such, my heart, thy world would be,
If no love did flow in thee.

"As a world without the sound
Of the rivulets underground;
Or the bubbling of the spring
Out of darkness wandering;
Or the mighty rush and flowing
Of the river's downward going;
Or the music-showers that drop
On the outspread beech's top;
Or the ocean's mighty voice,
When his lifted waves rejoice;—
Such, my soul, thy world would be,
If no love did sing in thee.

"Lady, keep thy world's delight;
Keep the waters in thy sight.
Love hath made me strong to go,
For thy sake, to realms below,
Where the water's shine and hum
Through the darkness never come:
Let, I pray, one thought of me
Spring, a little well, in thee;
Lest thy loveless soul be found
Like a dry and thirsty ground."

"Sing again, prince. It makes it less tedious," said the princess.

But the prince was too much overcome to sing any more, and a long pause followed.

"This is very kind of you, prince," said the princess at last, quite coolly, as she lay in the boat with her eyes shut.

"I am sorry I can't return the compliment," thought the prince; "but you are worth dying for, after all."

Again a wavelet, and another, and another flowed over the stone, and wetted both the prince's knees; but he did not speak or move. Two—three—four hours passed in this way, the princess apparently asleep, and the prince very patient. But he was much disappointed in his position, for he had none of the consolation he had hoped for.

At last he could bear it no longer.

"Princess!" said he.

But at the moment up started the princess, crying,—

"I'm afloat! I'm afloat!"

And the little boat bumped against the stone.

"Princess!" repeated the prince, encouraged by seeing her wide awake and looking eagerly at the water.

"Well?" said she, without looking round.

"Your papa promised that you should look at me, and you haven't looked at me once."

"Did he? Then I suppose I must. But I am so sleepy!"

"Sleep then, darling, and don't mind me," said the poor prince.

"Really, you are very good," replied the princess. "I think I will go to sleep again."

"Just give me a glass of wine and a biscuit first," said the prince, very humbly.

"With all my heart," said the princess, and gaped as she said it.

She got the wine and the biscuit, however, and leaning over the side of the boat towards him, was compelled to look at him.

"Why, prince," she said, "you don't look well! Are you sure you don't mind it?"

"Not a bit," answered he, feeling very faint indeed. "Only I shall die before it is of any use to you, unless I have something to eat."

"There, then," said she, holding out the wine to him.

"Ah! you must feed me. I dare not move my hands. The water would run away directly."

"Good gracious!" said the princess; and she began at once to feed him with bits of biscuit and sips of wine.

As she fed him, he contrived to kiss the tips of her fingers now and then. She did not seem to mind it, one way or the other. But the prince felt better.

"Now, for your own sake, princess," said he, "I cannot let you go to sleep. You must sit and look at me, else I shall not be able to keep up."

"Well, I will do anything I can to oblige you," answered she, with condescension; and, sitting down, she did look at him, and kept looking at him with wonderful steadiness, considering all things.

The sun went down, and the moon rose, and, gush after gush, the waters were rising up the prince's body. They were up to his waist now.

"Why can't we go and have a swim?" said the princess. "There seems to be water enough just about here."

"I shall never swim more," said the prince.

"Oh, I forgot," said the princess, and was silent.

So the water grew and grew, and rose up and up on the prince. And the princess sat and looked at him. She fed him now and then. The night wore on. The waters rose and rose. The moon rose likewise higher and higher, and shone full on the face of the dying prince. The water was up to his neck.

"Will you kiss me, princess?" said he feebly. The nonchalance was all gone now.

"Yes, I will," answered the princess, and kissed him with a long, sweet, cold kiss.

"Now," said he, with a sigh of content, "I die happy."

He did not speak again. The princess gave him some wine for the last time: he was past eating. Then she sat down again, and looked at him. The water rose and rose. It touched his chin. It touched his lower lip. It touched between his lips. He shut them hard to keep it out. The princess began to feel strange. It touched his upper lip. He breathed through his nostrils. The princess looked wild. It covered his nostrils. Her eyes looked scared, and shone strange in the moonlight. His head fell back; the water closed over it, and the bubbles of his last breath bubbled up through the water. The princess gave a shriek, and sprang into the lake.

She laid hold first of one leg, and then of the other, and pulled and tugged, but she could not move either. She stopped to take breath, and that made her think that he could not get any breath. She was frantic. She got hold of him, and held his head above the water, which was possible now his hands were no longer on the hole. But it was of no use, for he was past breathing.

Love and water brought back all her strength. She got under the water, and pulled and pulled with her whole might, till at last she got one leg out. The other easily followed. How she got him into the boat she never could tell; but when she did, she fainted away. Coming to herself, she seized the oars, kept herself steady as best she could, and rowed and rowed, though she had never rowed before. Round rocks, and over shallows, and through mud she rowed, till she got to the landing-stairs of the palace. By this time her people were on the shore, for they had heard her shriek. She made them carry the prince to her own room, and lay him in her bed, and light a fire, and send for the doctors.

"But the lake, your highness!" said the chamberlain, who, roused by the noise, came in, in his nightcap.

"Go and drown yourself in it!" she said.

This was the last rudeness of which the princess was ever guilty; and one must allow that she had good cause to feel provoked with the lord chamberlain.

Had it been the king himself, he would have fared no better. But both he and the queen were fast asleep. And the chamberlain went back to his bed. Somehow, the doctors never came. So the princess and her old nurse were left with the prince. But the old nurse was a wise woman, and knew what to do.

They tried everything for a long time without success. The princess was nearly distracted between hope and fear, but she tried on and on, one thing after another, and everything over and over again.

At last, when they had all but given it up, just as the sun rose, the prince opened his eyes.

XV. LOOK AT THE RAIN!

The princess burst into a passion of tears, and *fell* on the floor. There she lay for an hour, and her tears never ceased. All the pent-up crying of her life was spent now. And a rain came on, such as had never been seen in that country. The sun shone all the time, and the great drops, which fell straight to the earth, shone likewise. The palace was in the heart of a rainbow. It was a rain of rubies, and sapphires, and emeralds, and topazes. The torrents poured from the mountains like molten gold; and if it had not been for its subterranean outlet, the lake would have overflowed and inundated the country. It was full from shore to shore.

But the princess did not heed the lake. She lay on the floor and wept. And this rain within doors was far more wonderful than the rain out of doors. For when it abated a little, and she proceeded to rise, she found, to her astonishment, that she could not. At length, after many efforts, she succeeded in getting upon her feet. But she tumbled down again directly. Hearing her fall, her old nurse uttered a yell of delight, and ran to her, screaming,—

"My darling child! she's found her gravity!"

"Oh, that's it! is it?" said the princess, rubbing her shoulder and her knee alternately. "I consider it very unpleasant. I feel as if I should be crushed to pieces."

"Hurrah!" cried the prince from the bed. "If you've come round, princess, so have I. How's the lake?"

"Brimful," answered the nurse.

"Then we're all happy."

"That we are indeed!" answered the princess, sobbing.

And there was rejoicing all over the country that rainy day. Even the babies forgot their past troubles, and danced and crowed amazingly. And the king told stories, and the queen listened to them. And he divided the money in his box, and she the honey in her pot, to all the children. And there was such jubilation as was never heard of before.

Of course the prince and princess were betrothed at once. But the princess had to learn to walk, before they could be married with any propriety. And this was not so easy at her time of life, for she could walk no more than a baby. She was always falling down and hurting herself.

"Is this the gravity you used to make so much of?" said she one day to the prince, as he raised her from the floor. "For my part, I was a great deal more comfortable without it."

"No, no, that's not it. This is it," replied the prince, as he took her up, and carried her about like a baby, kissing her all the time. "This is gravity."

"That's better," said she. "I don't mind that so much."

And she smiled the sweetest, loveliest smile in the prince's face. And she gave him one little kiss in return for all his; and he thought them overpaid, for he was beside himself with delight. I fear she complained of her gravity more than once after this, notwithstanding.

It was a long time before she got reconciled to walking. But the pain of learning it was quite counterbalanced by two things, either of which would have been sufficient consolation. The first was, that the prince himself was her teacher; and the second, that she could tumble into the lake as often as she pleased. Still, she preferred to have the prince jump in with her; and the splash they made before was nothing to the splash they made now.

The lake never sank again. In process of time, it wore the roof of the cavern quite through, and was twice as deep as before.

The only revenge the princess took upon her aunt was to tread pretty hard on her gouty toe the next time she saw her. But she was sorry for it the very next day, when she heard that the water had undermined her house, and that it had fallen in the night, burying her in its ruins; whence no one ever ventured to dig up her body. There she lies to this day.

So the prince and princess lived and were happy; and had crowns of gold, and clothes of cloth, and shoes of leather, and children of boys and girls, not one of whom was ever known, on the most critical occasion, to lose the smallest atom of his or her due proportion of gravity.

THE GIANT'S HEART[1]

There was once a giant who lived on the borders of Giantland where it touched on the country of common people.

Everything in Giantland was so big that the common people saw only a mass of awful mountains and clouds; and no living man had ever come from it, as far as anybody knew, to tell what he had seen in it.

Somewhere near the borders, on the other side, by the edge of a great forest, lived a labourer with his wife and a great many children. One day Tricksey-Wee, as they called her, teased her brother Buffy-Bob, till he could not bear it any longer, and gave her a box on the ear. Tricksey-Wee cried; and Buffy-Bob was so sorry and so ashamed of himself that he cried too, and ran off into the wood. He was so long gone that Tricksey-Wee began to be frightened, for she was very fond of her brother; and she was so distressed that she had first teased him and then cried, that at last she ran into the wood to look for him, though there was more chance of losing herself than of finding him.

And, indeed, so it seemed likely to turn out; for, running on without looking, she at length found herself in a valley she knew nothing about. And no wonder; for what she thought was a valley with round, rocky sides, was no other than the space between two of the roots of a great tree that grew on the borders of Giantland. She climbed over the side of it, and went towards what she took for a black, round-topped mountain, far away; but which she soon discovered to be close to her, and to be a hollow place so great that she could not tell what it was hollowed out of. Staring at it, she found that it was a doorway; and going nearer and staring harder, she saw the door, far in, with a knocker of iron upon it, a great many yards above her head, and as large as the anchor of a big ship. Now nobody had ever been unkind to Tricksey-Wee, and therefore she was not afraid of anybody. For Buffy-Bob's box on the ear she did not think worth considering. So spying a little hole at the bottom of the door which had been nibbled by some giant mouse, she crept through it, and found

---

1   "The Giant's Heart" was first published as "Tell Us a Story" in *The Illustrated London News*, 19 December 1863, pp. 626-30. It later appeared in *Adela Cathcart* (1864), *Dealings with the Fairies* (1867), and *The Light Princess and Other Fairy Stories* (1890). The text reproduced here is based on that published in *Dealings with the Fairies*.

herself in an enormous hall. She could not have seen the other end of it at all, except for the great fire that was burning there, diminished to a spark in the distance. Towards this fire she ran as fast as she could, and was not far from it when something fell before her with a great clatter, over which she tumbled, and went rolling on the floor. She was not much hurt, however, and got up in a moment. Then she saw that what she had fallen over was not unlike a great iron bucket. When she examined it more closely, she discovered that it was a thimble; and looking up to see who had dropped it, beheld a huge face, with spectacles as big as the round windows in a church, bending over her, and looking everywhere for the thimble. Tricksey-Wee immediately laid hold of it in both her arms, and lifted it about an inch nearer to the nose of the peering giantess. This movement made the old lady see where it was, and, her finger popping into it, it vanished from the eyes of Tricksey-Wee, buried in the folds of a white stocking like a cloud in the sky, which Mrs. Giant was busy darning. For it was Saturday night, and her husband would wear nothing but white stockings on Sunday. To be sure, he did eat little children, but only *very* little ones; and if ever it crossed his mind that it was wrong to do so, he always said to himself that he wore whiter stockings on Sunday than any other giant in all Giantland.

At the same instant Tricksey-Wee heard a sound like the wind in a tree full of leaves, and could not think what it could be; till, looking up, she found that it was the giantess whispering to her; and when she tried very hard she could hear what she said well enough.

"Run away, dear little girl," she said, "as fast as you can; for my husband will be home in a few minutes."

"But I've never been naughty to your husband," said Tricksey-Wee, looking up in the giantess's face.

"That doesn't matter. You had better go. He is fond of little children, particularly little girls."

"Oh, then he won't hurt me."

"I am not sure of that. He is so fond of them that he eats them up; and I am afraid he couldn't help hurting you a little. He's a very good man though."

"Oh! then—" began Tricksey-Wee, feeling rather frightened; but before she could finish her sentence she heard the sound of footsteps very far apart and very heavy. The next moment, who should come running towards her, full speed, and as pale as death, but Buffy-Bob. She held out her arms, and he ran into them. But when she tried to kiss him, she only kissed the back of his head; for his white face and round eyes were turned to the door.

"Run, children; run and hide," said the giantess.

"Come, Buffy," said Tricksey; "yonder's a great brake; we'll hide in it."

The brake was a big broom; and they had just got into the bristles of it when they heard the door open with a sound of thunder, and in stalked the giant. You would have thought you saw the whole earth through the door when he opened it, so wide was it; and when he closed it, it was like nightfall.

"Where is that little boy?" he cried, with a voice like the bellowing of a cannon. "He looked a very nice boy indeed. I am almost sure he crept through the mousehole at the bottom of the door. Where is he, my dear?"

"I don't know," answered the giantess.

"But you know it is wicked to tell lies; don't you, my dear?" retorted the giant.

"Now, you ridiculous old Thunderthump!" said his wife, with a smile as broad as the sea in the sun, "how can I mend your white stockings and look after little boys? You have got plenty to last you over Sunday, I am sure. Just look what good little boys they are!"

Tricksey-Wee and Buffy-Bob peered through the bristles, and discovered a row of little boys, about a dozen, with very fat faces and goggle eyes, sitting before the fire, and looking stupidly into it. Thunderthump intended the most of these for pickling, and was feeding them well before salting them. Now and then, however, he could not keep his teeth off them, and would eat one by the bye, without salt.

He strode up to the wretched children. Now what made them very wretched indeed was, that they knew if they could only keep from eating, and grow thin, the giant would dislike them, and turn them out to find their way home; but notwithstanding this, so greedy were they, that they ate as much as ever they could hold. The giantess, who fed them, comforted herself with thinking that they were not real boys and girls, but only little pigs pretending to be boys and girls.

"Now tell me the truth," cried the giant, bending his face down over them. They shook with terror, and every one hoped it was somebody else the giant liked best. "Where is the little boy that ran into the hall just now? Whoever tells me a lie shall be instantly boiled."

"He's in the broom," cried one dough-faced boy. "He's in there, and a little girl with him."

"The naughty children," cried the giant, "to hide from *me*!" And he made a stride towards the broom.

"Catch hold of the bristles, Bobby. Get right into a tuft, and hold on," cried Tricksey-Wee, just in time.

The giant caught up the broom, and seeing nothing under it, set it down again with a force that threw them both on the floor. He then made two strides to the boys, caught the dough-faced one by the neck, took the lid off a great pot that was boiling on the fire, popped him in as if he had been a trussed chicken, put the lid on again, and saying, "There, boys! See what comes of lying!" asked no more questions; for, as he always kept his word, he was afraid he might have to do the same to them all; and he did not like boiled boys. He like to eat them crisp, as radishes, whether forked or not, ought to be eaten. He then sat down, and asked his wife if his supper was ready. She looked into the pot, and throwing the boy out with the ladle, as if he had been a black beetle that had tumbled in and had had the worst of it, answered that she thought it was. Whereupon he rose to help her; and taking the pot from the fire, poured the whole contents, bubbling and splashing, into a dish like a vat. Then they sat down to supper. The children in the broom could not see what they had; but it seemed to agree with them; for the giant talked like thunder, and the giantess answered like the sea, and they grew chattier and chattier. At length the giant said,—

"I don't feel quite comfortable about that heart of mine." And as he spoke, instead of laying his hand on his bosom, he waved it away towards the corner where the children were peeping from the broom-bristles, like frightened little mice.

"Well, you know, my darling Thunderthump," answered his wife, "I always thought it ought to be nearer home. But you know best, of course."

"Ha! ha! You don't know where it is, wife. I moved it a month ago."

"What a man you are, Thunderthump! You trust any creature alive rather than your own wife."

Here the giantess gave a sob which sounded exactly like a wave going flop into the mouth of a cave up to the roof.

"Where have you got it now?" she resumed, checking her emotion.

"Well, Doodlem, I don't mind telling *you*," answered the giant, soothingly. "The great she-eagle has got it for a nest egg. She sits on it night and day, and thinks she will bring the greatest eagle out of it that ever sharpened his beak on the rocks of Mount Skycrack. I can warrant no one else will touch it while she has got it. But she is rather capricious, and I confess I am not easy about it; for the least scratch of one of her claws would do for me at once. And she *has* claws."

I refer any one who doubts this part of my story to certain chronicles of Giantland preserved among the Celtic nations. It was quite a common thing for a giant to put his heart out to nurse, because he did not like the trouble and responsibility of doing it himself; although I must confess it was a dangerous sort of plan to take, especially with such a delicate viscus as the heart.

All this time Buffy-Bob and Tricksey-Wee were listening with long ears.

"Oh!" thought Tricksey-Wee, "if I could but find the giant's cruel heart, wouldn't I give it a squeeze!"

The giant and giantess went on talking for a long time. The giantess kept advising the giant to hide his heart somewhere in the house; but he seemed afraid of the advantage it would give her over him.

"You could hide it at the bottom of the flour-barrel," said she.

"That would make me feel chokey," answered he.

"Well, in the coal-cellar. Or in the dust-hole—that's the place! No one would think of looking for your heart in the dust-hole."

"Worse and worse!" cried the giant.

"Well, the water-butt," suggested she.

"No, no; it would grow spongy there," said he.

"Well, what *will* you do with it?"

"I will leave it a month longer where it is, and then I will give it to the Queen of the Kangaroos, and she will carry it in her pouch for me. It is best to change its place, you know, lest my enemies should scent it out. But, dear Doodlem, it's a fretting care to have a heart of one's own to look after. The responsibility is too much for me. If it were not for a bite of a radish now and then, I never could bear it."

Here the giant looked lovingly towards the row of little boys by the fire, all of whom were nodding, or asleep on the floor.

"Why don't you trust it to me, dear Thunderthump?" said his wife. "I would take the best possible care of it."

"I don't doubt it, my love. But the responsibility would be too much for *you*. You would no longer be my darling, light-hearted, airy, laughing Doodlem. It would transform you into a heavy, oppressed woman, weary of life—as I am."

The giant closed his eyes and pretended to go to sleep. His wife got his stockings, and went on with her darning. Soon the giant's pretence became reality, and the giantess began to nod over her work.

"Now, Buffy," whispered Tricksey-Wee, "now's our time. I think it's moonlight, and we had better be off. There's a door with a hole for the cat just behind us."

"All right," said Bob; "I'm ready."

So they got out of the broom-brake and crept to the door. But to their great disappointment, when they got through it, they found themselves in a sort of shed. It was full of tubs and things, and, though it was built of wood only, they could not find a crack.

"Let us try this hole," said Tricksey; for the giant and giantess were sleeping behind them, and they dared not go back.

"All right," said Bob.

He seldom said anything else than *All right*.

Now this hole was in a mound that came in through the wall of the shed, and went along the floor for some distance. They crawled into it, and found it very dark. But groping their way along, they soon came to a small crack, through which they saw grass, pale in the moonshine. As they crept on, they found the hole began to get wider and lead upwards.

"What is that noise of rushing?" said Buffy-Bob.

"I can't tell," replied Tricksey; "for, you see, I don't know what we are in."

The fact was, they were creeping along a channel in the heart of a giant tree; and the noise they heard was the noise of the sap rushing along in its wooden pipes. When they laid their ears to the wall, they heard it gurgling along with a pleasant noise.

"It sounds kind and good," said Tricksey. "It is water running. Now it must be running from somewhere to somewhere. I think we had better go on, and we shall come somewhere."

It was now rather difficult to go on, for they had to climb as if they were climbing a hill; and now the passage was wide. Nearly worn out, they saw light overhead at last, and creeping through a crack into the open air, found themselves on the fork of a huge tree. A great, broad, uneven space lay around them, out of which spread boughs in every direction, the smallest of them as big as the biggest tree in the country of common people. Overhead were leaves enough to supply all the trees they had ever seen. Not much moonlight could come through, but the leaves would glimmer white in the wind at times. The tree was full of giant birds. Every now and then, one would sweep through, with a great noise. But, except an occasional chirp, sounding like a shrill pipe in a great organ, they made no noise. All at once an owl began to hoot. He thought he was singing. As soon as he began, other birds replied, making rare game of him. To their astonishment, the children found they could understand every word they sang. And what they sang was something like this:—

"I will sing a song.
I'm the Owl."
"Sing a song, you sing-song
Ugly fowl!
What will you sing about,
Night in and Day out?"

"Sing about the night;
I'm the Owl."
"You could not see for the light,
Stupid fowl!"
"Oh! the moon! and the dew!
And the shadows!—tu-whoo!"

The owl spread out his silent, soft, sly wings, and lighting between Tricksey-Wee and Buffy-Bob, nearly smothered them, closing up one under each wing. It was like being buried in a down bed. But the owl did not like anything between his sides and his wings, so he opened his wings again, and the children made haste to get out. Tricksey-Wee immediately went in front of the bird, and looking up into his huge face, which was as round as the eyes of the giantess's spectacles, and much bigger, dropped a pretty courtesy, and said,—

"Please, Mr. Owl, I want to whisper to you."

"Very well, small child," answered the owl, looking important, and stooping his ear towards her. "What is it?"

"Please tell me where the eagle lives that sits on the giant's heart."

"Oh, you naughty child! That's a secret. For shame!"

And with a great hiss that terrified them, the owl flew into the tree. All birds are fond of secrets; but not many of them can keep them so well as the owl.

So the children went on because they did not know what else to do. They found the way very rough and difficult, the tree was so full of humps and hollows. Now and then they plashed into a pool of rain; now and then they came upon twigs growing out of the trunk where they had no business, and they were as large as full-grown poplars. Sometimes they came upon great cushions of soft moss, and on one of them they lay down and rested. But they had not lain long before they spied a large nightingale sitting on a branch, with its bright eyes looking up at the moon. In a moment more he began to sing, and the birds about him began to reply, but in a very different tone from that in which they had replied to the owl. Oh, the birds did call the nightingale such pretty names! The nightingale sang, and the birds replied like this:—

> "I will sing a song.
> I'm the nightingale."
> "Sing a song, long, long,
> Little Neverfail!
> What will you sing about,
> Light in or light out?"

> "Sing about the light
> Gone away;
> Down, away, and out of sight—
> Poor lost day!
> Mourning for the day dead,
> O'er his dim bed."

The nightingale sang so sweetly, that the children would have fallen asleep but for fear of losing any of the song. When the nightingale stopped they got up and wandered on. They did not know where they were going, but they thought it best to keep going on, because then they might come upon something or other. They were very sorry they had forgotten to ask the nightingale about the eagle's nest, but his music had put everything else out of their heads. They resolved, however, not to forget the next time they had a chance. So they went on and on, till they were both tired, and Tricksey-Wee said at last, trying to laugh,—

"I declare my legs feel just like a Dutch doll's."

"Then here's the place to go to bed in," said Buffy-Bob.

They stood at the edge of a last year's nest, and looked down with delight into the round, mossy cave. Then they crept gently in, and, lying down in each other's arms, found it so deep, and warm, and comfortable, and soft, that they were soon fast asleep.

Now close beside them, in a hollow, was another nest, in which lay a lark and his wife; and the children were awakened, very early in the morning, by a dispute between Mr. and Mrs. Lark.

"Let me up," said the lark.

"It is not time," said the lark's wife.

"It is," said the lark, rather rudely. "The darkness is quite thin. I can almost see my own beak."

"Nonsense!" said the lark's wife. "You know you came home yesterday morning quite worn out—you had to fly so very high before you saw him. I am sure he would not mind if you took it a little easier. Do be quiet and go to sleep again."

"That's not it at all," said the lark. "He doesn't want me. I want him. Let me up, I say."

He began to sing; and Tricksey-Wee and Buffy-Bob, having now learned the way, answered him:—

> "I will sing a song.
>   I'm the Lark."
> "Sing, sing, Throat-strong,
>   Little Kill-the-dark.
> What will you sing about,
> Now the night is out?"

> "I can only call;
>   I can't think.
> Let me up—that's all.
>   Let me drink!
> Thirsting all the long night
> For a drink of light."

By this time the lark was standing on the edge of his nest and looking at the children.

"Poor little things! You can't fly," said the lark.

"No; but we can look up," said Tricksey.

"Ah, you don't know what it is to see the very first of the sun."

"But we know what it is to wait till he comes. He's no worse for your seeing him first, is he?"

"Oh no, certainly not," answered the lark, with condescension; and then, bursting into his *Jubilate*,[1] he sprang aloft, clapping his wings like a clock running down.

"Tell us where—" began Buffy-Bob.

But the lark was out of sight. His song was all that was left of him. That was everywhere, and he was nowhere.

---

1   "A call to rejoice; an outburst of joyous triumph" (*OED*).

"Selfish bird!" said Buffy. "It's all very well for larks to go hunting the sun, but they have no business to despise their neighbours, for all that."

"Can I be of any use to you?" said a sweet bird-voice out of the nest.

This was the lark's wife, who stayed at home with the young larks while her husband went to church.

"Oh! thank you. If you please," answered Tricksey-Wee.

And up popped a pretty brown head; and then up came a brown feathery body; and last of all came the slender legs on to the edge of the nest. There she turned, and, looking down into the nest, from which came a whole litany of chirpings for breakfast, said, "Lie still, little ones." Then she turned to the children.

"My husband is King of the Larks," she said.

Buffy-Bob took off his cap, and Tricksey-Wee courtesied very low.

"Oh, it's not me," said the bird, looking very shy. "I am only his wife. It's my husband." And she looked up after him into the sky, whence his song was still falling like a shower of musical hailstones. Perhaps *she* could see him.

"He's a splendid bird," said Buffy-Bob; "only you know he *will* get up a little too early."

"Oh, no! he doesn't. It's only his way, you know. But tell me what I can do for you."

"Tell us, please, Lady Lark, where the she-eagle lives that sits on Giant Thunderthump's heart."

"Oh! that is a secret."

"Did you promise not to tell?"

"No; but larks ought to be discreet. They see more than other birds."

"But you don't fly up high like your husband, do you?"

"Not often. But it's no matter. I come to know things for all that."

"Do tell me, and I will sing you a song," said Tricksey-Wee.

"Can you sing too?—You have got no wings!"

"Yes. And I will sing you a song I learned the other day about a lark and his wife."

"Please do," said the lark's wife. "Be quiet, children, and listen."

Tricksey-Wee was very glad she happened to know a song which would please the lark's wife, at least, whatever the lark himself might have thought of it, if he had heard it. So she sang,—

"'Good morrow, my lord!' in the sky alone,
Sang the lark, as the sun ascended his throne.
'Shine on me, my lord; I only am come,
Of all your servants, to welcome you home.
I have flown a whole hour, right up, I swear,
To catch the first shine of your golden hair!'

"'Must I thank you, then,' said the king, 'Sir Lark,
For flying so high, and hating the dark?
You ask a full cup for half a thirst:
Half is love of me, and half love to be first.
There's many a bird that makes no haste,
But waits till I come. That's as much to my taste.'

"And the king hid his head in a turban of cloud;
And the lark stopped singing, quite vexed and cowed.
But he flew up higher, and thought, 'Anon,
The wrath of the king will be over and gone;
And his crown, shining out of its cloudy fold,
Will change my brown feathers to a glory of gold.'

"So he flew, with the strength of a lark he flew.
But as he rose the cloud rose too;
And not a gleam of the golden hair
Came through the depth of the misty air;
Till, weary with flying, with sighing sore,
The strong sun-seeker could do no more.

"His wings had had no chrism of gold,
And his feathers felt withered and worn and old;
So he quivered and sank, and dropped like a stone.
And there on his nest, where he left her, alone,
Sat his little wife on her little eggs,
Keeping them warm with wings and legs.

"Did I say alone? Ah, no such thing!
Full in her face was shining the king.
'Welcome, Sir Lark! You look tired,' said he.
'*Up* is not always the best way to me.
While you have been singing so high and away,
I've been shining to your little wife all day.'

"He had set his crown all about the nest,
And out of the midst shone her little brown breast;
And so glorious was she in russet gold,
That for wonder and awe Sir Lark grew cold.
He popped his head under her wing, and lay
As still as a stone, till the king was away."

As soon as Tricksey-Wee had finished her song, the lark's wife began a low, sweet, modest little song of her own; and after she had piped away for two or three minutes, she said,—

"You dear children, what can I do for you?"

"Tell us where the she-eagle lives, please," said Tricksey-Wee.

"Well, I don't think there can be much harm in telling such wise, good children," said Lady Lark; "I am sure you don't want to do any mischief."

"Oh, no; quite the contrary," said Buffy-Bob.

"Then I'll tell you. She lives on the very topmost peak of Mount Skycrack; and the only way to get up is to climb on the spiders' webs that cover it from top to bottom."

"That's rather serious," said Tricksey-Wee.

"But you don't want to go up, you foolish little thing! You can't go. And what do you want to go up for?"

"That is a secret," said Tricksey-Wee.

"Well, it's no business of mine," rejoined Lady Lark, a little offended, and quite vexed that she had told them. So she flew away to find some breakfast for her little ones, who by this time were chirping very impatiently. The children looked at each other, joined hands, and walked off.

In a minute more the sun was up, and they soon reached the outside of the tree. The bark was so knobby and rough, and full of twigs, that they managed to get down, though not without great difficulty. Then, far away to the north they saw a huge peak, like the spire of a church, going right up into the sky. They thought this must be Mount Skycrack, and turned their faces towards it. As they went on, they saw a giant or two, now and then, striding about the fields or through the woods, but they kept out of their way. Nor were they in much danger; for it was only one or two of the border giants that were so very fond of children.

At last they came to the foot of Mount Skycrack. It stood in a plain alone, and shot right up, I don't know how many thousand feet, into the air, a long, narrow, spearlike mountain. The whole face of it, from top to bottom, was covered with a network of spiders' webs, the threads of various sizes, from that of silk to that of whipcord. The webs shook, and quivered, and waved in the sun, glittering like silver. All about ran huge greedy spiders, catching huge silly flies, and devouring them.

Here they sat down to consider what could be done. The spiders did not heed them, but ate away at the flies.—Now at the foot of the mountain, and all round it, was a ring of water, not very broad, but very deep. As they sat watching them, one of the spiders, whose web was woven across this water, somehow or other lost his hold, and fell in on his back. Tricksey-Wee and Buffy-Bob ran to his assistance, and laying hold each of one of his legs, succeeded, with the help of the other legs, which struggled spiderfully, in getting him out upon dry land. As soon as he had shaken himself, and dried himself a little, the spider turned to the children, saying,—

"And now, what can I do for you?"

"Tell us, please," said they, "how we can get up the mountain to the she-eagle's nest."

"Nothing is easier," answered the spider. "Just run up there, and tell them all I sent you, and nobody will mind you."

"But we haven't got claws like you, Mr. Spider," said Buffy.

"Ah! no more you have, poor unprovided creatures! Still, I think we can manage it. Come home with me."

"You won't eat us, will you?" said Buffy.

"My dear child," answered the spider, in a tone of injured dignity, "I eat nothing but what is mischievous or useless. You have helped me, and now I will help you."

The children rose at once, and climbing as well as they could, reached the spider's nest in the centre of the web. Nor did they find it very difficult; for whenever too great a gap came, the spider spinning a strong cord stretched it just where they would have chosen to put their feet next. He left them in his nest, after bringing them two enormous honey-bags, taken from bees that he had caught; but presently about six of the wisest of the spiders came back with him. It was rather horrible to look up and see them all round the mouth of the nest, looking down on them in contemplation, as if wondering whether they would be nice eating. At length one of them said,—"Tell us truly what you want with the eagle, and we will try to help you."

Then Tricksey-Wee told them that there was a giant on the borders who treated little children no better than radishes, and that they had narrowly escaped being eaten by him; that they had found out that the great she-eagle of Mount Skycrack was at present sitting on his heart; and that, if they could only get hold of the heart, they would soon teach the giant better behaviour.

"But," said their host, "if you get at the heart of the giant, you will find it as large as one of your elephants. What can you do with it?"

"The least scratch will kill it," replied Buffy-Bob.

"Ah! but you might do better than that," said the spider.— "Now we have resolved to help you. Here is a little bag of spider-juice. The giants cannot bear spiders, and this juice is dreadful poison to them. We are all ready to go up with you, and drive the eagle away. Then you must put the heart into this other bag, and bring it down with you; for then the giant will be in your power."

"But how can we do that?" said Buffy. "The bag is not much bigger than a pudding-bag."

"But it is as large as you will be able to carry."

"Yes; but what are we to do with the heart?"

"Put it in the bag, to be sure. Only, first, you must squeeze a drop out of the other bag upon it. You will see what will happen."

"Very well; we will do as you tell us," said Tricksey-Wee. "And now, if you please, how shall we go?"

"Oh, that's our business," said the first spider. "You come with me, and my grandfather will take your brother. Get up."

So Tricksey-Wee mounted on the narrow part of the spider's back, and held fast. And Buffy-Bob got on the grandfather's back. And up they scrambled, over one web after another, up and up—so fast! And every spider followed; so that, when Tricksey-Wee looked back, she saw a whole army of spiders scrambling after them.

"What can we want with so many?" she thought; but she said nothing.

The moon was now up, and it was a splendid sight below and around them. All Giantland was spread out under them, with its great hills, lakes, trees, and animals. And all above them was the clear heaven, and Mount Skycrack rising into it, with its endless ladders of spider-webs, glittering like cords made of moonbeams. And up the moonbeams went, crawling, and scrambling, and racing, a huge army of huge spiders.

At length they reached all but the very summit, where they stopped. Tricksey-Wee and Buffy-Bob could see above them a great globe of feathers, that finished off the mountain like an ornamental knob.

"But how shall we drive her off?" said Buffy.

"We'll soon manage that," answered the grandfather-spider. "Come on you, down there."

Up rushed the whole army, past the children, over the edge of the nest, on to the she-eagle, and buried themselves in her feathers. In a moment she became very restless, and went pecking about with her beak. All at once she spread out her wings, with a sound like a whirlwind, and flew off to bathe in the sea; and then the spiders began to drop from her in all directions on their gossamer wings. The children had to hold fast to keep the wind of the eagle's flight from blowing them off. As soon as it was over, they looked into the nest, and there lay the giant's heart—an awful and ugly thing.

"Make haste, child!" said Tricksey's spider.

So Tricksey took her bag, and squeezed a drop out of it upon the heart. She thought she heard the giant give a far-off roar of pain, and she nearly fell from her seat with terror. The heart instantly began to shrink. It shrunk and shrivelled till it was nearly gone; and Buffy-Bob caught it up and put it into his bag. Then the two spiders turned and went down again as fast as they could. Before they got to the bottom, they heard the shrieks of the she-eagle over the loss of her egg; but the spiders told them not to be alarmed, for her eyes were too big to see them.—By the time they reached the foot of the mountain, all the spiders had got home, and were busy again catching flies, as if nothing had happened.

After renewed thanks to their friends, the children set off, carrying the giant's heart with them.

"If you should find it at all troublesome, just give it a little more spider-juice directly," said the grandfather, as they took their leave.

Now, the giant had given an awful roar of pain the moment they anointed his heart, and had fallen down in a fit, in which he lay so long that all the boys might have escaped if they had not been so fat. One did, and got home in safety. For days the giant was unable to speak. The first words he uttered were,—

"Oh, my heart! my heart!"

"Your heart is safe enough, dear Thunderthump," said his wife. "Really, a man of your size ought not to be so nervous and apprehensive. I am ashamed of you."

"You have no heart, Doodlem," answered he. "I assure you that at this moment mine is in the greatest danger. It has fallen into the hands of foes, though who they are I cannot tell."

Here he fainted again; for Tricksey-Wee, finding the heart begin to swell a little, had given it the least touch of spider-juice.

Again he recovered, and said,—

"Dear Doodlem, my heart is coming back to me. It is coming nearer and nearer."

After lying silent for hours, he exclaimed,—

"It is in the house, I know!"

And he jumped up and walked about, looking in every corner.

As he rose, Tricksey-Wee and Buffy-Bob came out of the hole in the tree-root, and through the cat-hole in the door, and walked boldly towards the giant. Both kept their eyes busy watching him. Led by the love of his own heart, the giant soon spied them, and staggered furiously towards them.

"I will eat you, you vermin!" he cried. "Here with my heart!"

Tricksey gave the heart a sharp pinch. Down fell the giant on his knees, blubbering, and crying, and begging for his heart.

"You shall have it, if you behave yourself properly," said Tricksey.

"How shall I behave myself properly?" asked he, whimpering.

"Take all those boys and girls, and carry them home at once."

"I'm not able; I'm too ill. I should fall down."

"Take them up directly."

"I can't, till you give me my heart."

"Very well!" said Tricksey; and she gave the heart another pinch.

The giant jumped to his feet, and catching up all the children, thrust some into his waistcoat-pockets, some into his breast-pocket, put two or three into his hat, and took a bundle of them under each arm. Then he staggered to the door.

All this time poor Doodlem was sitting in her arm-chair, crying, and mending a white stocking.

The giant led the way to the borders. He could not go so fast but that Buffy and Tricksey managed to keep up with him. When they reached the borders, they thought it would be safer to let the children find their own way home. So they told him to set them down. He obeyed.

"Have you put them all down, Mr. Thunderthump?" asked Tricksey-Wee.

"Yes," said the giant.

"That's a lie!" squeaked a little voice; and out came a head from his waistcoat-pocket.

Tricksey-Wee pinched the heart till the giant roared with pain.

"You're not a gentleman. You tell stories," she said.

"He was the thinnest of the lot," said Thunderthump, crying.

"Are you all there now, children?" asked Tricksey.

"Yes, ma'am," returned they, after counting themselves very carefully, and with some difficulty; for they were all stupid children.

"Now," said Tricksey-Wee to the giant, "will you promise to carry off no more children, and never to eat a child again all your life?"

"Yes, yes! I promise," answered Thunderthump, sobbing.

"And you will never cross the borders of Giantland?"

"Never."

"And you shall never again wear white stockings on a Sunday, all your life long.—Do you promise?"

The giant hesitated at this, and began to expostulate; but Tricksey-Wee, believing it would be good for his morals, insisted; and the giant promised.

Then she required of him, that, when she gave him back his heart, he should give it to his wife to take care of for him for ever after.

The poor giant fell on his knees, and began again to beg. But Tricksey-Wee giving the heart a slight pinch, he bawled out,—

"Yes, yes! Doodlem shall have it, I swear. Only she must not put it in the flour-barrel, or in the dust-hole."

"Certainly not. Make your own bargain with her.—And you promise not to interfere with my brother and me, or to take any revenge for what we have done?"

"Yes, yes, my dear children; I promise everything. Do, pray, make haste and give me back my poor heart."

"Wait there, then, till I bring it to you."

"Yes, yes. Only make haste, for I feel very faint."

Tricksey-Wee began to undo the mouth of the bag. But Buffy-Bob, who had got very knowing on his travels, took out his knife with the pretence of cutting the string; but, in reality, to be prepared for any emergency.

No sooner was the heart out of the bag, than it expanded to the size of a bullock; and the giant, with a yell of rage and vengeance, rushed on the two children, who had stepped sideways from the terrible heart. But Buffy-Bob was too quick for Thunderthump. He sprang to the heart, and buried his knife in it, up to the hilt. A fountain of blood spouted from it; and with a dreadful groan the giant fell dead at the feet of little Tricksey-Wee, who could not help being sorry for him after all.

THE GOLDEN KEY[1]

There was a boy who used to sit in the twilight and listen to his great-aunt's stories.

She told him that if he could reach the place where the end of the rainbow stands he would find there a golden key.

"And what is the key for?" the boy would ask. "What is it the key of? What will it open?"

"That nobody knows," his aunt would reply. "He has to find that out."

"I suppose, being gold," the boy once said, thoughtfully, "that I could get a good deal of money for it if I sold it."

"Better never find it than sell it," returned his aunt. And then the boy went to bed and dreamed about the golden key.

Now all that his great-aunt told the boy about the golden key would have been nonsense, had it not been that their little house stood on the borders of Fairyland. For it is perfectly well known that out of Fairyland nobody ever can find where the rainbow stands. The creature takes such good care of its golden key, always flitting from place to place, lest any one should find it! But in Fairyland it is quite different. Things that look real in this country look very thin indeed in Fairyland, while some of the things that here cannot stand still for a moment, will not move there. So it was not in the least absurd of the old lady to tell her nephew such things about the golden key.

"Did you ever know anybody find it?" he asked, one evening.

"Yes. Your father, I believe, found it."

"And what did he do with it, can you tell me?"

"He never told me."

"What was it like?"

"He never showed it to me."

"How does a new key come there always?"

"I don't know. There it is."

"Perhaps it is the rainbow's egg."

"Perhaps it is. You will be a happy boy if you find the nest."

"Perhaps it comes tumbling down the rainbow from the sky."

"Perhaps it does."

---

1 "The Golden Key" was first published in *Dealings with the Fairies* (1867) and later in *The Light Princess and Other Fairy Stories* (1890). The text reproduced here is based on that published in *Dealings with the Fairies*.

One evening, in summer, he went into his own room, and stood at the lattice-window, and gazed into the forest which fringed the outskirts of Fairyland. It came close up to his great-aunt's garden, and, indeed, sent some straggling trees into it. The forest lay to the east, and the sun, which was setting behind the cottage, looked straight into the dark wood with his level red eye. The trees were all old, and had few branches below, so that the sun could see a great way into the forest; and the boy, being keen-sighted, could see almost as far as the sun. The trunks stood like rows of red columns in the shine of the red sun, and he could see down aisle after aisle in the vanishing distance. And as he gazed into the forest he began to feel as if the trees were all waiting for him, and had something they could not go on with till he came to them. But he was hungry, and wanted his supper. So he lingered.

Suddenly, far among the trees, as far as the sun could shine, he saw a glorious thing. It was the end of a rainbow, large and brilliant. He could count all the seven colours, and could see shade after shade beyond the violet; while before the red stood a colour more gorgeous and mysterious still. It was a colour he had never seen before. Only the spring of the rainbow-arch was visible. He could see nothing of it above the trees.

"The golden key!" he said to himself, and darted out of the house, and into the wood.

He had not gone far before the sun set. But the rainbow only glowed the brighter. For the rainbow of Fairyland is not dependent upon the sun as ours is. The trees welcomed him. The bushes made way for him. The rainbow grew larger and brighter; and at length he found himself within two trees of it.

It was a grand sight, burning away there in silence, with its gorgeous, its lovely, its delicate colours, each distinct, all combining. He could now see a great deal more of it. It rose high into the blue heavens, but bent so little that he could not tell how high the crown of the arch must reach. It was still only a small portion of a huge bow.

He stood gazing at it till he forgot himself with delight—even forgot the key which he had come to seek. And as he stood it grew more wonderful still. For in each of the colours, which was as large as the column of a church, he could faintly see beautiful forms slowly ascending as if by the steps of a winding stair. The forms appeared irregularly—now one, now many, now several, now none—men and women and children—all different, all beautiful.

He drew nearer to the rainbow. It vanished. He started back a step in dismay. It was there again, as beautiful as ever. So he contented himself with standing as near it as he might, and watching the forms that ascended the glorious colours towards the unknown height of the arch, which did not end abruptly, but faded away in the blue air, so gradually that he could not say where it ceased.

When the thought of the golden key returned, the boy very wisely proceeded to mark out in his mind the space covered by the foundation of the rainbow, in order that he might know where to search, should the rainbow disappear. It was based chiefly upon a bed of moss.

Meantime it had grown quite dark in the wood. The rainbow alone was visible by its own light. But the moment the moon rose the rainbow vanished. Nor could any change of place restore the vision to the boy's eyes. So he threw himself down upon the mossy bed, to wait till the sunlight would give him a chance of finding the key. There he fell fast asleep.

When he woke in the morning the sun was looking straight into his eyes. He turned away from it, and the same moment saw a brilliant little thing lying on the moss within a foot of his face. It was the golden key. The pipe of it was of plain gold, as bright as gold could be. The handle was curiously wrought and set with sapphires. In a terror of delight he put out his hand and took it, and had it.

He lay for a while, turning it over and over, and feeding his eyes upon its beauty. Then he jumped to his feet, remembering that the pretty thing was of no use to him yet. Where was the lock to which the key belonged? It must be somewhere, for how could anybody be so silly as make a key for which there was no lock? Where should he go to look for it? He gazed about him, up into the air, down to the earth, but saw no keyhole in the clouds, in the grass, or in the trees.

Just as he began to grow disconsolate, however, he saw something glimmering in the wood. It was a mere glimmer that he saw, but he took it for a glimmer of rainbow, and went towards it.— And now I will go back to the borders of the forest.

Not far from the house where the boy had lived, there was another house, the owner of which was a merchant, who was much away from home. He had lost his wife some years before, and had only one child, a little girl, whom he left to the charge of two servants, who were very idle and careless. So she was neglected and left untidy, and was sometimes ill-used besides.

Now it is well known that the little creatures commonly called fairies, though there are many different kinds of fairies in Fairyland, have an exceeding dislike to untidiness. Indeed, they are quite spiteful to slovenly people. Being used to all the lovely ways of the trees and flowers, and to the neatness of the birds and all woodland creatures, it makes them feel miserable, even in their deep woods and on their grassy carpets, to think that within the same moonlight lies a dirty, uncomfortable, slovenly house. And this makes them angry with the people that live in it, and they would gladly drive them out of the world if they could. They want the whole earth nice and clean. So they pinch the maids black and blue, and play them all manner of uncomfortable tricks.

But this house was quite a shame, and the fairies in the forest could not endure it. They tried everything on the maids without effect, and at last resolved upon making a clean riddance, beginning with the child. They ought to have known that it was not her fault, but they have little principle and much mischief in them, and they thought that if they got rid of her the maids would be sure to be turned away.

So one evening, the poor little girl having been put to bed early, before the sun was down, the servants went off to the village, locking the door behind them. The child did not know she was alone, and lay contentedly looking out of her window towards the forest, of which, however, she could not see much, because of the ivy and other creeping plants which had straggled across her window. All at once she saw an ape making faces at her out of the mirror, and the heads carved upon a great old wardrobe grinning fearfully. Then two old spider-legged chairs came forward into the middle of the room, and began to dance a queer, old-fashioned dance. This set her laughing, and she forgot the ape and the grinning heads. So the fairies saw they had made a mistake, and sent the chairs back to their places. But they knew that she had been reading the story of Silverhair all day. So the next moment she heard the voices of the three bears upon the stair, big voice, middle voice, and little voice, and she heard their soft, heavy tread, as if they had had stockings over their boots, coming nearer and nearer to the door of her room, till she could bear it no longer. She did just as Silverhair did, and as the fairies wanted her to do: she darted to the window, pulled it open, got upon the ivy, and so scrambled to the ground. She then fled to the forest as fast as she could run.

Now, although she did not know it, this was the very best way she could have gone; for nothing is ever so mischievous in its own place as it is out of it; and, besides, these mischievous creatures were only the children of Fairyland, as it were, and there are many other beings there as well; and if a wanderer gets in among them, the good ones will always help him more than the evil ones will be able to hurt him.

The sun was now set, and the darkness coming on, but the child thought of no danger but the bears behind her. If she had looked round, however, she would have seen that she was followed by a very different creature from a bear. It was a curious creature, made like a fish, but covered, instead of scales, with feathers of all colours, sparkling like those of a humming-bird. It had fins, not wings, and swam through the air as a fish does through the water. Its head was like the head of a small owl.

After running a long way, and as the last of the light was disappearing, she passed under a tree with drooping branches. It dropped its branches to the ground all about her, and caught her as in a trap. She struggled to get out, but the branches pressed her closer and closer to the trunk. She was in great terror and distress, when the air-fish, swimming into the thicket of branches, began tearing them with its beak. They loosened their hold at once, and the creature went on attacking them, till at length they let the child go. Then the air-fish came from behind her, and swam on in front, glittering and sparkling all lovely colours; and she followed.

It led her gently along till all at once it swam in at a cottage-door. The child followed still. There was a bright fire in the middle of the floor, upon which stood a pot without a lid, full of water that boiled and bubbled furiously. The air-fish swam straight to the pot and into the boiling water, where it lay quiet. A beautiful woman rose from the opposite side of the fire and came to meet the girl. She took her up in her arms, and said,—

"Ah, you are come at last! I have been looking for you a long time."

She sat down with her on her lap, and there the girl sat staring at her. She had never seen anything so beautiful. She was tall and strong, with white arms and neck, and a delicate flush on her face. The child could not tell what was the colour of her hair, but could not help thinking it had a tinge of dark green. She had not one ornament upon her, but she looked as if she had just put off quantities of diamonds and emeralds. Yet here she was in the simplest, poorest little cottage, where she was evidently at home. She was dressed in shining green.

The girl looked at the lady, and the lady looked at the girl.

"What is your name?" asked the lady.

"The servants always call me Tangle."

"Ah, that was because your hair was so untidy. But that was their fault, the naughty women! Still it is a pretty name, and I will call you Tangle too. You must not mind my asking you questions, for you may ask me the same questions, every one of them, and any others that you like. How old are you?"

"Ten," answered Tangle.

"You don't look like it," said the lady.

"How old are you, please?" returned Tangle.

"Thousands of years old," answered the lady.

"You don't look like it," said Tangle.

"Don't I? I think I do. Don't you see how beautiful I am?"

And her great blue eyes looked down on the little Tangle, as if all the stars in the sky were melted in them to make their brightness.

"Ah! but," said Tangle, "when people live long they grow old. At least I always thought so."

"I have no time to grow old," said the lady. "I am too busy for that. It is very idle to grow old.—But I cannot have my little girl so untidy. Do you know I can't find a clean spot on your face to kiss?"

"Perhaps," suggested Tangle, feeling ashamed, but not too much so to say a word for herself—"perhaps that is because the tree made me cry so."

"My poor darling!" said the lady, looking now as if the moon were melted in her eyes, and kissing her little face, dirty as it was, "the naughty tree must suffer for making a girl cry."

"And what is your name, please?" asked Tangle.

"Grandmother," answered the lady.

"Is it really?"

"Yes, indeed. I never tell stories, even in fun."

"How good of you!"

"I couldn't if I tried. It would come true if I said it, and then I should be punished enough." And she smiled like the sun through a summer-shower.

"But now," she went on, "I must get you washed and dressed, and then we shall have some supper."

"Oh! I had supper long ago," said Tangle.

"Yes, indeed you had," answered the lady—"three years ago. You don't know that it is three years since you ran away from the bears. You are thirteen and more now."

Tangle could only stare. She felt quite sure it was true.

"You will not be afraid of anything I do with you—will you?" said the lady.

"I will try very hard not to be; but I can't be certain, you know," replied Tangle.

"I like your saying so, and I shall be quite satisfied," answered the lady.

She took off the girl's night-gown, rose with her in her arms, and going to the wall of the cottage, opened a door. Then Tangle saw a deep tank, the sides of which were filled with green plants, which had flowers of all colours. There was a roof over it like the roof of the cottage. It was filled with beautiful clear water, in which swam a multitude of such fishes as the one that had led her to the cottage. It was the light their colours gave that showed the place in which they were.

The lady spoke some words Tangle could not understand, and threw her into the tank.

The fishes came crowding about her. Two or three of them got under her head and kept it up. The rest of them rubbed themselves all over her, and with their wet feathers washed her quite clean. Then the lady, who had been looking on all the time, spoke again; whereupon some thirty or forty of the fishes rose out of the water underneath Tangle, and so bore her up to the arms the lady held out to take her. She carried her back to the fire, and, having dried her well, opened a chest, and taking out the finest linen garments, smelling of grass and lavender, put them upon her, and over all a green dress, just like her own, shining like hers, and soft like hers, and going into just such lovely folds from the waist, where it was tied with a brown cord, to her bare feet.

"Won't you give me a pair of shoes too, grandmother?" said Tangle.

"No, my dear; no shoes. Look here. I wear no shoes."

So saying she lifted her dress a little, and there were the loveliest white feet, but no shoes. Then Tangle was content to go without shoes too. And the lady sat down with her again, and combed her hair, and brushed it, and then left it to dry while she got the supper.

First she got bread out of one hole in the wall; then milk out of another; then several kinds of fruit out of a third; and then she went to the pot on the fire, and took out the fish, now nicely cooked, and, as soon as she had pulled off its feathered skin, ready to be eaten.

"But," exclaimed Tangle. And she stared at the fish, and could say no more.

"I know what you mean," returned the lady. "You do not like to eat the messenger that brought you home. But it is the kindest return you can make. The creature was afraid to go until it saw me put the pot on, and heard me promise it should be boiled the moment it returned with you. Then it darted out of the door at once. You saw it go into the pot of itself the moment it entered, did you not?"

"I did," answered Tangle, "and I thought it very strange; but then I saw you, and forgot all about the fish."

"In Fairyland," resumed the lady, as they sat down to the table, "the ambition of the animals is to be eaten by the people; for that is their highest end in that condition. But they are not therefore destroyed. Out of that pot comes something more than the dead fish, you will see."

Tangle now remarked that the lid was on the pot. But the lady took no further notice of it till they had eaten the fish, which Tangle found nicer than any fish she had ever tasted before. It was as white as snow, and as delicate as cream. And the moment she had swallowed a mouthful of it, a change she could not describe began to take place in her. She heard a murmuring all about her, which became more and more articulate, and at length, as she went on eating, grew intelligible. By the time she had finished her share, the sounds of all the animals in the forest came crowding through the door to her ears; for the door still stood wide open, though it was pitch-dark outside; and they were no longer sounds only; they were speech, and speech that she could understand. She could tell what the insects in the cottage were saying to each other too. She had even a suspicion that the trees and flowers all about the cottage were holding midnight communications with each other; but what they said she could not hear.

As soon as the fish was eaten, the lady went to the fire and took the lid off the pot. A lovely little creature in human shape, with large white wings, rose out of it, and flew round and round the roof of the cottage; then dropped, fluttering, and nestled in the lap of the lady. She spoke to it some strange words, carried it to the door, and threw it out into the darkness. Tangle heard the flapping of its wings die away in the distance.

"Now have we done the fish any harm?" she said, returning.

"No," answered Tangle, "I do not think we have. I should not mind eating one every day."

"They must wait their time, like you and me too, my little Tangle."

And she smiled a smile which the sadness in it made more lovely.

"But," she continued, "I think we may have one for supper to-morrow."

So saying she went to the door of the tank, and spoke; and now Tangle understood her perfectly.

"I want one of you," she said,—"the wisest."

Thereupon the fishes got together in the middle of the tank, with their heads forming a circle above the water, and their tails a larger circle beneath it. They were holding a council, in which their relative wisdom should be determined. At length one of them flew up into the lady's hand, looking lively and ready.

"You know where the rainbow stands?" she asked.

"Yes, mother, quite well," answered the fish.

"Bring home a young man you will find there, who does not know where to go."

The fish was out of the door in a moment. Then the lady told Tangle it was time to go to bed; and, opening another door in the side of the cottage, showed her a little arbour, cool and green, with a bed of purple heath growing in it, upon which she threw a large wrapper made of the feathered skins of the wise fishes, shining gorgeous in the firelight.

Tangle was soon lost in the strangest, loveliest dreams. And the beautiful lady was in every one of her dreams.

In the morning she woke to the rustling of leaves over her head, and the sound of running water. But, to her surprise, she could find no door—nothing but the moss-grown wall of the cottage. So she crept through an opening in the arbour, and stood in the forest. Then she bathed in a stream that ran merrily through the trees, and felt happier; for having once been in her grandmother's pond, she must be clean and tidy ever after; and, having put on her green dress, felt like a lady.

She spent that day in the wood, listening to the birds and beasts and creeping things. She understood all that they said, though she could not repeat a word of it; and every kind had a different language, while there was a common though more limited understanding between all the inhabitants of the forest. She saw nothing of the beautiful lady, but she felt that she was near her all the time; and she took care not to go out of sight of the cottage. It was round, like a snow-hut or a wigwam; and she could see neither door nor window in it. The fact was, it had no windows; and though it was full of doors, they all opened from the inside, and could not even be seen from the outside.

She was standing at the foot of a tree in the twilight, listening to a quarrel between a mole and a squirrel, in which the mole told the squirrel that the tail was the best of him, and the squirrel called the mole Spade-fists, when, the darkness having deepened around her, she became aware of something shining in her face, and looking round, saw that the door of the cottage was open, and the red light of the fire flowing from it like a river through the darkness. She left Mole and Squirrel to settle matters as they might, and darted off to the cottage. Entering, she found the pot boiling on the fire, and the grand, lovely lady sitting on the other side of it.

"I've been watching you all day," said the lady. "You shall have something to eat by-and-by, but we must wait till our supper comes home."

She took Tangle on her knee, and began to sing to her—such songs as made her wish she could listen to them for ever. But at length in rushed the shining fish, and snuggled down in the pot. It was followed by a youth who had outgrown his worn garments. His face was ruddy with health, and in his hand he carried a little jewel, which sparkled in the firelight.

The first words the lady said were,—

"What is that in your hand, Mossy?"

Now Mossy was the name his companions had given him, because he had a favourite stone covered with moss, on which he used to sit whole days reading; and they said the moss had begun to grow upon him too.

Mossy held out his hand. The moment the lady saw that it was the golden key, she rose from her chair, kissed Mossy on the forehead, made him sit down on her seat, and stood before him like a servant. Mossy could not bear this, and rose at once. But the lady begged him, with tears in her beautiful eyes, to sit, and let her wait on him.

"But you are a great, splendid, beautiful lady," said Mossy.

"Yes, I am. But I work all day long—that is my pleasure; and you will have to leave me so soon!"

"How do you know that, if you please, madam?" asked Mossy.

"Because you have got the golden key."

"But I don't know what it is for. I can't find the key-hole. Will you tell me what to do?"

"You must look for the key-hole. That is your work. I cannot help you. I can only tell you that if you look for it you will find it."

"What kind of box will it open? What is there inside?"

"I do not know. I dream about it, but I know nothing."

"Must I go at once?"

"You may stop here to-night, and have some of my supper. But you must go in the morning. All I can do for you is to give you clothes. Here is a girl called Tangle, whom you must take with you."

"That *will* be nice," said Mossy.

"No, no!" said Tangle. "I don't want to leave you, please, grandmother."

"You must go with him, Tangle. I am sorry to lose you, but it will be the best thing for you. Even the fishes, you see, have to go into the pot, and then out into the dark. If you fall in with the Old Man of the Sea, mind you ask him whether he has not got some more fishes ready for me. My tank is getting thin."

So saying, she took the fish from the pot, and put the lid on as before. They sat down and ate the fish, and then the winged creature rose from the pot, circled the roof, and settled on the lady's lap. She talked to it, carried it to the door, and threw it out into the dark. They heard the flap of its wings die away in the distance.

The lady then showed Mossy into just such another chamber as that of Tangle; and in the morning he found a suit of clothes laid beside him. He looked very handsome in them. But the wearer of grandmother's clothes never thinks about how he or she looks, but thinks always how handsome other people are.

Tangle was very unwilling to go.

"Why should I leave you? I don't know the young man," she said to the lady.

"I am never allowed to keep my children long. You need not go with him except you please, but you must go some day; and I should like you to go with him, for he has the golden key. No girl need be afraid to go with a youth that has the golden key. You will take care of her, Mossy, will you not?"

"That I will," said Mossy.

And Tangle cast a glance at him, and thought she should like to go with him.

"And," said the lady, "if you should lose each other as you go through the—the—I never can remember the name of that country,—do not be afraid, but go on and on."

She kissed Tangle on the mouth and Mossy on the forehead, led them to the door, and waved her hand eastward. Mossy and Tangle took each other's hand and walked away into the depth of the forest. In his right hand Mossy held the golden key.

They wandered thus a long way, with endless amusement from the talk of the animals. They soon learned enough of their language to ask them necessary questions. The squirrels were always friendly, and gave them nuts out of their own hoards; but the bees were selfish and rude, justifying themselves on the ground that Tangle and Mossy were not subjects of their queen, and charity must begin at home, though indeed they had not one drone in their poorhouse at the time. Even the blinking moles would fetch them an earth-nut or a truffle now and then, talking as if their mouths, as well as their eyes and ears, were full of cotton wool, or their own velvety fur. By the time they got out of the forest they were very fond of each other, and Tangle was not in the least sorry that her grandmother had sent her away with Mossy.

At length the trees grew smaller, and stood farther apart, and the ground began to rise, and it got more and more steep, till the trees were all left behind, and the two were climbing a narrow path with rocks on each side. Suddenly they came upon a rude doorway, by which they entered a narrow gallery cut in the rock. It grew darker and darker, till it was pitch-dark, and they had to feel their way. At length the light began to return, and at last they came out upon a narrow path on the face of a lofty precipice. This path went winding down the rock to a wide plain, circular in shape, and surrounded on all sides by mountains. Those opposite to them were a great way off, and towered to an awful height, shooting up sharp, blue, ice-enamelled pinnacles. An utter silence reigned where they stood. Not even the sound of water reached them.

Looking down, they could not tell whether the valley below was a grassy plain or a great still lake. They had never seen any space look like it. The way to it was difficult and dangerous, but down the narrow path they went, and reached the bottom in safety. They found it composed of smooth, light-coloured sandstone, undulating in parts, but mostly level. It was no wonder to them now that they had not been able to tell what it was, for this surface was everywhere crowded with shadows. It was a sea of shadows. The mass was chiefly made up of the shadows of leaves innumerable, of all lovely and imaginative forms, waving to and fro, floating and quivering in the breath of a breeze whose motion was unfelt, whose sound was unheard. No forests clothed the mountain-sides, no trees were anywhere to be seen, and yet the shadows of the leaves, branches, and stems of all various trees covered the valley as far as their eyes could reach. They soon spied the shadows of flowers mingled with those of the leaves, and now and then the shadow of a bird with open beak, and throat distended with song. At times would appear the forms of strange, graceful creatures, running up and down the shadow-boles and along the branches, to disappear in the wind-tossed foliage. As they walked they waded knee-deep in the lovely lake. For the shadows were not merely lying on the surface of the ground, but heaped up above it like substantial forms of darkness, as if they had been cast upon a thousand different planes of the air. Tangle and Mossy often lifted their heads and gazed upwards to descry whence the shadows came; but they could see nothing more than a bright mist spread above them, higher than the tops of the mountains, which stood clear against it. No forests, no leaves, no birds were visible.

After a while, they reached more open spaces, where the shadows were thinner; and came even to portions over which shadows only flitted, leaving them clear for such as might follow. Now a wonderful form, half bird-like half human, would float across on outspread sailing pinions. Anon an exquisite shadow group of gambolling children would be followed by the loveliest female form, and that again by the grand stride of a Titanic[1] shape, each disappearing in the surrounding press of shadowy foliage. Sometimes a profile of unspeakable beauty or grandeur would appear for a moment and vanish. Sometimes they seemed lovers that passed linked arm in arm, sometimes father and son, sometimes brothers in loving contest, sometimes sisters entwined in gracefullest community of complex form. Sometimes wild horses would tear across, free, or bestrode by noble shadows of ruling men. But some of the things which pleased them most they never knew how to describe.

About the middle of the plain they sat down to rest in the heart of a heap of shadows. After sitting for a while, each, looking up, saw the other in tears: they were each longing after the country whence the shadows fell.

"We *must* find the country from which the shadows come," said Mossy.

"We must, dear Mossy," responded Tangle. "What if your golden key should be the key to *it*?"

"Ah! that would be grand," returned Mossy.—"But we must rest here for a little, and then we shall be able to cross the plain before night."

---

1 "Pertaining to, resembling, or characteristic of the Titans of mythology; gigantic, colossal; also, of the nature or character of the Titans" (*OED*).

So he lay down on the ground, and about him on every side, and over his head, was the constant play of the wonderful shadows. He could look through them, and see the one behind the other, till they mixed in a mass of darkness. Tangle, too, lay admiring, and wondering, and longing after the country whence the shadows came. When they were rested they rose and pursued their journey.

How long they were in crossing this plain I cannot tell; but before night Mossy's hair was streaked with gray, and Tangle had got wrinkles on her forehead.

As evening drew on, the shadows fell deeper and rose higher. At length they reached a place where they rose above their heads, and made all dark around them. Then they took hold of each other's hand, and walked on in silence and in some dismay. They felt the gathering darkness, and something strangely solemn besides, and the beauty of the shadows ceased to delight them. All at once Tangle found that she had not a hold of Mossy's hand, though when she lost it she could not tell.

"Mossy, Mossy!" she cried aloud in terror.

But no Mossy replied. A moment after, the shadows sank to her feet, and down under her feet, and the mountains rose before her. She turned towards the gloomy region she had left, and called once more upon Mossy. There the gloom lay tossing and heaving, a dark, stormy, foamless sea of shadows, but no Mossy rose out of it, or came climbing up the hill on which she stood. She threw herself down and wept in despair.

Suddenly she remembered that the beautiful lady had told them, if they lost each other in a country of which she could not remember the name, they were not to be afraid, but to go straight on.

"And besides," she said to herself, "Mossy has the golden key, and so no harm will come to him, I do believe."

She rose from the ground, and went on.

Before long she arrived at a precipice, in the face of which a stair was cut. When she had ascended half-way, the stair ceased, and the path led straight into the mountain. She was afraid to enter, and turning again towards the stair, grew giddy at sight of the depth beneath her, and was forced to throw herself down in the mouth of the cave.

When she opened her eyes, she saw a beautiful little creature with wings standing beside her, waiting.

"I know you," said Tangle. "You are my fish."

"Yes. But I am a fish no longer. I am an aëranth now."

"What is that?" asked Tangle.

"What you see I am," answered the shape. "And I am come to lead you through the mountain."

"Oh! thank you, dear fish—aëranth, I mean," returned Tangle, rising.

Thereupon the aëranth took to his wings, and flew on through the long, narrow passage, reminding Tangle very much of the way he had swum on before her when he was a fish. And the moment his white wings moved, they began to throw off a continuous shower of sparks of all colours, which lighted up the passage before them.—All at once he vanished, and Tangle heard a low, sweet sound, quite different from the rush and crackle of his wings. Before her was an open arch, and through it came light, mixed with the sound of sea-waves.

She hurried out, and fell, tired and happy, upon the yellow sand of the shore. There she lay, half asleep with weariness and rest, listening to the low plash and retreat of the tiny waves, which seemed ever enticing the land to leave off being land, and become sea. And as she lay, her eyes were fixed upon the foot of a great rainbow standing far away against the sky on the other side of the sea. At length she fell fast asleep.

When she awoke, she saw an old man with long white hair down to his shoulders, leaning upon a stick covered with green buds, and so bending over her.

"What do you want here, beautiful woman?" he said.

"Am I beautiful? I am so glad!" answered Tangle, rising. "My grandmother is beautiful."

"Yes. But what do you want?" he repeated, kindly.

"I think I want you. Are not you the Old Man of the Sea?"

"I am."

"Then grandmother says, have you any more fishes ready for her?"

"We will go and see, my dear," answered the old man, speaking yet more kindly than before. "And I can do something for you, can I not?"

"Yes—show me the way up to the country from which the shadows fall," said Tangle.

For there she hoped to find Mossy again.

"Ah! indeed, that would be worth doing," said the old man. "But I cannot, for I do not know the way myself. But I will send you to the Old Man of the Earth. Perhaps he can tell you. He is much older than I am."

Leaning on his staff, he conducted her along the shore to a steep rock, that looked like a petrified ship turned upside down.

The door of it was the rudder of a great vessel, ages ago at the bottom of the sea. Immediately within the door was a stair in the rock, down which the old man went, and Tangle followed. At the bottom the old man had his house, and there he lived.

As soon as she entered it, Tangle heard a strange noise, unlike anything she had ever heard before. She soon found that it was the fishes talking. She tried to understand what they said; but their speech was so old-fashioned, and rude, and undefined, that she could not make much of it.

"I will go and see about those fishes for my daughter," said the Old Man of the Sea.

And moving a slide in the wall of his house, he first looked out, and then tapped upon a thick piece of crystal that filled the round opening. Tangle came up behind him, and peeping through the window into the heart of the great deep green ocean, saw the most curious creatures, some very ugly, all very odd, and with especially queer mouths, swimming about everywhere, above and below, but all coming towards the window in answer to the tap of the Old Man of the Sea. Only a few could get their mouths against the glass; but those who were floating miles away yet turned their heads towards it. The old man looked through the whole flock carefully for some minutes, and then turning to Tangle, said,—

"I am sorry I have not got one ready yet. I want more time than she does. But I will send some as soon as I can."

He then shut the slide.

Presently a great noise arose in the sea. The Old Man opened the slide again, and tapped on the glass, whereupon the fishes were all as still as sleep.

"They were only talking about you," he said. "And they do speak such nonsense!—To-morrow," he continued, "I must show you the way to the Old Man of the Earth. He lives a long way from here."

"Do let me go at once," said Tangle.

"No. That is not possible. You must come this way first."

He led her to a hole in the wall, which she had not observed before. It was covered with the green leaves and white blossoms of a creeping plant.

"Only white-blossoming plants can grow under the sea," said the old man. "In there you will find a bath, in which you must lie till I call you."

Tangle went in, and found a smaller room or cave, in the further corner of which was a great basin hollowed out of a rock, and half-full of the clearest sea-water. Little streams were constantly running into it from cracks in the wall of the cavern. It was polished quite smooth inside, and had a carpet of yellow sand in the bottom of it. Large green leaves and white flowers of various plants crowded up and over it, draping and covering it almost entirely.

No sooner was she undressed and lying in the bath, than she began to feel as if the water were sinking into her, and she were receiving all the good of sleep without undergoing its forgetfulness. She felt the good coming all the time. And she grew happier and more hopeful than she had been since she lost Mossy. But she could not help thinking how very sad it was for a poor old man to live there all alone, and have to take care of a whole seaful of stupid and riotous fishes.

After about an hour, as she thought, she heard his voice calling her, and rose out of the bath. All the fatigue and aching of her long journey had vanished. She was as whole, and strong, and well as if she had slept for seven days.

Returning to the opening that led into the other part of the house, she started back with amazement, for through it she saw the form of a grand man, with a majestic and beautiful face, waiting for her.

"Come," he said; "I see you are ready."

She entered with reverence.

"Where is the Old Man of the Sea?" she asked, humbly.

"There is no one here but me," he answered, smiling. "Some people call me the Old Man of the Sea. Others have another name for me, and are terribly frightened when they meet me taking a walk by the shore. Therefore I avoid being seen by them, for they are so afraid, that they never see what I really am. You see me now.—But I must show you the way to the Old Man of the Earth."

He led her into the cave where the bath was, and there she saw, in the opposite corner, a second opening in the rock.

"Go down that stair, and it will bring you to him," said the Old Man of the Sea.

With humble thanks Tangle took her leave. She went down the winding-stair, till she began to fear there was no end to it. Still down and down it went, rough and broken, with springs of water bursting out of the rocks and running down the steps beside her. It was quite dark about her, and yet she could see. For after being in that bath, people's eyes always give out a light they can see by. There were no creeping things in the way. All was safe and pleasant though so dark and damp and deep.

At last there was not one step more, and she found herself in a glimmering cave. On a stone in the middle of it sat a figure with its back towards her—the figure of an old man bent double with age. From behind she could see his white beard spread out on the rocky floor in front of him. He did not move as she entered, so she passed round that she might stand before him and speak to him. The moment she looked in his face, she saw that he was a youth of marvellous beauty. He sat entranced with the delight of what he beheld in a mirror of something like silver, which lay on the floor at his feet, and which from behind she had taken for his white beard. He sat on, heedless of her presence, pale with the joy of his vision. She stood and watched him. At length, all trembling, she spoke. But her voice made no sound. Yet the youth lifted up his head. He showed no surprise, however, at seeing her—only smiled a welcome.

"Are you the Old Man of the Earth?" Tangle had said.

And the youth answered, and Tangle heard him, though not with her ears:—

"I am. What can I do for you?"

"Tell me the way to the country whence the shadows fall."

"Ah! that I do not know. I only dream about it myself. I see its shadows sometimes in my mirror: the way to it I do not know. But I think the Old Man of the Fire must know. He is much older than I am. He is the oldest man of all."

"Where does he live?"

"I will show you the way to his place. I never saw him myself."

So saying, the young man rose, and then stood for a while gazing at Tangle.

"I wish I could see that country too," he said. "But I must mind my work."

He led her to the side of the cave, and told her to lay her ear against the wall.

"What do you hear?" he asked.

"I hear," answered Tangle, "the sound of a great water running inside the rock."

"That river runs down to the dwelling of the oldest man of all—the Old Man of the Fire. I wish I could go to see him. But I must mind my work. That river is the only way to him."

Then the Old Man of the Earth stooped over the floor of the cave, raised a huge stone from it, and left it leaning. It disclosed a great hole that went plumb-down.

"That is the way," he said.

"But there are no stairs."

"You must throw yourself in. There is no other way."

She turned and looked him full in the face—stood so for a whole minute, as she thought: it was a whole year—then threw herself headlong into the hole.

When she came to herself, she found herself gliding down fast and deep. Her head was under water, but that did not signify, for, when she thought about it, she could not remember that she had breathed once since her bath in the cave of the Old Man of the Sea. When she lifted up her head a sudden and fierce heat struck her, and she sank it again instantly, and went sweeping on.

Gradually the stream grew shallower. At length she could hardly keep her head under. Then the water could carry her no farther. She rose from the channel, and went step for step down the burning descent. The water ceased altogether. The heat was terrible. She felt scorched to the bone, but it did not touch her strength. It grew hotter and hotter. She said, "I can bear it no longer." Yet she went on.

At the long last, the stair ended at a rude archway in an all but glowing rock. Through this archway Tangle fell exhausted into a cool mossy cave. The floor and walls were covered with moss—green, soft, and damp. A little stream spouted from a rent in the rock and fell into a basin of moss. She plunged her face into it and drank. Then she lifted her head and looked around. Then she rose and looked again. She saw no one in the cave. But the moment she stood upright she had a marvellous sense that she was in the secret of the earth and all its ways. Everything she had seen, or learned from books; all that her grandmother had said or sung to her; all the talk of the beasts, birds, and fishes; all that had happened to her on her journey with Mossy, and since then in the heart of the earth with the Old man and the Older man—all was plain: she understood it all, and saw that everything meant the same thing, though she could not have put it into words again.

The next moment she descried, in a corner of the cave, a little naked child, sitting on the moss. He was playing with balls of various colours and sizes, which he disposed in strange figures upon the floor beside him. And now Tangle felt that there was something in her knowledge which was not in her understanding. For she knew there must be an infinite meaning in the change and sequence and individual forms of the figures into which the child arranged the balls, as well as in the varied harmonies of their colours, but what it all meant she could not tell.[1] He went

---

1 I think I must be indebted to Novalis for these geometrical figures.
   [MacDonald's note. See Introduction, pp. 12-13.]

on busily, tirelessly, playing his solitary game, without looking up, or seeming to know that there was a stranger in his deep-with-drawn cell. Diligently as a lace-maker shifts her bobbins, he shifted and arranged his balls. Flashes of meaning would now pass from them to Tangle, and now again all would be not merely obscure, but utterly dark. She stood looking for a long time, for there was fascination in the sight; and the longer she looked the more an indescribable vague intelligence went on rousing itself in her mind. For seven years she had stood there watching the naked child with his coloured balls, and it seemed to her like seven hours, when all at once the shape the balls took, she knew not why, reminded her of the Valley of Shadows, and she spoke:—

"Where is the Old Man of the Fire?" she said.

"Here I am," answered the child, rising and leaving his balls on the moss. "What can I do for you?"

There was such an awfulness of absolute repose on the face of the child that Tangle stood dumb before him. He had no smile, but the love in his large gray eyes was deep as the centre. And with the repose there lay on his face a shimmer as of moonlight, which seemed as if any moment it might break into such a rav-ishing smile as would cause the beholder to weep himself to death. But the smile never came, and the moonlight lay there unbroken. For the heart of the child was too deep for any smile to reach from it to his face.

"Are you the oldest man of all?" Tangle at length, although filled with awe, ventured to ask.

"Yes, I am. I am very, very old. I am able to help you, I know. I can help everybody."

And the child drew near and looked up in her face so that she burst into tears.

"Can you tell me the way to the country the shadows fall from?" she sobbed.

"Yes. I know the way quite well. I go there myself sometimes. But you could not go my way; you are not old enough. I will show you how you can go."

"Do not send me out into the great heat again," prayed Tangle.

"I will not," answered the child.

And he reached up, and put his little cool hand on her heart.

"Now," he said, "you can go. The fire will not burn you. Come."

He led her from the cave, and following him through another archway, she found herself in a vast desert of sand and rock. The sky of it was of rock, lowering over them like solid thunderclouds; and the whole place was so hot that she saw, in bright rivulets, the yellow gold and white silver and red copper trickling molten from the rocks. But the heat never came near her.

When they had gone some distance, the child turned up a great stone, and took something like an egg from under it. He next drew a long curved line in the sand with his finger, and laid the egg in it. He then spoke something Tangle could not understand. The egg broke, a small snake came out, and, lying in the line in the sand, grew and grew till he filled it. The moment he was thus full-grown, he began to glide away, undulating like a sea-wave.

"Follow that serpent," said the child. "He will lead you the right way."

Tangle followed the serpent. But she could not go far without looking back at the marvellous Child. He stood alone in the midst of the glowing desert, beside a fountain of red flame that had burst forth at his feet, his naked whiteness glimmering a pale rosy red in the torrid fire. There he stood, looking after her, till, from the lengthening distance, she could see him no more. The serpent went straight on, turning neither to the right nor left.

Meantime Mossy had got out of the lake of shadows, and, following his mournful, lonely way, had reached the sea-shore. It was a dark, stormy evening. The sun had set. The wind was blowing from the sea. The waves had surrounded the rock within which lay the Old Man's house. A deep water rolled between it and the shore, upon which a majestic figure was walking alone.

Mossy went up to him and said,—

"Will you tell me where to find the Old Man of the Sea?"

"I am the Old Man of the Sea," the figure answered.

"I see a strong kingly man of middle age," returned Mossy.

Then the Old Man looked at him more intently, and said,—

"Your sight, young man, is better than that of most who take this way. The night is stormy: come to my house and tell me what I can do for you."

Mossy followed him. The waves flew from before the footsteps of the Old Man of the Sea, and Mossy followed upon dry sand.

When they had reached the cave, they sat down and gazed at each other.

Now Mossy was an old man by this time. He looked much older than the Old Man of the Sea, and his feet were very weary.

After looking at him for a moment, the Old Man took him by the hand and led him into his inner cave. There he helped him to undress, and laid him in the bath. And he saw that one of his hands Mossy did not open.

"What have you in that hand?" he asked.

Mossy opened his hand, and there lay the golden key.

"Ah!" said the Old Man, "that accounts for your knowing me. And I know the way you have to go."

"I want to find the country whence the shadows fall," said Mossy.

"I dare say you do. So do I. But meantime, one thing is certain.—What is that key for, do you think?"

"For a keyhole somewhere. But I don't know why I keep it. I never could find the keyhole. And I have lived a good while, I believe," said Mossy, sadly. "I'm not sure that I'm not old. I know my feet ache."

"Do they?" said the old man, as if he really meant to ask the question; and Mossy, who was still lying in the bath, watched his feet for a moment before he replied,

"No, they do not," he answered. "Perhaps I am not old either."

"Get up and look at yourself in the water."

He rose and looked at himself in the water, and there was not a gray hair on his head or a wrinkle on his skin.

"You have tasted of death now," said the Old Man. "Is it good?"

"It is good," said Mossy. "It is better than life."

"No," said the Old Man: "it is only more life.—Your feet will make no holes in the water now."

"What do you mean?"

"I will show you that presently."

They returned to the outer cave, and sat and talked together for a long time. At length the Old Man of the Sea rose, and said to Mossy,—

"Follow me."

He led him up the stair again, and opened another door. They stood on the level of the raging sea, looking towards the east. Across the waste of waters, against the bosom of a fierce black cloud, stood the foot of a rainbow, glowing in the dark.

"This indeed is my way," said Mossy, as soon as he saw the rainbow, and stepped out upon the sea. His feet made no holes in the water. He fought the wind, and clomb the waves, and went on towards the rainbow.

The storm died away. A lovely day and a lovelier night followed. A cool wind blew over the wide plain of the quiet ocean. And still Mossy journeyed eastward. But the rainbow had vanished with the storm.

Day after day he held on, and he thought he had no guide. He did not see how a shining fish under the waters directed his steps. He crossed the sea, and came to a great precipice of rock, up which he could discover but one path. Nor did this lead him farther than half-way up the rock, where it ended on a platform. Here he stood and pondered.—It could not be that the way stopped here, else what was the path for? It was a rough path, not very plain, yet certainly a path.—He examined the face of the rock. It was smooth as glass. But as his eyes kept roving hopelessly over it, something glittered, and he caught sight of a row of small sapphires. They bordered a little hole in the rock.

"The keyhole!" he cried.

He tried the key. It fitted. It turned. A great clang and clash, as of iron bolts on huge brazen caldrons, echoed thunderously within. He drew out the key. The rock in front of him began to fall. He retreated from it as far as the breadth of the platform would allow. A great slab fell at his feet. In front was still the solid rock, with this one slab fallen forward out of it. But the moment he stepped upon it, a second fell, just short of the edge of the first, making the next step of a stair, which thus kept dropping itself before him as he ascended into the heart of the precipice. It led him into a hall fit for such an approach—irregular and rude in formation, but floor, sides, pillars, and vaulted roof, all one mass of shining stones of every colour that light can show. In the centre stood seven columns, ranged from red to violet. And on the pedestal of one of them sat a woman, motionless, with her face bowed upon her knees. Seven years had she sat there waiting. She lifted her head as Mossy drew near. It was Tangle. Her hair had grown to her feet, and was rippled like the windless sea on broad sands. Her face was beautiful, like her grandmother's, and as still and peaceful as that of the Old Man of the Fire. Her form was tall and noble. Yet Mossy knew her at once.

"How beautiful you are, Tangle!" he said, in delight and astonishment.

"Am I?" she returned. "Oh, I have waited for you so long! But you, you are like the Old Man of the Sea. No. You are like the Old Man of the Earth. No, no. You are like the oldest man of all. You are like them all. And yet you are my own old Mossy! How did you come here? What did you do after I lost you? Did you find the key-hole? Have you got the key still?"

She had a hundred questions to ask him, and he a hundred more to ask her. They told each other all their adventures, and were as happy as man and woman could be. For they were younger and better, and stronger and wiser, than they had ever been before.

It began to grow dark. And they wanted more than ever to reach the country whence the shadows fall. So they looked about them for a way out of the cave. The door by which Mossy entered had closed again, and there was half a mile of rock between them and the sea. Neither could Tangle find the opening in the floor by which the serpent had led her thither. They searched till it grew so dark that they could see nothing, and gave it up.

After a while, however, the cave began to glimmer again. The light came from the moon, but it did not look like moonlight, for it gleamed through those seven pillars in the middle, and filled the place with all colours. And now Mossy saw that there was a pillar beside the red one, which he had not observed before. And it was of the same new colour that he had seen in the rainbow when he saw it first in the fairy forest. And on it he saw a sparkle of blue. It was the sapphires round the keyhole.

He took his key. It turned in the lock to the sound of Æolian[1] music. A door opened upon slow hinges, and disclosed a winding stair within. The key vanished from his fingers. Tangle went up. Mossy followed. The door closed behind them. They climbed out of the earth; and, still climbing, rose above it. They were in the rainbow. Far abroad, over ocean and land, they could see through its transparent walls the earth beneath their feet. Stairs beside stairs wound up together, and beautiful beings of all ages climbed along with them.

They knew that they were going up to the country whence the shadows fall.

And by this time I think they must have got there.

---

[1] "Of or relating to Aeolus, the Greek god of the winds; of, made by, or borne on the wind or currents of air; (also) like an Aeolian harp" (*OED*).

THE HISTORY OF PHOTOGEN AND NYCTERIS:
A DAY AND NIGHT MÄRCHEN[1]

CHAPTER I. WATHO.

There was once a witch who desired to know everything. But the wiser a witch is, the harder she knocks her head against the wall when she comes to it. Her name was Watho, and she had a wolf in her mind. She cared for nothing in itself—only for knowing it. She was not naturally cruel, but the wolf had made her cruel.

She was tall and graceful, with a white skin, red hair, and black eyes, which had a red fire in them. She was straight and strong, but now and then would fall bent together, shudder, and sit for a moment with her head turned over her shoulder, as if the wolf had got out of her mind onto her back.

CHAPTER II. AURORA.

This witch got two ladies to visit her. One of them belonged to the court, and her husband had been sent on a far and difficult embassy. The other was a young widow whose husband had lately died, and who had since lost her sight. Watho lodged them in different parts of her castle, and they did not know of each other's existence.

The castle stood on the side of a hill sloping gently down into a narrow valley, in which was a river, with a pebbly channel and a continual song. The garden went down to the bank of the river, enclosed by high walls, which crossed the river and there stopped. Each wall had a double row of battlements, and between the rows was a narrow walk.

In the topmost story of the castle the Lady Aurora occupied a spacious apartment of several large rooms looking southward.

---

1 Also known as "The Day Boy and the Night Girl," this story first appeared in the Christmas number of *The Graphic*, 1879. It was later reprinted in *The Gifts of the Child Christ and Other Tales* (1882) and *Fairy Tales* (1904). The text reproduced here is based on that published in *The Gifts of the Child Christ and Other Tales*. Märchen (the singular and plural form are the same) are folk or fairy tales, especially in the German tradition.

The windows projected oriel-wise[1] over the garden below, and there was a splendid view from them both up and down and across the river. The opposite side of the valley was steep, but not very high. Far away snowpeaks were visible. These rooms Aurora seldom left, but their airy spaces, the brilliant landscape and sky, the plentiful sunlight, the musical instruments, books, pictures, curiosities, with the company of Watho who made herself charming, precluded all dullness. She had venison and feathered game to eat, milk and pale sunny sparkling wine to drink.

She had hair of the yellow gold, waved and rippled; her skin was fair, not white like Watho's, and her eyes were of the blue of the heavens when bluest; her features were delicate but strong, her mouth large and finely curved, and haunted with smiles.

CHAPTER III. VESPER.

Behind the castle the hill rose abruptly; the north-eastern tower, indeed, was in contact with the rock, and communicated with the interior of it. For in the rock was a series of chambers, known only to Watho and the one servant whom she trusted, called Falca. Some former owner had constructed these chambers after the tomb of an Egyptian king, and probably with the same design, for in the center of one of them stood what could only be a sarcophagus, but that and others were walled off. The sides and roofs of them were carved in low relief, and curiously painted. Here the witch lodged the blind lady, whose name was Vesper. Her eyes were black, with long black lashes; her skin had a look of darkened silver, but was of purest tint and grain; her hair was black and fine and straight-flowing; her features were exquisitely formed, and if less beautiful yet more lovely from sadness; she always looked as if she wanted to lie down and not rise again. She did not know she was lodged in a tomb, though now and then she wondered she never touched a window. There were many couches, covered with richest silk, and soft as her own cheek, for her to lie upon; and the carpets were so thick, she might have cast herself down anywhere—as befitted a tomb. The place was dry and warm, and cunningly pierced for air, so that it was always fresh, and lacked only sunlight. There the witch fed her upon

---

1 An "oriel" is "a large polygonal recess with a window, projecting from a building, usually at an upper storey, and supported from the ground or on corbels" (*OED*).

milk, and wine dark as a carbuncle, and pomegranates, and purple grapes, and birds that dwell in marshy places; and she played to her mournful tunes, and caused wailful violins to attend her, and told her sad tales, thus holding her ever in an atmosphere of sweet sorrow.

CHAPTER IV. PHOTOGEN.

Watho at length had her desire, for witches often get what they want: a splendid boy was born to the fair Aurora. Just as the sun rose, he opened his eyes. Watho carried him immediately to a distant part of the castle, and persuaded the mother that he never cried but once, dying the moment he was born. Overcome with grief, Aurora left the castle as soon as she was able, and Watho never invited her again.

And now the witch's care was, that the child should not know darkness. Persistently she trained him until at last he never slept during the day, and never woke during the night. She never let him see anything black, and even kept all dull colors out of his way. Never, if she could help it, would she let a shadow fall upon him, watching against shadows as if they had been live things that would hurt him. All day he basked in the full splendour of the sun, in the same large rooms his mother had occupied. Watho used him to the sun, until he could bear more of it than any dark-blooded African. In the hottest of every day, she stripped him and laid him in it, that he might ripen like a peach; and the boy rejoiced in it, and would resist being dressed again. She brought all her knowledge to bear on making his muscles strong and elastic and swiftly responsive—that his soul, she said laughing, might sit in every fibre, be all in every part, and awake the moment of call. His hair was of the red gold, but his eyes grew darker as he grew, until they were as black as Vesper's. He was the merriest of creatures, always laughing, always loving, for a moment raging, then laughing afresh. Watho called him Photogen.

CHAPTER V. NYCTERIS.

Five or six months after the birth of Photogen, the dark lady also gave birth to a baby: in the windowless tomb of a blind mother, in the dead of night, under the feeble rays of a lamp in an alabaster globe, a girl came into the darkness with a wail. And just as she was born for the first time, Vesper was born for the second, and passed into a world as unknown to her as this was to her child—who would have to be born yet again before she could see her mother.

Watho called her Nycteris, and she grew as like Vesper as possible—in all but one particular. She had the same dark skin, dark eyelashes and brows, dark hair, and gentle sad look; but she had just the eyes of Aurora, the mother of Photogen, and if they grew darker as she grew older, it was only a darker blue. Watho, with the help of Falca, took the greatest possible care of her—in every way consistent with her plans, that is,—the main point in which was that she should never see any light but what came from the lamp. Hence her optic nerves, and indeed her whole apparatus for seeing, grew both larger and more sensitive; her eyes, indeed, stopped short only of being too large. Under her dark hair and forehead and eyebrows, they looked like two breaks in a cloudy night-sky, through which peeped the heaven where the stars and no clouds live. She was a sadly dainty little creature. No one in the world except those two was aware of the being of the little bat. Watho trained her to sleep during the day, and wake during the night. She taught her music, in which she was herself a proficient, and taught her scarcely anything else.

CHAPTER VI. HOW PHOTOGEN GREW.

The hollow in which the castle of Watho lay, was a cleft in a plain rather than a valley among hills, for at the top of its steep sides, both north and south, was a table-land, large and wide. It was covered with rich grass and flowers, with here and there a wood, the outlying colony of a great forest. These grassy plains were the finest hunting grounds in the world. Great herds of small, but fierce cattle, with humps and shaggy manes, roved about them, also antelopes and gnus, and the tiny roedeer, while the woods were swarming with wild creatures. The tables of the castle were mainly supplied from them. The chief of Watho's huntsmen was a fine fellow, and when Photogen began to outgrow the training she could give him, she handed him over to Fargu. He with a will set about teaching him all he knew. He got him pony after pony, larger and larger as he grew, every one less manageable than that which had preceded it, and advanced him from pony to horse, and from horse to horse, until he was equal to anything in that kind which the country produced. In similar fashion he trained him to the use of bow and arrow, substituting every three months a stronger bow and longer arrows; and soon he became, even on horseback, a wonderful archer. He was but fourteen when he killed his first bull, causing jubilation among the huntsmen, and, indeed, through all the castle, for there too he was the favourite. Every day, almost as soon as the sun was up, he went out hunting, and would in general be out nearly the whole of the day. But Watho had laid upon Fargu just one commandment, namely, that Photogen should on no account, whatever the plea, be out until sundown, or so near it as to wake in him the desire of seeing what was going to happen; and this commandment Fargu was anxiously careful not to break; for, although he would not have trembled had a whole herd of bulls come down upon him, charging at full speed across the level, and not an arrow left in his quiver, he was more than afraid of his mistress. When she looked at him in a certain way, he felt, he said, as if his heart turned to ashes in his breast, and what ran in his veins was no longer blood, but milk and water. So that, ere long, as Photogen grew older, Fargu began to tremble, for he found it steadily growing harder to restrain him. So full of life was he, as Fargu said to his mistress, much to her content, that he was more like a live thunderbolt than a human being. He did not know what fear was, and that not because he did not know danger; for he had had a severe laceration from the razor-like tusk of a boar—whose spine, however, he had severed with one blow of his hunting-knife, before Fargu could reach him with defence. When he would spur his horse into the midst of a herd of bulls, carrying only his bow and his short sword, or shoot an arrow into a herd, and go after it as if to reclaim it for a runaway shaft, arriving in time to follow it with a spear-thrust before the wounded animal knew which way to charge, Fargu thought with terror how it would be when he came to know the temptation of the huddle-spot leopards, and the knife-clawed lynxes, with which the forest was haunted. For the boy had been so steeped in the sun, from childhood so saturated with his influence, that he looked upon every danger from a sovereign height of courage. When, therefore, he was approaching his sixteenth year, Fargu ventured to beg of Watho that she would lay her commands upon the youth himself, and release him from responsibility for him. One might as soon hold a tawny-maned lion as Photogen, he said. Watho called the youth, and in the presence of Fargu laid her command upon him never to be out when the rim of the sun should touch the horizon, accompanying the prohibition with hints of consequences, none the less awful than they were obscure. Photogen listened respectfully, but, knowing neither the taste of fear nor the temptation of the night, her words were but sounds to him.

CHAPTER VII. HOW NYCTERIS GREW.

The little education she intended Nycteris to have, Watho gave her by word of mouth. Not meaning she should have light enough to read by, to leave other reasons unmentioned, she never put a book in her hands. Nycteris, however, saw so much better than Watho imagined, that the light she gave her was quite sufficient, and she managed to coax Falca into teaching her the letters, after which she taught herself to read, and Falca now and then brought her a child's book. But her chief pleasure was in her instrument. Her very fingers loved it, and would wander about over its keys like feeding sheep. She was not unhappy. She knew nothing of the world except the tomb in which she dwelt, and had some pleasure in everything she did. But she desired, nevertheless, something more or different. She did not know what it was, and the nearest she could come to expressing it to herself was—that she wanted more room. Watho and Falca would go from her beyond the shine of the lamp, and come again; therefore surely there must be more room somewhere. As often as she was left alone, she would fall to poring over the coloured bas-reliefs on the walls. These were intended to represent various of the powers of Nature under allegorical similitudes, and as nothing can be made that does not belong to the general scheme, she could not fail at least to imagine a flicker of relationship between some of them, and thus a shadow of the reality of things found its way to her.

There was one thing, however, which moved and taught her more than all the rest—the lamp, namely, that hung from the ceiling, which she always saw alight, though she never saw the flame, only the slight condensation towards the centre of the alabaster globe. And besides the operation of the light itself after its kind, the indefiniteness of the globe, and the softness of the light, giving her the feeling as if her eyes could go in and into its whiteness, were somehow also associated with the idea of space and room. She would sit for an hour together gazing up at the lamp, and her heart would swell as she gazed. She would wonder what had hurt her, when she found her face wet with tears, and then would wonder how she could have been hurt without knowing it. She never looked thus at the lamp except when she was alone.

CHAPTER VIII. THE LAMP.

Watho having given orders, took it for granted they were obeyed, and that Falca was all night long with Nycteris, whose day it was. But Falca could not get into the habit of sleeping through the day, and would often leave her alone half the night. Then it seemed to Nycteris that the white lamp was watching over her. As it was never permitted to go out—while she was awake at least—Nycteris, except by shutting her eyes, knew less about darkness than she did about light. Also, the lamp being fixed high overhead, and in the centre of everything, she did not know much about shadows either. The few there were fell almost entirely on the floor, or kept like mice about the foot of the walls.

Once, when she was thus alone, there came the noise of a far-off rumbling: she had never before heard a sound of which she did not know the origin, and here therefore was a new sign of something beyond these chambers. Then came a trembling, then a shaking; the lamp dropped from the ceiling to the floor with a great crash, and she felt as if both her eyes were hard shut and both her hands over them. She concluded that it was the darkness that had made the rumbling and the shaking, and rushing into the room, had thrown down the lamp. She sat trembling. The noise and the shaking ceased, but the light did not return. The darkness had eaten it up!

Her lamp gone, the desire at once awoke to get out of her prison. She scarcely knew what *out* meant; out of one room into another, where there was not even a dividing door, only an open arch, was all she knew of the world. But suddenly she remembered that she had heard Falca speak of the lamp *going out*: this must be what she had meant? And if the lamp had gone out, where had it gone? Surely where Falca went, and like her it would come again. But she could not wait. The desire to go out grew irresistible. She must follow her beautiful lamp! She must find it! She must see what it was about!

Now there was a curtain covering a recess in the wall, where some of her toys and gymnastic things were kept; and from behind that curtain Watho and Falca always appeared, and behind it they vanished. How they came out of solid wall, she had not an idea, all up to the wall was open space, and all beyond it seemed wall; but clearly the first and only thing she could do, was to feel her way behind the curtain. It was so dark that a cat could not have caught the largest of mice. Nycteris could see better than any cat, but now her great eyes were not of the smallest use to her. As she went she trod upon a piece of the broken lamp. She had never worn shoes or stockings, and the fragment, though, being of soft alabaster, it did not cut, yet hurt her foot. She did not know what it was, but as it had not been there before the darkness came, she suspected that it had to do with the lamp. She kneeled therefore, and searched with her hands, and bringing two large pieces together, recognized the shape of the lamp. Therewith it flashed upon her that the lamp was dead, that this brokenness was the death of which she had read without understanding, that the darkness had killed the lamp. What then could Falca have meant when she spoke of the lamp *going out*? There was the lamp—dead, indeed, and so changed that she would never have taken it for a lamp but for the shape! No, it was not the lamp anymore now it was dead, for all that made it a lamp was gone, namely, the bright shining of it. Then it must be the shine, the light, that had gone out! That must be what Falca meant—and it must be somewhere in the other place in the wall. She started afresh after it, and groped her way to the curtain.

Now she had never in her life tried to get out, and did not know how; but instinctively she began to move her hands about over one of the walls behind the curtain, half expecting them to go into it, as she supposed Watho and Falca did. But the wall repelled her with inexorable hardness, and she turned to the one opposite. In so doing, she set her foot upon an ivory die, and as it met sharply the same spot the broken alabaster had already hurt, she fell forward with her outstretched hands against the wall. Something gave way, and she tumbled out of the cavern.

CHAPTER IX. OUT.

But alas! *out* was very much like *in*, for the same enemy, the darkness, was here also. The next moment, however, came a great gladness—a firefly, which had wandered in from the garden. She saw the tiny spark in the distance. With slow pulsing ebb and throb of light, it came pushing itself through the air, drawing nearer and nearer, with that motion which more resembles swimming than flying, and the light seemed the source of its own motion.

"My lamp! my lamp!" cried Nycteris. "It is the shiningness of my lamp, which the cruel darkness drove out. My good lamp has been waiting for me here all the time! It knew I would come after it, and waited to take me with it."

She followed the firefly, which, like herself, was seeking the way out. If it did not know the way, it was yet light; and, because all light is one, any light may serve to guide to more light. If she was mistaken in thinking it the spirit of her lamp, it was of the same spirit as her lamp—and had wings. The gold-green jet-boat, driven by light, went throbbing before her through a long narrow passage. Suddenly it rose higher, and the same moment Nycteris fell upon an ascending stair. She had never seen a stair before, and found going-up a curious sensation. Just as she reached what seemed the top, the firefly ceased to shine, and so disappeared. She was in utter darkness once more. But when we are following the light, even its extinction is a guide. If the firefly had gone on shining, Nycteris would have seen the stair turn, and would have gone up to Watho's bedroom; whereas now, feeling straight before her, she came to a latched door, which after a good deal of trying she managed to open—and stood in a maze of wondering perplexity, awe, and delight. What was it? Was it outside of her, or something taking place in her head? Before her was a very long and very narrow passage, broken up she could not tell how, and spreading out above and on all sides to an infinite height and breadth and distance—as if space itself were growing out of a trough. It was brighter than her rooms had ever been—brighter than if six alabaster lamps had been burning in them. There was a quantity of strange streaking and mottling about it, very different from the shapes on her walls. She was in a dream of pleasant perplexity, of delightful bewilderment. She could not tell whether she was upon her feet or drifting about like the firefly, driven by the pulses of an inward bliss. But she knew little as yet of her inheritance. Unconsciously she took one step forward from the threshold, and the girl who had been from her very birth a troglodyte, stood in the ravishing glory of a southern night, lit by a perfect moon—not the moon of our northern clime, but a moon like silver glowing in a furnace—a moon one could see to be a globe—not far off, a mere flat disk on the face of the blue, but hanging down halfway, and looking as if one could see all round it by a mere bending of the neck.

"It is my lamp!" she said, and stood dumb with parted lips. She looked and felt as if she had been standing there in silent ecstasy from the beginning.

"No, it is not my lamp," she said after a while; "it is the mother of all the lamps."

And with that she fell on her knees, and spread out her hands to the moon. She could not in the least have told what was in her mind, but the action was in reality just a begging of the moon to be what she was—that precise incredible splendour hung in the far-off roof, that very glory essential to the being of poor girls born and bred in caverns. It was a resurrection—nay, a birth itself, to Nycteris. What the vast blue sky, studded with tiny sparks like the heads of diamond nails, could be; what the moon, looking so absolutely content with light—why, she knew less about them than you and I! but the greatest of astronomers might envy the rapture of such a first impression at the age of sixteen. Immeasurably imperfect it was, but false the impression could not be, for she saw with the eyes made for seeing, and saw indeed what many men are too wise to see.

As she knelt, something softly flapped her, embraced her, stroked her, fondled her. She rose to her feet, but saw nothing, did not know what it was. It was likest a woman's breath. For she knew nothing of the air even, had never breathed the still newborn freshness of the world. Her breath had come to her only through long passages and spirals in the rock. Still less did she know of the air alive with motion—of that thrice blessed thing, the wind of a summer night. It was like a spiritual wine, filling her whole being with an intoxication of purest joy. To breathe was a perfect existence. It seemed to her the light itself she drew into her lungs. Possessed by the power of the gorgeous night, she seemed at one and the same moment annihilated and glorified.

She was in the open passage or gallery that ran round the top of the garden walls, between the cleft battlements, but she did not once look down to see what lay beneath. Her soul was drawn to the vault above her, with its lamp and its endless room. At last she burst into tears, and her heart was relieved, as the night itself is relieved by its lightning and rain.

And now she grew thoughtful. She must hoard this splendour! What a little ignorance her gaolers had made of her! Life was a mighty bliss, and they had scraped hers to the bare bone! They must not know that she knew. She must hide her knowledge—hide it even from her own eyes, keeping it close in her bosom, content to know that she had it, even when she could not brood on its presence, feasting her eyes with its glory. She turned from the vision, therefore, with a sigh of utter bliss, and with soft quiet steps and groping hands, stole back into the darkness of the rock.

What was darkness or the laziness of Time's feet to one who had seen what she had that night seen? She was lifted above all weariness—above all wrong.

When Falca entered, she uttered a cry of terror. But Nycteris called to her not to be afraid, and told her how there had come a rumbling and a shaking, and the lamp had fallen. Then Falca went and told her mistress, and within an hour a new globe hung in the place of the old one. Nycteris thought it did not look so bright and clear as the former, but she made no lamentation over the change; she was far too rich to heed it. For now, prisoner as she knew herself, her heart was full of glory and gladness; at times she had to hold herself from jumping up, and going dancing and singing about the room. When she slept, instead of dull dreams, she had splendid visions. There were times, it is true, when she became restless, and impatient to look upon her riches, but then she would reason with herself, saying, "What does it matter if I sit here for ages with my poor pale lamp, when out there a lamp is burning at which ten thousand little lamps are glowing with wonder?"

She never doubted she had looked upon the day and the sun, of which she had read; and always when she read of the day and the sun, she had the night and the moon in her mind; and when she read of the night and the moon, she thought only of the cave and the lamp that hung there.

CHAPTER X. THE GREAT LAMP.

It was some time before she had a second opportunity of going out, for Falca, since the fall of the lamp, had been a little more careful, and seldom left her for long. But one night, having a little headache, Nycteris lay down upon her bed, and was lying with her eyes closed, when she heard Falca come to her, and felt she was bending over her. Disinclined to talk, she did not open her eyes, and lay quite still. Satisfied that she was asleep, Falca left her, moving so softly that her very caution made Nycteris open her eyes and look after her—just in time to see her vanish—through a picture, as it seemed, that hung on the wall a long way from the usual place of issue. She jumped up, her headache forgotten, and ran in the opposite direction; got out, groped her way to the stair, climbed, and reached the top of the wall.—Alas! the great room was not so light as the little one she had left. Why?—Sorrow of sorrows! the great lamp was gone! Had its globe fallen?

and its lovely light gone out upon great wings, a resplendent firefly, oaring itself through a yet grander and lovelier room? She looked down to see if it lay anywhere broken to pieces on the carpet below; but she could not even see the carpet. But surely nothing very dreadful could have happened—no rumbling or shaking, for there were all the little lamps shining brighter than before, not one of them looking as if any unusual matter had befallen. What if each of those little lamps was growing into a big lamp, and after being a big lamp for a while, had to go out and grow a bigger lamp still—out there, beyond this *out*?—Ah! here was the living thing that would not be seen, come to her again—bigger to-night! with such loving kisses, and such liquid strokings of her cheeks and forehead, gently tossing her hair, and delicately toying with it! But it ceased, and all was still. Had it gone out? What would happen next? Perhaps the little lamps had not to grow great lamps, but to fall one by one and go out first?—With that, came from below a sweet scent, then another, and another. Ah, how delicious! Perhaps they were all coming to her only on their way out after the great lamp!—Then came the music of the river, which she had been too absorbed in the sky to note the first time. What was it? Alas! alas! another sweet living thing on its way out. They were all marching slowly out in long lovely file, one after the other, each taking its leave of her as it passed! It must be so: here were more and more sweet sounds, following and fading! The whole of the *Out* was going out again; it was all going after the great lovely lamp! She would be left the only creature in the solitary day! Was there nobody to hang up a new lamp for the old one, and keep the creatures from going?—She crept back to her rock very sad. She tried to comfort herself by saying that anyhow there would be room out there; but as she said it she shuddered at the thought of *empty* room.

When next she succeeded in getting out, a half-moon hung in the east: a new lamp had come, she thought, and all would be well.

It would be endless to describe the phases of feeling through which Nycteris passed, more numerous and delicate than those of a thousand changing moons. A fresh bliss bloomed in her soul with every varying aspect of infinite nature. Ere long she began to suspect that the new moon was the old moon, gone out and come in again like herself; also that, unlike herself, it wasted and grew again; that it was indeed a live thing, subject like herself to caverns, and keepers, and solitudes, escaping and shining when it could. Was it a prison like hers it was shut in? and did it grow dark when the lamp left it? Where could be the way into it?—With that first she began to look below, as well as above and around her; and then first noted the tops of the trees between her and the floor. There were palms with their red-fingered hands full of fruit; eucalyptus trees crowded with little boxes of powder-puffs; oleanders with their half-caste roses; and orange trees with their clouds of young silver stars, and their aged balls of gold. Her eyes could see colours invisible to ours in the moonlight, and all these she could distinguish well, though at first she took them for the shapes and colours of the carpet of the great room. She longed to get down among them, now she saw they were real creatures, but she did not know how. She went along the whole length of the wall to the end that crossed the river, but found no way of going down. Above the river she stopped to gaze with awe upon the rushing water. She knew nothing of water but from what she drank and what she bathed in; and, as the moon shone on the dark, swift stream, singing lustily as it flowed, she did not doubt the river was alive, a swift rushing serpent of life, going—out?—whither? And then she wondered if what was brought into her rooms had been killed that she might drink it, and have her bath in it.

Once when she stepped out upon the wall, it was into the midst of a fierce wind. The trees were all roaring. Great clouds were rushing along the skies, and tumbling over the little lamps: the great lamp had not come yet. All was in tumult. The wind seized her garments and hair, and shook them as if it would tear them from her. What could she have done to make the gentle creature so angry? Or was this another creature altogether—of the same kind, but hugely bigger, and of a very different temper and behaviour? But the whole place was angry! Or was it that the creatures dwelling in it, the wind, and the trees, and the clouds, and the river, had all quarrelled, each with all the rest? Would the whole come to confusion and disorder? But, as she gazed wondering and disquieted, the moon, larger than ever she had seen her, came lifting herself above the horizon to look, broad and red as if she, too, were swollen with anger that she had been roused from her rest by their noise, and compelled to hurry up to see what her children were about, thus rioting in her absence, lest they should rack the whole frame of things. And as she rose, the loud wind grew quieter and scolded less fiercely, the trees grew stiller and moaned with a lower complaint, and the clouds hunted and hurled themselves less wildly across the sky. And as if she were pleased that her children obeyed her very presence, the moon grew smaller as she ascended the heavenly stair; her puffed cheeks sank, her complexion grew clearer, and a sweet smile spread over her countenance, as peacefully she rose and rose. But there was treason and rebellion in her court; for, ere she reached the top of her great stairs, the clouds had assembled, forgetting their late wars, and very still they were as they laid their heads together and conspired. Then combining, and lying silently in wait until she came near, they threw themselves upon her, and swallowed her up. Down from the roof came spots of wet, faster and faster, and they wetted the cheeks of Nycteris; and what could they be but the tears of the moon, crying because her children were smothering her? Nycteris wept too, and not knowing what to think, stole back in dismay to her room.

The next time, she came out in fear and trembling. There was the moon still! away in the west—poor, indeed, and old, and looking dreadfully worn, as if all the wild beasts in the sky had been gnawing at her—but there she was, alive still, and able to shine!

CHAPTER XI. THE SUNSET.

Knowing nothing of darkness, or stars, or moon, Photogen spent his days in hunting. On a great white horse he swept over the grassy plains, glorying in the sun, fighting the wind, and killing the buffaloes.

One morning, when he happened to be on the ground a little earlier than usual, and before his attendants, he caught sight of an animal unknown to him, stealing from a hollow into which the sunrays had not yet reached. Like a swift shadow it sped over the grass, slinking southward to the forest. He gave chase, noted the body of a buffalo it had half eaten, and pursued it the harder. But with great leaps and bounds the creature shot farther and farther ahead of him, and vanished. Turning therefore defeated, he met Fargu, who had been following him as fast as his horse could carry him.

"What animal was that, Fargu?" he asked. "How he did run!"

Fargu answered he might be a leopard, but he rather thought from his pace and look that he was a young lion.

"What a coward he must be!" said Photogen.

"Don't be too sure of that," rejoined Fargu. "He is one of the creatures the sun makes uncomfortable. As soon as the sun is down, he will be brave enough."

He had scarcely said it, when he repented; nor did he regret it the less when he found that Photogen made no reply. But alas! said was said.

"Then," said Photogen to himself, "that contemptible beast is one of the terrors of sundown, of which Madam Watho spoke!"

He hunted all day, but not with his usual spirit. He did not ride so hard, and did not kill one buffalo. Fargu to his dismay observed also that he took every pretext for moving farther south, nearer to the forest. But all at once, the sun now sinking in the west, he seemed to change his mind, for he turned his horse's head, and rode home so fast that the rest could not keep him in sight. When they arrived, they found his horse in the stable, and concluded that he had gone into the castle. But he had in truth set out again by the back of it. Crossing the river a good way up the valley, he reascended to the ground they had left, and just before sunset reached the skirts of the forest.

The level orb shone straight in between the bare stems, and saying to himself he could not fail to find the beast, he rushed into the wood. But even as he entered, he turned, and looked to the west. The rim of the red was touching the horizon, all jagged with broken hills. "Now," said Photogen, "we shall see"; but he said it in the face of a darkness he had not proved. The moment the sun began to sink among the spikes and saw-edges, with a kind of sudden flap at his heart a fear inexplicable laid hold of the youth; and as he had never felt anything of the kind before, the very fear itself terrified him. As the sun sank, it rose like the shadow of the world, and grew deeper and darker. He could not even think what it might be, so utterly did it enfeeble him. When the last flaming scimitar-edge of the sun went out like a lamp, his horror seemed to blossom into very madness. Like the closing lids of an eye—for there was no twilight, and this night no moon—the terror and the darkness rushed together, and he knew them for one. He was no longer the man he had known, or rather thought himself. The courage he had had was in no sense his own—he had only had courage, not been courageous; it had left him, and he could scarcely stand—certainly not stand straight, for not one of his joints could he make stiff or keep from trembling. He was but a spark of the sun, in himself nothing.

The beast was behind him—stealing upon him! He turned. All was dark in the wood, but to his fancy the darkness here and there broke into pairs of green eyes, and he had not the power even to raise his bow-hand from his side. In the strength of despair he strove to rouse courage enough—not to fight—that he did not even desire—but to run. Courage to flee home was all he could ever imagine, and it would not come. But what he had not, was ignominiously given him. A cry in the wood, half a screech, half a growl, sent him running like a boar-wounded cur. It was not even himself that ran, it was the fear that had come alive in his legs: he did not know that they moved. But as he ran he grew able to run—gained courage at least to be a coward. The stars gave a little light. Over the grass he sped, and nothing followed him. "How fallen, how changed," from the youth who had climbed the hill as the sun went down! A mere contempt to himself, the self that contemned was a coward with the self it contemned! There lay the shapeless black of a buffalo, humped upon the grass: he made a wide circuit, and swept on like a shadow driven in the wind. For the wind had arisen, and added to his terror: it blew from behind him. He reached the brow of the valley, and shot down the steep descent like a falling star. Instantly the whole upper country behind him arose and pursued him! The wind came howling after him, filled with screams, shrieks, yells, roars, laughter, and chattering, as if all the animals of the forest were careering with it. In his ears was a trampling rush, the thunder of the hoofs of the cattle, in career from every quarter of the wide plains to the brow of the hill above him! He fled straight for the castle, scarcely with breath enough to pant.

As he reached the bottom of the valley, the moon peered up over its edge. He had never seen the moon before—except in the daytime, when he had taken her for a thin bright cloud. She was a fresh terror to him—so ghostly! so ghastly! so gruesome!—so knowing as she looked over the top of her garden-wall upon the world outside! That was the night itself! the darkness alive—and after him! the horror of horrors coming down the sky to curdle his blood, and turn his brain to a cinder! He gave a sob, and made straight for the river, where it ran between the two walls, at the bottom of the garden. He plunged in, struggled through, clambered up the bank, and fell senseless on the grass.

CHAPTER XII. THE GARDEN.

Although Nycteris took care not to stay out long at a time, and used every precaution, she could hardly have escaped discovery so long, had it not been that the strange attacks to which Watho was subject had been more frequent of late, and had at last settled into an illness which kept her to her bed. But whether from an access of caution or from suspicion, Falca, having now to be much with her mistress both day and night, took it at length into her head to fasten the door as often as she went by her usual place of exit; so that one night, when Nycteris pushed, she found, to her surprise and dismay, that the wall pushed her again, and would not let her through; nor with all her searching could she discover wherein lay the cause of the change. Then first she felt the pressure of her prison-walls, and turning, half in despair, groped her way to the picture where she had once seen Falca disappear. There she soon found the spot by pressing upon which the wall yielded. It let her through into a sort of cellar, where was a glimmer of light from a sky whose blue was paled by the moon. From the cellar she got into a long passage, into which the moon was shining, and came to a door. She managed to open it, and, to her great joy, found herself in *the other place*, not on the top of the wall, however, but in the garden she had longed to enter. Noiseless as a fluffy moth she flitted away into the covert of the trees and shrubs, her bare feet welcomed by the softest of carpets, which, by the very touch, her feet knew to be alive, whence it came that it was so sweet and friendly to them. A soft little wind was out among the trees, running now here, now there, like a child that had got its will. She went dancing over the grass, looking behind her at her shadow, as she went. At first she had taken it for a little black creature that made game of her, but when she perceived that it was only where she kept the moon away, and that every tree, however great and grand a creature, had also one of these strange attendants, she soon learned not to mind it, and by and by it became the source of as much amusement to her, as to any kitten its tail. It was long before she was quite at home with the trees, however. At one time they seemed to disapprove of her; at another not even to know she was there, and to be altogether taken up with their own business. Suddenly, as she went from one to another of them, looking up with awe at the murmuring mystery of their branches and leaves, she spied one a little way off, which was very different from all the rest. It was white, and dark, and sparkling, and spread like a palm—a small slender palm, without much head; and it grew very fast, and sang as it grew. But it never grew any bigger, for just as fast as she could see it growing, it kept falling to pieces. When she got close to it, she discovered that it was a water-tree—made of just such water as she washed with—only it was alive of course, like the river—a different sort of water from that, doubtless, seeing the one crept swiftly along the floor, and the other shot straight up, and fell, and swallowed itself, and rose again. She put her feet into the marble basin, which was the flower-pot in which it grew. It was full of real water, living and cool—so nice, for the night was hot!

But the flowers! ah, the flowers! she was friends with them from the very first. What wonderful creatures they were!—and so kind and beautiful—always sending out such colours and such scents—red scent, and white scent, and yellow scent—for the other creatures! The one that was invisible and everywhere, took such a quantity of their scents, and carried it away! yet they did not seem to mind. It was their talk, to show they were alive, and not painted like those on the walls of her rooms, and on the carpets.

She wandered along down the garden, until she reached the river. Unable then to get any further—for she was a little afraid, and justly, of the swift watery serpent—she dropped on the grassy bank, dipped her feet in the water, and felt it running and pushing against them. For a long time she sat thus, and her bliss seemed complete, as she gazed at the river, and watched the broken picture of the great lamp overhead, moving up one side of the roof, to go down the other.

CHAPTER XIII. SOMETHING QUITE NEW.

A beautiful moth brushed across the great blue eyes of Nycteris. She sprang to her feet to follow it—not in the spirit of the hunter, but of the lover. Her heart—like every heart, if only its fallen sides were cleared away—was an inexhaustible fountain of love: she loved everything she saw. But as she followed the moth, she caught sight of something lying on the bank of the river, and not yet having learned to be afraid of anything, ran straight to see what it was. Reaching it, she stood amazed. Another girl like herself! But what a strange-looking girl!—so curiously dressed too!—and not able to move! Was she dead? Filled suddenly with pity, she sat down, lifted Photogen's head, laid it on her lap, and began stroking his face. Her warm hands brought him to himself. He opened his black eyes, out of which had gone all the fire, and looked up with a strange sound of fear, half moan, half gasp. But when he saw her face, he drew a deep breath, and lay motion-less—gazing at her: those blue marvels above him, like a better sky, seemed to side with courage and assuage his terror. At length, in a trembling, awed voice, and a half whisper, he said, "Who are you?"

"I am Nycteris," she answered.

"You are a creature of the darkness, and love the night," he said, his fear beginning to move again.

"I may be a creature of the darkness," she replied. "I hardly know what you mean. But I do not love the night. I love the day— with all my heart; and I sleep all the night long."

"How can that be?" said Photogen, rising on his elbow, but dropping his head on her lap again the moment he saw the moon; "—how can it be," he repeated, "when I see your eyes there— wide awake?"

She only smiled and stroked him, for she did not understand him, and thought he did not know what he was saying.

"Was it a dream then?" resumed Photogen, rubbing his eyes. But with that his memory came clear, and he shuddered, and cried, "Oh, horrible! horrible! to be turned all at once into a coward! a shameful, contemptible, disgraceful coward! I am ashamed—ashamed—and *so* frightened! It is all so frightful!"

"What is so frightful?" asked Nycteris, with a smile like that of a mother to her child waked from a bad dream.

"All, all," he answered; "all this darkness and the roaring."

"My dear," said Nycteris, "there is no roaring. How sensitive you must be! What you hear is only the walking of the water, and the running about of the sweetest of all the creatures. She is invisible, and I call her Everywhere, for she goes through all the other creatures and comforts them. Now she is amusing herself, and them too, with shaking them and kissing them, and blowing in their faces. Listen: do you call that roaring? You should hear her when she is rather angry though! I don't know why, but she is sometimes, and then she does roar a little."

"It is so horribly dark!" said Photogen, who, listening while she spoke, had satisfied himself that there was no roaring.

"Dark!" she echoed. "You should be in my room when an earthquake has killed my lamp. I do not understand. How *can* you call this dark? Let me see: yes, you have eyes, and big ones, bigger than Madam Watho's or Falca's—not so big as mine, I fancy— only I never saw mine. But then—oh, yes!—I know now what is the matter! You can't see with them because they are so black. Darkness can't see, of course. Never mind: I will be your eyes, and teach you to see. Look here—at these lovely white things in the grass, with red sharp points all folded together into one. Oh, I love them so! I could sit looking at them all day, the darlings!"

Photogen looked close at the flowers, and thought he had seen something like them before, but could not make them out. As

Nycteris had never seen an open daisy, so had he never seen a closed one.

Thus instinctively Nycteris tried to turn him away from his fear; and the beautiful creature's strange lovely talk helped not a little to make him forget it.

"You call it dark!" she said again, as if she could not get rid of the absurdity of the idea; "why, I could count every blade of the green hair—I suppose it is what the books call grass—within two yards of me! And just look at the great lamp! It is brighter than usual to-day, and I can't think why you should be frightened, or call it dark!"

As she spoke, she went on stroking his cheeks and hair, and trying to comfort him. But oh how miserable he was! and how plainly he looked it! He was on the point of saying that her great lamp was dreadful to him, looking like a witch, walking in the sleep of death; but he was not so ignorant as Nycteris, and knew even in the moonlight that she was a woman, though he had never seen one so young or so lovely before; and while she comforted his fear, her presence made him the more ashamed of it. Besides, not knowing her nature, he might annoy her, and make her leave him to his misery. He lay still therefore, hardly daring to move: all the little life he had seemed to come from her, and if he were to move, she might move; and if she were to leave him, he must weep like a child.

"How did you come here?" asked Nycteris, taking his face between her hands.

"Down the hill," he answered.

"Where do you sleep?" she asked.

He signed in the direction of the house. She gave a little laugh of delight.

"When you have learned not to be frightened, you will always be wanting to come out with me," she said.

She thought with herself she would ask her presently, when she had come to herself a little, how she had made her escape, for she must, of course, like herself have got out of a cave, in which Watho and Falca had been keeping her.

"Look at the lovely colours," she went on, pointing to a rose-bush, on which Photogen could not see a single flower. "They are far more beautiful—are they not?—than any of the colours upon your walls. And then they are alive, and smell so sweet!"

He wished she would not make him keep opening his eyes to look at things he could not see; and every other moment would start and grasp tight hold of her, as some fresh pang of terror shot into him.

"Come, come, dear!" said Nycteris; "you must not go on this way. You must be a brave girl, and—"

"A girl!" shouted Photogen, and started to his feet in wrath. "If you were a man, I should kill you."

"A man?" repeated Nycteris—"what is that? How could I be that? We are both girls—are we not?"

"No, I am not a girl," he answered; "—although," he added, changing his tone, and casting himself on the ground at her feet, "I have given you too good reason to call me one."

"Oh, I see!" returned Nycteris. "No, of course! you can't be a girl: girls are not afraid—without reason. I understand now: it is because you are not a girl that you are so frightened."

Photogen twisted and writhed upon the grass.

"No, it is not," he said sulkily; "it is this horrible darkness that creeps into me, goes all through me, into the very marrow of my bones—that is what makes me behave like a girl. If only the sun would rise!"

"The sun! what is it?" cried Nycteris, now in her turn conceiving a vague fear.

Then Photogen broke into a rhapsody, in which he vainly sought to forget his.

"It is the soul, the life, the heart, the glory of the universe," he said. "The worlds dance like motes in his beams. The heart of man is strong and brave in his light, and when it departs his courage grows from him—goes with the sun, and he becomes such as you see me now."

"Then that is not the sun?" said Nycteris, thoughtfully, pointing up to the moon.

"That!" cried Photogen, with utter scorn; "I know nothing about *that*, except that it is ugly and horrible. At best it can be only the ghost of a dead sun. Yes, that is it! That is what makes it look so frightful."

"No," said Nycteris, after a long, thoughtful pause; "you must be wrong there. I think the sun is the ghost of a dead moon, and that is how he is so much more splendid as you say.—Is there, then, another big room, where the sun lives in the roof?"

"I do not know what you mean," replied Photogen. "But you mean to be kind, I know, though you should not call a poor fellow in the dark a girl. If you will let me lie here, with my head in your lap, I should like to sleep. Will you watch me, and take care of me?"

"Yes, that I will," answered Nycteris, forgetting all her own danger.

So Photogen fell asleep.

CHAPTER XIV. THE SUN.

There Nycteris sat, and there the youth lay, all night long, in the heart of the great cone-shadow of the earth, like two Pharaohs in one pyramid. Photogen slept, and slept; and Nycteris sat motionless lest she should wake him, and so betray him to his fear.

The moon rode high in the blue eternity; it was a very triumph of glorious night; the river ran babble-murmuring in deep soft syllables; the fountain kept rushing moonward, and blossoming momently to a great silvery flower, whose petals were for ever falling like snow, but with a continuous musical clash, into the bed of its exhaustion beneath; the wind woke, took a run among the trees, went to sleep, and woke again; the daisies slept on their feet at hers, but she did not know they slept; the roses might well seem awake, for their scent filled the air, but in truth they slept also, and the odour was that of their dreams; the oranges hung like gold lamps in the trees, and their silvery flowers were the souls of their yet unembodied children; the scent of the acacia blooms filled the air like the very odour of the moon herself.

At last, unused to the living air, and weary with sitting so still and so long, Nycteris grew drowsy. The air began to grow cool. It was getting near the time when she too was accustomed to sleep. She closed her eyes just a moment, and nodded—opened them suddenly wide, for she had promised to watch.

In that moment a change had come. The moon had got round, and was fronting her from the west, and she saw that her face was altered, that she had grown pale, as if she too were wan with fear, and from her lofty place espied a coming terror. The light seemed to be dissolving out of her; she was dying—she was going out! And yet everything around looked strangely clear—clearer than ever she had seen anything before: how could the lamp be shedding more light when she herself had less? Ah, that was just it! See how faint she looked! It was because the light was forsaking her, and spreading itself over the room, that she grew so thin and pale! She was giving up everything! She was melting away from the roof like a bit of sugar in water.

Nycteris was fast growing afraid, and sought refuge with the face upon her lap. How beautiful the creature was!—what to call it she could not think, for it had been angry when she called it what Watho called her. And, wonder upon wonder! now, even in the cold change that was passing upon the great room, the colour as of a red rose was rising in the wan cheek. What beautiful yellow hair it was that spread over her lap! What great huge breaths the creature took! And what were those curious things it carried? She had seen them on her walls, she was sure.

Thus she talked to herself while the lamp grew paler and paler, and everything kept growing yet clearer. What could it mean? The lamp was dying—going out into the other place of which the creature in her lap had spoken, to be a sun! But why were the things growing clearer before it was yet a sun? That was the point. Was it her growing into a sun that did it? Yes! yes! it was coming death! She knew it, for it was coming upon her also! She felt it coming! What was she about to grow into? Something beautiful, like the creature in her lap? It might be! Anyhow, it must be death; for all her strength was going out of her, while all around her was growing so light she could not bear it! She must be blind soon! Would she be blind or dead first?

For the sun was rushing up behind her. Photogen woke, lifted his head from her lap, and sprang to his feet. His face was one radiant smile. His heart was full of daring—that of the hunter who will creep into the tiger's den. Nycteris gave a cry, covered her face with her hands, and pressed her eyelids close. Then blindly she stretched out her arms to Photogen, crying, "Oh, I am *so* frightened! What is this? It must be death! I don't wish to die yet. I love this room and the old lamp. I do not want the other place! This is terrible. I want to hide. I want to get into the sweet, soft, dark hands of all the other creatures. Ah me! ah me!"

"What is the matter with you, girl?" said Photogen, with the arrogance of all male creatures until they have been taught by the other kind. He stood looking down upon her over his bow, of which he was examining the string. "There is no fear of anything now, child. It is day. The sun is all but up. Look! he will be above the brow of yon hill in one moment more! Good-bye. Thank you for my night's lodging. I'm off. Don't be a goose. If ever I can do anything for you—and all that, you know!"

"Don't leave me; oh, don't leave me!" cried Nycteris. "I am dying! I am dying! I cannot move. The light sucks all the strength out of me. And oh, I am *so* frightened!"

But already Photogen had splashed through the river, holding high his bow that it might not get wet. He rushed across the level, and strained up the opposing hill. Hearing no answer, Nycteris removed her hands. Photogen had reached the top, and the same moment the sunrays alighted upon him: the glory of the king of day crowded blazing upon the golden-haired youth. Radiant as Apollo, he stood in mighty strength, a flashing shape in the midst of flame. He fitted a glowing arrow to a gleaming bow. The arrow parted with a keen musical twang of the bowstring, and Photogen darting after it, vanished with a shout. Up shot Apollo himself, and from his quiver scattered astonishment and exultation. But the brain of poor Nycteris was pierced through and through. She fell down in utter darkness. All around her was a flaming furnace. In despair and feebleness and agony, she crept back, feeling her way with doubt and difficulty and enforced persistence to her cell. When at last the friendly darkness of her chamber folded her about with its cooling and consoling arms, she threw herself on her bed and fell fast asleep. And there she slept on, one alive in a tomb, while Photogen, above in the sun-glory, pursued the buffaloes on the lofty plain, thinking not once of her where she lay dark and forsaken, whose presence had been his refuge, her eyes and her hands his guardians through the night. He was in his glory and his pride; and the darkness and its disgrace had vanished for a time.

CHAPTER XV. THE COWARD HERO.

But no sooner had the sun reached the noonstead, than Photogen began to remember the past night in the shadow of that which was at hand, and to remember it with shame. He had proved himself—and not to himself only, but to a girl as well—a coward!—one bold in the daylight, while there was nothing to fear, but trembling like any slave when the night arrived. There was, there must be, something unfair in it! A spell had been cast upon him! He had eaten, he had drunk something that did not agree with courage! In any case he had been taken unprepared! How was he to know what the going down of the sun would be like? It was no wonder he should have been surprised into terror, seeing it was what it was—in its very nature so terrible! Also, one could not see where danger might be coming from! You might be torn in pieces, carried off, or swallowed up, without even seeing where to strike a blow! Every possible excuse he caught at, eager as a self-lover to lighten his self-contempt. That day he astonished the huntsmen—terrified them with his reckless daring—all to prove to himself he was no coward. But nothing eased his shame.

One thing only had hope in it—the resolve to encounter the dark in solemn earnest, now that he knew something of what it was. It was nobler to meet a recognized danger than to rush contemptuously into what seemed nothing—nobler still to encounter a nameless horror. He could conquer fear and wipe out disgrace together. For a marksman and swordsman like him, he said, one with his strength and courage, there was but danger. Defeat there was not. He knew the darkness now, and when it came he would meet it as fearless and cool as now he felt himself. And again he said, "We shall see!"

He stood under the boughs of a great beech as the sun was going down, far away over the jagged hills: before it was half down, he was trembling like one of the leaves behind him in the first sigh of the night-wind. The moment the last of the glowing disc vanished, he bounded away in terror to gain the valley, and his fear grew as he ran. Down the side of the hill, an abject creature, he went bounding and rolling and running; fell rather than plunged into the river, and came to himself, as before, lying on the grassy bank in the garden.

But when he opened his eyes, there were no girl-eyes looking down into his; there were only the stars in the waste of the sunless Night—the awful all-enemy he had again dared, but could not encounter. Perhaps the girl was not yet come out of the water! He would try to sleep, for he dared not move, and perhaps when he woke he would find his head on her lap, and the beautiful dark face, with its deep blue eyes, bending over him. But when he woke he found his head on the grass, and although he sprang up with all his courage, such as it was, restored, he did not set out for the chase with such an *elan* as the day before; and, despite the sun-glory in his heart and veins, his hunting was this day less eager; he ate little, and from the first was thoughtful even to sadness. A second time he was defeated and disgraced! Was his courage nothing more than the play of the sunlight on his brain? Was he a mere ball tossed between the light and the dark? Then what a poor contemptible creature he was! But a third chance lay before him. If he failed the third time, he dared not foreshadow what he must then think of himself! It was bad enough now—but then!

Alas! it went no better. The moment the sun was down, he fled as if from a legion of devils.

Seven times in all, he tried to face the coming night in the strength of the past day, and seven times he failed—failed with such increase of failure, with such a growing sense of ignominy, overwhelming at length all the sunny hours and joining night to night, that, what with misery, self-accusation, and loss of confidence, his daylight courage too began to fade, and at length, from exhaustion, from getting wet, and then lying out of doors all night, and night after night,—worst of all, from the consuming of the deathly fear, and the shame of shame, his sleep forsook him, and on the seventh morning, instead of going to the hunt, he crawled into the castle, and went to bed. The grand health, over which the witch had taken such pains, had yielded, and in an hour or two he was moaning and crying out in delirium.

CHAPTER XVI. AN EVIL NURSE.

Watho was herself ill, as I have said, and was the worse tempered; and, besides, it is a peculiarity of witches, that what works in others to sympathy, works in them to repulsion. Also, Watho had a poor, helpless, rudimentary spleen of a conscience left, just enough to make her uncomfortable, and therefore more wicked. So, when she heard that Photogen was ill, she was angry. Ill, indeed! after all she had done to saturate him with the life of the system, with the solar might itself! He was a wretched failure, the boy! And because he was *her* failure, she was annoyed with him, began to dislike him, grew to hate him. She looked on him as a painter might upon a picture, or a poet upon a poem, which he had only succeeded in getting into an irrecoverable mess. In the hearts of witches, love and hate lie close together, and often tumble over each other. And whether it was that her failure with Photogen foiled also her plans in regard to Nycteris, or that her illness made her yet more of a devil's wife, certainly Watho now got sick of the girl too, and hated to know her about the castle.

She was not too ill, however, to go to poor Photogen's room and torment him. She told him she hated him like a serpent, and hissed like one as she said it, looking very sharp in the nose and chin, and flat in the forehead. Photogen thought she meant to kill him, and hardly ventured to take anything brought him. She ordered every ray of light to be shut out of his room; but by means of this he got a little used to the darkness. She would take one of his arrows, and now tickle him with the feather end of it, now prick him with the point till the blood ran down. What she meant finally I cannot tell, but she brought Photogen speedily to the determination of making his escape from the castle: what he should do then he would think afterwards. Who could tell but he might find his mother somewhere beyond the forest! If it were not for the broad patches of darkness that divided day from day, he would fear nothing!

But now, as he lay helpless in the dark, ever and anon would come dawning through it the face of the lovely creature who on that first awful night nursed him so sweetly: was he never to see her again? If she was, as he had concluded, the nymph of the river, why had she not re-appeared? She might have taught him not to fear the night, for plainly she had no fear of it herself! But then, when the day came, she did seem frightened:—why was that, seeing there was nothing to be afraid of then? Perhaps one so much at home in the darkness, was correspondingly afraid of the light! Then his selfish joy at the rising of the sun, blinding him to her condition, had made him behave to her, in ill return for her kindness, as cruelly as Watho behaved to him! How sweet and dear and lovely she was! If there were wild beasts that came out only at night, and were afraid of the light, why should there not be girls too, made the same way—who could not endure the light, as he could not bear the darkness? If only he could find her again! Ah, how differently he would behave to her! But alas! perhaps the sun had killed her—melted her—burned her up!—dried her up— that was it, if she was the nymph of the river!

CHAPTER XVII. WATHO'S WOLF.

From that dreadful morning Nycteris had never got to be herself again. The sudden light had been almost death to her; and now she lay in the dark with the memory of a terrific sharpness—a something she dared scarcely recall, lest the very thought of it should sting her beyond endurance. But this was as nothing to the pain which the recollection of the rudeness of the shining creature whom she had nursed through his fear caused her; for, the moment his suffering passed over to her, and he was free, the first use he made of his returning strength had been to scorn her! She wondered and wondered; it was all beyond her comprehension.

Before long, Watho was plotting evil against her. The witch was like a sick child weary of his toy: she would pull her to pieces, and see how she liked it. She would set her in the sun, and see her die, like a jelly from the salt ocean cast out on a hot rock. It would be a sight to soothe her wolf-pain. One day, therefore, a little before noon, while Nycteris was in her deepest sleep, she had a darkened litter brought to the door, and in that she made two of her men carry her to the plain above. There they took her out, laid her on the grass, and left her.

Watho watched it all from the top of her high tower, through her telescope; and scarcely was Nycteris left, when she saw her sit up, and the same moment cast herself down again with her face to the ground.

"She'll have a sunstroke," said Watho, "and that'll be the end of her."

Presently, tormented by a fly, a huge-humped buffalo, with great shaggy mane, came galloping along, straight for where she lay. At sight of the thing on the grass, he started, swerved yards aside, stopped dead, and then came slowly up, looking malicious. Nycteris lay quite still, and never even saw the animal.

"Now she'll be trodden to death!" said Watho. "That's the way those creatures do."

When the buffalo reached her, he sniffed at her all over, and went away; then came back, and sniffed again; then all at once went off as if a demon had him by the tail.

Next came a gnu, a more dangerous animal still, and did much the same; then a gaunt wild boar. But no creature hurt her, and Watho was angry with the whole creation.

At length, in the shade of her hair, the blue eyes of Nycteris began to come to themselves a little, and the first thing they saw was a comfort. I have told already how she knew the night-daisies, each a sharp-pointed little cone with a red tip; and once she had parted the rays of one of them, with trembling fingers, for she was afraid she was dreadfully rude, and perhaps was hurting it; but she did want, she said to herself, to see what secret it carried so carefully hidden; and she found its golden heart. But now, right under her eyes, inside the veil of her hair, in the sweet twilight of whose blackness she could see it perfectly, stood a daisy with its red tip opened wide into a carmine ring, displaying its heart of gold on a platter of silver. She did not at first recognize it as one of those cones come awake, but a moment's notice revealed what it was. Who then could have been so cruel to the lovely little creature, as to force it open like that, and spread it heart-bare to the terrible death-lamp? Whoever it was, it must be the same that had thrown her out there to be burned to death in its fire! But she had her hair, and could hang her head, and make a small sweet night of her own about her! She tried to bend the daisy down and away from the sun, and to make its petals hang about it like her hair, but she could not. Alas! it was burned and dead already! She did not know that it could not yield to her gentle force because it was drinking life, with all the eagerness of life, from what she called the death-lamp. Oh, how the lamp burned her!

But she went on thinking—she did not know how; and by and by began to reflect that, as there was no roof to the room except that in which the great fire went rolling about, the little Red-tip must have seen the lamp a thousand times, and must know it quite well! and it had not killed it! Nay, thinking about farther, she began to ask the question whether this, in which she now saw it, might not be its more perfect condition. For not only now did the whole seem perfect, as indeed it did before, but every part showed its own individual perfection as well, which perfection made it capable of combining with the rest into the higher perfection of a whole. The flower was a lamp itself! The golden heart was the light, and the silver border was the alabaster globe, skillfully broken, and spread wide to let out the glory. Yes; the radiant shape was plainly its perfection! If, then, it was the lamp which had opened it into that shape, the lamp could not be unfriendly to it, but must be of its own kind, seeing it made it perfect! And again, when she thought of it, there was clearly no little resemblance between them. What if the flower then was the little great-grandchild of the lamp, and he was loving it all the time? And what if the lamp did not mean to hurt her, only could not help it? The red tips looked as if the flower had some time or other been hurt: what if the lamp was making the best it could of her—opening her out somehow like the flower? She would bear it patiently, and see. But how coarse the colour of the grass was! Perhaps, however, her eyes not being made for the bright lamp, she did not see them as they were! Then she remembered how different were the eyes of the creature that was not a girl and was afraid of the darkness! Ah, if the darkness would only come again, all arms, friendly and soft everywhere about her! She would wait and wait, and bear, and be patient.

She lay so still that Watho did not doubt she had fainted. She was pretty sure she would be dead before the night came to revive her.

CHAPTER XVIII. REFUGE.

Fixing her telescope on the motionless form, that she might see it at once when the morning came, Watho went down from the tower to Photogen's room. He was much better by this time, and before she left him, he had resolved to leave the castle that very night. The darkness was terrible indeed, but Watho was worse than even the darkness, and he could not escape in the day. As soon, therefore, as the house seemed still, he tightened his belt, hung to it his hunting-knife, put a flask of wine and some bread in his pocket, and took his bow and arrows. He got from the house, and made his way at once up to the plain. But what with his illness, the terrors of the night, and his dread of the wild beasts, when he got to the level he could not walk a step further, and sat down, thinking it better to die than to live. In spite of his fears, however, sleep contrived to overcome him, and he fell at full length on the soft grass.

He had not slept long when he woke with such a strange sense of comfort and security, that he thought the dawn at last must have arrived. But it was dark night about him. And the sky—no, it was not the sky, but the blue eyes of his naiad looking down upon him! Once more he lay with his head in her lap, and all was well, for plainly the girl feared the darkness as little as he the day.

"Thank you," he said. "You are like live armour to my heart; you keep the fear off me. I have been very ill since then. Did you come up out of the river when you saw me cross?"

"I don't live in the water," she answered. "I live under the pale lamp, and I die under the bright one."

"Ah, yes! I understand now," he returned. "I would not have behaved as I did last time if I had understood; but I thought you were mocking me; and I am so made that I cannot help being frightened at the darkness. I beg your pardon for leaving you as I did, for, as I say, I did not understand. Now I believe you were really frightened. Were you not?"

"I was, indeed," answered Nycteris, "and shall be again. But why you should be, I cannot in the least understand. You must know how gentle and sweet the darkness is, how kind and friendly, how soft and velvety! It holds you to its bosom and loves you. A little while ago, I lay faint and dying under your hot lamp.—What is it you call it?"

"The sun," murmured Photogen: "How I wish he would make haste!"

"Ah! do not wish that. Do not, for my sake, hurry him. I can take care of you from the darkness, but I have no one to take care of me from the light.—As I was telling you, I lay dying in the sun. All at once I drew a deep breath. A cool wind came and ran over my face. I looked up. The torture was gone, for the death-lamp itself was gone. I hope he does not die and grow brighter yet. My terrible headache was all gone, and my sight was come back. I felt as if I were new made. But I did not get up at once, for I was tired still. The grass grew cool about me, and turned soft in colour. Something wet came upon it, and it was now so pleasant to my feet, that I rose and ran about. And when I had been running about a long time, all at once I found you lying, just as I had been lying a little while before. So I sat down beside you to take care of you, till your life—and my death—should come again."

"How good you are, you beautiful creature!—Why, you forgave me before ever I asked you!" cried Photogen.

Thus they fell a-talking, and he told her what he knew of his history, and she told him what she knew of hers, and they agreed they must get away from Watho as far as ever they could.

"And we must set out at once," said Nycteris.

"The moment the morning comes," returned Photogen.

"We must not wait for the morning," said Nycteris; "for then I shall not be able to move, and what would you do the next night? Besides, Watho sees best in the daytime. Indeed, you must come now, Photogen.—You must."

"I cannot; I dare not," said Photogen. "I cannot move. If I but lift my head from your lap, the very sickness of terror seizes me."

"I shall be with you," said Nycteris soothingly. "I will take care of you till your dreadful sun comes, and then you may leave me, and go away as fast as you can. Only please put me in a dark place first, if there is one to be found."

"I will never leave you again, Nycteris," cried Photogen. "Only wait till the sun comes, and brings me back my strength, and we will go away together, and never, never part any more."

"No, no," persisted Nycteris; "we must go now. And you must learn to be strong in the dark as well as in the day, else you will always be only half brave. I have begun already—not to fight your sun, but to try to get at peace with him, and understand what he really is, and what he means with me—whether to hurt me or to make the best of me. You must do the same with my darkness."

"But you don't know what mad animals there are away there towards the south," said Photogen. "They have huge green eyes, and they would eat you up like a bit of celery, you beautiful creature!"

"Come, come! you must," said Nycteris, "or I shall have to pretend to leave you, to make you come. I have seen the green eyes you speak of, and I will take care of you from them."

"You! How can you do that? If it were day now, I could take care of you from the worst of them. But as it is, I can't even see them for this abominable darkness. I could not see your lovely eyes but for the light that is in them; that lets me see straight into heaven through them. They are windows into the very heaven beyond the sky. I believe they are the very place where the stars are made."

"You come then, or I shall shut them," said Nycteris, "and you shan't see them anymore till you are good. Come. If you can't see the wild beasts, I can."

"You can! and you ask me to come!" cried Photogen.

"Yes," answered Nycteris. "And more than that, I see them long before they can see me, so that I am able to take care of you."

"But how?" persisted Photogen. "You can't shoot with bow and arrow, or stab with a hunting-knife."

"No, but I can keep out of the way of them all. Why, just when I found you, I was having a game with two or three of them at once. I see, and scent them too, long before they are near me— long before they can see or scent me."

"You don't see or scent any now, do you?" said Photogen, uneasily, rising on his elbow.

"No—none at present. I will look," replied Nycteris, and sprang to her feet.

"Oh, oh! do not leave me—not for a moment," cried Photogen, straining his eyes to keep her face in sight through the darkness.

"Be quiet, or they will hear you," she returned. "The wind is from the south, and they cannot scent us. I have found out all about that. Ever since the dear dark came, I have been amusing myself with them, getting every now and then just into the edge of the wind, and letting one have a sniff of me."

"Oh, horrible!" cried Photogen. "I hope you will not insist on doing so anymore. What was the consequence?"

"Always, the very instant, he turned with flashing eyes, and bounded towards me—only he could not see me, you must remember. But my eyes being so much better than his, I could see him perfectly well, and would run away round him until I scented him, and then I knew he could not find me anyhow. If the wind were to turn, and run the other way now, there might be a whole army of them down upon us, leaving no room to keep out of their way. You had better come."

She took him by the hand. He yielded and rose, and she led him away. But his steps were feeble, and as the night went on, he seemed more and more ready to sink.

"Oh dear! I am so tired! and so frightened!" he would say.

"Lean on me," Nycteris would return, putting her arm round him, or patting his cheek. "Take a few steps more. Every step away from the castle is clear gain. Lean harder on me. I am quite strong and well now."

So they went on. The piercing night-eyes of Nycteris descried not a few pairs of green ones gleaming like holes in the darkness, and many a round she made to keep far out of their way; but she never said to Photogen she saw them. Carefully she kept him off the uneven places, and on the softest and smoothest of the grass, talking to him gently all the way as they went—of the lovely flowers and the stars—how comfortable the flowers looked, down in their green beds, and how happy the stars up in their blue beds!

When the morning began to come, he began to grow better, but was dreadfully tired with walking instead of sleeping, especially after being so long ill. Nycteris too, what with supporting him, what with growing fear of the light which was beginning to ooze out of the east, was very tired. At length, both equally exhausted, neither was able to help the other. As if by consent they stopped. Embracing each the other, they stood in the midst of the wide grassy land, neither of them able to move a step, each supported only by the leaning weakness of the other, each ready to fall if the other should move. But while the one grew weaker still, the other had begun to grow stronger. When the tide of the night began to ebb, the tide of the day began to flow; and now the sun was rushing to the horizon, borne upon its foaming billows. And ever as he came, Photogen revived. At last the sun shot up into the air, like a bird from the hand of the Father of Lights. Nycteris gave a cry of pain, and hid her face in her hands.

"Oh me!" she sighed; "I am so frightened! The terrible light stings so!"

But the same instant, through her blindness, she heard Photogen give a low exultant laugh, and the next felt herself caught up: she who all night long had tended and protected him like a child, was now in his arms, borne along like a baby, with her head lying on his shoulder. But she was the greater, for, suffering more, she feared nothing.

CHAPTER XIX. THE WEREWOLF.

At the very moment when Photogen caught up Nycteris, the telescope of Watho was angrily sweeping the table-land. She swung it from her in rage, and running to her room, shut herself up.

There she anointed herself from top to toe with a certain ointment; shook down her long red hair, and tied it round her waist; then began to dance, whirling round and round faster and faster, growing angrier and angrier, until she was foaming at the mouth with fury. When Falca went looking for her, she could not find her anywhere.

As the sun rose, the wind slowly changed and went round, until it blew straight from the north. Photogen and Nycteris were drawing near the edge of the forest, Photogen still carrying Nycteris, when she moved a little on his shoulder uneasily, and murmured in his ear,

"I smell a wild beast—that way, the way the wind is coming."

Photogen turned, looked back towards the castle, and saw a dark speck on the plain. As he looked, it grew larger: it was coming across the grass with the speed of the wind. It came nearer and nearer. It looked long and low, but that might be because it was running at a great stretch. He set Nycteris down under a tree, in the black shadow of its bole, strung his bow, and picked out his heaviest, longest, sharpest arrow. Just as he set the notch on the string, he saw that the creature was a tremendous wolf, rushing straight at him. He loosened his knife in its sheath, drew another arrow half-way from the quiver, lest the first should fail, and took his aim—at a good distance, to leave time for a second chance. He shot. The arrow rose, flew straight, descended, struck the beast, and started again into the air, doubled like a letter V. Quickly Photogen snatched the other, shot, cast his bow from him, and drew his knife. But the arrow was in the brute's chest, up to the feather; it tumbled heels over head with a great thud of its back on the earth, gave a groan, made a struggle or two, and lay stretched out motionless.

"I've killed it, Nycteris," cried Photogen. "It is a great red wolf."

"Oh, thank you!" answered Nycteris feebly from behind the tree. "I was sure you would. I was not a bit afraid."

Photogen went up to the wolf. It *was* a monster! But he was vexed that his first arrow had behaved so badly, and was the less willing to lose the one that had done him such good service: with a long and a strong pull, he drew it from the brute's chest. Could he believe his eyes? There lay—no wolf, but Watho, with her hair tied round her waist! The foolish witch had made herself invulnerable, as she supposed, but had forgotten that, to torment Pho-

togen therewith, she had handled one of his arrows. He ran b
to Nycteris and told her.

She shuddered and wept, and would not look.

CHAPTER XX. ALL IS WELL.

There was now no occasion to fly a step farther. Neither of them
feared any one but Watho. They left her there, and went back. A
great cloud came over the sun, and rain began to fall heavily, and
Nycteris was much refreshed, grew able to see a little, and with
Photogen's help walked gently over the cool wet grass.

They had not gone far before they met Fargu and the other
huntsmen. Photogen told them he had killed a great red wolf,
and it was Madam Watho. The huntsmen looked grave, but gladness shone through.

"Then," said Fargu, "I will go and bury my mistress."

But when they reached the place, they found she was already
buried—in the maws of sundry birds and beasts which had made
their breakfast of her.

Then Fargu, overtaking them, would, very wisely, have Photogen go to the king, and tell him the whole story. But Photogen,
yet wiser than Fargu, would not set out until he had married
Nycteris; "for then," he said, "the king himself can't part us; and
if ever two people couldn't do the one without the other, those
two are Nycteris and I. She has got to teach me to be a brave man
in the dark, and I have got to look after her until she can bear the
heat of the sun, and he helps her to see, instead of blinding her."

They were married that very day. And the next day they went
together to the king, and told him the whole story. But whom
should they find at the court but the father and mother of Photogen, both in high favour with the king and queen. Aurora nearly
died for joy, and told them all how Watho had lied, and made her
believe her child was dead.

No one knew anything of the father or mother of Nycteris; but
when Aurora saw in the lovely girl her own azure eyes shining
through night and its clouds, it made her think strange things,
and wonder how even the wicked themselves may be a link to join
together the good. Through Watho, the mothers, who had never
seen each other, had changed eyes in their children.

The king gave them the castle and lands of Watho, and there
they lived and taught each other for many years that were not

long. But hardly had one of them passed, before Nycteris had come to love the day best, because it was the clothing and crown of Photogen, and she saw that the day was greater than the night, and the sun more lordly than the moon; and Photogen had come to love the night best, because it was the mother and home of Nycteris.

"But who knows," Nycteris would say to Photogen, "that, when we go out, we shall not go into a day as much greater than your day as your day is greater than my night?"

Appendix A: Contemporary Reviews

[This selection of reviews offers a sense of both the publishing context in which MacDonald's fairy tales appeared and the growing sophistication of the critical response to children's books in the late Victorian period. Sidney Colvin's review for *Academy* offers an omnibus analysis of four new works by names that are now instantly recognizable in the canon of nineteenth-century children's literature: Lewis Carroll, Edward Lear, Christina Rossetti, and MacDonald himself. Neta Syrett's 1903 retrospective identifies precisely the difference between the imaginative worlds of Carroll and MacDonald, and considers as well the aesthetic case to be made for Arthur Hughes's black and white illustrations even as the colour printing familiar in Walter Crane's Toy Books has taken over the market. The responses to *Dealings with the Fairies* and *The Light Princess and Other Tales* demonstrate the appreciation of cross-written works for children, as reviewers clearly identify the presence of dual audience.]

1. *The Princess and the Goblin*

a. From "Christmas Books," *Saturday Review of Politics, Literature, Science and Art* 32.843 (1871): 823-25

This is a clever and original little story, and is very prettily illustrated. We should infer, however, that the artist, whoever he may be, for he does not give his name, never had children of his own. For though he can draw children very well indeed, yet now and then he gives such a frightful picture of a goblin that no child who had not "robur et æs triplex circa pectus,"[1] after looking at it, would dare to trust himself in a dark room. No one surely who had seen how timid children suffer from the dark would willingly increase their suffering. Terror certainly is the nurse's recognized and approved prescription for sleeplessness. The other day in one of the Assize Courts a gentleman who was later on sentenced to fifteen years' penal servitude, by way of proving his thoroughly domestic nature, said that on the very evening on which he was accused of trying to murder his wife, he had, when asked to assist in getting his wakeful child to sleep, done his best, as he had called out to it, "If you don't go to sleep at once, I will come and cut your head off." In spite of his example, and that of nurses in general, we trust that

---

1   Horace, *Odes* I: "both oak and a triple layer of bronze around the heart."

so clever an artist as the illustrator of Mr. MacDonald's book will leave off frightening children.

b. Sidney Colvin, *Academy* 3.40 (1872): 23-24[1]

It is pleasant to see children's literature get better as it does year by year in England. This season in particular has produced a crop of books that are delightful for them—for the children—but more delightful still, perhaps, for some among their elders; since no child, in the most enchanted eagerness of its single-minded attention and fancy, knows so full or so subtly mingled a pleasure in the best of these things as the properly constituted grown-up reader. The adult spirit here finds the reward of its affliction of self-consciousness. While the attention, the fancy, can let themselves go, and be as those of a child, following the fun or movement of the tale with all the old mirth, the old breathlessness, there lingers, beneath such abeyance of criticism, a more complex self looking on somewhere in the background, aware of the revival of ancient spells, and pleased to feel them work:—you have your own enjoyment to enjoy as well as its object, you have a hundred causes of pathetic entertainment side by side with the old absorption.

The volume written by Miss Rossetti, and illustrated by Mr. Hughes (not, by the way, a matter of story-telling but of song-singing), is one of the most exquisite of its class ever seen, in which the poet and artist have continually had parallel felicities of inspiration—each little rhyme having its separate and carefully engraved head-piece. In the form of the poetry the book answers literally to its title, and consists of nothing but short rhymes as simple in sound as those immemorially sung in nurseries—one only, of exceptional length, containing as many as nine verses—and having always a music suited to baby ears, though sometimes a depth of pathos or suggestion far enough transcending baby apprehension. But both in pictures and poetry, provided they have the simple turn, and the appeal to everyday experience and curiosity, which makes them attractive to children at first sight and hearing, the ulterior, intenser quality of many of these must in an unrealized way constitute added value, we should say, even for children. The pieces range, indeed, as to matter, from the extreme of infant punning and catchy triviality to the extreme, in an imaginative sense, of delicate penetration and pregnancy, with an almost equal grace of manner in either case; here is an example of the latter:—

---

1 In this review essay, Colvin looks at Christina Rossetti's *Sing-Song: A Nursery-Rhyme Book* with illustrations by Arthur Hughes, MacDonald's *Princess and the Goblin*, Lewis Carroll's *Through the Looking-Glass, and What Alice Saw There*, and Edward Lear's *More Nonsense: Pictures, Rhymes, Botany, &c.*

"What are heavy? sea-sand and sorrow:
What are brief? to-day and to-morrow:
What are frail? spring blossoms and youth:
What are deep? the ocean and truth."

And this is illustrated with one of the best of Mr. Hughes' landscape cuts—a still, flat sea flooded with moonlight, under a black sky, with a child's sand-castle going to pieces at its edge. There are some dealing with death—a motherless baby, a ring of three dancers from which one is caught away—in just the right mood of tender thought and plaintive wonder, striking the mere note of loss, unexplained disappearance, the falling of an unknown shadow, with the loveliest feeling; and many about out-door things, birds and flowers, animated with an intimate fanciful charity, or having sometimes a little ethical conclusion, of which the lesson cannot fail to find its way home. In tuning the simplest fancies or hints of fragmentary idea, Miss Rossetti cannot lose the habit or instinct of an artist; and the style and cadence of these tiny verses are as finished and individual, sometimes as beautiful in regard of their theme, as they can be, and not much recalling any precedent, except in a few cases that of Blake.... Mr. Hughes' illustrations, many of them lovely and full of imagination as we have said, and always seconding the suggestion of the verse, are not quite equal, and the sentiment is sometimes in advance of the design: but what can be more delightful than the child feeding birds at the winter window on p. 8, or its *vis-à-vis* supping porridge in the ingle,[1] or the lambs and ducklings of pp. 27 and 29, or the landscapes of pp. 35 and 79, or the pathetic dance of p. 73, or the pancake-making (79), or, indeed, a full half of them all.

Mr. George MacDonald is a poet also, and in his *Light Princess* had already achieved a humorous and imaginative success in that most difficult of all tasks, the invention of contemporary mythology for children. We should say that with this writer, more than most, it was hit or miss; other pieces in the volume containing *The Light Princess* we should count misses. Here, again, and on a larger scale than before, the hit is palpable and delightful. *The Princess and the Goblin* does not perhaps contain any invention so felicitous as that of the child to whom an evil fairy had denied the physical property of gravity; but it is a thoroughly beautiful and enjoyable story, and its machinery of princess and nurse, heroic miner-boy, evil subterranean goblins, and beneficent supernatural grandmother in her tower, thoroughly calculated to take hold of the imagination of readers of all ages. The sup-

---

1 "In the ingle" means "by the fire."

pressed personage within our grown-up reader will be knowing enough to observe, from his background, that there is allegory in all this; aware of the religious and ethical pre-occupations of the writer's genius, he will guess what the beneficent grandmother is meant more or less explicitly to stand for—will, if he chooses, be able to note how it is even the moral and religious foundation that has stimulated the writer's invention and developed the turns and incidents of the story. But all this really does not at all spoil this charming fable, as it has so many others; the narrative and scenic parts of it are conceived with a vividness of their own, alongside of the ethical part of the conception; the characters are delightfully dramatic, and there is nothing strained in the tone of purity and elevation which is given to them. Against unction, when unction passes into such bright imaginative devices as these, and only gives a peculiar ring and fervour to their pathos or their humour, the most uncompromising opponent of moral story-writing can have nothing to protest. Mr. MacDonald in this story is long, detailed; but he has the art of having been there (so to speak); and the attention never flags during all the adventures of the little Irene with her mystic friend in the tower, and the brave Curdie with his goblin enemies in the mine. The sympathetic talent of Mr. Hughes in this volume again has been employed in furtherance of the writer's fancy, and his designs (though not so fully in his choicest manner, perhaps, as those we last spoke of) are very delicate and ingenious.

We pass from poetical enchantment to prose fun in passing from the work of Mr. MacDonald to that of Mr. "Lewis Carroll"—from the transformation scene to the harlequinade,[1] if one may venture that imperfect parallel. *Through the Looking-glass* is a sequel to *Alice in Wonderland*, and has the misfortune of all sequels—that it is not a commencement. An author who continues himself loses the effect, although not the merit, of his originality; and in its originality lay half the charm of the old "Alice." No reader will have the sense of freshness and the unforeseen, amid the burlesque combinations which the little lady encounters in her new dreamland, which he had amid those of the old; hence the inevitable injustice of a comparison. But, making allowance for the sense of repetition, we think the invention here shows no falling-off in ingenuity or in the peculiar humour, which mixes up untransformed fragments of familiar experience with the bewilderment of the polite child amid people of irregular manners and a topsy-turvy order of existence. There is perhaps a little too much complication in the machinery of chess-board geography prevailing in Looking-glass Land, and a somewhat meaningless eccentricity in

---

1 A harlequinade derives from pantomime theatre in which the character Harlequin performs, hence "Buffoonery; fantastic procedure" (*OED*).

some of the transformations; but the ingenuity which traces out the remotest consequences of its data cannot be too much praised,—as the property of space in Looking-glass Land by which to walk towards a thing is to move away from it, and the inverse disposition of the letters in the amazing nonsense-poem of "Jabberwocky." The introduction and conclusion of the adventure are particularly well devised and written. Every reader will be charmed to meet his old friends the Hare and the Hatter (still engaged upon his tea and bread and butter) dignified with the Anglo-Saxon orthography Haigha and Hatta (Alice has evidently been having lessons in English history); and amused at the forms under which the child's matter-of-fact dream realises the ideas of Tweedle-dum and Tweedle-dee, Humpty Dumpty, and all the provoking brotherhood of mythic personages who insist on taking all words literally, and regarding every question as a riddle. If this prose extravaganza, this matter-of-fact absurdity, has a certain ugliness at times which seems to run near the edge of the vulgar, that is its only weak point. The clever and mannered humour of Mr. Tenniel's designs illustrates their theme to perfection.

The stout, jovial book of *More Nonsense*, by Mr. Edward Lear, transcends criticism as usual. We may just indicate the interest of the preface, in which the author explains the genesis of this class of composition; we may point out the great felicity of some of the new botanical figures and names—"Nastycreechia Krorluppia," "Stunnia Dinnerbellia," and the rest; we may protest, with deference, against the absence of the charms of rhyme in the alliterative pieces at the end of the volume; and then leave the reader to his unmolested entertainment.

c. From "Christmas Books," *Athenaeum* 2304 (1871): 834-36

Those who delighted in Mr. MacDonald's last year's Christmas book, "At the Back of the North Wind,"[1] will not be less glad of *The Princess and the Goblin* (Strahan & Co.). It is a graceful story, full of romance and adventure, with a deep meaning underlying the beauty of the surface, which gives it the life and mystery that form the subtle charm which Mr. MacDonald weaves into all his works, but especially into those he writes for the young. Faith in that which is invisible, and the courage to live for that which we believe, are what he tries to teach. He speaks with a tender, earnest eloquence, that draws a response from the heart of the reader, like perfume from the flowers, or music from

---

1 One of MacDonald's early works for children, first serialized in *Good Words for the Young* in 1868-69 and later published as a separate volume in 1871. For more information, see *At the Back of the Northwind*, ed. Roderick McGillis (Peterborough: Broadview, 2011).

the harp under the touch of a master minstrel. We hope Mr. Mac-
Donald will keep his promise, and tell us the further history of the
beautiful Princess and Curdie the miner; but more than all, we desire
to be told more about the mysterious and lovely lady who lived in the
turret, and whose surroundings were as beautiful and wonderful as the
clouds at sunset.

d. From "Belles Lettres," *Westminster Review* 41 (1872): 581-89

We now come to a number of children's books, gleaming in blue,
purple, crimson and gold. As far as we have been able to watch their
effects, they act precisely as Sydney Smith says really good novels
should—make children forget, not only the time, but their dinners.[1] It
is really wonderful the amount of ability which is now employed upon
children's books. Here, for instance, is "Lilliput Legends," "got up" in
an exquisite binding, good paper, clear type, and with an artistic care
and excellence which a few years ago would only have been bestowed
upon the works of some of the world's greatest poets. Nor are the contents unworthy of the outside. Both author and artist have done their
best.

Equally good as "Lilliput Legends" is Mr. George MacDonald's
"The Princess and the Goblin." The author is known not merely as a
novelist who holds a unique position, but as a poet of quaint grace and
fancy. He has managed to unite his poetical fancies with a delicate and
fantastic humour, which will we think have charms for others besides
children.

e. Netta Syrett, "On the Right Choice of Books for Children," *Academy and Literature* 1648 (1903): 641

The season of juvenile books is upon us and the mothers and aunts of
Christendom are once more face to face with the task of deciding what
the children like. "Fairy tales!" they cry hopefully, reading the title on
one or other of the pink, green or purple volumes pressed upon them.
"Surely that will do. All children like fairy tales." But do they? Per-

---

1 An allusion to Sydney Smith's (1771-1845) comments on effective novel
writing in a review of *Granby* (1826) by Thomas Henry Lister (1800-42):
"The main question to a novel is—did it amuse? Were you surprised at dinner
coming so soon? Did you mistake eleven for ten? Were you too late to dress?
And did you sit up beyond the usual hour? If a novel produces these effects, it
is good; if it does not—story, language, love, scandal itself cannot save it. It is
only meant to please; and it must do that or it does nothing" (*Edinburgh
Review or Critical Journal* 43 [1826]: 395).

sonally I divide children into two classes, one loving and the other detesting them, and to the non-recognition of this clear distinction we owe that distressing hybrid, the "comic" fairy story. "Children like fun," says the hasty generalizer, "and everyone knows they like fairy tales. Let me, therefore, write a funny fairy tale." This he proceeds to do, urging on the clown with wild shouts and brandishing the sausages, while the transformation scene—and every fairy tale worthy the name is a transformation scene—clumsily managed at best, fades into insignificance before the cries of "Here we are again!" My contention is that not only do certain children find this clown-and-sausage treatment of the fairy world the abomination of desolation, but that even by the more practical minded it is at best merely tolerated. It is a compromise, and matter-of-fact children infinitely prefer frankly realistic fiction.

The devotee of fairy tales is quick to feel the mystic atmosphere:—

"For Kilmeny had been, she kenned not where,
And Kilmeny had seen what she could not declare.
Kilmeny had been where the cock never crew,
Where the rain never fell, and the wind never blew."[1]

How significant too, that on returning to the world of every day "no smile was seen on Kilmeny's face." She had been to the *real* land of faërie, that Land of Heart's Desire which must be dear and familiar to anyone who would guide the children thither.

And of all the writers who know that "dim green, well-beloved isle,"[2] with the exception, perhaps of Hans Andersen, it is still George MacDonald I would choose as guide if I were once more a child. He should take me there "At the Back of the North Wind," and once more I should know that mystic lady of the streaming hair and starry eyes, and in "The Princess and the Goblin" I should meet again the old-young "grandmother" with her fire of roses and her silver bath, in whose depths, for me, the stars are still shining. For George Mac-Donald, like every other true teller of fairy tales, takes his fairyland seriously. Not that taking it seriously means of necessity an absence of gaiety. Some of the best stories I know combine beauty and mystery, with a charming playfulness which never jars even upon the most serious-minded reader. Their writer, long since dead, took her book to publishers in vain, and her non-success is only to be explained by the false idea which prevails of what children really like. It depends upon

---

1 James Hogg (1770-1835), "Kilmeny," lines 38-41.
2 William Butler Yeats (1865-1939), "The Man Who Dreamed of Fairyland," line 8.

the children. For the devotee of fairy tales you must go the whole fairy; for the practical child you need not write fairy tales at all.

But there is "Alice in Wonderland" someone exclaims triumphantly. "There you have joking—the best imaginable joking—there the atmosphere is anything but mystic, yet all children love 'Alice.'" Precisely. But then "Alice" is not a fairy tale at all. It is an extremely realistic story. Wonderland is not Fairyland, as Lewis Carroll well knew. There are mad hatters, delightful dormice, immortal Cheshire cats in "Wonderland," but never a fairy, or except for the moment when Alice emerges from the rabbit-hole passage into the garden of roses is there a single passage of "faërie" charm in the whole book. I yield to none in my admiration of the inimitable "Alice," and sorrowfully regret that others have not taken the adjective literally. For to the influence of this masterpiece, falsely considered a fairy tale, we owe almost all the third-rate "funny" fairy stories of the past thirty years. And for the other children—the children who are bored by the magic country and find the real world good enough? Well, theirs is no hard case. It is not the domestic story which has fallen upon evil days. Mr. E.V. Lucas, indeed, has gone so far as to provide a special and very delightful series for the matter-of-fact child, and one at least of the stories contained in his "Little Blue Books" ("The Castaways of Meadow Bank") is as good a piece of realistic fiction as one would wish to find in or out of a child's book;[1] while, of the innumerable school stories, Evelyn Sharp's "Youngest Girl in the School" always strikes me as a charming example.[2] It is here, of course, that the devotee of fairy tales is to be envied, for delight in the magic country does not exclude interest in the "Land of Every Day," and the "fairy-tale child" enters both worlds with equal if with different pleasure.

With regard to the vexed question of the sort of illustrations which please children, my views are again heterodox. All children, one hears, "like bright colours, and are confused by detail in a picture." I do not agree. That baby children love violent reds and yellows is doubtless true, but my experience tends to show that directly a child is old enough to understand a story at all, it prefers an elaborate black and white drawing in which it gradually discovers a fresh flower on the Princess's robe; a new window or another mysterious door in the castle—to the flat, plain, coloured illustrations nowadays beloved of

---

1   Edward Verral Lucas (1868-1938), essayist and biographer, had over 180 publications during his lifetime ranging from biographies, general essays, travel writing, and children's literature (*ODNB*).

2   Evelyn Sharp (1869-1955), children's writer and suffragette, published *The Youngest Girl in the School* in 1901. Her first publication, *Fairy Tales as They Are, as They Were and as They Should Be* (1889), is a non-fictional defence of fairy tales (*ODNB*).

publishers. Of course, if a quite little child can get the same amount of detail, *combined* with colour, as in the delightful picture books of Walter Crane,[1] so much the greater is its joy. But by older children the coloured illustration is often considered babyish, unworthy the dignity of the sort of fairy-tale they love. Imagine "The Princess and the Goblin" with coloured pictures. Perish the thought! My memory goes back to its beautifully mysterious drawings and again the glamour of the fairy tale is upon me, and I envy the child for whom, out of a thousand books, a mother or an aunt has "chosen right."

2. *Dealings with the Fairies*

a. *London Review of Politics, Society, Literature, Art, and Science* 14 (1867): 549

This is a little book of the wisest fooling. Mr. MacDonald has put as much thought, fancy, and tenderness into its pages as would suffice to enrich a work of far more imposing dimensions. There is an exquisite sympathy with the child-mind in every line of it, and a grave underlying humour—the humour of genius—showing itself here and there for the pleasure of those who can no longer believe in fairies. Of the five stories we give the palm to the "Light Princess." We sincerely trust that Mr. MacDonald will carry out his half-promise expressed in the appropriate dedication "to his children," and that the condition upon which he rests his future performance will be amply satisfied.[2] The illustrations, by Mr. Hughes, are occasionally hard, but on the whole are fair translations of the text, but only translations. It would be difficult for any artist to catch the subtle grace and spirit of Mr. Mac-Donald's delicate conceptions.

b. "*Dealings with the Fairies*, 'Where more is meant than meets the Ear,'" *The British Quarterly Review* 46.91 (1867): 247

It would be a pleasant task to try and teach in homely prose the lessons which Mr. MacDonald has clothed in this gorgeous, grotesque, fantastic dress. These vivid parables of the great things of the moral world, adapted for the weird and wild imagination of childhood,

---

1 Walter Crane (1845-1915), illustrator, designer, and painter, illustrated books for children from the mid-Victorian period onward and demonstrated a well-defined and very popular style with emphasis on fantasy, especially in the use of anthropomorphic animals.
2 In his Preface, MacDonald "promises" "If plenty of children like this volume, you shall have another soon."

before it has learned the agonies of improbability, or knows how to separate the natural from the supernatural, are worthy of the subtle and potent pen of the author. He has succeeded in effecting a glorious "Mitchinmalico,"[1] a daring commingling of the two worlds of Fancy and Fact, and in leaving some healthy, wise, elevated impression on the minds of his youthful readers. Arthur Hughes has illustrated the fairy tales with much skill; and the charming little volume, if it did not make us wish to be young again, did more, for while we were reading, so great was the magic of the enchanter's wand, we became young once more, and clapped our venerable hands over the tears of the light princess, and the groans of Mr. Thunderthump.

c. From "Our Book Club," *Eclectic Review* 13 (1867): 224-36

Pretty little volumes are *The Will-o-the-Wisps are in Town; and other New Tales, by Hans Christian Andersen* (Alexander Strahan) and *Dealings with the Fairies, by George MacDonald* (Alexander Strahan). Hans Andersen[2] is always welcome, and always delightful, but in this volume not equal to most of his rememberable little tales, though the "Silver Coin," and the "Windmill," seem to be all himself too; but the *Dealings with the Fairies* contains some of Mr. MacDonald's happiest, brightest, fancies. The *Golden Key* is a most strengthening and touching piece in the old fantastic vein, the mystical and weird dealing with the place where the end of the rainbow stands, and the land the shadows come from, with forest, and trees, and water, and those singular people, the old man of the Sea, the old man of the Earth, and the old man of the Fire, a wonderful little piece altogether, which if the reader has the right stuff of fairy blood in him, will make the heart ache, and the eyes to lighten with tears, and brighten with hopes; the author fulfils the promise of his title page, which says, "There is more meant than meets the eye."[3]

---

1 Presumably a reference to the phrase "miching malicho" used by Hamlet to describe the actions depicted by the players in III.ii.131. Without offering a precise definition, the *OED* states that the phrase is "taken to be generally suggestive of dark deeds, mystery, or intrigue, and used in these senses" (see *OED* definition for "malicho," noun).

2 Hans Christian Andersen (1805-75), Danish author best known for his fairy tales.

3 The reviewer misremembers the epigraph "Where more is meant than meets the ear," From John Milton, "Il Penseroso," line 120.

d. *Athenaeum* 3452 (1893): 881

Though nothing to that effect appears on the title-page or elsewhere, *The Light Princess, and other Fairy Tales*, by Dr. George MacDonald (Putnam's Sons), is a reproduction of the charming little book published by Mr. Alexander Strahan in 1868, under the name of "Dealings with the Fairies,"[1] and with very good illustrations by Mr. Arthur Hughes. Is it quite fair of Mr. Putnam to ignore this? Dr. George MacDonald is a master of the art of story-telling both to old and young; indeed, there is not one of these tales which will not be read with pleasure by children of a larger growth. Two good stories have been added in this edition, and a preface widely different from the simplicity of the first addressed by the author to his children, and informing them in a line or two that as he never told them stories he gave them a book of stories, and that if "plenty of children" liked that volume they should soon have another. In one of the new stories Mr. MacDonald says:—

"I never knew of any interference on the part of a wicked fairy that did not turn out a good thing in the end. What a good thing, for instance, it was that one princess should sleep for a hundred years! Was she not saved from all the plague of young men who were not worthy of her? And did she not come awake exactly at the right moment when the right prince kissed her? For my part, I can't help wishing a good many girls would sleep till just the same fate overtook them. It would be happier for them, and more agreeable to their friends."

He forgets, however, that their friends would have to sleep a hundred years also. This new edition is prettily illustrated by Miss (?) Maud Humphrey.[2]

---

1 *The Light Princess* was published in America by G.P. Putnam's Sons but, as the reviewer notes, adds two stories and a preface not included in *Dealings with the Fairies*. The two additional stories are "The Carasoyn" (which first appeared in *Works of Fancy and Imagination* in 1871) and "Little Daylight" (which was originally part of *At the Back of the North Wind* published in 1871 and which also appeared in *Works of Fancy and Imagination* in 1871). *The Light Princess* also included a preface that was later to become "The Fantastic Imagination." (See Shaberman, *George MacDonald*, p. 33.)

2 Maud Humphrey (1868-1940) was an American commercial artist and illustrator.

Appendix B: MacDonald on the Imagination

[MacDonald published two essays concerning the imagination as an essential faculty in human experience. First published as a preface to an American edition of *The Light Princess*, "The Fantastic Imagination" is MacDonald's response to repeated inquiries for explanations of the meaning of his stories. In his avoidance of offering definitive answers, MacDonald makes clear the value he finds in the search for meaning, and in the process he articulates his understanding of the relationship between the form of fantasy that develops its own laws to fit the imaginary world created and the moral content of fantasy that must conform to the highest values of this world. As befits its origin as an accompaniment to a volume of tales, the essay is both accessible and light in tone. Structured in large part as a question-and-answer exchange between imaginative writer and unimaginative reader, this essay stays focused on the fairy tale. MacDonald had published a much more substantial essay on "The Imagination: Its Functions and Its Culture" in the *British Quarterly Review* nearly three decades earlier. Ambitious in scope, this essay presents an apologia for the place of imagination in human experience. Quoting liberally from Shakespeare and the Romantic poets as well as from German philosophers Goethe and Novalis, MacDonald constructs a compelling case for imagination as the primary human faculty. Both essays usually appear only in excerpts, but are here included in their entirety.]

1. "The Fantastic Imagination" (1893)[1]

That we have in English no word corresponding to the German *Märchen*, drives us to use the word *Fairytale*, regardless of the fact that the tale may have nothing to do with any sort of fairy. The old use of

---

1 In the preface to *A Dish of Orts*, MacDonald writes: "The paper on 'The Fantastic Imagination' had its origin in the repeated request of readers for an explanation of things in certain shorter stories I had written. It forms the preface to an American edition of my so-called Fairy Tales." The "so-called Fairly Tales" in which the essay appeared as a preface is *The Light Princess and Other Fairy Tales*, published in New York by G.P. Putnam's Sons in 1893. The essay also appeared in the same year in *A Dish of Orts*. The text followed here is the one included in *A Dish of Orts*.

the word *Fairy*, by Spenser[1] at least, might, however, well be adduced, were justification or excuse necessary where *need must*.

Were I asked, what is a fairytale? I should reply, *Read Undine: that is a fairytale; then read this and that as well, and you will see what is a fairytale*.[2] Were I further begged to describe the *fairytale*, or define what it is, I would make answer, that I should as soon think of describing the abstract human face, or stating what must go to constitute a human being. A fairytale is just a fairytale, as a face is just a face; and of all fairytales I know, I think *Undine* the most beautiful.

Many a man, however, who would not attempt to define *a man*, might venture to say something as to what a man ought to be: even so much I will not in this place venture with regard to the fairytale, for my long past work in that kind might but poorly instance or illustrate my now more matured judgment. I will but say some things helpful to the reading, in right-minded fashion, of such fairytales as I would wish to write, or care to read.

Some thinkers would feel sorely hampered if at liberty to use no forms but such as existed in nature, or to invent nothing save in accordance with the laws of the world of the senses; but it must not therefore be imagined that they desire escape from the region of law. Nothing lawless can show the least reason why it should exist, or could at best have more than an appearance of life.

The natural world has its laws, and no man must interfere with them in the way of presentment any more than in the way of use; but they themselves may suggest laws of other kinds, and man may, if he pleases, invent a little world of his own, with its own laws; for there is that in him which delights in calling up new forms—which is the nearest, perhaps, he can come to creation. When such forms are new embodiments of old truths, we call them products of the Imagination; when they are mere inventions, however lovely, I should call them the work of the Fancy: in either case, Law has been diligently at work.

His world once invented, the highest law that comes next into play is, that there shall be harmony between the laws by which the new

---

1 Sir Edmund Spenser (c. 1552-99) published *The Fairie Queene* books I-III in 1590 and books IV-VI in 1596. The poem is a mixture of allegory, Italian romance, and classical epic, involving knights in a variety of marvellous adventures.

2 *Undine: A Romance* (1811) by German writer Friedrich, baron de la Motte Fouqué (1777-1843). Undine is a water nymph who receives a soul by marrying a knight, Huldbrand. Her husband becomes unfaithful and forsakes Undine for Bertalda. Just as Huldbrand is about to marry Bertalda, Undine reappears and kills him. The work was very popular, being adapted as an opera and a play.

world has begun to exist; and in the process of his creation, the inventor must hold by those laws. The moment he forgets one of them, he makes the story, by its own postulates, incredible. To be able to live a moment in an imagined world, we must see the laws of its existence obeyed. Those broken, we fall out of it. The imagination in us, whose exercise is essential to the most temporary submission to the imagination of another, immediately, with the disappearance of Law, ceases to act. Suppose the gracious creatures of some childlike region of Fairyland talking either cockney or Gascon! Would not the tale, however lovelily begun, sink at once to the level of the Burlesque[1]—of all forms of literature the least worthy? A man's inventions may be stupid or clever, but if he do not hold by the laws of them, or if he make one law jar with another, he contradicts himself as an inventor, he is no artist. He does not rightly consort his instruments, or he tunes them in different keys. The mind of man is the product of live Law; it thinks by law, it dwells in the midst of law, it gathers from law its growth; with law, therefore, can it alone work to any result. Inharmonious, unconsorting ideas will come to a man, but if he try to use one of such, his work will grow dull, and he will drop it from mere lack of interest. Law is the soil in which alone beauty will grow; beauty is the only stuff in which Truth can be clothed; and you may, if you will, call Imagination the tailor that cuts her garments to fit her, and Fancy his journeyman that puts the pieces of them together, or perhaps at most embroiders their button-holes. Obeying law, the maker works like his creator; not obeying law, he is such a fool as heaps a pile of stones and calls it a church.

In the moral world it is different: there a man may clothe in new forms, and for this employ his imagination freely, but he must invent nothing. He may not, for any purpose, turn its laws upside down. He must not meddle with the relations of live souls. The laws of the spirit of man must hold, alike in this world and in any world he may invent. It were no offence to suppose a world in which everything repelled instead of attracted the things around it; it would be wicked to write a tale representing a man it called good as always doing bad things, or a man it called bad as always doing good things: the notion itself is absolutely lawless. In physical things a man may invent; in moral things he must obey—and take their laws with him into his invented world as well.

"You write as if a fairytale were a thing of importance: must it have a meaning?"

---

1 "That species of literary composition, or of dramatic representation, which aims at exciting laughter by caricature of the manner or spirit of serious works, or by ludicrous treatment of their subjects" (*OED*).

It cannot help having some meaning; if it have proportion and harmony it has vitality, and vitality is truth. The beauty may be plainer in it than the truth, but without the truth the beauty could not be, and the fairytale would give no delight. Everyone, however, who feels the story, will read its meaning after his own nature and development: one man will read one meaning in it, another will read another.

"If so, how am I to assure myself that I am not reading my own meaning into it, but yours out of it?"

Why should you be so assured? It may be better that you should read your meaning into it. That may be a higher operation of your intellect than the mere reading of mine out of it: your meaning may be superior to mine.

"Suppose my child ask me what the fairytale means, what am I to say?"

If you do not know what it means, what is easier than to say so? If you do see a meaning in it, there it is for you to give him. A genuine work of art must mean many things; the truer its art, the more things it will mean. If my drawing, on the other hand, is so far from being a work of art that it needs THIS IS A HORSE written under it, what can it matter that neither you nor your child should know what it means? It is there not so much to convey a meaning as to wake a meaning. If it do not even wake an interest, throw it aside. A meaning may be there, but it is not for you. If, again, you do not know a horse when you see it, the name written under it will not serve you much. At all events, the business of the painter is not to teach zoology.

But indeed your children are not likely to trouble you about the meaning. They find what they are capable of finding, and more would be too much. For my part, I do not write for children, but for the childlike, whether of five, or fifty, or seventy-five.

A fairytale is not an allegory. There may be allegory in it, but it is not an allegory. He must be an artist indeed who can, in any mode, produce a strict allegory that is not a weariness to the spirit. An allegory must be Mastery or Moorditch.[1]

A fairytale, like a butterfly or a bee, helps itself on all sides, sips at every wholesome flower, and spoils not one. The true fairytale is, to my mind, very like the sonata. We all know that a sonata means something; and where there is the faculty of talking with suitable vagueness, and choosing metaphor sufficiently loose, mind may approach mind, in the interpretation of a sonata, with the result of a more or less contenting consciousness of sympathy. But if two or three

---

1   Associated with melancholy by Prince Hal in Shakespeare's *Henry IV*, part 1 (I.ii.75), Moorditch was a narrow, stagnant ditch outside the walls of London, designed to drain the swampy area of Moorfields.

men sat down to write each what the sonata meant to him, what approximation to definite idea would be the result? Little enough— and that little more than needful. We should find it had roused related, if not identical, feelings, but probably not one common thought. Has the sonata therefore failed? Had it undertaken to convey, or ought it to be expected to impart anything defined, anything notionally recognisable?

"But words are not music; words at least are meant and fitted to carry a precise meaning!"

It is very seldom indeed that they carry the exact meaning of any user of them! And if they can be so used as to convey definite meaning, it does not follow that they ought never to carry anything else. Words are live things that may be variously employed to various ends. They can convey a scientific fact, or throw a shadow of her child's dream on the heart of a mother. They are things to put together like the pieces of a dissected map, or to arrange like the notes on a stave. Is the music in them to go for nothing? It can hardly help the definiteness of a meaning: is it therefore to be disregarded? They have length, and breadth, and outline: have they nothing to do with depth? Have they only to describe, never to impress? Has nothing any claim to their use but the definite? The cause of a child's tears may be altogether undefinable: has the mother therefore no antidote for his vague misery? That may be strong in colour which has no evident outline. A fairytale, a sonata, a gathering storm, a limitless night, seizes you and sweeps you away: do you begin at once to wrestle with it and ask whence its power over you, whither it is carrying you? The law of each is in the mind of its composer; that law makes one man feel this way, another man feel that way. To one the sonata is a world of odour and beauty, to another of soothing only and sweetness. To one, the cloudy rendezvous is a wild dance, with a terror at its heart; to another, a majestic march of heavenly hosts, with Truth in their centre pointing their course, but as yet restraining her voice. The greatest forces lie in the region of the uncomprehended.

I will go farther.—The best thing you can do for your fellow, next to rousing his conscience, is—not to give him things to think about, but to wake things up that are in him; or say, to make him think things for himself. The best Nature does for us is to work in us such moods in which thoughts of high import arise. Does any aspect of Nature wake but one thought? Does she ever suggest only one definite thing? Does she make any two men in the same place at the same moment think the same thing? Is she therefore a failure, because she is not definite? Is it nothing that she rouses the something deeper than the understanding—the power that underlies thoughts? Does she not set feeling, and so thinking at work? Would it be better that she did this after one fashion and not after many fashions? Nature is mood-engendering, thought-provoking: such ought the sonata, such ought the fairytale to be.

"But a man may then imagine in your work what he pleases, what you never meant!"

Not what he pleases, but what he can. If he be not a true man, he will draw evil out of the best; we need not mind how he treats any work of art! If he be a true man, he will imagine true things; what matter whether I meant them or not? They are there none the less that I cannot claim putting them there! One difference between God's work and man's is, that, while God's work cannot mean more than he meant, man's must mean more than he meant. For in everything that God has made, there is layer upon layer of ascending significance; also he expresses the same thought in higher and higher kinds of that thought: it is God's things, his embodied thoughts, which alone a man has to use, modified and adapted to his own purposes, for the expression of his thoughts; therefore he cannot help his words and figures falling into such combinations in the mind of another as he had himself not foreseen, so many are the thoughts allied to every other thought, so many are the relations involved in every figure, so many the facts hinted in every symbol. A man may well himself discover truth in what he wrote; for he was dealing all the time with things that came from thoughts beyond his own.

"But surely you would explain your idea to one who asked you?"

I say again, if I cannot draw a horse, I will not write THIS IS A HORSE under what I foolishly meant for one. Any key to a work of imagination would be nearly, if not quite, as absurd. The tale is there, not to hide, but to show: if it show nothing at your window, do not open your door to it; leave it out in the cold. To ask me to explain, is to say, "Roses! Boil them, or we won't have them!" My tales may not be roses, but I will not boil them.

So long as I think my dog can bark, I will not sit up to bark for him.

If a writer's aim be logical conviction, he must spare no logical pains, not merely to be understood, but to escape being misunderstood; where his object is to move by suggestion, to cause to imagine, then let him assail the soul of his reader as the wind assails an æolian harp.[1] If there be music in my reader, I would gladly wake it. Let fairytale of mine go for a firefly that now flashes, now is dark, but may flash again. Caught in a hand which does not love its kind, it will turn to an insignificant, ugly thing, that can neither flash nor fly.

---

1 "A stringed instrument producing musical sounds on exposure to a current of air" (*OED*).

The best way with music, I imagine, is not to bring the forces of our intellect to bear upon it, but to be still and let it work on that part of us for whose sake it exists. We spoil countless precious things by intellectual greed. He who will be a man, and will not be a child, must—he cannot help himself—become a little man, that is, a dwarf. He will, however, need no consolation, for he is sure to think himself a very large creature indeed.

If any strain of my "broken music" make a child's eyes flash, or his mother's grow for a moment dim, my labour will not have been in vain.

2. "The Imagination: Its Functions and Its Culture" (1867)[1]

There are in whose notion education would seem to consist in the production of a certain repose through the development of this and that faculty, and the depression, if not eradication, of this and that other faculty. But if mere repose were the end in view, an unsparing depression of all the faculties would be the surest means of approaching it, provided always the animal instincts could be depressed likewise, or, better still, kept in a state of constant repletion. Happily, however, for the human race, it possesses in the passion of hunger even, a more immediate saviour than in the wisest selection and treatment of its faculties. For repose is not the end of education; its end is a noble unrest, an ever renewed awaking from the dead, a ceaseless questioning of the past for the interpretation of the future, an urging on of the motions of life, which had better far be accelerated into fever, than retarded into lethargy.

By those who consider a balanced repose the end of culture, the imagination must necessarily be regarded as the one faculty before all others to be suppressed. "Are there not facts?" say they. "Why forsake them for fancies? Is there not that which may be *known?* Why forsake it for inventions? What God hath made, into that let man inquire."

We answer: To inquire into what God has made is the main function of the imagination. It is aroused by facts, is nourished by facts, seeks for higher and yet higher laws in those facts; but refuses to regard science as the sole interpreter of nature, or the laws of science as the only region of discovery.

We must begin with a definition of the word *imagination*, or rather some description of the faculty to which we give the name.

The word itself means an *imaging* or a *making of likenesses*. The imagination is that faculty which gives form to thought—not nec-

---

1 First published in *British Quarterly Review* 46.91 (July 1867): 45-70; republished in *Orts* (1882). The essay was also included in *A Dish of Orts* (1893). The text reproduced here is based on that published in *A Dish of Orts*.

essarily uttered form, but form capable of being uttered in shape or in sound, or in any mode upon which the senses can lay hold. It is, therefore, that faculty in man which is likest to the prime operation of the power of God, and has, therefore, been called the *creative* faculty, and its exercise *creation*. *Poet* means *maker*. We must not forget, however, that between creator and poet lies the one unpassable gulf which distinguishes—far be it from us to say *divides*—all that is God's from all that is man's; a gulf teeming with infinite revelations, but a gulf over which no man can pass to find out God, although God needs not to pass over it to find man; the gulf between that which calls, and that which is thus called into being; between that which makes in its own image and that which is made in that image. It is better to keep the word *creation* for that calling out of nothing which is the imagination of God; except it be as an occasional symbolic expression, whose daring is fully recognized, of the likeness of man's work to the work of his maker. The necessary unlikeness between the creator and the created holds within it the equally necessary likeness of the thing made to him who makes it, and so of the work of the made to the work of the maker. When therefore, refusing to employ the word *creation* of the work of man, we yet use the word *imagination* of the work of God, we cannot be said to dare at all. It is only to give the name of man's faculty to that power after which and by which it was fashioned. The imagination of man is made in the image of the imagination of God. Everything of man must have been of God first; and it will help much towards our understanding of the imagination and its functions in man if we first succeed in regarding aright the imagination of God, in which the imagination of man lives and moves and has its being.

As to *what* thought is in the mind of God ere it takes form, or what the form is to him ere he utters it; in a word, what the consciousness of God is in either case, all we can say is, that our consciousness in the resembling conditions must, afar off, resemble his. But when we come to consider the acts embodying the Divine thought (if indeed thought and act be not with him one and the same), then we enter a region of large difference. We discover at once, for instance, that where a man would make a machine, or a picture, or a book, God makes the man that makes the book, or the picture, or the machine. Would God give us a drama? He makes a Shakespere. Or would he construct a drama more immediately his own? He begins with the building of the stage itself, and that stage is a world—a universe of worlds. He makes the actors, and they do not act,—they *are* their part. He utters them into the visible to work out their life—his drama. When he would have an epic, he sends a thinking hero into his drama, and the epic is the soliloquy of his Hamlet. Instead of writing his lyrics, he sets his birds and his maidens a-singing. All the processes of the ages are God's science; all the flow of history is his poetry. His sculpture is not in marble, but in living and speech-giving forms, which pass away, not to yield place to those that come after, but to be perfected in a nobler studio. What he has done remains, although it vanishes; and he never either forgets what he has once done, or does it even once again. As the thoughts move in the mind of a man, so move the worlds of men and women in the mind of God, and make no confusion there, for there they had their birth, the offspring of his imagination. Man is but a thought of God.

If we now consider the so-called creative faculty in man, we shall find that in no *primary* sense is this faculty creative. Indeed, a man is rather *being thought* than *thinking*, when a new thought arises in his mind. He knew it not till he found it there, therefore he could not even have sent for it. He did not create it, else how could it be the surprise that it was when it arose? He may, indeed, in rare instances foresee that something is coming, and make ready the place for its birth; but that is the utmost relation of consciousness and will he can bear to the dawning idea. Leaving this aside, however, and turning to the *embodiment* or revelation of thought, we shall find that a man no more *creates* the forms by which he would reveal his thoughts, than he creates those thoughts themselves.

For what are the forms by means of which a man may reveal his thoughts? Are they not those of nature? But although he is created in the closest sympathy with these forms, yet even these forms are not born in his mind. What springs there is the perception that this or that form is already an expression of this or that phase of thought or of feeling. For the world around him is an outward figuration of the condition of his mind; an inexhaustible storehouse of forms whence he may choose exponents—the crystal pitchers that shall protect his thought and not need to be broken that the light may break forth. The meanings are in those forms already, else they could be no garment of unveiling. God has made the world that it should thus serve his creature, developing in the service that imagination whose necessity it meets. The man has but to light the lamp within the form: his imagination is the light, it is not the form. Straightway the shining thought makes the form visible, and becomes itself visible through the form.[1]

In illustration of what we mean, take a passage from the poet Shelley.

In his poem *Adonais*, written upon the death of Keats, representing death as the revealer of secrets, he says:—

---

1 We would not be understood to say that the man works consciously even in this. Oftentimes, if not always, the vision arises in the mind, thought and form together. [MacDonald's note]

"The one remains; the many change and pass;
   Heaven's light for ever shines; earth's shadows fly;
Life, like a dome of many coloured glass,
   Stains the white radiance of eternity,
Until death tramples it to fragments."[1]

This is a new embodiment, certainly, whence he who gains not, for the moment at least, a loftier feeling of death, must be dull either of heart or of understanding. But has Shelley created this figure, or only put together its parts according to the harmony of truths already embodied in each of the parts? For first he takes the inventions of his fellow-men, in glass, in colour, in dome: with these he represents life as finite though elevated, and as an analysis although a lovely one. Next he presents eternity as the dome of the sky above this dome of coloured glass—the sky having ever been regarded as the true symbol of eternity. This portion of the figure he enriches by the attribution of whiteness, or unity and radiance. And last, he shows us Death as the destroying revealer, walking aloft through the upper region, treading out this life-bubble of colours, that the man may look beyond it and behold the true, the uncoloured, the all-coloured.

But although the human imagination has no choice but to make use of the forms already prepared for it, its operation is the same as that of the divine inasmuch as it does put thought into form. And if it be to man what creation is to God, we must expect to find it operative in every sphere of human activity. Such is, indeed, the fact, and that to a far greater extent than is commonly supposed.

The sovereignty of the imagination, for instance, over the region of poetry will hardly, in the present day at least, be questioned; but not every one is prepared to be told that the imagination has had nearly as much to do with the making of our language as with "Macbeth" or the "Paradise Lost." The half of our language is the work of the imagination.

For how shall two agree together what name they shall give to a thought or a feeling? How shall the one show the other that which is invisible? True, he can unveil the mind's construction in the face—that living eternally changeful symbol which God has hung in front of the unseen spirit—but that without words reaches only to the expression of present feeling. To attempt to employ it alone for the conveyance of the intellectual or the historical would constantly mislead; while the expression of feeling itself would be misinterpreted, especially with

---

1 Lines 460-64.

regard to cause and object: the dumb show[1] would be worse than dumb.

But let a man become aware of some new movement within him. Loneliness comes with it, for he would share his mind with his friend, and he cannot; he is shut up in speechlessness. Thus

> He *may* live a man forbid
> Weary seven nights nine times nine,[2]

or the first moment of his perplexity may be that of his release. Gazing about him in pain, he suddenly beholds the material form of his immaterial condition. There stands his thought! God thought it before him, and put its picture there ready for him when he wanted it. Or, to express the thing more prosaically, the man cannot look around him long without perceiving some form, aspect, or movement of nature, some relation between its forms, or between such and himself which resembles the state or motion within him. This he seizes as the symbol, as the garment or body of his invisible thought, presents it to his friend, and his friend understands him. Every word so employed with a new meaning is henceforth, in its new character, born of the spirit and not of the flesh, born of the imagination and not of the under-standing, and is henceforth submitted to new laws of growth and modification.

"Thinkest thou," says Carlyle in "Past and Present," "there were no poets till Dan Chaucer? No heart burning with a thought which it could not hold, and had no word for; and needed to shape and coin a word for—what thou callest a metaphor, trope, or the like? For every word we have there was such a man and poet. The coldest word was once a glowing new metaphor and bold questionable originality. Thy very ATTENTION, does it not mean an *attentio*, a STRETCHING-TO? Fancy that act of the mind, which all were conscious of, which none had yet named,—when this new poet first felt bound and driven to name it. His questionable originality and new glowing metaphor was found adoptable, intelligible, and remains our name for it to this day."[3]

All words, then, belonging to the inner world of the mind, are of the imagination, are originally poetic words. The better, however, any such word is fitted for the needs of humanity, the sooner it loses its poetic

---

1   "In the early drama, a part of a play represented by action without speech, chiefly in order to exhibit more of the story than could otherwise be included, but sometimes merely emblematical" (*OED*).

2   Shakespeare, *Macbeth*, I.iii.21-22.

3   Thomas Carlyle, *Past and Present* (1843) Book II, chap. XVII.

aspect by commonness of use. It ceases to be heard as a symbol, and appears only as a sign. Thus thousands of words which were originally poetic words owing their existence to the imagination, lose their vitality, and harden into mummies of prose. Not merely in literature does poetry come first, and prose afterwards, but poetry is the source of all the language that belongs to the inner world, whether it be of passion or of metaphysics, of psychology or of aspiration. No poetry comes by the elevation of prose; but the half of prose comes by the "massing into the common clay"[1] of thousands of winged words, whence, like the lovely shells of by-gone ages, one is occasionally disinterred by some lover of speech, and held up to the light to show the play of colour in its manifold laminations.

For the world is—allow us the homely figure—the human being turned inside out. All that moves in the mind is symbolized in Nature. Or, to use another more philosophical, and certainly not less poetic figure, the world is a sensuous analysis of humanity, and hence an inexhaustible wardrobe for the clothing of human thought. Take any word expressive of emotion—take the word *emotion* itself—and you will find that its primary meaning is of the outer world. In the swaying of the woods, in the unrest of the "wavy plain," the imagination saw the picture of a well-known condition of the human mind; and hence the word *emotion*.[2]

But while the imagination of man has thus the divine function of putting thought into form, it has a duty altogether human, which is paramount to that function—the duty, namely, which springs from his immediate relation to the Father, that of following and finding out the divine imagination in whose image it was made. To do this, the man must watch its signs, its manifestations. He must contemplate what the Hebrew poets call the works of His hands.

"But to follow those is the province of the intellect, not of the imagination."—We will leave out of the question at present that poetic interpretation of the works of Nature with which the intellect has almost nothing, and the imagination almost everything, to do. It is unnecessary to insist that the higher being of a flower even is dependent for its reception upon the human imagination; that science may pull the snowdrop to shreds, but cannot find out the idea of

---

1 Cf. Percy Bysshe Shelley, "The Sensitive Plant": "And Indian plants, of scent and hue / The sweetest that ever were fed on dew, / Leaf by leaf, day after day, / Were massed into the common clay" (lines 30-33).

2 This passage contains only a repetition of what is far better said in the preceding extract from Carlyle, but it was written before we had read (if reviewers may be allowed to confess such ignorance) the book from which that extract is taken. [MacDonald's note]

suffering hope and pale confident submission, for the sake of which that darling of the spring looks out of heaven, namely, God's heart, upon us his wiser and more sinful children; for if there be any truth in this region of things acknowledged at all, it will be at the same time acknowledged that that region belongs to the imagination. We confine ourselves to that questioning of the works of God which is called the province of science.

"Shall, then, the human intellect," we ask, "come into readier contact with the divine imagination than that human imagination?" The work of the Higher must be discovered by the search of the Lower in degree which is yet similar in kind. Let us not be supposed to exclude the intellect from a share in every highest office. Man is not divided when the manifestations of his life are distinguished. The intellect "is all in every part."[1] There were no imagination without intellect, however much it may appear that intellect can exist without imagination. What we mean to insist upon is, that in finding out the works of God, the Intellect must labour, workman-like, under the direction of the architect, Imagination. Herein, too, we proceed in the hope to show how much more than is commonly supposed the imagination has to do with human endeavour; how large a share it has in the work that is done under the sun.

"But how can the imagination have anything to do with science? That region, at least, is governed by fixed laws."

"True," we answer. "But how much do we know of these laws? How much of science already belongs to the region of the ascertained—in other words, has been conquered by the intellect? We will not now dispute your vindication of the *ascertained* from the intrusion of the imagination; but we do claim for it all the undiscovered, all the unexplored." "Ah, well! There it can do little harm. There let it run riot if you will." "No," we reply. "Licence is not what we claim when we assert the duty of the imagination to be that of following and finding out the work that God maketh. Her part is to understand God ere she attempts to utter man. Where is the room for being fanciful or riotous here? It is only the ill-bred, that is, the uncultivated imagination that will amuse itself where it ought to worship and work."

"But the facts of Nature are to be discovered only by observation and experiment." True. But how does the man of science come to think of his experiments? Does observation reach to the non-present, the possible, the yet unconceived? Even if it showed you the ex-

---

1 John Dryden (1631-1700), "Eleonora: A Panegyrical Poem, Dedicated to the Memory of the Late Countess of Abingdon": "Yet as the soul is all in every part, / So God and he might each have all her heart" (lines 91-92).

periments which *ought* to be made, will observation reveal to you the experiments which *might* be made? And who can tell of which kind is the one that carries in its bosom the secret of the law you seek? We yield you your facts. The laws we claim for the prophetic imagination. "He hath set the world *in* man's heart,"[1] not in his understanding. And the heart must open the door to the understanding. It is the far-seeing imagination which beholds what might be a form of things, and says to the intellect: "Try whether that may not be the form of these things;" which beholds or invents *a* harmonious relation of parts and operations, and sends the intellect to find out whether that be not *the* harmonious relation of them—that is, the law of the phenomenon it contemplates. Nay, the poetic relations themselves in the phenomenon may suggest to the imagination the law that rules its scientific life. Yea, more than this: we dare to claim for the true, childlike, humble imagination, such an inward oneness with the laws of the universe that it possesses in itself an insight into the very nature of things.

Lord Bacon tells us that a prudent question is the half of knowledge.[2] Whence comes this prudent question? we repeat. And we answer, From the imagination. It is the imagination that suggests in what direction to make the new inquiry—which, should it cast no immediate light on the answer sought, can yet hardly fail to be a step towards final discovery. Every experiment has its origin in hypothesis; without the scaffolding of hypothesis, the house of science could never arise. And the construction of any hypothesis whatever is the work of the imagination. The man who cannot invent will never discover. The

---

1 Francis Bacon (1561-1626), *Valerius Terminus or The Interpretation of Nature*: "And lest any man should retain a scruple as if this thirst of knowledge were rather an humour of the mind than an emptiness or want in nature and an instinct from God, the same author [Solomon] defineth of it fully, saying, *God hath made every thing in beauty according to season; also he hath set the world in man's heart, yet can he not find out the work which God worketh from beginning to end.*" (James Spedding, Robert Leslie Ellis, and Douglas Denon Heath, eds., *The Works of Francis Bacon* [Boston: Brown and Taggard, 1860] vol. III, p. 220.)

2 Francis Bacon, *The Advancement of Learning*: "Nor is its office [that of analysis into general and particular topics] only confined to the suggesting or admonishing us of what should be affirmed or asserted, but also what we should examine or question; a prudent questioning being a kind of half knowledge" (Book V, chap. III). (The later books of *The Advancement of Learning* were written in Latin. MacDonald appears to have quoted from Joseph Devey, ed., *The Physical and Metaphysical Works of Lord Bacon, Including the Advancement of Learning and Nouvum Organum*, Bohn's Philosophical Library [London: G. Bell, 1904], p. 199.)

imagination often gets a glimpse of the law itself long before it is or can be *ascertained* to be a law.[1]

The region belonging to the pure intellect is straitened: the imagination labours to extend its territories, to give it room. She sweeps across the borders, searching out new lands into which she may guide her plodding brother. The imagination is the light which redeems from the darkness for the eyes of the understanding. Novalis says, "The imagination is the stuff of the intellect"—affords, that is, the material upon which the intellect works. And Bacon, in his "Advancement of Learning," fully recognizes this its office, corresponding to the foresight of God in this, that it beholds afar

---

1 This paper was already written when, happening to mention the present subject to a mathematical friend, a lecturer at one of the universities, he gave us a corroborative instance. He had lately *guessed* that a certain algebraic process could be shortened exceedingly if the method which his imagination suggested should prove to be a true one—that is, an algebraic law. He put it to the test of experiment—committed the verification, that is, into the hands of his intellect—and found the method true. It has since been accepted by the Royal Society. Noteworthy illustration we have lately found in the record of the experiences of an Edinburgh detective, an Irishman of the name of McLevy. That the service of the imagination in the solution of the problems peculiar to his calling is well known to him, we could adduce many proofs. He recognizes its function in the construction of the theory which shall unite this and that hint into an organic whole, and he expressly sets forth the need of a theory before facts can be serviceable:—

"I would wait for my 'idea'.... I never did any good without mine.... Chance never smiled on me unless I poked her some way; so that my 'notion,' after all, has been in the getting of it my own work only perfected by a higher hand."

"On leaving the shop I went direct to Prince's Street,—of course with an idea in my mind; and somehow I have always been contented with one idea when I could not get another; and the advantage of sticking by one is, that the other don't jostle it and turn you about in a circle when you should go in a straight line." [MacDonald's note. MacDonald adds the following note to the last paragraph in this note:] "Since quoting the above I have learned that the book referred to is unworthy of confidence. But let it stand as illustration where it cannot be proof."

[According to Raphael Shaberman, the "mathematical friend" is C.L. Dodgson, also known as Lewis Carroll (*George MacDonald*, p. 71).

James McLevy (1793/4-1873), police officer and author, was noted for his abilities to spot and arrest criminals as part of the Edinburgh police force. Later in life, he produced *Curiousities of Crime in Edinburgh* (1861), whose stories were based on investigations he had actively pursed after the 1830s (*ODNB*).]

off. And he says: "Imagination is much akin to miracle-working faith."[1]

In the scientific region of her duty of which we speak, the Imagination cannot have her perfect work; this belongs to another and higher sphere than that of intellectual truth—that, namely, of full-globed humanity, operating in which she gives birth to poetry—truth in beauty. But her function in the complete sphere of our nature, will, at the same time, influence her more limited operation in the sections that belong to science. Coleridge says that no one but a poet will make any further *great* discoveries in mathematics;[2] and Bacon says that

---

1 We are sorry we cannot verify this quotation, for which we are indebted to Mr. Oldbuck the Antiquary, in the novel of that ilk. There is, however, little room for doubt that it is sufficiently correct. [MacDonald's note]

    [In Sir Walter Scott's *The Antiquary* (1816), Jonathan Oldbuck, the antiquary, states, "But I rather opine with Lord Bacon, who says that imagination is much akin to miracle-working faith." Cf. Bacon, *The Advancement of Learning*: "Fascination is the power and act of imagination intentive upon other bodies than the body of the imagination, for of that we spake in the proper place: wherein the school of Paracelsus, and the disciples of pretended Natural Magic have been so intemperate, as they have exalted the power of the imagination to be much one with the power of miracle-working faith" (Book I, sect. 11, para. 3).]

2 Likely a reference to Samuel Taylor Coleridge's "Prospectus and Specimen of a Translation of Euclid" first found in a letter to his brother, the Reverend George Coleridge, 31 March 1791:

    I have often been surprized, that Mathematics, the quintessence of Truth, should have found admirers so few and so languid.—Frequent consideration and minute scrutiny have at length unravelled the cause—viz.—that though Reason is feasted, Imagination is starved; whilst Reason is luxuriating in it's proper Paradise, Imagination is wearily travelling on a dreary desart. To assist *Reason* by the stimulus of *Imagination* is the *Design* of the following production. In the *execution* of it much may be objectionable. The verse (particularly in the introduction of the Ode) may be accused of unwarrantable liberties; but they are liberties equally homogeneal with the exactness of Mathematical disquisition, and the boldness of *Pindaric* Daring. I have three strong champions to defend me against the attacks of Criticism: the Novelty, the Difficulty, and the Utility of the Work. I may justly plume myself, that I first have drawn the Nymph Mathesis from the visionary caves of Abstracted Idea, and caused her to unite with Harmony. The first-born of this Union I now present to you: with interested motives indeed—as I expect to receive in return the more valuable offspring of your Muse—.

    This statement is then followed by a poem, "This is now—This was erst / Proposition the first and Problem the first," illustrating his introductory prose remarks. MacDonald could have encountered this material in Henry Nelson Coleridge's edition of STC's *Poetical Works* (1834).

"wonder," that faculty of the mind especially attendant on the child-like imagination, "is the seed of knowledge."[1] The influence of the poetic upon the scientific imagination is, for instance, especially present in the construction of an invisible whole from the hints afforded by a visible part; where the needs of the part, its uselessness, its broken relations, are the only guides to a multiplex harmony, completeness, and end, which is the whole. From a little bone, worn with ages of death, older than the man can think, his scientific imagination dashed with the poetic, calls up the form, size, habits, periods, belonging to an animal never beheld by human eyes, even to the mingling contrasts of scales and wings, of feathers and hair. Through the combined lenses of science and imagination, we look back into ancient times, so dreadful in their incompleteness, that it may well have been the task of seraphic faith, as well as of cherubic imagination, to behold in the wallowing monstrosities of the terror-teeming earth, the prospective, quiet, age-long labour of God preparing the world with all its humble, graceful service for his unborn Man. The imagination of the poet, on the other hand, dashed with the imagination of the man of science, revealed to Goethe the prophecy of the flower in the leaf.[2] No other than an artistic imagination, however, fulfilled of science, could have attained to the discovery of the fact that the leaf is the imperfect flower.

When we turn to history, however, we find probably the greatest operative sphere of the intellectuo-constructive imagination. To discover its laws; the cycles in which events return, with the reasons of their return, recognizing them notwithstanding metamorphosis; to perceive the vital motions of this spiritual body of mankind; to learn from its facts the rule of God; to construct from a succession of broken indications a whole accordant with human nature; to approach a scheme of the forces at work, the passions overwhelming or

---

1 Bacon, *The Advancement of Learning*: "for all knowledge and wonder (which is the seed of knowledge) is an impression of pleasure in itself" (Book I, sect. 1, para. 3).

2 A reference to Goethe's conception of the *Urpflanze* or principle of unity among all plants. He describes the emergence of this concept in his *Italian Journal*: "While walking in the Public Gardens of Palermo, it came to me in a flash that in the organ of the plant which we are accustomed to call the leaf lies the true Proteus who can hide or reveal himself in vegetal forms. From first to last, the plant is nothing but leaf, which is so inseparable from the future germ that one cannot think of one without the other" ([Harmondsworth, UK: Penguin, 1970], p. 366). The concept is explored in Goethe's poem, "The Metamorphosis of Plants" (see Johann Wolfgang von Goethe, *The Metamorphosis of Plants* [Cambridge, MA: MIT Press, 2009]).

upheaving, the aspirations securely upraising, the selfishnesses debasing and crumbling, with the vital interworking of the whole; to illuminate all from the analogy with individual life, and from the predominant phases of individual character which are taken as the mind of the people—this is the province of the imagination. Without her influence no process of recording events can develop into a history. As truly might that be called the description of a volcano which occupied itself with a delineation of the shapes assumed by the smoke expelled from the mountain's burning bosom. What history becomes under the full sway of the imagination may be seen in the "History of the French Revolution," by Thomas Carlyle, at once a true picture, a philosophical revelation, a noble poem.[1]

There is a wonderful passage about *Time* in Shakespere's "Rape of Lucrece," which shows how he understood history. The passage is really about history, and not about time; for time itself does nothing— not even "blot old books and alter their contents."[2] It is the forces at work in time that produce all the changes; and they are history. We quote for the sake of one line chiefly, but the whole stanza is pertinent.

> "Time's glory is to calm contending kings,
> To unmask falsehood, and bring truth to light,
> To stamp the seal of time in aged things,
> To wake the morn and sentinel the night,
> *To wrong the wronger till he render right*;
> To ruinate proud buildings with thy hours,
> And smear with dust their glittering golden towers."[3]

To wrong the wronger till he render right. Here is a historical cycle worthy of the imagination of Shakespere, yea, worthy of the creative imagination of our God—the God who made the Shakespere with the imagination, as well as evolved the history from the laws which that imagination followed and found out.

In full instance we would refer our readers to Shakespere's historical plays; and, as a side-illustration, to the fact that he repeatedly represents his greatest characters, when at the point of death, as relieving their overcharged minds by prophecy. Such prophecy is the

---

1 *A History of the French Revolution*, a three-volume work published by Thomas Carlyle in 1837, describes the Revolution in France from the death of Louis XV in 1774 to the fall of Robespierre and the actions of Bonaparte to stop the insurrection of the Vendémiaire in 1795. Although actually a prose narrative, MacDonald attests to the creative inspiration behind the work in calling it a "noble poem."

2 Shakespeare, *The Rape of Lucrece*, line 948.

3 Ibid., lines 939-45.

result of the light of imagination, cleared of all distorting dimness by the vanishing of earthly hopes and desires, cast upon the facts of experience. Such prophecy is the perfect working of the historical imagination.

In the interpretation of individual life, the same principles hold; and nowhere can the imagination be more healthily and rewardingly occupied than in endeavouring to construct the life of an individual out of the fragments which are all that can reach us of the history of even the noblest of our race. How this will apply to the reading of the gospel story we leave to the earnest thought of our readers.

We now pass to one more sphere in which the student imagination works in glad freedom—the sphere which is understood to belong more immediately to the poet.

We have already said that the forms of Nature (by which word *forms* we mean any of those conditions of Nature which affect the senses of man) are so many approximate representations of the mental conditions of humanity. The outward, commonly called the material, is *informed* by, or has form in virtue of, the inward or immaterial—in a word, the thought. The forms of Nature are the representations of human thought in virtue of their being the embodiment of God's thought. As such, therefore, they can be read and used to any depth, shallow or profound. Men of all ages and all developments have discovered in them the means of expression; and the men of ages to come, before us in every path along which we are now striving, must likewise find such means in those forms, unfolding with their unfolding necessities. The man, then, who, in harmony with nature, attempts the discovery of more of her meanings, is just searching out the things of God. The deepest of these are far too simple for us to understand as yet. But let our imagination interpretive reveal to us one severed significance of one of her parts, and such is the harmony of the whole, that all the realm of Nature is open to us henceforth—not without labour—and in time. Upon the man who can understand the human meaning of the snowdrop, of the primrose, or of the daisy, the life of the earth blossoming into the cosmical flower of a perfect moment will one day seize, possessing him with its prophetic hope, arousing his conscience with the vision of the "rest that remaineth," and stirring up the aspiration to enter into that rest:

"Thine is the tranquil hour, purpureal Eve!
But long as godlike wish, or hope divine,
Informs my spirit, ne'er can I believe
That this magnificence is wholly thine!
—From worlds not quickened by the sun
A portion of the gift is won;

An intermingling of Heaven's pomp is spread
On ground which British shepherds tread!"[1]

Even the careless curve of a frozen cloud across the blue will calm some troubled thoughts, may slay some selfish thoughts. And what shall be said of such gorgeous shows as the scarlet poppies in the green corn, the likest we have to those lilies of the field which spoke to the Saviour himself of the care of God, and rejoiced His eyes with the glory of their God-devised array? From such visions as these the imagination reaps the best fruits of the earth, for the sake of which all the science involved in its construction, is the inferior, yet willing and beautiful support.

From what we have now advanced, will it not then appear that, on the whole, the name given by our Norman ancestors is more fitting for the man who moves in these regions than the name given by the Greeks? Is not the *Poet*, the *Maker*, a less suitable name for him than the *Trouvère*, the *Finder*? At least, must not the faculty that finds precede the faculty that utters?

But is there nothing to be said of the function of the imagination from the Greek side of the question? Does it possess no creative faculty? Has it no originating power?

Certainly it would be a poor description of the Imagination which omitted the one element especially present to the mind that invented the word *Poet*.—It can present us with new thought-forms—new, that is, as revelations of thought. It has created none of the material that goes to make these forms. Nor does it work upon raw material. But it takes forms already existing, and gathers them about a thought so much higher than they, that it can group and subordinate and harmonize them into a whole which shall represent, unveil that thought.[2] The nature of this process we will illustrate by an examination of the well-known *Bugle Song* in Tennyson's "Princess."

---

1 William Wordsworth (1770-1850), "Composed upon an Evening of Extraordinary Splendour and Beauty," lines 33-40.

2 Just so Spenser describes the process of the embodiment of a human soul in his Platonic "Hymn in Honour of Beauty."

"She frames her house in which she will be placed
Fit for herself....
And the gross matter by a sovereign might
Tempers so trim....
For of the soul the body form doth take;
For soul is form, and doth the body make." [MacDonald's note]

[Lines 117-18, 124-25, 132-33.]

First of all, there is the new music of the song, which does not even remind one of the music of any other. The rhythm, rhyme, melody, harmony are all an embodiment in sound, as distinguished from word, of what can be so embodied—the *feeling* of the poem, which goes before, and prepares the way for the following thought—tunes the heart into a receptive harmony. Then comes the new arrangement of thought and figure whereby the meaning contained is presented as it never was before. We give a sort of paraphrastical synopsis of the poem, which, partly in virtue of its disagreeableness, will enable the lovers of the song to return to it with an increase of pleasure.

The glory of midsummer mid-day upon mountain, lake, and ruin. Give nature a voice for her gladness. Blow, bugle.

Nature answers with dying echoes, sinking in the midst of her splendour into a sad silence.

Not so with human nature. The echoes of the word of truth gather volume and richness from every soul that re-echoes it to brother and sister souls.

With poets the *fashion* has been to contrast the stability and rejuvenescence of nature with the evanescence and unreturning decay of humanity:—

> "Yet soon reviving plants and flowers, anew shall deck the
> plain;
> The woods shall hear the voice of Spring, and flourish green
> again.
> But man forsakes this earthly scene, ah! never to return:
> Shall any following Spring revive the ashes of the urn?"

But our poet vindicates the eternal in humanity:—

> "O Love, they die in yon rich sky,
> They faint on hill or field or river:
> Our echoes roll from soul to soul,
> And grow for ever and for ever.
> Blow, bugle, blow, set the wild echoes flying;
> And answer, echoes, answer, Dying, dying, dying."[1]

Is not this a new form to the thought—a form which makes us feel the truth of it afresh? And every new embodiment of a known truth must be a new and wider revelation. No man is capable of seeing for himself the whole of any truth: he needs it echoed back to him from

---

1 Alfred, Lord Tennyson (1809-92), "Bugle Song," from "The Princess," lines 13-18.

every soul in the universe; and still its centre is hid in the Father of Lights. In so far, then, as either form or thought is new, we may grant the use of the word Creation, modified according to our previous definitions.

This operation of the imagination in choosing, gathering, and vitally combining the material of a new revelation, may be well illustrated from a certain employment of the poetic faculty in which our greatest poets have delighted. Perceiving truth half hidden and half revealed in the slow speech and stammering tongue of men who have gone before them, they have taken up the unfinished form and completed it; they have, as it were, rescued the soul of meaning from its prison of uninformed crudity, where it sat like the Prince in the "Arabian Nights," half man, half marble;[1] they have set it free in its own form, in a shape, namely, which it could "through every part impress."[2] Shakespere's keen eye suggested many such a rescue from the tomb—of a tale drearily told—a tale which no one now would read save for the glorified form in which he has re-embodied its true contents. And from Tennyson we can produce one specimen small enough for our use, which, a mere chip from the great marble re-embodying the old legend of Arthur's death, may, like the hand of Achilles holding his spear in the crowded picture,

"Stand for the whole to be imagined."[3]

In the "History of Prince Arthur," when Sir Bedivere returns after hiding Excalibur the first time, the king asks him what he has seen, and he answers—

"Sir, I saw nothing but waves and wind."

The second time, to the same question, he answers—

---

1 "The History of the Young King of the Black Isles" provides the story of a young man who marries his cousin on his accession to the throne. He later finds that she is an enchantress who has been carrying on an affair with her Moorish lover. When he grievously wounds the lover, she speaks: "By virtue of my enchantments, I command thee to become half marble and half man." *The Arabian Nights' Entertainments* (London: J. Limbard, 1827) 37.

2 Spenser, "A Hymn to Beauty": "When she [Beauty] in fleshly seed is eft enraced, / Through every part she doth the same impress" (lines 114-15).

3 Shakespeare, *The Rape of Lucrece*, line 1428.

"Sir, I saw nothing but the water[1] wap, and the waves wan."[2]

This answer Tennyson has expanded into the well-known lines—

"I heard the ripple washing in the reeds,
And the wild water lapping on the crag;"

slightly varied, for the other occasion, into—

"I heard the water lapping on the crag,
And the long ripple washing in the reeds."[3]

But, as to this matter of *creation*, is there, after all, I ask yet, any genuine sense in which a man may be said to create his own thought-forms? Allowing that a new combination of forms already existing might be called creation, is the man, after all, the author of this new combination? Did he, with his will and his knowledge, proceed wittingly, consciously, to construct a form which should embody his thought? Or did this form arise within him without will or effort of his—vivid if not clear—certain if not outlined? Ruskin (and better authority we do not know) will assert the latter, and we think he is right: though perhaps he would insist more upon the absolute perfection of the vision than we are quite prepared to do. Such embodiments are not the result of the man's intention, or of the operation of his conscious nature. His feeling is that they are given to

---

1   The word *wap* is plain enough; the word *wan* we cannot satisfy ourselves about. Had it been used with regard to the water, it might have been worth remarking that *wan*, meaning dark, gloomy, turbid, is a common adjective to a river in the old Scotch ballad. And it might be an adjective here; but that is not likely, seeing it is conjoined with the verb *wap*. The Anglo-Saxon *wanian*, to decrease, might be the root-word, perhaps, (in the sense of *to ebb*,) if this water had been the sea and not a lake. But possibly the meaning is, "I heard the water *whoop* or *wail aloud*" (from *Wópan*); and "the waves *whine* or *bewail*" (from *Wánian* to lament). But even then the two verbs would seem to predicate of transposed subjects. [MacDonald's note]

2   This quotation and the one above it are derived from the William Caxton translation of Sir Thomas Malory's *Le Morte Darthur*. (See James W. Spisak, William Matthews, and Bert Dillon, eds., *Caxton's Malory: A New Edition of Sir Thomas Malory's Le Morte Darthur; Based on the Pierpont Morgan Copy of William Caxton's Edition of 1485* [Berkeley: U of California P, 1983], p. 591.)

3   Tennyson, "Morte D'Arthur," lines 116-17.

him; that from the vast unknown, where time and space are not, they suddenly appear in luminous writing upon the wall of his consciousness. Can it be correct, then, to say that he created them? Nothing less so, as it seems to us. But can we not say that they are the creation of the unconscious portion of his nature? Yes, provided we can understand that that which is the individual, the man, can know, and not know that it knows, can create and yet be ignorant that virtue has gone out of it. From that unknown region we grant they come, but not by its own blind working. Nor, even were it so, could any amount of such production, where no will was concerned, be dignified with the name of creation. But God sits in that chamber of our being in which the candle of our consciousness goes out in darkness, and sends forth from thence wonderful gifts into the light of that understanding which is His candle. Our hope lies in no most perfect mechanism even of the spirit, but in the wisdom wherein we live and move and have our being. Thence we hope for endless forms of beauty informed of truth. If the dark portion of our own being were the origin of our imaginations, we might well fear the apparition of such monsters as would be generated in the sickness of a decay which could never feel— only declare—a slow return towards primeval chaos. But the Maker is our Light.

One word more, ere we turn to consider the culture of this noblest faculty, which we might well call the creative, did we not see a something in God for which we would humbly keep our mighty word:—the fact that there is always more in a work of art—which is the highest human result of the embodying imagination—than the producer himself perceived while he produced it, seems to us a strong reason for attributing to it a larger origin than the man alone—for saying at the last, that the inspiration of the Almighty shaped its ends.

We return now to the class which, from the first, we supposed hostile to the imagination and its functions generally. Those belonging to it will now say: "It was to no imagination such as you have been setting forth that we were opposed, but to those wild fancies and vague reveries in which young people indulge to the damage and loss of the real in the world around them."

"And," we insist, "you would rectify the matter by smothering the young monster at once—because he has wings, and, young to their use, flutters them about in a way discomposing to your nerves, and destructive to those notions of propriety of which this creature—you stop not to inquire whether angel or pterodactyle—has not yet learned even the existence. Or, if it is only the creature's vagaries of which you disapprove, why speak of them as *the* exercise of the

All that has been said, then, tends to enforce the culture of the imagination. But the strongest argument of all remains behind. For, if the whole power of pedantry should rise against her, the imagination will yet work; and if not for good, then for evil; if not for truth, then for falsehood; if not for life, then for death; the evil alternative becoming the more likely from the unnatural treatment she has experienced from those who ought to have fostered her. The power that might have gone forth in conceiving the noblest forms of action, in realizing the lives of the true-hearted, the self-forgetting, will go forth in building airy castles of vain ambition, of boundless riches, of unearned admiration. The imagination that might be devising how to make home blessed or to help the poor neighbour, will be absorbed in the invention of the new dress, or worse, in devising the means of procuring it. For, if she be not occupied with the beautiful, she will be occupied by the pleasant; that which goes not out to worship, will remain at home to be sensual. Cultivate the mere intellect as you may, it will never reduce the passions: the imagination, seeking the ideal in everything, will elevate them to their true and noble service. Seek not that your sons and your daughters should not see visions, should not dream dreams; seek that they should see true visions, that they should dream noble dreams. Such out-going of the imagination is one with aspiration, and will do more to elevate above what is low and vile than all possible inculcations of morality. Nor can religion herself ever rise up into her own calm home, her crystal shrine, when one of her wings, one of the twain with which she flies, is thus broken or paralyzed.

"The universe is infinitely wide,
And conquering Reason, if self-glorified,
Can nowhere move uncrossed by some new wall
Or gulf of mystery, which thou alone,
Imaginative Faith! canst overleap,
In progress towards the fount of love."[1]

The danger that lies in the repression of the imagination may be well illustrated from the play of "Macbeth." The imagination of the hero (in him a powerful faculty), representing how the deed would appear to others, and so representing its true nature to himself, was his great impediment on the path to crime. Nor would he have succeeded in reaching it, had he not gone to his wife for help—sought refuge from his troublesome imagination with her. She, possessing far less of the faculty, and having dealt more destructively with what she had,

---

1 William Wordsworth, "Desire we past illusions to recall?" lines 6-11.

took his hand, and led him to the deed. From her imagination, again, she for her part takes refuge in unbelief and denial, declaring to herself and her husband that there is no reality in its representations; that there is no reality in anything beyond the present effect it produces on the mind upon which it operates; that intellect and courage are equal to any, even an evil emergency; and that no harm will come to those who can rule themselves according to their own will. Still, however, finding her imagination, and yet more that of her husband, troublesome, she effects a marvellous combination of materialism and idealism, and asserts that things are not, cannot be, and shall not be more or other than people choose to think them. She says,—

"These deeds must not be thought
After these ways; so, it will make us mad."
"The sleeping and the dead
Are but as pictures."[1]

But she had over-estimated the power of her will, and under-estimated that of her imagination. Her will was the one thing in her that was bad, without root or support in the universe, while her imagination was the voice of God himself out of her own unknown being. The choice of no man or woman can long determine how or what he or she shall think of things. Lady Macbeth's imagination would not be repressed beyond its appointed period—a time determined by laws of her being over which she had no control. It arose, at length, as from the dead, over-shadowing her with all the blackness of her crime. The woman who drank strong drink that she might murder, dared not sleep without a light by her bed; rose and walked in the night, a sleepless spirit in a sleeping body, rubbing the spotted hand of her dreams, which, often as water had cleared it of the deed, yet smelt so in her sleeping nostrils, that all the perfumes of Arabia would not sweeten it.[2] Thus her long down-trodden imagination rose and took vengeance, even through those senses which she had thought to subordinate to her wicked will.

But all this is of the imagination itself, and fitter, therefore, for illustration than for argument. Let us come to facts.—Dr. Pritchard, lately executed for murder, had no lack of that invention, which is, as it were, the intellect of the imagination—its lowest form.[3] One of the

---

1 Shakespeare, *Macbeth*, II.ii.33-34, 52-53.

2 Shakespeare, *Macbeth*, "Here's the smell of the blood still; all the perfumes of Arabia will not but sweeten this little hand" (V.i.47-48).

3 Edward William Pritchard (1825-65), a surgeon who poisoned both his wife and mother-in-law, admitted to the crimes, was hanged on 28 July 1865 in front of 100,000 people. His was the last public execution in Glasgow (*ODNB*).

clergymen who, at his own request, attended the prisoner, went through indescribable horrors in the vain endeavour to induce the man simply to cease from lying: one invention after another followed the most earnest asseverations of truth. The effect produced upon us by this clergyman's report of his experience was a moral dismay, such as we had never felt with regard to human being, and drew from us the exclamation, "The man could have had no imagination." The reply was, "None whatever." Never seeking true or high things, caring only for appearances, and, therefore, for inventions, he had left his imagination all undeveloped, and when it represented his own inner condition to him, had repressed it until it was nearly destroyed, and what remained of it was set on fire of hell.[1]

Man is "the roof and crown of things."[2] He is the world, and more. Therefore the chief scope of his imagination, next to God who made him, will be the world in relation to his own life therein. Will he do better or worse in it if this imagination, touched to fine issues and having free scope, present him with noble pictures of relationship and duty, of possible elevation of character and attainable justice of behaviour, of friendship and of love; and, above all, of all these in that life to understand which as a whole, must ever be the loftiest aspiration of this noblest power of humanity? Will a woman lead a more or a less troubled life that the sights and sounds of nature break through the crust of gathering anxiety, and remind her of the peace of the lilies and the well-being of the birds of the air? Or will life be less interesting to her, that the lives of her neighbours, instead of passing like shadows upon a wall, assume a consistent wholeness, forming themselves into stories and phases of life? Will she not hereby love more and talk less? Or will she be more unlikely to make a good match—? But here we arrest ourselves in bewilderment over the word *good*, and seek to re-arrange our thoughts. If what mothers mean by a *good* match, is the alliance of a man of position and means—or let them throw intellect, manners, and personal advantages into the same scale—if this be all, then we grant the daughter of cultivated imagination may not be manageable, will probably be obstinate. We hope she will be obstinate enough.[3] But will the girl be less likely to

---

1 One of the best weekly papers in London, evidently as much in ignorance of the man as of the facts of the case, spoke of Dr. Macleod as having been engaged in "white-washing the murderer for heaven." So far is this from a true representation, that Dr. Macleod actually refused to pray with him, telling him that if there was a hell to go to, he must go to it. [MacDonald's note]

2 Tennyson, "The Lotos-Eaters," line 69.

3 Let women who feel the wrongs of their kind teach women to be high-minded in their relation to men, and they will do more for the social *(continued)*

marry a *gentleman*, in the grand old meaning of the sixteenth century? when it was no irreverence to call our Lord

"The first true gentleman that ever breathed;"[1]

or in that of the fourteenth?—when Chaucer teaching "whom is worthy to be called gentill," writes thus:—

> "The first stocke was full of rightwisnes,
> Trewe of his worde, sober, pitous and free,
> Clene of his goste, and loved besinesse,
> Against the vice of slouth in honeste;
> And but his heire love vertue as did he,
> He is not gentill though he rich seme,
> All weare he miter, crowne, or diademe."[2]

Will she be less likely to marry one who honours women, and for their sakes, as well as his own, honours himself? Or to speak from what many would regard as the mother's side of the question—will the girl be more likely, because of such a culture of her imagination, to refuse the wise, true-hearted, generous rich man, and fall in love with the talking, verse-making fool, *because* he is poor, as if that were a virtue for which he had striven? The highest imagination and the lowliest common sense are always on one side.

For the end of imagination is *harmony*. A right imagination, being the reflex of the creation, will fall in with the divine order of things as the highest form of its own operation; "will tune its instrument here at the door"[3] to the divine harmonies within; will be content alone with growth towards the divine idea, which includes all that is beautiful in the imperfect imaginations of men; will know that every deviation from that growth is downward; and will therefore send the man forth from its loftiest representations to do the commonest duty of the most wearisome

---

elevation of women, and the establishment of their rights, whatever those rights may be, than by any amount of intellectual development or assertion of equality. Nor, if they are other than mere partisans, will they refuse the attempt because in its success men will, after all, be equal, if not greater gainers, if only thereby they should be "feelingly persuaded" what they are. [MacDonald's note]

1 Thomas Dekker and Thomas Middleton, *The Honest Whore*, V.ii.494.
2 Chaucer, "Gentilesse," lines 8-14.
3 John Donne, "Hymne to God My God, in My Sickness": "I tune the Instrument here at the dore," line 4.

calling in a hearty and hopeful spirit. This is the work of the right imagination; and towards this work every imagination, in proportion to the rightness that is in it, will tend. The reveries even of the wise man will make him stronger for his work; his dreaming as well as his thinking will render him sorry for past failure, and hopeful of future success.

To come now to the culture of the imagination. Its development is one of the main ends of the divine education of life with all its efforts and experiences. Therefore the first and essential means for its culture must be an ordering of our life towards harmony with its ideal in the mind of God. As he that is willing to do the will of the Father, shall know of the doctrine, so, we doubt not, he that will do the will of THE POET, shall behold the Beautiful. For all is God's; and the man who is growing into harmony with His will, is growing into harmony with himself; all the hidden glories of his being are coming out into the light of humble consciousness; so that at the last he shall be a pure microcosm, faithfully reflecting, after his manner, the mighty macrocosm. We believe, therefore, that nothing will do so much for the intellect or the imagination as *being good*—we do not mean after any formula or any creed, but simply after the faith of Him who did the will of his Father in heaven.

But if we speak of direct means for the culture of the imagination, the whole is comprised in two words—food and exercise. If you want strong arms, take animal food, and row. Feed your imagination with food convenient for it, and exercise it, not in the contortions of the acrobat, but in the movements of the gymnast. And first for the food.

Goethe has told us that the way to develop the aesthetic faculty is to have constantly before our eyes, that is, in the room we most frequent, some work of the best attainable art.[1] This will teach us to

---

1 Johann Peter Eckermann (1792-1854), German poet and author, describes his experience of examining drawings and engravings with Goethe. He recounts that

> Goethe, in such matters, takes great pains on my account, and I see that it is his intention to give me a higher degree of penetration in the observation of works of arts. He shows me only what is perfect in its kind, and endeavours to make me apprehend the intention and merit of the artist, that I may learn to pursue the thoughts of the best, and feel like the best. "This," said he, "is the way to cultivate what we call taste. Taste is only to be educated by contemplation, not of the tolerably good, but of the truly excellent. I, therefore, show you only the best works; and when you are grounded in these, you will have a standard for the rest, which you will know how to value, without overrating them."

Johann Peter Eckermann, *Conversations of Goethe with Eckermann and Soret*, trans. John Oxenford, 2 vols. (London: Smith, Elder & Co., 1850), vol. 1, p. 137.

refuse the evil and choose the good. It will plant itself in our minds and become our counsellor. Involuntarily, unconsciously, we shall compare with its perfection everything that comes before us for judgment. Now, although no better advice could be given, it involves one danger, that of narrowness. And not easily, in dread of this danger, would one change his tutor, and so procure variety of instruction. But in the culture of the imagination, books, although not the only, are the readiest means of supplying the food convenient for it, and a hundred books may be had where even one work of art of the right sort is unattainable, seeing such must be of some size as well as of thorough excellence. And in variety alone is safety from the danger of the convenient food becoming the inconvenient model.

Let us suppose, then, that one who himself justly estimates the imagination is anxious to develop its operation in his child. No doubt the best beginning, especially if the child be young, is an acquaintance with nature, in which let him be encouraged to observe vital phenomena, to put things together, to speculate from what he sees to what he does not see. But let earnest care be taken that upon no matter shall he go on talking foolishly. Let him be as fanciful as he may, but let him not, even in his fancy, sin against fancy's sense; for fancy has its laws as certainly as the most ordinary business of life. When he is silly, let him know it and be ashamed.

But where this association with nature is but occasionally possible, recourse must be had to literature. In books, we not only have store of all results of the imagination, but in them, as in her workshop, we may behold her embodying before our very eyes, in music of speech, in wonder of words, till her work, like a golden dish set with shining jewels, and adorned by the hands of the cunning workmen, stands finished before us. In this kind, then, the best must be set before the learner, that he may eat and not be satisfied; for the finest products of the imagination are of the best nourishment for the beginnings of that imagination. And the mind of the teacher must mediate between the work of art and the mind of the pupil, bringing them together in the vital contact of intelligence; directing the observation to the lines of expression, the points of force; and helping the mind to repose upon the whole, so that no separable beauties shall lead to a neglect of the scope—that is the shape or form complete. And ever he must seek to *show* excellence rather than talk about it, giving the thing itself, that it may grow into the mind, and not a eulogy of his own upon the thing; isolating the point worthy of remark rather than making many remarks upon the point.

Especially must he endeavour to show the spiritual scaffolding or skeleton of any work of art; those main ideas upon which the shape is constructed, and around which the rest group as ministering dependencies.

But he will not, therefore, pass over that intellectual structure without which the other could not be manifested. He will not forget the builder while he admires the architect. While he dwells with delight on the relation of the peculiar arch to the meaning of the whole cathedral, he will not think it needless to explain the principles on which it is constructed, or even how those principles are carried out in actual process. Neither yet will the tracery of its windows, the foliage of its crockets, or the fretting of its mouldings be forgotten. Every beauty will have its word, only all beauties will be subordinated to the final beauty—that is, the unity of the whole.

Thus doing, he shall perform the true office of friendship. He will introduce his pupil into the society which he himself prizes most, surrounding him with the genial presence of the high-minded, that this good company may work its own kind in him who frequents it.

But he will likewise seek to turn him aside from such company, whether of books or of men, as might tend to lower his reverence, his choice, or his standard. He will, therefore, discourage indiscriminate reading, and that worse than waste which consists in skimming the books of a circulating library. He knows that if a book is worth reading at all, it is worth reading well; and that, if it is not worth reading, it is only to the most accomplished reader that it *can* be worth skimming. He will seek to make him discern, not merely between the good and the evil, but between the good and the not so good. And this not for the sake of sharpening the intellect, still less of generating that self-satisfaction which is the closest attendant upon criticism, but for the sake of choosing the best path and the best companions upon it. A spirit of criticism for the sake of distinguishing only, or, far worse, for the sake of having one's opinion ready upon demand, is not merely repulsive to all true thinkers, but is, in itself, destructive of all thinking. A spirit of criticism for the sake of the truth—a spirit that does not start from its chamber at every noise, but waits till its presence is desired—cannot, indeed, garnish the house, but can sweep it clean. Were there enough of such wise criticism, there would be ten times the study of the best writers of the past, and perhaps one-tenth of the admiration for the ephemeral productions of the day. A gathered mountain of misplaced worships would be swept into the sea by the study of one good book; and while what was good in an inferior book would still be admired, the relative position of the book would be altered and its influence lessened.

Speaking of true learning, Lord Bacon says: "It taketh away vain admiration of anything, *which is the root of all weakness.*"[1]

---

1 Francis Bacon, *The Advancement of Learning*, Book I, sect. 8, para. 1.

The right teacher would have his pupil easy to please, but ill to satisfy; ready to enjoy, unready to embrace; keen to discover beauty, slow to say, "Here I will dwell."[1]

But he will not confine his instructions to the region of art. He will encourage him to read history with an eye eager for the dawning figure of the past. He will especially show him that a great part of the Bible is only thus to be understood; and that the constant and consistent way of God, to be discovered in it, is in fact the key to all history.

In the history of individuals, as well, he will try to show him how to put sign and token together, constructing not indeed a whole, but a probable suggestion of the whole.

And, again, while showing him the reflex of nature in the poets, he will not be satisfied without sending him to Nature herself; urging him in country rambles to keep open eyes for the sweet fashionings and blendings of her operation around him; and in city walks to watch the "human face divine."[2]

Once more: he will point out to him the essential difference between reverie and thought; between dreaming and imagining. He will teach him not to mistake fancy, either in himself or in others for imagination, and to beware of hunting after resemblances that carry with them no interpretation.

Such training is not solely fitted for the possible development of artistic faculty. Few, in this world, will ever be able to utter what they feel. Fewer still will be able to utter it in forms of their own. Nor is it necessary that there should be many such. But it is necessary that all should feel. It is necessary that all should understand and imagine the good; that all should begin, at least, to follow and find out God.

"The glory of God is to conceal a thing, but the glory of the king is to find it out," says Solomon.[3] "As if," remarks Bacon on the passage, "according to the innocent play of children, the Divine Majesty took delight to hide his works, to the end to have them found out; and as if kings could not obtain a greater honour than to be God's playfellows in that game."[4]

One more quotation from the book of Ecclesiastes, setting forth both the necessity we are under to imagine, and the comfort that our imagining cannot outstrip God's making.

"I have seen the travail which God hath given to the sons of men to be exercised in it. He hath made everything beautiful in his time; also

---

1 Psalms, 132:14.
2 John Milton, *Paradise Lost*: "Or flocks, or herds, or human face divine" (III, line 44).
3 Proverbs, 25:2.
4 Francis Bacon, *The Advancement of Learning*, Book I, sect. 6, para. 11.

he hath set the world in their heart, so that no man can find out the work that God maketh from the beginning to the end."[1]

Thus to be playfellows with God in this game, the little ones may gather their daisies and follow their painted moths; the child of the kingdom may pore upon the lilies of the field, and gather faith as the birds of the air their food from the leafless hawthorn, ruddy with the stores God has laid up for them; and the man of science

> "May sit and rightly spell
> Of every star that heaven doth shew,
> And every herb that sips the dew;
> Till old experience do attain
> To something like prophetic strain."[2]

---

1 Ecclesiastes, 3:10-11.
2 John Milton, "Il Penseroso," lines 170-74.

Appendix C: Victorian Fairy Tales

[George MacDonald's fairy tales are best understood in the context of a Victorian approach to literary fairy tales that combined the supernatural elements associated with traditional fairy tales with either the comedy of social satire or a deep Christian mysticism. The three tales excerpted here reflect the key elements that MacDonald shared with his fellow authors. John Ruskin's *The King of the Golden River* (1851) offers a Christian allegory of kindness and communal concern that elevates the traditional three brothers tale of European folklore through equating the individual success of the unlikely youngest brother with the well-being of all elements of his community. In a twist on the traditional animal helper motif, the piteous dog with whom Gluck shares his water transforms into the King of the Golden River himself who rewards his kindness and punishes the selfish older brothers by turning them to stone as hard as their hearts. In the second selection, William Makepeace Thackeray's *The Rose and the Ring* (1855), subtitled "A Fire-side Pantomime for Great and Small Children," provides a witty parallel to the satirical social banter MacDonald adopts in "The Light Princess," though Thackeray is on the whole more pointed in his critique and more evidently writing for an adult as well as a child audience.

Finally, in *The Gold Thread: A Story for the Young* (1861), Norman Macleod, then editor of *Good Words for the Young*, offers an allegory of the invisible thread of Christian faith that holds the true believer to the path of virtue. Note, however, that Macleod retains the traditional paternalist structure, and Eric's golden thread comes from his caring father, not the mysterious great-great-grandmother MacDonald imagines as spinning the gossamer thread herself.

MacDonald's shorter fairy tales then, form part of a larger cultural discussion of the place of fantasy as a genre and the function of the imagination in works for younger readers.]

1. From John Ruskin, *The King of the Golden River* (1851), Chapter V[1]

Yet, when he had climbed for another hour, his thirst became intolerable again; and, when he looked at his bottle, he saw that there were

---

1 This text is based on John Ruskin, *King of the Golden River or the Black Brothers, a Legend of Stiriam* illustrated by Richard Doyle, 4th ed. (London: Smith, Elder, 1859).

only five or six drops left in it, and he could not venture to drink. And, as he was hanging the flask to his belt again, he saw a little dog lying on the rocks, gasping for breath—just as Hans had seen it on the day of his ascent. And Gluck stopped and looked at it, and then at the Golden River, not five hundred yards above him; and he thought of the dwarf's words, "that no one could succeed, except in his first attempt; and he tried to pass the dog, but it whined piteously, and Gluck stopped again. "Poor beastie," said Gluck, "it'll be dead when I come down again, if I don't help it." Then he looked closer and closer at it, and its eye turned on him so mournfully, that he could not stand it. "Confound the King and his gold too," said Gluck; and he opened the flask, and poured all the water into the dog's mouth.

The dog sprang up and stood on its hind legs. Its tail disappeared; its ears became longer, longer, silky, golden; its nose became very red; its eyes became very twinkling; in three seconds the dog was gone, and before Gluck stood his old acquaintance, the King of the Golden River.

"Thank you," said the monarch, "but don't be frightened, it's all right"; for Gluck showed manifest symptoms of consternation at this unlooked-for reply to his last observation. "Why didn't you come before," continued the dwarf, "instead of sending me those rascally brothers of yours, for me to have the trouble of turning into stones? Very hard stones they make too."

"Oh dear me!" said Gluck, "have you really been so cruel?"

"Cruel!" said the dwarf, "they poured unholy water into my stream: do you suppose I'm going to allow that?"

"Why," said Gluck, "I am sure, sir—your majesty, I mean—they got the water out of the church font."

"Very probably," replied the dwarf; "but," and his countenance grew stern as he spoke, "the water which has been refused to the cry of the weary and dying, is unholy, though it had been blessed by every saint in heaven; and the water which is found in the vessel of mercy is holy, though it had been defiled with corpses."

So saying, the dwarf stooped and plucked a lily that grew at his feet. On its white leaves there hung three drops of clear dew. And the dwarf shook them into the flask which Gluck held in his hand. "Cast these into the river," he said, "and descend on the other side of the mountains into the Treasure Valley. And so good speed."

As he spoke, the figure of the dwarf became indistinct. The playing colours of his robe formed themselves into a prismatic mist of dewy light: he stood for an instant veiled with them as with the belt of a broad rainbow. The colours grew faint, the mist rose into the air; the monarch had evaporated.

And Gluck climbed to the brink of the Golden River, and its waves were as clear as crystal, and as brilliant as the sun. And, when he cast the three drops of dew into the stream, there opened where they fell a small circular whirlpool, into which the waters descended with a musical noise. Gluck stood watching it for some time, very much disappointed, because not only the river was not turned into gold, but its waters seemed much diminished in quantity. Yet he obeyed his friend the dwarf, and descended the other side of the mountains, towards the Treasure Valley; and, as he went, he thought he heard the noise of water working its way under the ground. And, when he came in sight of the Treasure Valley, behold, a river, like the Golden River, was springing from a new cleft of the rocks above it, and was flowing in innumerable streams along the dry heaps of red sand. And as Gluck gazed, fresh grass sprang beside the new streams, and creeping plants grew and climbed among the moistening soil. Young flowers opened suddenly along the river-sides, as stars leap out when twilight is deepening, and thickets of myrtle, and tendrils of vine, cast lengthening shadows over the valley as they grew. And thus the Treasure Valley became a garden again, and the inheritance, which had been lost by cruelty, was regained by love. And Gluck went, and dwelt in the valley, and the poor were never driven from his door; so that his barns became full of corn, and his house of treasure. And, for him, the river had, according to the dwarf's promise, become a River of Gold. And, to this day, the inhabitants of the valley point out the place where the three drops of holy dew were cast into the stream, and trace the course of the Golden River under the ground, until it emerges in the Treasure Valley. And, at the top of the cataract of the Golden River, are still to be seen two BLACK STONES, round which the waters howl mournfully every day at sunset; and these stones are still called by the people of the valley, THE BLACK BROTHERS.

2. From William Makepeace Thackeray, *The Rose and the Ring or The History of Prince Giglio and Prince Bulbo* (1855)[1]

I Shows How the Royal Family Sate Down to Breakfast

This is Valoroso XXIV, King of Paflagonia, seated with his Queen and only child at their royal breakfast-table, and receiving the letter which

---

1   This text is based on William Makepeace Thackeray, *The Rose and the Ring: Or, the History of Prince Giglio and Prince Bulbo. A Fire-Side Pantomime for Great and Small Children* (London: Smith, Elder, 1855).

announces to his majesty a proposed visit from Prince Bulbo, heir of Padella, reigning King of Crim Tartary.[1] Remark the delight upon the monarch's royal features. He is so absorbed in the perusal of the King of Crim Tartary's letter, that he allows his eggs to get cold, and leaves his august muffins untasted.

"What! that wicked, brave, delightful Prince Bulbo!" cries Princess Angelica—"so handsome, so accomplished, so witty,—the conqueror of Rimbombamento,[2] where he slew ten thousand giants!"

"Who told you of him, my dear?" asks his Majesty.

"A little bird," says Angelica.

"Poor Giglio!" says mamma, pouring out the tea.

"Bother Giglio!" cries Angelica, tossing up her head, which rustled with a thousand curl-papers.

"I wish," growls the King—"I wish Giglio was ..."

"Was better? Yes, dear, he is better," says the Queen. "Angelica's little maid, Betsinda, told me so when she came to my room this morning with my early tea."

"You are always drinking tea," said the monarch, with a scowl.

"It is better than drinking port or brandy-and-water," replies her Majesty.

"Well, well, my dear, I only said you were fond of drinking tea," said the King of Paflagonia, with an effort as if to command his temper. "Angelica! I hope you have plenty of new dresses; your milliners' bills are long enough. My dear Queen, you must see and have some parties. I prefer dinners, but of course you will be for balls. Your everlasting blue velvet quite tires me: and, my love, I should like you to have a new necklace. Order one. Not more than a hundred or a hundred and fifty thousand pounds."

"And Giglio, dear," says the Queen.

"GIGLIO MAY GO TO THE—"

"Oh, sir," screams her Majesty. "Your own nephew! our late King's only son."

"Giglio may go to the tailor's, and order the bills to be sent in to Glumboso to pay. Confound him! I mean bless his dear heart. He need want for nothing; give him a couple of guineas for pocket-money, my dear, and you may as well order yourself bracelets while you are about the necklace, Mrs. V."

---

1 Paflagonia and Crim Tartary are regions on the coast of the Black Sea. Paflago-nia was an ancient country in what is now Turkey; Crim Tartary included the Crimean Peninsula and part of the north coast of the Black Sea in what is now the Ukraine. Britain was engaged in the Crimean War between 1853 and 1856.

2 Not a real place—in Spanish, *rimbombante* is an adjective meaning resounding or echoing, but also pompous or bombastic.

Her Majesty, or *Mrs. V*, as the monarch facetiously called her (for even royalty will have its sport, and this august family were very much attached), embraced her husband, and, twining her arm round her daughter's waist, they quitted the breakfast-room in order to make all things ready for the princely stranger.

When they were gone, the smile that had lighted up the eyes of the *husband* and *father* fled—the pride of the *King* fled—the MAN was alone. Had I the pen of a G.P.R. James,[1] I would describe Valoroso's torments in the choicest language; in which I would also depict his flashing eye, his distended nostril—his dressing-gown, pocket-handkerchief, and boots. But I need not say I have *not* the pen of that novelist; suffice it to say, Valoroso was alone.

He rushed to the cupboard, seizing from the table one of the many egg-cups with which his princely board was served for the matin meal, drew out a bottle of right Nantz[2] or Cognac, filled and emptied the cup several times, and laid it down with a hoarse "Ha, ha, ha! now Valoroso is a man again!"

"But oh!" he went on (still sipping, I am sorry to say), "ere I was a king, I needed not this intoxicating draught; once I detested the hot brandy wine, and quaffed no other fount but nature's rill. It dashes not more quickly o'er the rocks, than I did, as, with blunderbuss in hand, I brushed away the early morning dew, and shot the partridge, snipe, or antlered deer! Ah! well may England's dramatist remark, 'Uneasy lies the head that wears a crown!'[3] Why did I steal my nephew's, my young Giglio's—? Steal! said I; no, no, no, not steal, not steal. Let me withdraw that odious expression. I took, and on my manly head I set, the royal crown of Paflagonia; I took, and with my royal arm I wield, the sceptral rod of Paflagonia; I took, and in my outstretched hand I hold, the royal orb of Paflagonia! Could a poor boy, a snivelling, drivelling boy—was in his nurse's arms but yesterday, and cried for

---

1 George Payne Rainsford James (1799-1860) was one of the most prolific novelists of the nineteenth century, his works totalling more than 100 volumes. *The Cambridge History of English and American Literature* comments "Without a particle of Scott's genius, James was a quick, patient, indefatigable worker. He poured forth historical novel after historical novel, all conscientiously accurate in historical fact, all dressed in well-invented incident, all diffuse and pompous in style, and all lifeless, humourless and characterless. James fell an easy victim to Thackeray's gift for parody; but the modern reader will wonder why Thackeray took the trouble to parody James, unless it were that the task was agreeably easy and that James's popularity was worth a shaft of ridicule" (Vol. 12).

2 Like Cognac, Nantz is a type of fine brandy.

3 Shakespeare, *Henry IV, Part 2*, III.i.31.

sugar plums and puled for pap—bear up the awful weight of crown, orb, sceptre? Gird on the sword my royal fathers wore, and meet in fight the tough Crimean foe?"

And then the monarch went on to argue in his own mind (though we need not say that blank verse is not argument) that what he had got it was his duty to keep, and that, if at one time he had entertained ideas of a certain restitution, which shall be nameless, the prospect by a *certain marriage* of uniting two crowns and two nations which had been engaged in bloody and expensive wars, as the Paflagonians and the Crimeans had been, put the idea of Giglio's restoration to the throne out of the question: nay, were his own brother, King Savio, alive, he would certainly will away the crown from his own son in order to bring about such a desirable union.

Thus easily do we deceive ourselves! Thus do we fancy what we wish is right! The King took courage, read the papers, finished his muffins and eggs, and rang the bell for his Prime Minister. The Queen, after thinking whether she should go up and see Giglio, who had been sick, thought, "Not now. Business first; pleasure afterwards. I will go and see dear Giglio this afternoon; and now I will drive to the jeweller's, to look for the necklace and bracelets." The Princess went up into her own room, and made Betsinda, her maid, bring out all her dresses; and as for Giglio, they forgot him as much as I forget what I had for dinner last Tuesday twelvemonth.

3. From Norman Macleod, *The Gold Thread: A Story for the Young* (1861)[1]

TO MY CHILDREN [v-vii]

I dedicate this story to you, because it was for you I first wrote it, to you I first read it among the green hills of Moffat. It was afterwards printed in *Good Words*,[2] and now you see it again appears as a little book for other children, who, I hope, will like it as much as you do.

I wish to help and encourage you, and all who read this story, to learn the great lesson which it is intended to teach; that lesson is, that we should always trust God and do what is right, and thus hold fast our gold thread in spite of every temptation and danger, being certain

---

1   This text is based on Norman Macleod, *The Gold Thread: A Story for the Young*, 7th ed. (London: Alexander Strahan, 1867). It was first serialized in *Good Words*.

2   Macleod was founding editor of *Good Words for the Young* (begun as *Good Words* in 1860), the periodical MacDonald would edit from 1870 to 1872.

that in this way only will God lead us in safety and peace to His home.

Now, God gives each of you this gold thread to hold fast in your own house or in school, in the nursery or in the play-ground, on every day and in every place. His voice in your heart, and in His Word, will also tell you always what is right, if you only listen to it. You, too, will be constantly tempted in some way or other to give up your gold thread, and to be selfish, disobedient, lazy, or untruthful. Many things, in short, will tempt you to do your own will rather than God's will.

You already know, and I hope you will always love and remember, those true stories in the Bible about the good men of the olden time, whose lives are there written. Now, what shewed that they were good? It was this, that *they trusted God, and did what was right.* If they ever let this their gold thread go, they lost their way and became unhappy; but when they held it fast, it led them in a way of peace and safety. To see how true this is, you have only to recall such stories as those of Noah, Abraham, Joseph, Moses, Job, Caleb and Joshua, Samuel, David and Jonathan, Elijah and Elisha, Hezekiah, Jeremiah, Daniel and his three companions, &c., &c., with those told you in the book of Acts, not to mention the history of Jesus Christ, the perfect example for us all.

That you, my dear children, may be "followers of those who through faith and patience now inherit the promises,"[1] and thus be "followers of God as dear children,"[2] is the constant prayer of your mother, and of your father.

NORMAN MACLEOD

Chapter III

Eric knew not how long he slept, but, as in a dream, he heard a sweet voice singing these words:—

> "Rest thee, boy, rest thee, boy, lonely and dreary,
> Thy little heart breaking from losing the way;
> Thy father has not left thee friendless, though weary,
> When learning through suffering to fear and obey."

Eric opened his eyes, but moved not a limb, as if under some strange fascination. It was early morning. High over head a lark was

---

1 Hebrews 6:12: "That ye be not slothful, but followers of them who through faith and patience inherit the promises."
2 Ephesians 5:1: "Be ye therefore followers of God, as dear children."

"singing like an angel in the clouds."[1] The mysterious voice went on in the same beautiful and soothing strain—

> "Oh, sweet is the lark as she sings o'er her nest,
>   And warbles unseen in the clear morning light;
> But sweeter by far is the song in the breast
>   When in life's early morning we do what is right!"

Eric could neither move nor speak; but in his heart he confessed with sorrow that he had done what was wrong. And again the voice sang—

> "Now, darling, awaken, thou art not forsaken!
>   The old night is past and a new day begun;
> Let thy journey with love to thy father be taken,
>   And at evening thy father will welcome thee home."

"I will arise and go to my father!" said Eric, springing to his feet. He saw beside him a beautiful lady, who looked like a picture he once saw of his mother, or like one of those angels from heaven about whom he had often read. And the lady said, "Fear not! I know you, Eric, and how it came to pass that you are here. Your father sent you for a wise and good purpose through the forest, and gave you hold of a gold thread to guide you, and told you never to let it go. It was your duty to him to have held it fast; but instead of doing your duty, trusting and obeying your father, and keeping hold of the thread, you let it go to chase butterflies, and gather wild-berries, and to amuse yourself. This you did more than once. You neglected your father's counsels and warnings, and because of your self-confidence and self-pleasing, you lost your thread, and then you lost your way. What dangers and troubles have you thus got into through disobedience to your father's commands, and want of trust in his love and wisdom! For had you only followed your father's directions, the gold thread would have brought you to his beautiful castle, where there is to be a happy meeting of your friends, with all your brothers and sisters." Poor little Eric began to weep! "Listen to me, child," said the lady, kindly, "for *you cannot have peace but by doing what is right.* Know, then, that all your brothers and sisters made this very journey by help of the gold

---

1 From Coleridge, "Fears in Solitude" (lines 25-28):

> And so, his senses gradually wrapped
> In a half sleep, he dreams of better worlds,
> And dreaming hears thee still, O singing lark,
> That singest like an angel in the clouds!

thread, and they are at home with great joy." "Oh, save me! save me!" cried Eric, and caught the lady's hand. "Yes, I will save you," said she, "if you will learn obedience. I know and love you, dear boy, I know and love your father, and have been sent by him to deliver you. I heard what you said, and know all you did, last night, and I was very glad that you proved, in trial, your love to your father, your love of truth, and your love of others, and this makes me hope all good of you for the future. Come now with me!" And so the beautiful woman took him by the hand. The storm had passed away, and the sun was shining on the green leaves of the trees, and every drop of dew sparkled like a diamond. The birds were all warbling their morning hymns, and feeding their young ones in their nests. The streams were dancing down the rocks and through the glens. "The mountains broke forth into singing, and all the trees clapped their hands with joy." Everything thus seemed beautiful and happy to Eric, for he himself was happy at the thought of doing what was right, and of going home. The lady led him to a sunny glade in the wood, covered with wild-flowers, from which the bees were busy gathering their honey, and she said, "Now, child, are you willing to do your father's will?" "Oh, yes!" "Will you do it, whatever dangers may await you?" "Yes!" "Well, then, I must tell you that your father has given me the gold thread which you lost; and he bids me again tell you, with his warm love, that if you keep hold of it, and follow it wherever it leads, you are sure to come to him at sunset; but if you let it go, you may wander on in this dark forest till you die, or are again taken prisoner by robbers. Know, also, that there is no other possible way of saving you, but by your following the gold thread." "I am resolved to do my duty, come what may," said Eric. "May you be helped to do it!" said the lady. She then gave him a cake, to support him in his journey. "And now, child," she added, "one advice more I will give you, and it was given you by your father, though you forgot it; it is this—if ever you feel the thread slipping from your hands, or are yourself tempted to let it go, pray immediately, and you will get wisdom and strength to find it, to lay hold of it, and to follow it. Before we part, kneel down and ask assistance to be good and obedient, brave and patient, until you meet your father." The little boy knelt down and repeated the Lord's Prayer; and as he said, "Thy will be done on earth, as it is done in heaven," he felt calm and happy as he used to do when he knelt at his mother's knee, and he thought her hand was waving over him, as if to bless him. When he lifted up his head there was no one there but himself; but he saw an old gray cross, and a GOLD THREAD was tied to it, and passed away, away, shining through the woods.

With a firm hold of his gold thread, the boy began his journey home. He passed along pathways on which the brown leaves of last year's growth were thickly strewn, and from among which flowers of every colour were springing. He crossed little brooks that ran like silver threads, and tinkled like silver bells. He passed under trees with great trunks, and huge branches that swept down to the ground, and waved far up in the blue sky. The birds hopped about him, and looked down upon him from among the green leaves, and they sang him songs, and some of them seemed to speak to him. He thought one large bird like a crow cried, "Good boy! Good boy!" and another whistled, "Cheer up! cheer up!" and so he went merrily on and very often he gave the robins and blackbirds that came near him bits of his cake. After awhile, he came to a green spot in the middle of the wood, without trees, and a footpath went direct across it, to the place where the gold thread was leading him, and there he saw a sight that made him wonder and pause. It was a bird about the size of a pigeon, with feathers like gold and a crown like silver, and it was slowly walking near him, and he saw gold eggs glittering in a nest among the grass a few yards off. Now, he thought, it would be such a nice thing to bring home a nest with gold eggs! The bird did not seem afraid of him, but stopped and looked at him with a calm blue eye, as if she said, "Surely you would not rob me?" He could not, however, reach the nest with his hand, and though he pulled and pulled the thread, it would not yield one inch, but seemed as stiff as a wire. "I see the thread quite plain," said the boy to himself, "and the very place where it enters the dark wood on the other side. I will just leap to the nest, and in a moment I shall have the eggs in my pocket, and then spring back and catch the thread again. I cannot lose it here, with the sun shining; and, besides, I see it a long way before me." So he took one step to seize the eggs; but he was in such haste that he fell and crushed the nest, breaking the eggs to pieces, and the little bird screamed and flew away, and then suddenly the birds in the trees began to fly about, and a large owl swept out of a dark glade, and cried, "Whoo—whoo—whoo-oo-oo;" and a cloud came over the sun! Eric's heart beat quick, and he made a grasp at his gold thread, but it was not there! Another, and another grasp, but it was not there! and soon he saw it waving far above his head, like a gossamer thread in the breeze. You would have pitied him, while you could not have helped being angry with him for having been so silly and disobedient when thus tried, had you only seen his pale face, as he looked above him for his thread, and about him for the road, but could see neither! And he became so confused with his fall, that he did not know which side of the open glade he had entered, nor to which point he was travelling. But at last he thought he heard a bird chirping, "Seek—seek—seek!" and another repeating, "Try again—try again—try—try!" and then he remembered what the lady had said to him, and he fell on his knees and told all his grief, and cried, "Oh, give me back my thread! and help me never, never, to let it go again!" As he lifted up his eyes, he saw the thread come slowly, slowly down; and when it came near, he sprang to it and caught it, and he did not know whether to laugh, or cry, or sing, he was so thankful and happy! "Ah!" said he, "I hope I shall never forget this fall!" That part of the Lord's Prayer came into his mind which says, "Lead us not into temptation, but deliver us from evil." "Who would have thought," said he to himself, "that I was in any danger in such a beautiful, green, sunny place as this, and so very early, too, in my journey! Oh! shame upon me!" As he proceeded with much more thought and caution, a large crow up a tree was hoarsely croaking, and seemed to say, "Beware, beware!" "Thank you, Mr. Crow," said the boy, "I shall;" and he threw him a bit of bread for his good advice. But now the thread led him through the strangest places. One was a very dark, deep ravine, with a steam that roared and rushed far down, and overhead the rocks seemed to meet, and thick bushes concealed the light, and nothing could Eric see but the gold thread, that looked like a thread of fire, though even that grew dim sometimes, until he could only feel it in his hand. And whither he was going he know not. At one time he seemed to be on the edge of a precipice, until it seemed as if the next step *must* lead him over, and plunge him down; but when he came to the very edge, the thread led him quite safely along it. At another, a rock which looked like a wall rose before him, and he said to himself, "Well, I must be stopped here! I shall never be able to climb up!" But just as he touched it, he found steps cut in it, and up, up, the thread guided him to the top! Then it would bring him down, down, until he once stood beside a raging stream, and the water foamed and dashed. "Now," he thought, "I must be drowned; but come what may, I will not let my thread go." And so it was, that when he came so near the stream as to feel the spray upon his cheek, and was sure that he must leap in if he followed his thread, what did he see but a little bridge that passed from bank to bank, and by which he crossed in perfect safety; until at last he began to lose fear, and to believe more and more that he would always be in the right road, so long as he did not trust mere appearances, but kept hold of his thread!

Appendix D: MacDonald's Composition and the Manuscript of The Princess and the Goblin

[The George MacDonald Collection of the Brander Library in Huntly, Aberdeenshire, holds the manuscript of *The Princess and the Goblin*.[1] The first version of the story published in the periodical *Good Words for the Young* was probably set from these pages, which include such elements as marginal instructions to set the metatextual conversation between "Mr. Editor" and his reader in italics (see Figure 32), and the letters "G.W.Y." at the beginning of four of the eight sections, each with its own sequential numbering,[2] into which the manuscript is divided. The text is virtually complete, missing only the final paragraph of Chapter 20 and pages 2-12 of the seventh manuscript segment, which constitute much of Chapter 21.[3]

The manuscript has been heavily revised, and offers a fascinating glimpse of the author at work. MacDonald deleted words, phrases, and passages with a bold stroke. Some deletions are clearly the second thoughts typical of composition on the fly, as he writes a word or phrase, then thinks better of it, crosses out the offending material, and substitutes his preferred wording on the same line: on the third page of the manuscript, for example, he initially writes that the princess had eyes "like little bits of the sky" but immediately changes the phrase to "like two bits of night-sky, each with a star melted down," which he then changes to "Like two bits of night-sky, each with a star dissolved in the blue" (see Figure 33). Other changes involve later interlineal revisions, usually to clarify a point or to create a more forceful expression, as in Chapter 6 when he changes the simple phrase "was too white to look at" to "was almost too white for the eyes to bear," giving a more precise description of the painful brilliance of the sheep's wool in the sunlight (Figure 34). At other points MacDonald revises to eliminate the redundancies often associated with rapid composition,

---

1   The manuscript is digitally available at
    http://www.aberdeenshire.gov.uk/libraries/information/georgemacdonald/ebooks
    /The%20Princess%20and%20The%20Goblin/index.htm#/-2/.

2   The sections can be identified as I: 1-22; II: 1-24; III: 1-31; IV: 1-16; V: 1-31; VI: 1-31; VII: 1, 13-40; and VIII: 1-4[6].

3   The first manuscript page of Chapter 21 is present, ending with the description of the Grandmother's thread "shooting hither & thither as"; the manuscript resumes with a sheet numbered 13 which begins "I can though, and you must be glad for both of us."

such as when adjectives are repeated too close together, indicating his concern for the literary quality of his prose. There are also instances of more substantial revisions, presumably carried out some time after the initial composition. In Chapter 4, for example, MacDonald inserts a symbol at the end of the first paragraph followed by the words "See Back," (Figure 35) where on the verso of manuscript page 5 he adds the lengthy dialogue between Lootie and the Princess concerning the nurse's hurt feelings at being seen as less attractive than Irene's "beautiful grandmother" (see Figure 36). Taken together, the 207 manuscript pages offer an excellent opportunity to observe MacDonald's creative process.]

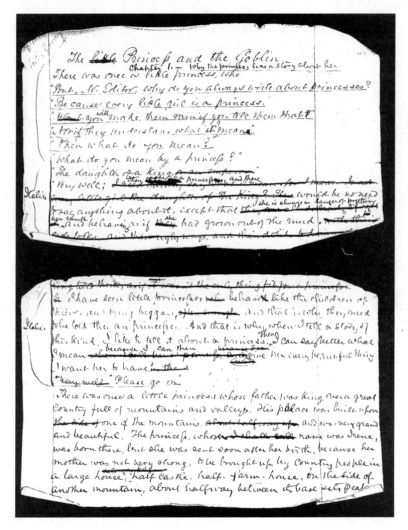

Figure 32

The princess was a sweet little creature, and at the time my story begins,
~~she~~ was about eight years old, I think, but she ~~gets~~ got older very fast. Her
face was very fair and pretty, with eyes ~~the~~ like ~~little bits of the sky,~~ two bits
of night-sky, each with a star ~~melted down~~ dissolved in the blue.
Those eyes ^ You would have thought ~~they~~ must have known they came from there,
so often they ~~were~~ turned up in that direction. ~~but last I tell for~~ The
ceiling of her nursery was blue, with stars in it, as like the sky as they
could make it. But I doubt if ever she saw the real sky with the stars
in it, for a reason which I had better mention at once.

These mountains were ~~full~~ of hollow places underneath; ~~as only natural~~
~~one great~~ huge caverns, ^though winding ways, some with water running ~~in~~ them,
and some shining ~~everywhere~~ with all colours of the rainbow when
a light was taken ~~into them~~ There would not have been much known
about them, had there not been mines there, great deep ~~pits, with~~
long galleries and winding passages, dug ~~by~~ to get at the ~~copper~~ ore
of which the mountains were full. In the course of digging, ~~and~~
~~the~~ miners came upon many of these natural caverns.

A few of them had far off openings out on the side of a mountain; ~~4~~
~~from some of which there was, an~~ opening here and there ~~out out~~
~~on in the mountain side~~ or into a ravine, ~~or out of these there were as~~
~~many~~
~~Now down in these~~ subterranean ~~underground~~ caverns, ~~some which one of great~~
~~big also~~ lived a strange race of beings, called by some gnomes,
by some kobolds, by some goblins. There was a legend current
in the country, that they ~~once~~ ^attractive lived above ground, ~~and only~~ ~~were very like other people~~
~~made use of ~~both~~ of the caves, ~~or go ~~~~to~~ in for houses~~
~~But they were a selfish & cruel people, for when travellers of this~~
~~nation ~~~~~~ But for some reason or other, concerning which
there were different legendary theories, and the king had ~~laid what they thought~~ ^ laid what they thought
~~several taxes,~~ of ten ^ they did not like,
upon them, or ^required ~~and~~ observance, ~~from them, or~~
had begun to treat them with more severity and impose stricter laws; ~~in the conse~~
quence ~~being~~ that they had all ~~by degrees~~ disappeared from the face of the
country. The legend ~~said,~~ ^according to however, ~~that~~ instead of going ~~down~~ elsewhere,
they had all taken refuge in the subterranean caverns, where to

lasted very long. But she wondered whether she should ever find her again. And she thought ... and it ... to find her ... when she wanted ... that she learned today nothing more to her ... on the subject ... seeing it was so little in her power to prove her words ...

Chapter 7. The little Miner.

The next day the great clouds still hung over the mountain, and the rain poured down like water from a full sponge. ... was very fond of ... keeping out of doors, and she nearly cried when she ... saw that ... the state of the weather ... was no ... touch a dark dreary gray; there was light in it; and as the hours went on, it grew brighter and brighter until ... was almost too brilliant to look at; and ... in the afternoon, the sun broke out so gloriously brilliant that Irene clapped her hands, crying

"See, see, Lootie! the sun has had his face washed. Look how brightly he is! Do get my hat, and let us go out for a walk. Oh dear! oh dear! how happy I am!"

Lootie was very glad to please the princess. She got her ... cloak, and they set out together for a walk up the mountain; for the road was so hard and steep that the water could not lie upon it, and it was dry enough for walking a few minutes after the rain ceased. ... clapping her hands with delight. The great clouds were rolling away in broken pieces, like great over-woolly sheep whose wool the sun had bleached till it was too white to look at. Between them shone the sky, blue because of the rain. The trees on the roadside were hung all over with rain-drops, which sparkled in the sun like jewels. The only things that were not brighter for the rain, were the brooks that ran down the mountain; they had changed from the clearness of crystal to a muddy brown; but what they lost in colour they gained in sound — or at least in noise, for every swollen brook was now so musical ... But Irene was in raptures with the great brown streams tumbling down everywhere; and

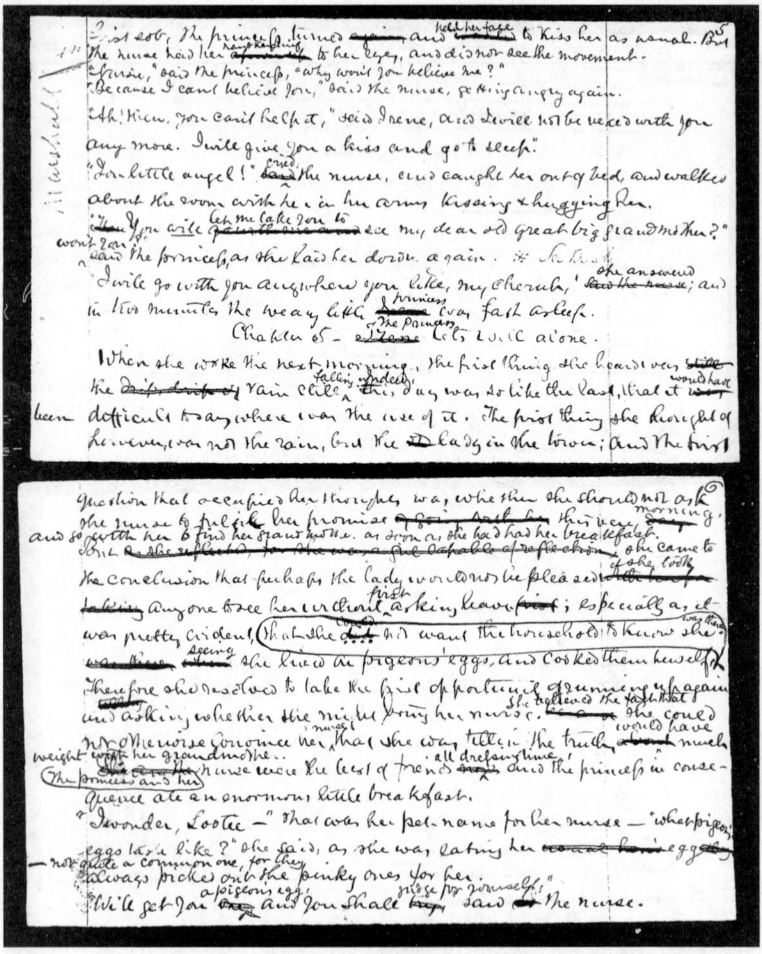

Figure 35

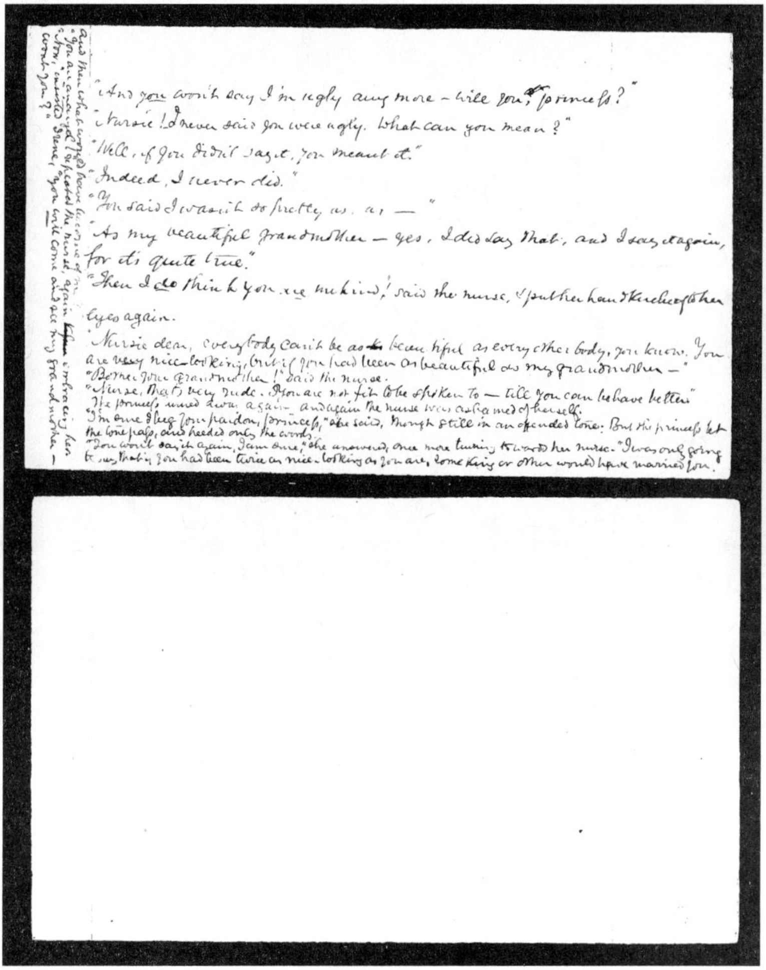
"And you won't say I'm ugly any more — will you, princess?"
"Nursie! I never said you were ugly. What can you mean?"
"Well, if you didn't say it, you meant it."
"Indeed, I never did."
"You said I wasn't so pretty as, as —"
"As my beautiful grandmother — yes, I did say that; and I say it again, for it's quite true."
"Then I do think you are unkind!" said the nurse, & put her handkerchief to her eyes again.
"Nursie dear, everybody can't be as beautiful as every other body, you know. You are very nice-looking, but if you had been as beautiful as my grandmother —"
"Bother your grandmother!" said the nurse.
"Nurse, that's very rude. You are not fit to be spoken to — till you can behave better."
The princess turned away again, and again the nurse was ashamed of herself.
"I'm sure I beg your pardon, princess," she said, though still in an offended tone. But the princess let the tone pass, and heeded only the words.
"You won't say it again, I am sure," she answered, once more turning towards her nurse. "I was only going to say, that if you had been twice as nice-looking as you are, some king or other would have married you.
And then what would have become of me?"
"You are an angel!" repeated the nurse, again embracing her.
"Now," insisted Irene, "you will come and see my grandmother — won't you?"

Figure 36

Select Bibliography

Primary Sources

MacDonald, George. *Adela Cathcart*. 3 vols. London: Hurst and Blackett, 1864.

——. "The Day Boy and the Night Girl." *Fairy Tales by George MacDonald*. Ed. Greville MacDonald. London: Arthur C. Fifield, 1904.

——. *Dealings with the Fairies*. London: Alexander Strahan, 1867.

——. *A Dish of Orts. Chiefly Papers on the Imagination, and on Shakspere*. Enlarged ed. London: Sampson Low, Marston, 1893.

——. "The Fantastic Imagination." *A Dish of Orts. Chiefly Papers on the Imagination, and on Shakspere*. Enlarged ed. London: Sampson Low, Marston, 1893. 313-22.

——. "The Giant's Heart." *Adela Cathcart*. Vol. 3. London: Hurst and Blackett, 1864. 25-85.

——. "The Giant's Heart." *Dealings with the Fairies*. London: Alexander Strahan, 1867. 100-40.

——. "The Giant's Heart." *The Light Princess and Other Fairy Stories*. London: Blackie, 1890. 95-133.

——. *The Gifts of the Child Christ, and Other Tales*. 2 vols. London: Sampson Low, Marston, Searle, & Rivington, 1882.

——. "The Golden Key." *Dealings with the Fairies*. London: Alexander Strahan, 1867. 248-308.

——. "The Golden Key." *The Light Princess and Other Fairy Stories*. London: Blackie, 1890. 135-92.

——. "The History of Photogen and Nycteris, a Day and Night Märchen." *The Gifts of the Child Christ, and Other Tales*. Vol. 1. London: Sampson Low, Marston, Searle, & Rivington, 1882. 85-196.

——. "The History of Photogen and Nycteris: A Day and Night Märchen." *The Graphic* 20 December 1879.

——. "The Imagination: Its Functions and Its Culture." *British Quarterly Review* 46.91 (1867): 45-70.

——. "The Imagination: Its Functions and Its Culture." *Orts*. London: Sampson Low, Marston, Searle, & Rivington, 1882. 1-42.

——. "The Imagination: Its Functions and Its Culture." *A Dish of Orts. Chiefly Papers on the Imagination, and on Shakspere*. Enlarged ed. London: Sampson Low, Marston, 1893. 1-42.

——. "The Light Princess." *Adela Cathcart*. Vol. 1. London: Hurst and Blackett, 1864. 118-228.

———. "The Light Princess." *Dealings with the Fairies*. London: Alexander Strahan, 1867. 1-99.

———. "The Light Princess." *The Light Princess and Other Fairy Stories*. London: Blackie, 1890. 9-94.

———. *The Light Princess and Other Fairy Stories*. London: Blackie, 1890.

———. *Orts*. London: Sampson, Low, Marston, Searle, & Rivington, 1882.

———. *The Princess and Curdie*. London: Chatto & Windus, 1883 [1882].

———. "The Princess and Curdie." *Good Things: A Picturesque Magazine for Boys and Girls* 6 (1877): 1-5, 57-63, 65-68, 177-80, 193-200, 321-52.

———. "The Princess and the Goblin." *Good Words for the Young* 3 (1870-71): 1-5, 65-72, 129-36, 185-91, 279-86, 297-305, 353-63, 409-20.

———. *The Princess and the Goblin*. New York: Routledge, 1871.

———. *The Princess and the Goblin and, the Princess and Curdie*. Ed. Roderick McGillis. Oxford: Oxford UP, 1990.

———. *The Princess and the Goblin. With 30 Illustrations by Arthur Hughes*. London: Strahan, 1872.

———. *The Princess and the Goblin. With Thirty Illustrations by Arthur Hughes*. New ed. London: Blackie & Son, 1888.

———. *The Princess and the Goblin. With Twelve Full-Page Illustrations in Colour, and Thirty Text Illustrations in Black-and-White*. New ed. London: Blackie & Son, 1911.

———. "Tell Us a Story [the Giant's Heart]." *The Illustrated London News* 19 December 1863: 626-30.

———. *Works of Fancy and Imagination*. 10 vols. London: Strahan, 1871.

Biography

Hein, Rolland. *George MacDonald: Victorian Mythmaker*. Whitehorn, CA: Star Song Publishing, 1993.

MacDonald, Greville. *George MacDonald and His Wife with an Introduction by G.K. Chesterton*. London: G. Allen & Unwin, 1924.

Raeper, William. *George MacDonald*. Tring: Lion, 1987.

Reis, Richard. *George MacDonald*. New York: Twayne, 1972.

Triggs, Kathy. *The Stars and the Stillness: A Portrait of George MacDonald*. Cambridge: Lutterworth, 1986.

Bibliography

Bulloch, John Malcolm. "A Bibliography of George MacDonald." *Aberdeen University Library Bulletin* 5 (1925): 679-745.

Sháberman, Raphael B. *George MacDonald: A Bibliographical Study.* Winchester: St. Paul's Bibliographies, 1990.

———. *George MacDonald's Books for Children: A Bibliography of First Editions.* London: Cityprint Business Centres, 1979.

Selected Criticism Related to *The Princess and the Goblin*

Bodmer, George. "Arthur Hughes, Walter Crane, and Maurice Sendak: The Picture as Literary Fairy Tale." *Marvels & Tales: Journal of Fairy-Tale Studies* 17.1 (2003): 120-37.

Bubel, Katharine. "Knowing God 'Other-Wise': The Wise Old Woman Archetype in George MacDonald's *The Princess and the Goblin, The Princess and Curdie* and 'the Golden Key'." *North Wind: A Journal of George MacDonald Studies* 25 (2006): 1-17.

Burns, Marjorie. "Saintly and Distant Mothers." *The Ring and the Cross: Christianity and the Lord of the Rings.* Ed. Paul E. Kerry. Madison, NJ: Fairleigh Dickinson UP, 2011. 246-58.

Davies, Maria Gonzalez. "A Spiritual Presence in Fairyland: The Great-Great-Grandmother in the Princess Books." *North Wind: A Journal of George MacDonald Studies* 12 (1993): 60-65.

Devey, Joseph, ed. *The Physical and Metaphysical Works of Lord Bacon, Including His Dignity and Advancement of Learning in Nine Books and His Novum Organum; or, Precepts for the Interpretation of Nature.* London: Henry G. Bohn, 1853.

Gray, William. *Death and Fantasy: Essays on Phillip Pullman, C.S. Lewis, George MacDonald and R.L. Stevenson.* Newcastle-Upon-Tyne: Cambridge Scholars, 2008.

———. *Fantasy, Art and Life: Essays on George MacDonald, Robert Louis Stevenson and Other Fantasy Writers.* Newcastle-Upon-Tyne: Cambridge Scholars, 2011.

Grenby, M.O. "'A Conservative Woman Doing Radical Things': Sarah Trimmer and the Guardian of Education." *Culturing the Child, 1690-1914: Essays in Memory of Mitzi Meyers.* Ed. Donelle Ruwe. Lanham: Children's Literature Association and Scarecrow, 2005. 137-61.

Hayward, Deirdre. "The Mystical Sophia: More on the Great Grandmother in the Princess Books." *North Wind: A Journal of George MacDonald Studies* 13 (1994): 29-33.

Hilder, Monika. "George MacDonald's Education into Mythic Wonder: A Recovery of the Transcendent." *Sublimer Aspects: Inter-*

faces between Literature, Aesthetics, and Theology. Ed. Natasha Duquette. Cambridge: Cambridge Scholars, 2007. 176-93.

Hunt, Caroline. "Form as Fantasy—Fantasy as Form." *Children's Literature Association Quarterly* 12.1 (1987): 7-10.

Hutton, Muriel. "Sour Grapeshot: Fault-Finding in a *Centennial Bibliography of George MacDonald.*" *Aberdeen University Review* 41 (1965): 85-88.

Jarrar, Osama. "MacDonald's Fairy Tales and Fantasy Novels as a Critique of Victorian Middle-Class Ideology." *North Wind: A Journal of George MacDonald Studies* 30 (2011): 13-24.

Jenkins, Ruth Y. "'I Am Spinning This for You, My Child': Voice and Identity Formation in George MacDonald's Princess Books." *The Lion and the Unicorn* 28.3 (2004): 325-44.

——. "Imagining the Abject in Kingsley, MacDonald, and Carroll: Disrupting Dominant Values and Cultural Identity in Children's Literature." *The Lion and the Unicorn* 35.1 (2011): 67-87.

John, Judith Gero. "Searching for Great-Great-Grandmother: Powerful Women in George MacDonald's Fantasies." *The Lion and the Unicorn* 15.2 (1991): 27-34.

Kotzin, Michael C. "C.S. Lewis and George MacDonald: The Silver Chair and the Princess Books." *Mythlore: A Journal of J.R.R. Tolkien, C.S. Lewis, Charles Williams, and the Genres of Myth and Fantasy Studies* 8.1 [27] (1981): 5-15.

Lang, Marjory. "Childhood's Champions: Mid-Victorian Children's Periodicals and the Critics." *Victorian Periodicals Review* 13.1/2 (1980): 17-31.

Lathey, Gillian. *The Role of Translators in Children's Literature: Invisible Storytellers.* London: Routledge, 2010.

Long, Josh. "Clinamen, Tessera, and the Anxiety of Influence: Swerving from and Completing George MacDonald." *Tolkien Studies* 6 (2009): 127-50.

Manlove, Colin. "The Princess and the Goblin and the Princess and Curdie." *North Wind: A Journal of George MacDonald Studies* 26 (2007): 1-36.

——. "Tolkien on Fairy-Stories: Expanded Edition, with Commentary and Notes." *Tolkien Studies* 6 (2009): 241-48.

McCulloch, Fiona. "'A Strange Race of Beings': Undermining Innocence in the Princess and the Goblin." *Scottish Studies Review* 7.1 (Spring 2006): 53-67.

McGillis, Roderick. "Criticism in the Wilderness: Fairy Tales as Poetry." *Children's Literature Association Quarterly* 7.2 (Summer 1982): 2-8.

——. "Fantasy as Adventure: Nineteenth Century Children's Fiction." *Children's Literature Association Quarterly* 8.3 (Fall 1983): 18-22.

——. "George MacDonald's Princess Books: High Seriousness." *Touchstones: Reflections on the Best in Children's Literature, Volume One*. Ed. Perry Nodelman and Jill P. May. Lafayette: Children's Lit. Assoc., 1985. 146-62.

——. "'If You Call Me Grandmother, That Will Do'." *Mythlore: A Journal of J. R. R. Tolkien, C. S. Lewis, Charles Williams, and the Genres of Myth and Fantasy Studies* 6.3 [21] (1979): 27-28.

Mendelson, Michael. "The Fairy Tales of George MacDonald and the Evolution of a Genre." *For the Childlike: George MacDonald's Fantasies for Children*. Ed. Roderick McGillis. Metuchen, NJ: Scarecrow, 1992. 31-49.

Merglesky, Natalie L. "Getting Lost in *The Princess and the Goblin*." *North Wind: A Journal of George MacDonald Studies* 29 (2010): 24-39.

Moss, Anita West. "Crime and Punishment, or Development, in Fairy Tales." *Proceedings of the Seventh Annual Conference of the Children's Literature Association, Baylor University, March 1980*. Ed. Priscilla Ord. New Rochelle: Department of English, Iona College 1982. 132-38.

——. "Varieties of Literary Fairy Tale." *Children's Literature Association Quarterly* 7.2 (1982): 15-17.

Patterson, Nancy-Lou. "Kore Motifs in *The Princess and the Goblin*." *For the Childlike: George MacDonald's Fantasies for Children*. Ed. Roderick McGillis. Metuchen, NJ: Scarecrow, 1992. 169-82.

Pennington, John. "Muscular Spirituality in George MacDonald's Curdie Books." *Muscular Christianity: Embodying the Victorian Age*. Ed. Donald E. Hall. Cambridge Studies in Nineteenth-Century Literature and Culture. Cambridge: Cambridge UP, 1994. 133-49.

Prickett, Stephen. "Fictions and Metafictions: *Phantastes*, *Wilhelm Meister*, and the Idea of the *Bildungsroman*." *The Golden Thread: Essays on George MacDonald*. Ed. William Raeper. Edinburgh: Edinburgh UP, 1990. 109-25.

——. "The Two Worlds of George MacDonald." *For the Childlike: George MacDonald's Fantasies for Children*. Ed. Roderick McGillis. Metuchen, NJ: Scarecrow, 1992. 17-29.

——. *Victorian Fantasy*. 2nd rev. and expanded ed. Waco, TX: Baylor UP, 2005.

Reiter, Geoffrey. "'Travelling Beastward': George MacDonald's Princess Books and Late Victorian Supernatural Degeneration Fiction." *George MacDonald: Literary Heritage and Heirs*. Ed. Roderick McGillis. Wayne, PA: Zossima, 2008. 217-26.

Rigsbee, Sally Adair. "Fantasy Places and Imaginative Belief: *The Lion, the Witch, and the Wardrobe* and *The Princess and the Goblin*." *Children's Literature Association Quarterly* 8.1 (1983): 10-11.

Rowe, Karen E. "Virtue in the Guise of Vice: The Making and Unmaking of Morality from Fairy Tale Fantasy." *Culturing the Child, 1690-1914: Essays in Memory of Mitzi Meyers*. Ed. Donelle Ruwe. Lanham: Children's Literature Association and Scarecrow, 2005. 22-66.

Sherman, Cordelia. "The Princess and the Wizard: The Fantasy Worlds of Ursula K. Le Guin and George MacDonald." *Children's Literature Association Quarterly* 12.1 (1987): 24-28.

Sigman, Joseph. "The Diamond in the Ashes: A Jungian Reading of the 'Princess' Books." *For the Childlike: George MacDonald's Fantasies for Children*. Ed. Roderick McGillis. Metuchen, NJ: Scarecrow, 1992. 183-94.

Soto, Fernando. "Kore Motifs in the Princess Books: Mythic Threads between Irenes and Eirinys." *George MacDonald: Literary Heritage and Heirs*. Ed. Roderick McGillis. Wayne, PA: Zossima, 2008. 65-81.

——. "Some Linguistic Moves in the Carroll-MacDonald 'Literary Game'." *North Wind: A Journal of George MacDonald Studies* 18 (1999): 45-53.

Stelle, Ginger. "Fracturing MacDonald: *The Princess and the Goblin* and 'Fractured Fairy Tales'." *North Wind: A Journal of George MacDonald Studies* 26 (2007): 121-25.

Stohler, Sara J. "The Mythic World of Childhood." *Children's Literature Association Quarterly* 12.1 (1987): 28-32.

Thacker, Deborah. "Feminine Language and the Politics of Children's Literature." *Lion and the Unicorn* 25.1 (2001): 3-16.

Willis, Lesley. "'Born Again': The Metamorphosis of Irene in George MacDonald's *The Princess and the Goblin*." *Scottish Literary Journal* 12.1 (1985): 24-39.

Wolff, Robert Lee. *The Golden Key: A Study of the Fiction of George MacDonald*. New Haven, CT: Yale UP, 1961.

Websites

North Wind, A Journal of George MacDonald Studies.
   http://www.snc.edu/northwind/
The George MacDonald Collection.
   http://www.aberdeenshire.gov.uk/libraries/information
   /georgemacdonald/index.asp (including the manuscript of *The Princess and the Goblin* http://www.aberdeenshire.gov.uk/libraries
   /information/georgemacdonald/childrens/princess/princess.asp).

from the publisher

A name never says it all, but the word "broadview" expresses a good deal of the philosophy behind our company. We are open to a broad range of academic approaches and political viewpoints. We pay attention to the broad impact book publishing and book printing has in the wider world; we began using recycled stock more than a decade ago, and for some years now we have used 100% recycled paper for most titles. As a Canadian-based company we naturally publish a number of titles with a Canadian emphasis, but our publishing program overall is internationally oriented and broad-ranging. Our individual titles often appeal to a broad readership too; many are of interest as much to general readers as to academics and students.

Founded in 1985, Broadview remains a fully independent company owned by its shareholders—not an imprint or subsidiary of a larger multinational.

If you would like to find out more about Broadview and about the books we publish, please visit us at **www.broadviewpress.com**. And if you'd like to place an order through the site, we'd like to show our appreciation by extending a special discount to you: by entering the code below you will receive a 20% discount on purchases made through the Broadview website.

Discount code: **broadview20%**

Thank you for choosing Broadview.

Please note: this offer applies only to sales of
bound books within the United States or Canada.

The interior of this book is printed on 100% recycled paper.